TIGER TAIL SOUP

a novel of China at War

by
Nicki Chen

No part of this publication may be reproduced, stored in a retrieval system, or transmitted, in any form or by any means, electronic, mechanical, photocopying, recording, or otherwise, without the written permission of the author.

First published by Dog Ear Publishing
4010 W. 86th Street, Ste H
Indianapolis, IN 46268
www.dogearpublishing.net

dog ear
<u>PUBLISHING</u>

ISBN: 978-1-4575-2675-6

This book is printed on acid-free paper.

Printed in the United States of America

For Eugene

Acknowledgments

This book would not have been possible without the inspiration of my late husband, Eugene Yu-wei Chen. Although I didn't start writing *Tiger Tail Soup* until after his death, he'd been teaching me about Chinese culture and telling me stories about his early childhood on Kulangsu since we first met. This book is for him.

My critique group in Port Angeles ushered me through the early days of the novel, providing invaluable support, suggestions and friendship. Thank you Patrick Loafman, Kathy Gonzales, Peggy deBroux, Diana Somerville, and Ken Gurney. Later, my critique group in Edmonds helped me finish the book. Thank you to my good friends and fellow writers: Maureen Rogers, Emily Hill, Gretchen Houser, Paddy Eger, Rona Besterman, and Sandra Walker.

Julian Chiu and Robert Chiu, thanks for sharing your memories of Kulangsu.

I owe a big debt of gratitude to Ellen Lesser, Francois Camoin, and Robin Ireland for their encouragement and editorial advice.

Thank you to everyone at Dog Ear Publishing, particularly Mark Jackson, Adrienne Miller, and Christy Phillipe.

To my family, thank you for your love and support. And thank you, Christine, for giving me the push I needed to finally get this book published.

1946

*D*odging a low-hanging pine, I settle back into my sedan chair. This washed-out road, like the mountains themselves and the tigers that hide in their shadows, is all beauty and treachery. We start up another slope, my neck straining to support my suddenly heavy head. Finally we reach a level spot.

"A moment's rest, ma'am?" the lead man asks, and I nod. These carriers use their rest periods to lick the opium they carry in their belts. I use the time to look back.

Walking along the trail, I search for a break in the trees, but we've come too far. Mountains are blocking the view of my home now. Kulangsu. Island of pianos they call it, drum-surf isle, egret island. Every detail of its contours is carved into my memory—trees everywhere, tile-roofed houses, cottages painted gold and peacock blue, sandy beaches the color of a ripe peach, and the surrounding sea, blue or green, gray or white, depending on the weather. My beloved home, and for nearly eight years of war, my prison.

"Ma'am." The amah comes up behind me, my son and daughter at her side. "They're ready to go, ma'am."

I search my children's eyes for the strength I know is there. My ox girl, my tiger boy. Too small for their ages. Still startled by loud noises. And yet the might of their ancestors shines through.

"Get in your sedan chair," I tell them. "We have a long way to go."

Our journey to Foochew won't be over tonight or even tomorrow night. I settle back for another leg in the long, uncomfortable journey, and as my chair jostles and jolts, my thoughts bounce from one memory to another. The Japanese guns and bombs. My tiger dreams. My mother, my mother-in-law, and of course, my husband, Yu-ming, so long absent from my bed.

Spring 1938

1

I was pregnant when Yu-ming went missing. And though I longed for a dream that would lead me to him, night after night the white tigers meant for the child I carried entered my dreams instead.

Tails swishing and eyes flashing, they led me through the forest, past a monk's fire pit and up to a clearing with white pillars at its center.

As the sun rose and my dream began to fade, the tigers flicked their ears and growled one last time. I shivered and opened my eyes. Enough with the tiger dreams!

Shaking the dampness from my hair, I dangled my feet over the side of the bed. Surely, I told myself, Yu-ming was still alive. All I had to do was wait for him. I fluffed the quilt, freshening equally the sweaty and the unused sides of the bed. I'd assumed when Yu-ming went to work for Siemens that the powerful German company would protect him from China's sorrows. Now I wasn't so sure. After all, why would bandits care whether the throat they slit belonged to a Siemens engineer? And the bow-legged invaders? I stuffed my fingers in my hair and yanked at it as I padded across the cool tile. It was ludicrous to think the Japanese would ask the affiliation of a Chinese before shooting him between the eyes.

Blinking the thought away, I opened the French doors and stepped onto the balcony. Below me a rice straw broom whispered on the paving stones. A rooster crowed. And in the distance, a rumbling boom and then another. I leaned out over the railing and looked for lightning. The booming sounded more like bombs, though, than thunder.

No, I thought, it can't be bombs. The Japanese are still in the north, and these sounds are coming from the south.

"Po-ping," I called to the amah. "Come out here."

She shuffled onto the balcony, my daughter's head resting on her shoulder.

"What do you hear?"

She squinted into the rising sun. "Thunder," she said.

"No, listen once more."

"I hear thunder, Young Mistress," she said again, impatiently bouncing Ah Mei on her hip. "May I go now?"

Before long the distant booms were drowned out by the sounds of shouting and laughter, chickens and birds. A crow swooped down and scattered a flock of chickadees. A vendor selling sweetened soymilk and crispy fried ghosts called at the gate. And once again, it seemed that everything was back to normal on the charmed little island of my birth.

Everything, except that my husband was missing and the Japanese invaders had within the past three months captured Shanghai to the north of us and the capital at Nanking.

Now, I wondered, were they also bombarding cities to the south?

I dressed and went downstairs, intending to ask one of the maids for a poached egg. As I turned a corner, Su-lee nearly ran me down. Only her legs showed as she hobbled toward me carrying a potted Japanese bamboo.

"Oh, Young Mistress," she said through the foliage. "Look at these flowers. They bloomed during the night." The small white flowers bursting from a center point in each cluster looked like miniature fireworks. "I want to put them outside," she said. "Very bad luck. When the bamboo flowers, someone is sure to die."

I held the door for her, and she staggered, half-running, through the laundry area and across the yard to the far side of the fishpond. As far from our house as possible, I thought as I followed her outside.

2

*I*found my mother-in-law in the back patio cultivating the soil around a potted lime tree. In her long black skirt and padded green tunic, her dark hair falling to her waist in a heavy braid, she was a sad, graceful figure. As I approached, she picked a fallen lime blossom from the lip of her pot and placed it in the palm of my hand. Then we wished each other a good morning—yet another morning with no news of her only son, my husband.

To all appearances my mother-in-law and I were opposites. She was tall with a long face and high forehead; I was short and moon-faced. She presented an imperturbable face to the world, I, a volatile one. The first time I saw her I was a child and she was still the favored second wife of Ambassador Han Gang. In my child's mind, she was a princess who used to live inside the Forbidden City as a guest of the emperor. People said the emperor gave her in marriage to Ambassador Han Gang as a reward for his success in the finals of the Civil Service Examination. If true, her life was like a story from an opera.

One day when I was no more than six years old, I saw her standing at her gate, noble in her yellow silk gown, her high forehead and long face smooth as silken tofu. She held her head high so that at first I thought she was looking at something beyond me. "Are you a princess?" I asked before I could stop myself.

Her lips curled into a smile. "No," she said. "Are you a boy?"

In accordance with my father's wishes, I was still dressing like a boy, wearing my hair in a boyish cut. "No," I said. "I'm a girl."

"You see, we are not always what we appear." She stepped closer and touched my cheek with her long fingers. "It's all right," she said. "Girls should not be too girlish. It makes them weak."

My father could have married a second wife to give him a son. Instead, he contented himself with me. He gave me books, a tutor, a large collection of toy soldiers, and, best of all, an enormous model of a British luxury liner, the construction of which Father had commissioned for me in Kuala Lumpur. It was an exact scale model of the HMS *Queen Elizabeth*. One whole side of it could be opened up to show the cabins, galley, laundry, engine room. Everything. Until that day in front of the elegant lady's gate, I was a willing conspirator in my father's pretense. Being treated like a boy was a privilege. Besides, it suited me. I loved reading stories of chivalry and spending summer afternoons at the opera with my father. And yet, when the Mongolian woman touched my face, the sympathy in her fingers brought tears to my eyes.

In the weeks following our meeting I had sudden fits of tears, and before spring turned to summer I decided to confront my father. I was a girl, I told him finally. A girl! I refused to dress like a boy ever again. And to my surprise, Father nodded. "You are right," he said. "It's time you dressed like a girl." Suddenly I was frightened. What if he took away my toy soldiers or my books and tutor? I was certain I'd made a serious mistake. I waited and worried, but other than my dress the only thing that changed was that in the fall, at the age of six and a half, I started going to school.

On my way to and from school I would pass by Ambassador Han's house and stare up at the second-story windows. Once his first wife, a heavy woman with a large head and angry eyes, saw me and told me to go away. After that, I hurried past, watching for the Mongolian princess from the sides of my eyes. Finally one day she was there, standing at their gate.

"Well," she said, "I see you're a girl now."

I bowed in what I thought was a girlish way.

"And still a bit of a boy," she said. "It's good to be both."

Once again she had interpreted my heart. It was exactly what I wanted to hear. Emboldened by her forthright manner and the affinity we seemed to share, I spoke my mind. "People say you lived in the emperor's palace," I said. "But why would you live there if you're not a princess?"

She looked off into the distance. Then, in a curious, low voice, she began her story. "My mother and I lived in splendor within the Forbidden City. We were served the finest dishes, clothed in silk,

7

entertained by the emperor's own eunuchs. Nevertheless, the palace was a prison for us. I was still a child, younger than you are now, and I longed for my village, for the grasslands and the open skies of the steppe. I missed my grandparents, my aunts, uncles, and cousins; and I missed my fine dappled pony. But my mother and I could not leave. We were the emperor's hostages, kept inside the palace to ensure the loyalty of my father, who was the general in charge of the Mongolian Regiment."

She looked away. "One day my father was killed. His army had been commanded to storm the gates of an enemy-occupied city. He led the charge. Unfortunately, only his horse and his body entered that city. His head remained outside."

I shivered to think of his bloody head rolling in the dirt.

"After his death I was of no further use to the emperor, so he gave me in marriage to my husband, a champion in that year's Civil Service Examination." She squeezed my arm and looked into my eyes as though to warn me that her story was for my ears only.

That evening I closed my bedroom door and proceeded to set the scene for my play. On the top shelf of my armoire I found some long-neglected wooden dolls. I chose one to be the general's only daughter and placed her on the camphor chest with her fine dappled pony. I arranged my toy soldiers in a long column. Then I moved them onto the chest. "No," the general's daughter cried as the soldiers carried her away. "I won't go. You can't make me. I will never leave my pony." I turned other soldiers into eunuchs, wrapping them round with hair-ribbons and handkerchief robes. I fashioned a many-roomed, multi-storied palace with pillows and ribbons and lengths of rice paper.

I marched my cavalry down from the camphor chest and over to my desk. Lacking a doll whose head could be removed, I found a ball to serve as the general's bloody, severed head and sent it rolling on the floor, where it was lost in the dust amidst the hooves of his soldiers' galloping horses. It was long past my bedtime when the general's daughter finally left her palace/prison to marry the soon-to-be wealthy, handsome, and brilliant champion of the civil service examinations.

Before the summer was over, however, the dashing Han Gang, Mandarin First Class, Consul General to the Philippines and all the colonies of Spain, took to his bed. By the middle of winter he was dead.

When he was alive, Ambassador Han had favored his second wife, gradually paying less and less attention to his first. The woman known on Kulangsu as Watermelon Head had been his wife during the years of study for the civil service examinations, first the county, then the provincial and regional, and finally the national. But she was a simple woman, uncultured, and as time went by and her husband rose to a life she couldn't fit into, she became bad tempered.

It was only natural that Ambassador Han would prefer the general's daughter. Watermelon Head didn't see it that way, though, and when he died, she saw her opportunity to take revenge. Citing her position as First Wife, she took control of all their late husband's assets. She forced the general's daughter and her son, my future husband, to sleep in the storage shed and fed them whatever was left after the maids and dogs had their fill.

It wasn't long before the news of their mistreatment was whispered from servant to servant and servant to mistress. I was in Mother's room when our old maid, Ah Kwai, passed on the shameful details. From that day forward, I stopped making a child's game out of Madam Han's life. I went back to reading and attending the opera, where the heroines' suffering eventually came to an end.

Now that she lived in our house, my mother-in-law no longer had to contend with Watermelon Head. And yet, even here, she still preferred to wait until the maids were done before eating breakfast. I looked at the lime blossom she'd placed in my hand and raised it to my nose.

"You must be hungry, dear." She pierced the hardened dirt with her trowel and turned it over.

I nodded. She wouldn't flinch if I mentioned the booming sounds. She might already have heard them and formed her own opinion. Still, I couldn't bring myself to disturb her peace. I sniffed the lime blossom and turned away. Today I would eat breakfast with my own mother. In the privacy of her room, the two of us could discuss what I thought I'd heard.

9

3

*T*he hazy morning sunlight filtering through the French doors
softened the appearance of Mother's room. Later, a harsher light
would accentuate all the details in this space filled with too many
objects—shelves crammed with books and bottles and jars, a statue of
the Buddha, landscape paintings, the screen she dressed behind, her
bed with its intricately carved dark posts and headboard. Mother was
sitting on the bed now, rocking gently, her eyes closed as she chanted
her morning prayers. After a moment of silent emptiness, she opened
her eyes. "Good morning, sweetheart," she said. My daily benedic-
tion.

I took a jar of jasmine-scented oil off the shelf and rubbed it
between my palms. "Did you hear anything this morning?"

"No. What did you hear?"

"I don't know for sure." I smoothed oil over her arms. Then I
held her elbow as she lowered her tiny, crippled feet to the floor and
shuffled over to her chair.

"What did it sound like?"

"Bombs, or naval artillery." This was crazy, discussing bombs as
though they were a flock of geese. I walked to the window and stared
at the horizon. Until now, the distant rumbling had been nothing
more than thoughts and sounds, invisible and bloodless. Suddenly I
felt the reality of it all. "It came from the south, Mother. That means
the invaders are on both sides of us now." I clenched my fists. "What
in the name of heaven is our bloody army doing?" It was an unfair
question, since only weeks before, in the Battle of Taierhchuang, the
Chinese Army had shown the whole world the warrior spirit of our
men. Against tremendous odds, they had held the old walled city,

annihilating two of Japan's best divisions and sending the rest scurrying away in defeat.

"Ours is a vast land," Mother said. "The foreign dwarfs imagine they can conquer and hold it, but in time, you will see, their pride will bring them down. Remember, what is going to be diminished must first be allowed to inflate."

"Aren't they inflated enough already?" Whether she was quoting from a Buddhist tract or from the *Five-Thousand-Word Classic*, I didn't like the sentiment. "Certainly by now the Japanese are puffed up beyond the bursting point."

"Wars aren't concluded in weeks, An Lee, or even months. Why don't you come and sit down."

"In a minute." I unlatched the French doors and gave them a shove. Stepping into the morning air, I raised my empty hands to the sky. All my heroes had horses and armor, a double-bladed sword or an eighteen-foot-long spear. They had their blood brothers to save the day. And I? My spindly arms fell to my sides. I should have been a man. Instead, here I was three months' pregnant and alone in the house with a toddler, some maids, and two old women—one, impassive in her suffering, the other a semi-invalid. And, despite the fire burning in my chest, I, too, was only a woman. No father or father-in-law. No horse, no sword. No blood brothers. And my husband, nowhere to be found.

On the lane below, three girls and a boy laughed under their umbrellas. How ordinary they looked, the boy with his straight-legged walk, heels first, toes up! Farther up, a man came into view. My heart leapt. His gait and posture, the shape of his head, all looked so familiar. Then I wasn't sure. He was slender like Yu-ming, but was he too short? He came closer, and I realized that what I'd taken for a firm, purposeful stride was, instead, a rigid lack of grace. I blinked. He was close enough now for me to see that his skin was too dark, his nose too wide.

How could I have mistaken such a man for my husband? Every cell in Yu-ming's body was known to me. It was inconceivable that I could have confused him with someone else, even from a distance, even with my nearsighted eyes and through the branches of our sandalwood tree. Seeing the way he held his shoulders, I could tell he lacked courage, something that was second nature to Yu-ming. I'd seen it demonstrated over and over.

One day on the playground, for example, I saw him save a little harelipped boy from his own high-school classmates. Yu-ming was the only one brave enough to confront the bullies. None of the others dared, even when their classmates went beyond teasing and started kicking the boy. If I could have stopped them, I would have, but what could a six-year-old girl do against ten or twelve big boys? Yu-ming didn't even pause. He walked into the center of their circle, extended his hand to the boy, lifted him up, and took him away.

"An Lee, you're letting in the damp."

The man who wasn't my husband was so close now that I could hear the tune he was singing, a marching song. I closed the French doors just as Su-lee arrived with our breakfast tray. She seemed relaxed now that the flowering bamboo was far enough from the house to save us from its ill effects.

"I'm sorry," I said as she arranged the food in front of Mother. "I forgot to mention that I wanted a soft-boiled egg."

"Yes, ma'am." She gave me a warning look as she left the room, and I nodded to reassure her that I wouldn't mention the bamboo to Mother.

"How old is she now?" Mother asked.

I subtracted from my age and added Su-lee's as I poured our tea. "Sixteen. I was six years old when you bought her." I remembered because it was the year I began to dress as a girl, the year I met my mother-in-law and started to love Yu-ming. There'd been floods in the north, and Su-lee's parents had followed other refugees south looking for work. Along the way, threatened with starvation, they'd been forced to sell the other three children. All they had left was Su-lee, and no one wanted to feed a useless one-year-old girl. It was Su-lee's good luck and ours that they found their way to our gate.

"Sixteen?" Mother picked up a steamed bun and broke it open. "Then I should start looking for a husband for her."

I spread butter and orange marmalade on my toast and took a bite. For a moment—the toast crunching between my teeth and Mother's dumpling shining white and round between her chopsticks while steam rose from our teacups—the world around our breakfast table was small and particular and sweet.

When Su-lee returned, she was carrying my egg, half-shelled and jiggling in its eggcup-throne at the center of a tray held waiter-wise above her shoulder.

"Su-lee," Mother said, "I think it's time we start looking for a husband for you."

Quickly, before my egg could topple off its cup, I jumped up and grabbed the tilting tray.

"A husband, ma'am? You mean you want me to leave your house?"

"That's not what I mean, dear. But you are old enough now to be someone's wife and start your own family."

Su-lee fell to her knees in front of me. "Oh, Young Mistress, you tell her. This is the only home I know."

I sighed. Didn't every young woman eventually have to marry and leave her parents' house or her master's? She knew Mother would give her a generous dowry and investigate the prospective bride-groom. Even after the marriage she would make inquiries to be sure Su-lee wasn't mistreated. I picked up my spoon and cut through the slithery white of my egg. "Don't worry. It won't happen immediately," I said. "And I'm sure you will find that marriage has many pleasures."

"Oh," she sobbed, collapsing on the floor like a wet mop.

"Now, now." I took her hands and lifted her up. "We'll talk about this later. We have more than enough to worry about today."

Little did she or even my mother know that—besides the obvious problems of the distant booms and a missing husband—I had one more thing to worry about today. As soon as I finished breakfast, I had an appointment at the beauty parlor to get a permanent wave. It was the first of my life, and though I was determined to do it for Yu-ming's sake, I hated the idea.

It didn't occur to me that I should change my hairstyle until he'd been missing for seven days. At first I thought he was merely late. By the second day, I began to worry. I walked to the ferry landing and asked everyone I saw if they'd seen him. Then I took the ferry across to Amoy and asked more questions. I sent a cable to his boss in Foochew. *Han Yu-ming expected yesterday stop did not arrive stop send news to Madam Han Yu-ming.* His reply was short: *Sorry no news stop will investigate stop Johann K Metzler.* On each of the four succeeding days I sent him another cable. His last reply read: *Siemens can do nothing more stop Johann K Metzler.*

After that, I didn't know where to turn. I dragged myself home from the telegraph office and went straight to bed, where I stayed for the next two days. I didn't eat or even speak to my daughter. Then, just before dawn on the third morning, I had a dream in which Yu-ming was standing in a forest, healthy and alive. He seemed to want to tell me he was all right and that he would come home as soon as he could. He didn't speak, but the message was unmistakable. He was alive.

I pushed my quilt aside and ran into the hallway. Despite the early hour, I called down to Ah Kwai to prepare my breakfast. Then I opened my camphor chest and took out a dress-length piece of powder-pink silk with an all-over design of white chrysanthemums. Like Mr. Metzler, I could do nothing more to find my husband, but my dream had shown me that he would come back. And if the dressmaker hurried, at least then I would have a new spring *chipao* in which to greet him. I was already designing it in my head, a slim, ankle-length dress with cap sleeves and white piping around the mandarin collar.

When I finished at the dressmaker's shop, I walked to the beauty parlor. I'd had my hair trimmed only four weeks earlier, but I wanted it perfect for Yu-ming. The beautician seemed to know because she took great pains to cut it straight. When she finished, she parted and brushed it. Then she looked at me in the mirror and sighed. I didn't understand. Even though my eyes were still a little puffy, my face looked normal. My newly trimmed hair, which made a triangle outside the oval of my face, was as shiny as a pond in moonlight. I raised my eyebrows and looked at her reflection.

She frowned and pushed out her lower lip—not an attractive expression on her sallow, square face. "This straight hair makes you too plain," she said.

I turned away from the mirror and addressed her directly. "My hair," I said, "does not have the ability to make me anything at all."

"I'm sorry, Madam Han. I only meant that a permanent wave would look good on you. All the modern young women are getting one."

"And why would I want to do what everyone else is doing?"

"I don't know, ma'am. I just thought..." She removed my cape and whisked my shoulders and neck with a brush full of talcum powder. Then she made one last attempt. "If you change your mind, ma'am, I'm sure your husband will be pleased with the new you."

"My husband is lost," I said, jumping to my feet.

The idea of wavy hair stayed with me, though. Yu-ming was a modern man, an engineer, a graduate of Chiao-tung University in Shanghai. He spoke four Chinese dialects as well as English and German.

Another day passed, and though Yu-ming didn't come home, I still believed he was alive and that it couldn't be much longer before he returned to me. When he did, I decided, he should have a modern-looking wife.

4

*T*he sky was overcast as I started for the beauty parlor, the lanes
and houses gray and shadowless. My red coat was a touch of
color, but everything else was dull—the moss-edged brick and stone
walls on either side, the steps and inclines that followed the contours
of the land, and the open concrete gutters molded to the earth beside
the lane. A sensible landscape, I thought, plain and serious as a
straight-haired woman. I walked quickly by habit, my white T-strap
shoes slapping against the wet pavement.

The Widow Ng's fifth son was standing in the doorway of their
noodle shop, feet wide, his arms crossed over his chest. How like a
fighter! I thought as he raised a muscular arm in greeting. He was
every bit as broad-shouldered as his older brothers, all of whom had
grown strong from the daily work of stretching and cutting the long,
heavy strips of dough. Amoy and Kulangsu were as full of work-hard-
ened men as our mountains were full of granite. My own son (for
that's what he would be, this child due to be born in the Year of the
Tiger) would be as strong as any of them—a fighter as well as a
scholar.

A *trained* fighter, I decided, as I approached a young monk sitting
straight-backed in an alcove next to the pastry shop and dropped a
coin in his begging bowl. A man like him would be capable of springing on an unsuspecting enemy as quickly and lethally as any tiger.

"Bless you, Young Mistress," he said, his words falling heavily on
my unworthy ears as I hurried off to my frivolous pursuit.

From the street, the beauty parlor looked peaceful. I opened the
door, and a blast of feminine chatter and pungent smells hit me in the
face. When I saw my beautician from the previous week's haircut

smirking at me, I almost changed my mind. But then a modest-looking older woman asked what I wanted and I blurted out the answer.

"A permanent wave," I said.

She led me to a sink where she shampooed and towel-dried my hair. Then, after ushering me over to a table cluttered with the tools of her trade, she began the long, tedious process of waving my hair. First she parted it into thin, perfect segments, sometimes parting it two or three times to divide off exactly the right amount of hair. Then she picked up a metal roller and a small rectangular tissue, taking care not to pick up two tissues by mistake. She folded the tissue over the ends of my hair and wrapped it around the roller, which she spun tightly against my head and ratcheted into place, a process she silently repeated over and over until my head was covered with rollers, hard, unnatural contraptions that pushed against my skull and pulled on the roots of my hair. Next she squirted something on each of the rollers that made my eyes smart and my nose burn.

On my way to and from the sink, I'd exchanged pleasantries with a friend who was having a manicure and pedicure as she sat under the hair dryer. I couldn't see Ling when I sat down again, but throughout the ordeal of parting, wrapping, rolling, and squirting, I could hear the conversation she and her sister Chi-chi were having.

"I should have counted," my friend said, her voice high and theatrical. "Ben-hui has four sisters and only one brother."

"That doesn't mean anything."

"Oh? But look at his older brother—three daughters, no sons."

"Still, the fortune-teller said you would have a son."

"And the Buddhist monk assured me I would have a daughter."

"You haven't gone back to the old abbot at the Chang Chou Monastery yet."

"I have no good dreams to relate to him. That's what he wants."

Ling and her sister spent the next few minutes trying to come up with a method for capturing Ling's dreams. Would it help to tie a bell on her finger? Which finger? The ring finger? The pinkie? Maybe her thumb. What should she eat before bed? Congee, warmed goat's milk, pomegranate berries, nothing? Would nap dreams be as good as night dreams? If I hadn't felt so immobilized by the frowning concentration of my beautician, I would have shaken my head in disbelief. Didn't Ling know that the kind of dream she desired couldn't be forced? It came or it didn't come. And once dreamed, it didn't melt away like ordinary dreams.

Sitting under the hair dryer, hot air blowing across my ears, I thought about my tiger dreams, how powerful they were, how indelible their imprint upon my mind. The beautician rinsed the solution from my hair and rolled it in a new set of curlers. And as I sat under the dryer again, I thought about my dream of Yu-ming. It was a different brand of dream, not from heaven, but from Yu-ming himself. That was why the images were so meager—only him, some mud, and a few trees. Even if the desire in his heart was strong, his skepticism would have canceled it out.

When it was time to remove my second set of curlers, the old beautician came to life. She loosened them two at a time and unrolled them with both hands. "Beautiful!" she exclaimed, noisily dropping them into a bucket.

Beautiful? I wanted to cry.

She combed the bent disfiguring mop of hair until it winged out from the sides of my head like a bird in flight. "How glamorous!" she squealed. "Elegant!"

The girls on either side agreed, dropping their combs and clapping. "One hundred percent modern!"

What could I do now? It was a *permanent* wave. All the way to my scalp.

As I prepared to leave, the beautician from the previous week appeared with my coat. "You made a good decision, ma'am," she said smugly. "Now you truly look like a woman of the modern world."

"That I do," I said, thinking that neither my stupid hairstyle nor the events of our times were any improvement at all over the past. "And now," I said under my breath, "we shall see what the so-called modern world has in store for us." I paid my bill and for the second week in a row left the beauty parlor in a huff.

If only I'd brought a head scarf. I thought of putting my coat over my head, but it was past noon, already starting to warm up, so I put it over my arm instead. People were coming out of the bakery with flaky pastries filled with sweet bean paste and rice-flour squares stuffed with ground peanuts, honey, and sesame seeds. The young monk was still sitting in the alcove, his begging bowl beside him. I hurried past, wishing him a good day but assuming he wouldn't recognize the new me.

"Good day again, Young Mistress," he said softly.

I stopped and turned around. "Tell me, Brother," I asked suddenly, "are you acquainted with the Chang Chou Monastery?"

He sprang effortlessly to his feet. "Yes, indeed, Young Mistress. I live there."

"Do any of your monks interpret dreams?"

"Yes, several."

"Which one has the most skill?"

"Abbot Zhang, of course."

"Then he's the one I must speak to."

The monk swayed and tilted his head. "I don't know if he'll consent to see you. But if you tell me something about your dreams, I'll see if he's interested."

I bristled. How could he not be interested in my dreams?

"I dream of white tigers," I told the young monk. "Three white tigers and a monk who eats dog meat." I didn't tell him about the white pillars the tigers climbed on the mountaintop or how they blinked at me from their perch, daring me to understand their significance for my unborn child.

"Oh?" The young monk raised his eyebrows. "When did your dreams begin?"

I placed a hand on my belly and looked down.

"Ah, I see."

I felt my cheeks redden and hurried on, identifying myself as Liu An Lee since my own name was better known in some quarters than my husband's.

"I know your mother," he said. "Old Mistress Liu is a generous contributor to our temple."

Suddenly the wind shifted, bringing garden smells with it—dirt, mold, jasmine, and orange blossoms overlaid with the promise of rain. When it came, the rain was in small drops that only dampened my permanently waved hair without straightening it in the slightest.

*　*　*

Jit, nung, sa, shi, go. The numbers echoed in my head. Six, seven, eight, nine, ten. Eleven. Already eleven. When the sun rose, it would be the eleventh day since he was due to return. First an hour late, then two . . . then a day. And the days kept coming, one after the other. At some point, the numbers would become too large. The way they had when I was a schoolgirl counting the number of times he spoke to me.

A crazy thought. How could I compare the two? Counting our meetings in those days had been like collecting jewels, wrapping each in a square of silk, gathering them into the treasure chest of my heart. Then, when the meetings became too many to count, it was cause only for rejoicing.

He was a high school teacher in those days, out of reach for a schoolgirl. His future, they said, lay somewhere beyond the classroom. He should have gone to university, such a brilliant student. His father, Ambassador Han Gang, had been a renowned scholar. But his father's first wife, Watermelon Head, had control of her late husband's fortune, and she refused to spend a single copper of it on Yu-ming's education. It scandalized his father's old friends, who knew how much Han Gang had adored his Mongolian wife and her only son. They'd tried to reason with Watermelon Head, appealing to her sense of justice and shame, but she wouldn't budge. Finally the friends collected money among themselves and sent Yu-ming to Chiao-tung University in Shanghai.

Such was his destiny. And mine, since it was during those years when he had no money for college that he began to notice me. At first, for me, it was just a crush. I loved him the way I loved colorful birds and opera stars and courageous generals. Then one afternoon in the early spring my perspective changed.

Father had returned from Malaya laden with gifts—fresh mangoes wrapped in tissue paper, Danish biscuits in painted tins, and jars of Scottish jam and British marmalade. He always brought me something special. This time it was a porcelain figurine, a European woman with painted lips and a full skirt that hid everything except one dainty foot. Unwrapping the figurine reminded me of all the toys and treasures he'd brought me when I was a child, so I was unprepared for what I heard the following day.

He and Mother were in the parlor with their backs to the open window. They didn't know I was reading under the sandalwood tree. "With both you and Goh Dang-ben at home," my mother was saying, "this would be a good time to broach the subject." I was only half-listening at that point. Goh Dang-ben was Father's friend, a wealthy merchant who'd made his fortune in Malaya.

"What does An Lee think of the young man?" my father asked. I could tell them what I thought of the young man if they were referring to the only son of Goh Dang-ben. He was a pale-faced fool who laughed like a donkey and spent his time gambling and spouting empty-headed nonsense.

"It's too soon to involve her," Mother said.

"I disagree. I don't want to jeopardize my good relations with Goh by approaching him before I know whether An Lee would consent to it."

Consent to it! I thought, finally understanding. I dropped my book and covered my mouth.

"Consent to it!" Mother said. "What are you talking about? What young woman if given the choice would agree to leave her parents' home for the home of a stranger? What would you expect her to say?"

While they argued, I thought about the man I would marry. He wouldn't be a pale-faced fool like Goh Dang-ben's son. Not in a million years. I closed my eyes, and suddenly, like rice water overflowing its pot, all my previously unknown desires came spilling out. The man I married would have high ideals, I nearly shouted. Like the hero, Liu Pei, he would treasure high enterprise and stand up for the weak and the poor. He would be a scholar, a man of deep learning. Not bookish, though.

I opened my eyes, and there were the fresh sandalwood leaves lying against one another, rubbing back and forth in the breeze, sunlight illuminating their delicately veined undersides. My husband would have red lips and long ears, I thought. He would have a fine straight nose and eyebrows like silkworms. The man I married would be as irresistible as a runaway horse. I closed my eyes, and immediately I saw his face. It was Yu-ming's.

*　　*　　*

Light was beginning to show at the window. Another day. It was time to stop counting and remembering. I stepped onto the balcony and listened. Nothing. I focused on the faint line to the east where the China Sea met the light of the pre-dawn sky. Pure silence, the earth holding its breath.

Then they began—the low, lazy booms, so muffled by the air between there and here that they seemed imagined. I counted eight explosions.

Only then, as I was turning to go inside, did I see the monk from Chang Chou Monastery. He was standing at the gate, his head bowed. I called for Ah Mei's amah to let him in and to tell Ah Kwai to serve him tea. Then I got dressed.

Before his teacup was half-empty, I was ready to go.

I should have told someone where I was going, I thought as we walked across the island to the ferry landing. Oh well. They didn't need to know everything, and besides, Ah Kwai saw me with the monk.

On the crossing, the monk and I stood near a window, watching the blue-green water. "Did you hear the explosions in the south?" I asked as we approached Amoy City.

He nodded.

"And what do you make of them?"

"Japanese bombs," he said, his monkish expression disappearing. His mouth and eyebrows twisted downward and his flushed face took on the angry red and black look of an operatic mask.

We still had a long way to go, traveling through the city and across Amoy Island on foot and by bus, to Jimei on another ferry and the rest of the way by rickshaw. By the time we reached the monastery, the morning was half-gone.

A tall, narrow-eyed monk greeted us at the gate. He ushered us through an anteroom and into a courtyard. My companion took his leave there, and the gatekeeper led me through a corridor that brought us, after several turns, to another courtyard. At the far side was a small wooden door. We ducked through it and started up a path that led into the forest and up a hillside. The monk looked over his shoulder several times to see if I was keeping up. Eventually, seeing that I had more energy than the average woman, he stopped checking on me and scaled the hill at his own brisk pace.

For a time, we kept the hill to our right. All we could see on the left were treetops and the distant sky. Then the trail took us across a stream and through a grove of giant bamboo. We emerged within view of a hut. In the packed-dirt yard in front of it, a swordsman was performing exercises—posing, knees deeply bent, sword horizontal over his head. A moment later, he was twirling and leaping, his dark blue robes flying. Strangely, although his movements were those of a young man, his eyebrows and his wispy beard were pure white.

"Wait here," the slit-eyed monk said. "I'll tell the abbot we've arrived."

So, this was the famous Abbot Zhang—eighty-five years old, they said, and still a top martial arts practitioner.

He completed his set, bowed, and presented his sword to the slit-eyed monk. Then he strode, gown flapping, toward the hut. The monk signaled for me to follow. On the porch, the abbot stood for a moment gazing out over the pine forests and foothills. "Please," he said finally. He indicated two wooden stools and waited for me to sit down. He smoothed the back of his skirt and joined me on the other stool. "The dreams?" he asked.

"They started, Father, soon after this child was conceived." I placed a hand on my belly. "They weren't the kind of dreams that melt away in the morning."

He watched me without expression, his eyes almost black under his white eyebrows.

"Always I dream of a monk and three white tigers. The monk watches the tigers, but he has no fear of them; in fact, he usually ignores them, sitting down instead beside his fire where he proceeds to eat his meal of roasted dog meat. The tigers pass him on their way up the mountain. They climb until they reach a clearing with three white pillars at the center. They circle the pillars, snarling first at me and then at each other until finally each one chooses a pillar and climbs to the top."

The abbot stood up. "The tiger is a symbol of fierceness and courage," he said, "the masculine principle of nature and the lord of all land animals. The five-hundred-year-old white tiger controls the wind. Look below you, and you will see Amoy's inner harbor. You know what the knolls on either side of it are called, don't you?"

"Of course, Father. Tiger-head Hill and Dragon-head Hill."

"The tiger and dragon who control wind and water are the lucky combination that has brought prosperity to Amoy. The monk is Ch'i Kung, a holy man in life, later an immortal who was often seen riding a tiger. The white tiger of your dreams is a powerful sign, more so three white tigers. Without a doubt, dear lady, your child will be a leader of men. In wartime he will be a field marshal; in times of peace, a prime minister."

Yes. That was the way I'd interpreted the dreams. My heart raced. My son was going to be a great man. A hero. Abbot Zhang's interpretation had confirmed it.

"Ch'i Kung is one of the most powerful immortals," he said, holding me with his eyes. "But he was a difficult man, rebellious and scornful of the accepted disciplines. Your dreams are not of comfort or peace. And the tiger signifies not only strength, but also violence and turmoil."

I tightened my lips. Of course. Would I be so foolish as to assume that a hero could escape the world's fury? My son would suffer if he must, but he would suffer for the people and for justice.

"I cannot tell you more until after the child is born," the abbot concluded.

I stood up and bowed. "Thank you," I said. "It was good of you to see me."

Making my way down the shaded path and through the hidden corridors and courtyards of the monastery, I thought only of my son and his illustrious future.

Once outside in the muggy heat of early afternoon, I looked around for the rickshaw puller. Seeing me first, he jumped up and grabbed the poles of his tumbledown rickshaw.

After discussing the price, I got in and we started down the hill. The puller's bare feet plop-plopped on the dusty road as my backbone played its own song on the wooden backrest. After a kilometer or so, the land leveled out, the forests and hills giving way to fields of newly planted rice, brilliant green in every direction. A beautiful, lonely expanse. By now the puller was wheezing with every breath. I pictured him falling, the rickshaw wedged over his lifeless body.

"Not so fast," I said. "I have plenty of time." He slowed slightly and then—in a hurry I supposed to fit as many passengers into his day as possible—returned to his former speed. "You needn't run. I'll give you a good tip when we get to the Kulangsu ferry landing." This time he did slow down, and soon his breathing sounded better. The image of him collapsing under his rickshaw stayed with me, though—him, dead on the road and me, sitting there, helpless and alone.

"Stop!" I shouted.

"What?" The poor man jolted to a stop. We were nearing the outskirts of Jimei. An old farmer herding ducks paused to stare at me. Behind him was a vendor carrying pipe tobacco and cigarettes in a wooden box.

"I need to buy cigarettes for my mother," I said quickly, waving the man over.

"Baby brand cigarettes," the vendor sang. "Golden Dragon brand."

"Baby brand," I said, holding out my money.

"Sorry, miss. That's not enough. The price went up again two days ago."

"Golden Dragon brand then."

"The same. It's the taxes, miss. Do you want Sun-brand? No tax."

"Not on your life. Give me the Baby brand. And some matches." I took out some more coins.

"I only have matches from the *Friendly Power*."

"Then you can keep your bloody matches." What nerve? It was bad enough he tried to push Japanese cigarettes and matches on me. He didn't need to use that stinking Japanese euphemism. *Friendly Power*, my eye!

"It's easy enough for you to be high-minded," he said as he grabbed my money, "but this is my rice bowl. If people want to buy cheap cigarettes and matches from the dwarf devils, what can I do?"

My heart pounding, I snatched the cigarettes. He was right. I knew that. For the past three years Japanese goods had been flooding the market. The island of Quemoy had become one huge warehouse. If I didn't buy Sun-brand matches, our own servants would. Maybe by now nothing else was available. I stuffed the cigarettes in my pocket and closed my eyes.

When I opened them, we were already approaching Jimei. All across the tide flats, workers were gathering the seaweed they'd spread on the beach earlier, and fishermen, their small boats scattered across the water like willow leaves, were pulling in their nets. I hadn't eaten all day. I told the puller to stop at the first stand he saw. They had no ordinary snacks, so I bought a paper cone of freshly shelled raw oysters.

The Jimei-Amoy ferry was larger than our ferry, and dirtier. The lower deck was for carts, rickshaws, lorries, and the occasional automobile. Most of the passengers at this hour were city dwellers returning home—day laborers and merchants, government officials, students, soldiers on leave. With my back to a window, holding the dripping raw oysters away from my body, I watched their faces. Which one, I wondered, was a Chinese traitor? Which merchant had made deals with the smugglers? Which government official was on the payroll of the Japanese imperialists? Which student had arranged for the dissemination of *flying and leaping propaganda*? I studied their faces, and, even though they may have thought they were inconspicuous, by the time we were halfway to Amoy I felt I could recognize them. Their twitches and fidgets gave them away, their smug expressions and wavering gazes.

While I was busy examining my fellow passengers, it seemed that two old women, not ten feet away, had been staring at me. Our eyes met, and they looked away. "Fake foreign devil," one of them whispered.

How dare she? I was about to step forward and confront her when I remembered that my hair was sticking out from my head with more waves than a typhoon-whipped sea. I leaned out the open window and let the sea air cool my burning face.

At the landing, a boy hawking a three-day-old copy of the Shanghai paper *Xinwen bao* caught up with us. "You want to buy?" he asked.

I shook my head and read the headline. "General Tang turns and fights."

"Only two copper coins to rent it for an hour."

I shook my head again. General Tang, a hero of Taierhchuang, was still fighting in the north near Hsuchow, according to the *Amoy Times*. "In death's grip," its headline read. "Through village and field."

Soon we were inside Amoy City, weaving through the crowded streets, my rickshaw driver dodging donkey carts, handcarts, soldiers, and other rickshaws. A blinding sun flashed between the three- and four-story buildings along the main street. When I get home, I thought, it will be dark already.

5

Su-lee was standing inside our gate, frowning—or so it seemed in the yellow glare of the streetlight. "Have you eaten rice?" she asked as she swung the gate open. In our dialect, "Have you eaten rice?" is a greeting, a "hello," not a serious question. But seeing her sour face, I was tempted to confound her by replying that, no, I hadn't eaten. Instead, I wished her a good evening and handed her the paper cone of raw oysters. She took them and turned away. "Why are you so late?" she asked over her shoulder. It wasn't like her to be rude. But I was tired and weak from hunger, so I let it go.

I was about to run upstairs and change my blouse when my mother-in-law stepped in front of me. "Where have you been?" she demanded, not even asking if I'd eaten. Before I had a chance to answer, she turned imperiously on the heel of her large, unbound foot and strode through the vestibule.

I'd always been an erratic eater, forgetting to nourish myself until I was so hungry I was frantic. Following my mother-in-law to the living room, I had to clench my teeth to keep from lashing out. Why was she treating me this way?

"An Lee," Mother scolded the moment she saw me. "You've been out all day."

"What!" I shouted. "Am I a child that I need to answer to each of you?" The words flew out before I had time to register the strangeness of the scene. Mother, who usually stayed in her room, was seated on the wicker love seat, embroidered cushions tucked behind her back, her tiny lotus feet resting on her favorite padded stool. She had her arm around Ah Mei, who—although it was an ordinary day—was wearing her best dress and her favorite pink hair ribbon. My eyes were

27

still adjusting to the light when I noticed a man at the far end of the room. He was looking out the window into the near-darkness. An army officer, the bulge of a pistol showing beneath his jacket.

He turned to face me, and... Ay! Blessed Mazu! It was Yu-ming. He was alive. Even before I lifted my foot off the floor, I could see myself running to him.

"An Lee," he said, his voice stopping me, "where have you been?"

"Where have *I* been? You're asking *me* where *I* have been?" The fear I'd felt these past days exploded into anger.

"Ma, Ma." Ah Mei ran to me. Then everyone was talking at once, excusing Yu-ming and blaming me.

"He's been here since morning. We've been waiting all day."

"You didn't tell anyone where you were going. Didn't you know we'd be worried?"

"These aren't ordinary times. You should know that."

I felt faint. "You! All of you!" I started toward Yu-ming, whether to pound on his chest or fall into his arms, I wasn't sure. Ah Mei darted in front of me. I would have tripped over her if Yu-ming hadn't caught me.

"I'm sorry," he said. "I had no chance to contact you. As you can see, I was drafted into the army."

"In the middle of a business trip?" It didn't make sense. Ordinarily it was common soldiers, not officers, who were rounded up. They were weighed and measured. Then they were forced to draw a slip of paper from a bamboo tube. My mind raced. In my dream he had been wearing work clothes, not a uniform.

"Engineers go out in the field." He smiled, trying to make light of it. "And, coincidentally, so does the army. I ran into an old university classmate, General Li. Let us just say, he was very persuasive."

I grasped the back of the love seat. My husband was home. Yu-ming, here with me. I was burning with the joy of it. And yet, I couldn't forget how hungry I was. "Can't we eat?" I moaned.

"Certainly." Mother kicked her stool aside and waited for Yu-ming to help her up. Oh, how I longed to touch him, to crash into him, to wipe out the windy canyon between us! I reached for his hand, and despite the presence of the mothers and maids, he let me take it. All too soon, though, he had to let go so he could help Mother into the dining room.

After seating her, he turned to me. "Your hair looks different."

"I had a permanent wave." *Different,* was all he had to say? I lifted Ah Mei into her high chair and sat down.

"How long will it be this way?"

"Forever," I snapped. "Until it grows and I cut it off."

He looked perplexed, as though his question had been simply about the science of waving hair. "Mm," he said belatedly. "It's very stylish."

The cold dishes were already on the table, the ginger-pickled radish mounds, spiced hazelnuts, and roast duck—special food prepared for Yu-ming's homecoming. I poured tea for him and a little tea in water for Ah Mei while he and Mother reached with their chopsticks for choice bites of radish pickles and duck to place on his mother's plate. Yu-ming put a slice of duck on my plate and I placed some radish on his. It was a common courtesy, taken for granted on ordinary days. Today, however, the simple acts of serving while being served were pleasant beyond the ordinary.

"I sent cables to Mr. Metzler." How could he not have told his boss? Yu-ming, who was always so conscientious and capable. I was the one who did the right thing. Kept my head. Didn't panic—those first few days anyway. Yu-ming didn't need to know how overwhelmed I'd been after the last cable.

"I contacted Mr. Metzler this morning," he said. "It was my first opportunity."

The fragrance of roast duck filled my head as I lifted a slice to my mouth.

"An Lee, where did you go with that monk?" Mother asked.

"To Chang Chou Monastery." I swallowed the duck and then I described the abbot's *kongfu* practice for them, how agile and strong he still was.

Yu-ming smiled. "Our recruits, on the other hand, don't even know their right feet from their left. The only way you can train a peasant to march is by making him wear a shoe on his left foot and a sandal on his right. Then instead of 'left, left, left-right-left,' the drill instructor shouts, 'shoe, shoe, shoe-sandal-shoe.'"

We all laughed, although it was, in fact, neither strange nor funny that a peasant shouldn't know left from right.

"An Lee," my mother-in-law said after the laughter died down, "you still haven't told us why you went to Chang Chou Monastery."

I was surprised at the note of disapproval in her voice. Surely my mother-in-law, who had feet large enough to run on and a spirit meant to ride free across the open plains, should have understood my desire to go where and when I wished without a chaperone. "The abbot sent word that he would hear my dreams," I said, my attention focused on the steaming platter Su-lee was placing on the lazy Susan—grouper and tofu topped with black beans and thin strips of ginger and spring onions.

"And what did the abbot say?" my mother-in-law persisted.

I watched Yu-ming pick out cubes of fish for his mother and then for me. "That our son would grow up to be a great leader—a prime minister or a field marshal," I said.

Yu-ming replaced the serving spoon and shook his head. "That's just superstition. A wild guess without a shred of scientific evidence. The best one could say is that there's an even chance the abbot is right about the child being a boy."

Mother sighed. "An Lee cares too much about having a son."

"Did I choose my dreams?" She was right, though. I did care, immensely. I wanted a son to please Yu-ming. But also for myself. Mother, I think, would have been content with another granddaughter, satisfied to live in a house filled with women and girls. I glanced at Ah Mei, but she was too busy watching her father to notice what we were talking about.

"Ah, the bread," my mother-in-law said as Su-lee put a plate of steamed buns and a platter of sliced fatty pork with pickled vegetables on the table.

"Bring the goat's milk for my mother-in-law," I told Su-lee before she returned to the kitchen. "And tell Ah Kwai to make an omelet with the oysters."

Finally we dished up the rice and everyone settled down to eat. Rice, heavenly rice. Where the duck and fish had failed to tame my hunger, the rice succeeded. I scooped a clump into my mouth, and another. Then, beginning to relax, I glanced at Yu-ming. He's home, I thought happily. He really is home. Tomorrow I'll make spring rolls for him. I'll send Ah Kwai out early to buy pork and vegetables, fresh tofu, tiny live shrimp, and delicate, lacy seaweed. I'll roll the skins paper-thin while Ah Kwai slices the pork and vegetables. Then I'll fry the raw peanuts and grind them fine and even.

"I'm going to make spring rolls for you tomorrow," I announced. Oh, how I longed to rid him of that stiff uniform!

"I'm sorry, An Lee," he said softly. "I can't wait for your spring rolls."

"Why?" Didn't he know I could fly around the kitchen faster than a seabird in a typhoon?

"I have to leave by sunrise."

"No!" A great wind seemed to suck the air from my lungs.

"It's not my choice. I have orders."

"No!"

"An Lee, you're just making it more difficult for everyone."

"You can't interfere with his orders."

Before I had a chance to apologize, again our mothers had joined forces in berating me.

"I'm sorry," I told them. "I'm sorry, sweetheart." I saw his eyes soften. Then I noticed something else. Somehow his eyes had become as restless as a cat's in mid-hunt. "Where have you been?" I asked.

"I can't tell you."

Of course. He couldn't say anything. How fearful it was, this soldiering! I shivered, suddenly understanding how soldiering would separate us as his engineering never had.

"Ah, the oysters," Yu-ming said as Su-lee entered carrying a platter mounded with oysters and sun-yellow eggs smelling of garlic and the sea. He spooned some onto his mother's plate and then mine.

I turned the lazy Susan, and Mother scooped up some oysters. "Oysters, dumpling?" she asked, turning to Ah Mei.

Ah Mei's head dropped to the side and her eyes fluttered shut.

"I'll get her," I said. As I lifted her out of the high chair, she clamped her legs around my waist and laid her sweaty, warm head on my shoulder. "Ah Mei, Ah Mei," I sang in her ear. "Daddy is home. Your daddy is home." I patted her back, and as I started up the stairs, I sang her another song, about the morning when her daddy would be gone again.

*   *   *

That night, our bed was turned back on both sides, the down comforter showing the underside of its duvet in two rosy triangles against the lacy white top. Two small lamps spread welcoming circles of light out from the desk and bureau. As I shut the bedroom door, I felt the perfection of the space—this warm, familiar pocket of a room. "Your jacket," I said.

He undid the buttons and took it off. Finally. "The enemy is moving toward Fukien Province," he said, handing me his jacket.

"I know. Their ships and airplanes are shelling the coast."

He looked at me with surprise. "How did you know?"

I shrugged and opened the closet door. Why should he be surprised whenever I knew something?

"While I'm away," he said, "you must stay here in the International Settlement. As long as the Western powers continue to claim their neutrality, Kulangsu and other treaty ports like it will be safe from invasion. There are many dangers out there, An Lee. It's not only the Japanese. Communist bandits regularly come out from their camps in the mountains. Refugees from Nanking and Shanghai have taken to the roads, mostly to the west, but some will find their way here."

I hung up his jacket and waited. He wouldn't want to be touched until he was finished giving advice.

"Tell the maids not to buy smuggled goods," he continued. "People will take us for Chinese traitors."

"I'll tell them," I said, touching his arm.

He hadn't finished, though. He walked across the room, the leather heels of his boots tapping softly on the wooden floor. Even in boots, his step was light. Yu-ming was not a man to impose himself on the earth unnecessarily. "You must stock up on food," he said, turning again. And now I could see something of the soldier in the neatness of his turn. "You must have a good store of rice and flour, sugar, salt, and soybeans. Dried meat," he said, pacing the room again, naming off the items on his mental list. "Dried fish and shrimp, pickled vegetables, peanut oil, sesame oil, salted eggs, preserved fruits, canned goods."

Jam, I thought, and dried mushrooms and noodles. Also he forgot to mention candles and matches, but I held my tongue. The less I interrupted, the more quickly he would be able to fulfill what he considered his obligation and the more quickly we could touch. Although I was inclined to feel insulted that he thought I'd need his help in choosing the contents of a well-stocked larder, I understood. Yu-ming was a Confucian gentleman, honorable and duty-bound to protect his family and country. I took his pajamas out of the bureau drawer. "I'll take inventory first thing in the morning," I said.

He nodded, allowing himself to relax just enough for his lips to plump. I couldn't help smiling, for I loved his soft, full lips. I doubted he could appreciate how much I loved the contradiction in his face—so serious and long like his mother's, his intelligent eyes and narrow, straight nose leading to those sensuous lips. My Yu-ming, like Liu Pei in *Romance of the Three Kingdoms*, was as irresistible as a runaway horse. "At university," he said, his lips tightening again, "people called us fanatics for taking over the president's office and preaching a boycott of Japanese goods. But even we, the vanguard, those of us who thought we understood Japanese ambition, had no concept of its extent. Who could have imagined then how insatiable their appetite for Chinese blood and territory would be?" He sighed and sat down on the edge of the bed.

He was right. Ten months ago we couldn't possibly have conceived of Peking falling to the Japanese, and then Shanghai and Taiyuan and finally the capital at Nanking. I took out my nightgown and switched off one lamp so that only the small desk light across the room was left on. Sitting down beside him, I made my fingers soft as a hummingbird's wing and unbuttoned his shirt. "How did it happen that you crossed paths with General Li?" I asked. So close, and now it was I—my mind and body competing for satisfaction—who was slowing things down.

"I was investigating sites for a hydroelectric dam on the Jiulong River." He stood up and stepped out of his pants. "General Li was camped near one of the potential sites."

"But how did he convince you to join him?"

He draped his pants over the back of a chair. "He said his unit was sorely in need of engineers."

An unsatisfactory explanation, but I accepted it then because we were coming together, our bodies softening, our blood racing. And, oh, the relief of it, the pure lightness! My stony earthen self dropped away, and as he lowered me onto the bed, life-fire filled my veins and cavities and the *wind and rain* took us away.

Afterward, I draped myself across his body—my leg over his leg, my arm around his chest, my head on his shoulder. I kissed his cheek. He kissed my lips. Then he closed his eyes, and I rose weakly on one elbow and kissed his eyelids.

* * *

The next morning, he was up before dawn. I opened my eyes and watched him button his shirt. Then I pushed back the covers and sat up.

"It's too early," he said. "Go back to sleep." A feeble attempt to command me in light of our still-fresh bond.

"No. I want to walk you to the ferry."

He shrugged, and we continued dressing, I in a simple cotton dress, the color as dark and tangled as the hour, he in the plain brown uniform of a Chinese army officer. Then he strapped on his pistol, and when he turned to me, I could see from his eyes that we were separate beings again.

"I leave our mothers in your care," he said. "Watch over Ah Mei, and look after your own body for the sake of the baby. Remember, An Lee, the maids are dependent on you for their safekeeping."

"I'll take good care of everyone," I promised.

I put on a sweater, and he tightened the strap on his duffel bag. Then, without a word to either of our mothers, we tiptoed down the stairs and out the door.

As we walked, crossing the sleeping island in near silence, my curiosity about his soldier's life and my need to share the mundane details of my own melted away, and I was left with only one question. I saved it until we were at the ferry landing. By then, a thin light was spreading up from the sea beyond Amoy Island. Dark figures were scurrying around, preparing the ferry for its first run of the day. "When will I see you again?" I asked.

He glanced at the ferry. "I don't know."

"Make an estimate. Engineers are trained to make estimates."

"Yes, but we're taught to base them on scientific data, and I have none."

"Make a guess."

Chains clanked. An engine sputtered to a start. "Instead of a guess," he said, "I'll make an intention. If I can, I'll spend a few days at home sometime next month. I can't promise anything, but I'll try my best."

I opened my mouth. There was something I needed to say. So many things. "Yu-ming." All my thoughts flew away like leaves in a high wind. "Please," I whispered. "Please come back to me."

6

*S*oggy clouds were gathering overhead. A gust of wind blew my hair. I pushed it back, and in a flash of lightning I saw him boarding the ferry—his upheld hand, his straight nose, the pistol bulge in his soldier's uniform. I waved and waved. And then he was gone and I started back, dragging my feet and then running. Away from him— up the hill and past the shops with their metal shutters rolled to the ground. Gone. Gone again. I slowed to catch my breath. The glow from an electric light spread across the lane where the first shopkeeper of the morning was noisily raising his shutter.

Suddenly, it was raining, fat, cold drops hitting my head and shoulders, setting off another, saltier shower. By the time I reached our gate, I was soaking wet, my tear streams swallowed up by the river of rain.

All day it rained, water cascading off roof tiles and splattered on the paving stones. The sound of thunder was deafening, even in the pantry where I went to make an inventory of our emergency supplies. When I finished, it was still raining, so I took the mending basket into the sitting room. Sifting through it, I found one of Yu-ming's stockings. I held it to my face for a moment. Then I took out the darning ball and got to work. Unlike those gentle women in days of old, I did not sit at a window embroidering pillow covers. I darned his worn stocking instead.

When I was finished, it was as good as new. I tested the heel and toe with my fingers. Then I placed it on the side table. Sighing, I rifled through the basket again and found a pair of cloth soles small enough to fit my mother's once-bound feet. Yu-ming told me that his mother used to line his shoes with newspaper because she had no cloth. On rainy days the paper would turn to mush. And in the evening, she'd have to stuff the shoes again with dry newspaper. It was a disgrace, the way Watermelon Head treated them after his father's death!

I chose a needle, but my stomach knotted up at the thought of all the tiny stitches I'd need to make around the edge of the cloth soles. Throwing the soles back in the basket, I walked to the window and stared out at the noisy-quiet world of drumming rain, slick paving stones, and drooping tree branches. What was I supposed to do? How does a woman wait for her husband? How does a patriot fight an enemy who hasn't yet arrived? I searched the world beyond our rain-streaked window for an answer.

Finding none, I returned to my chair. Retrieving the cloth soles and cotton lining for my mother's shoes, I threaded my needle and proceeded to sew them together with the smallest, neatest stitches I could manage.

In the afternoon, I played with Ah Mei and read aloud from a book of poetry and practiced my calligraphy. What more could a woman like me do on such a day?

That night, I curled up in bed and listened to the rain. How short our time together had been: Only a day, and then he was gone, his side of the bed as cold as before. Half a day actually. I hugged my knees and thought about all those hours I'd missed out on when I was at the monastery. Enough for Ah Kwai and Su-lee to prepare half a dozen dishes, enough for everyone's anger against me to reach fever-pitch. What had I been thinking, leaving the house when I knew Yu-ming could have returned any day?

I rolled onto my back and flung my arms out. What a fool I was! I shouldn't have gone out. I kicked off the covers. I put my palms on my belly. The child inside me was as small and silent as a nut. Next month when Yu-ming came back, he'd be bigger. Yu-ming would put his hand on me and feel the baby kick. Next time things would be better. Yu-ming would have a perfect homecoming.

I turned over again. Thunder rumbled over the mainland, reverberating in my breast like a distant bomb. Sleep was beginning to paralyze my limbs, but my mind was still active. It jumped from the bombs to General Li and the puzzle of how he'd convinced Yu-ming to join the army. Hadn't Yu-ming already been serving the war effort? Didn't the army need the roads and railways, the electric power and bridges companies like Siemens built? So what did General Li say?

And why couldn't Yu-ming explain it to me? With sleep scattering my thoughts, I only knew that he was far from me and growing ever more distant.

The next morning, the feeling was gone. Sunshine was pouring through the window. Birds were chirping. The air smelled of orange blossoms. Okay, I told myself, he *did* promise to return. And we *were* safe here on our little island. So why not enjoy the day? I put on some loose pants and a tunic and ran to catch Ah Kwai, who was already out the gate and heading for the market.

Ah Kwai had been with us since I was born. She was my wet nurse and later my amah. Even when her husband was alive, she and her daughter had stayed in our house. Later, with her daughter married and living so far away that she could visit only twice a year, Ah Kwai had focused her motherly attentions on me.

The market was busy with the usual early morning commerce. Housewives and cooks eased past each other, scanning the produce, smelling the melons, lifting the fish's gills to look for fresh blood. Ah Kwai and I bought a bunch of finger-sized sweet bananas. We leaned down to sniff lemons and limes. We stopped in front of the live squid to watch their inky spots dance and change color. The price was high, but, just the same, we bought enough squid for one small dish.

Beyond the squid and the shrimp, two women wearing wooden clogs and wide sleeves bowed ninety degrees to each other. We were used to seeing the Japanese bullies we referred to as *ronin* openly giving orders to smugglers and skulking in the shadows while their Chinese lackeys stood on street corners repeating the lies they'd been fed about the so-called culture of the "Kingly Way." But the Japanese women who lived in the International Settlement usually sent their maids to the market. Why today were they here, blocking the aisle with their bowing, laughing behind their hands, pointing their fingers at our seafood? And all the while, their armies were bombing our cities and killing and raping our citizens. Even as my husband was putting his life at risk, a vendor was selling Japanese sugar for five dollars, Chinese sugar for eight.

"Last week it was only seven," Ah Kwai complained as we started home. "Where will it stop?"

"We will buy less. Wait!" I said, remembering that I'd planned to buy a newspaper.

"Look," Ah Kwai said, raising her eyebrows as I paid for my copy of that morning's *Amoy Times*. "Your opera is coming to town again."

On the wall behind the stack of newspapers was a poster advertising next month's performance of a traveling opera: *Love beside the River*. "*My* opera?" I paid the vendor and turned on my heel.

"Ha, Young Mistress," Ah Kwai said, hurrying to catch up. "You know what I mean. You're just like Tian Ying."

I rolled my eyes. "How can you say that, Ah Kwai? We're nothing alike. I was a child when I dressed like a boy. She was a young woman. Besides, she not only dressed like a young man, she deceived the man she loved." I smiled in spite of myself, enjoying the sweet pleasure Tian Ying must have felt in passing herself off as a male student.

The brothers who must part sit by the river where Mandarin ducks swim in pairs.

How sad that they must part, she sang in reply.

We laughed, shaking our heads at how funny her old voice sounded singing the young woman's part. "We'll bring Su-lee and my mother-in-law to the opera," I said. "Mother can go by sedan chair." Why not! I thought, striding ahead. Why not enjoy ourselves while we can? An answer clinging to my question could not be ignored. Because of Yu-ming, it whispered. Because he has no chance to enjoy himself.

Ah Kwai caught up to me and took my arm. By the time we entered the kitchen, we were humming again. I plucked carrots from my bag and sang a couplet.

The river shines bright and clear.

Reflecting their faces as in a mirror.

Ah Kwai pulled pieces of pork from her bag and replied in a forced soprano.

The tongue-tied reflection,

Speaks not a word.

"Bravo," Su-lee shouted from the doorway. "Sing it again. I want to learn."

"Here," Ah Kwai said, slapping a chunk of pork belly on the cutting board and handing Su-lee a cleaver. "Cut this into chunks the size of my two fists."

We repeated the couplets three times, washing and drying mangoes as we sang.

"*Love beside the River,*" my mother-in-law commented from the doorway.

"Mother-in-law, it's good you're here." She knew all the operas— the lines and arias of every hero and heroine, villain, and clown who sang for the Young Emperor or the Empress Dowager while she was a prisoner in their palace. It was the one compensation she and the other female "guests" enjoyed for their contributions to national security—being allowed to watch the rehearsals and sometimes the performances of the country's greatest opera stars. "What comes next," I asked her, "after the reflection in the river?"

"First give me an apron and some work to do."

I emptied a bag of shrimp onto the counter.

She rolled up her sleeves and tied the apron around her waist. Then, breaking the head off a shiny, blue-gray shrimp, she sang in the rich, full voice of a young man:

> *The brothers who must part walk side by side*
>
> *As the Mandarin ducks take flight.*

Even without the exaggerated gestures of an actor, my mother-in-law's voice and the expression on her face were capable of bringing the characters to life.

Later, when Ah Mei and I found her in the garden, her face was once again as deep and impenetrable as well water. Seeing Ah Mei, though, she put down her watering can and held out her arms. Thank goodness for Ah Mei. It was for her sake that my mother-in-law had finally been persuaded to move in with us. I only wished we could have convinced her sooner. She suffered too long under the tyranny of her husband's first wife.

"Take your finger out of your mouth," she told Ah Mei, "and you can sing with Grandma. I'll teach you a new song. Listen."

Drop the string string

And the kite flies away.

Ah Mei sang with her grandmother, matching tone for tone in her sweet, pure voice.

You can't be heavyhearted and fearful all the time—at least in those days I couldn't. It was April. All around me the world bloomed green and yellow, pink, coral, and lavender. The suffering of my countrymen and the danger surrounding my husband and, in fact, all of us, were out of sight and earshot. Words in a newspaper, hearsay. Even the opera with its centuries-old story seemed more real. On a sunny spring day, it was easier to believe in lovers.

That afternoon, as I sat at my desk recording the prices of what Ah Kwai and I bought at the market, the opera was on my mind—Ying-tai and her young man, their verse-making on the road, and their pledge under the willows. I wrote today's date at the top of the page. Then, chewing on the end of the ballpoint pen, I thought about Ying-tai's father. It was his greed that had kept the young lovers apart, his refusal to give up his plan of marrying her to a rich man's son.

Three hundred grams of squid, I wrote, and, unbidden, my old grudge against my mother insinuated itself into my thoughts. She was the one who had wanted me to marry the son of Goh Dang-ben and then the son of Yu Teng-sui and after that the son of Li Beng. All rich men's sons. Mother was the landowner in our family. She used to sit at her big red desk, tallying up the rental income from the property she inherited from her father. In recent years, she worked from a padded chair with a portable desk rolled into place over her knees. On some days she worked from her bed using a large mahogany bed table. True, she was generous with the poor, but she always knew where each dollar went.

One catty of onions, I wrote, *forty cents. . .*

As I carried the list downstairs to her room, a bitter taste rose in my throat. I remembered how she'd reminded me not only about Yu-ming's poverty, but also about his mixed blood. "If you marry him," she said, and even now I recalled the outrage in her voice, "your children will not be pure Chinese. They'll be one-quarter Mongolian."

"They will be sons of Genghis Khan!" I shouted. I was so angry I threw my teacup on the tile floor and ran from the room.

"Spoiled child!" she yelled after me. "Do you think chinaware grows out of my skin?"

That was years ago, though. She'd long since come around, even blessed our marriage. I knocked on her door. "The marketing list," I said as I stepped inside.

"Thank you, dear. You can put it on my desk."

"We spent eight dollars for sugar," I added, unable to resist challenging her.

"So much?"

"For Chinese sugar," I said. "Would you have us support the Japanese to save three dollars?"

"Of course not. Come here, dear." She took my hand. "Times are different now. We have to be like water and flow around these obstacles. How is your mother-in-law today?"

"She's well."

"Good. Didn't I hear Ah Mei singing some songs from an opera? Could you bring her in to sing for me?"

I was ashamed. How could I forget how kind she'd been to my mother-in-law? I squeezed her hand. "I'll go get her."

7

*I*n those early days, despite Yu-ming's absence, despite the Japanese women bowing at the market, our world didn't seem all that different. Even our storing up of emergency supplies was familiar, indistinguishable from the preparations we often made for typhoons. There were the bombs and the news we heard on the radio and read in the newspaper. But it all seemed so distant.

Whether Mother was able to anticipate how much things would change, I couldn't say, but she'd already begun taking action to preserve our wealth. She had her lawyer set up accounts in London, New York, and Toronto. Then she sent me to the bank with instructions on how much money to transfer.

By the third week of April, with most of her money safely out of the country, she started on her next project: burying her gold. One night after dinner she called Ah Kwai, Su-lee, and me into her room and told us about the holes she wanted dug in the backyard. "Make them two hands deeper than the length of your arm," she told them. "And remember, you must never mention to anyone what you are doing." She gave them strict instructions about waiting for dark nights and working in silence. After they left, she explained my responsibilities. I was to make one bag for every twenty coins using heavy cotton and a sturdy drawstring. Then I was to place each bag full of coins in a tin box and supervise its burial.

That first moonless night was cool. I groped my way to the center of the yard where the maids were waiting. "Young Mistress," Ah Kwai whispered, taking my hand. "Su-lee thinks we should dig in the far corner near the wall. I say we should make our first hole under the clothesline."

42

I tried to remember how the ground looked in the daytime, whether there was any indication of what lay beneath. Kulangsu was rocky, and we shouldn't start a hole we couldn't finish. "Probe the ground first with some bamboo stakes," I whispered. They found stakes and a mallet leaning against the fence in the vegetable garden. It took several tries and a few broken stakes before we found a place to dig our first hole. When it was ready, Su-lee dropped in the tin box I gave her. She and Ah Kwai filled it with dirt. Then we stamped on it and started searching for another spot.

In the morning, before they sprinkled sand and pebbles on the disturbed earth, I marked the location on my map and composed a couplet that described where the gold was buried. At two holes a night, the job was completed in less than two weeks. I added a final couplet. Then Mother and I memorized it and I destroyed the map.

Just in time. Only a few days later, we had our first close encounter with the enemy. I was out walking near the American consulate with Ah Mei and her amah, Po-ping, when we heard the hum of airplanes. They were approaching from the southeast, flying close enough that I could see the red suns emblazoned on their wings.

"Flying ship! Flying ship!" Ah Mei shouted.

"Red-eyed airplanes," Po-ping told Ah Mei, as though she was adding a new word to her vocabulary.

"Red eye, red eye," Ah Mei sang, twirling her skirt out like a parasol.

Suddenly one of the planes descended. When it was directly over us, it pulled up and dropped something that scattered in the wind like bits of confetti. "My... It mine," Ah Mei squealed, holding her hands up to a fluttering yellow paper.

I grabbed it away. It was the same kind of flyer I'd seen in the hands of the *ronin* and the Chinese traitors who stood on the street corners trying to lead honest people astray. *Land of Happiness* it shouted in bold characters, *Coexistence and Co-prosperity, The Helping Hand*. I ripped it up and threw it into the wind, not bothering to object when Ah Mei chased the now harmless fragments.

*   *   *

When the first bombs landed, I was sound asleep. Running to the window, I threw open the doors and shutters. The red flashes streaking across the night sky were accompanied by a barrage of tooth-jangling whistles, each one followed by a heavy *boom*. I couldn't see where the bombs were landing. My windows were facing the wrong way. Dashing down the hall to my mother-in-law's room, I found her already at her window.

"Look," she said, pointing at the house of Goh Dang-ben, the man who had been Mother's first choice for my father-in-law. In the flickering glow reflecting off the clouds, we could see the whole Goh family climbing onto their roof for a better view.

"Idiots," I said under my breath.

My mother-in-law shook her head. "They even bring their children."

We craned our necks to peer over the houses and trees at the glowing streaks from shells that appeared to be falling somewhere beyond the city of Amoy, close to Amoy Fortress.

"Young Miss . . . Han tai- . . . Please . . ." Su-lee was calling us from the stairway, her words coming in bits and pieces between the explosions.

"You go," my mother-in-law said. "I have to get my robe."

"I've been yelling myself hoarse," Mother said when she saw me. She was sitting on her bed, Ah Mei beside her, the amah leaning across the bed to hold Ah Mei's little hand. "Where's your mother-in-law?"

"On her way."

"Su-lee, go get her."

Mother's shutters were closed, but they couldn't shut out the sounds. I looked up as my mother-in-law stood, hesitating, in the doorway.

"Please, Han tai-tai," Mother said, "don't stand on ceremony." She fluttered her fingers. "Come on in."

Another bomb exploded, louder than the others. I ducked my head, and when I looked up, Ah Mei was hiding her head in Mother's lap.

"The Japanese aren't here yet," she said. "We still have time to make some decisions."

I opened the window a crack. "What?" I swung around and frowned at her. "If you're talking about leaving, we already discussed that last summer after Peking fell." Even Yu-ming thought we should stay. The Japanese would be crazy to invade Kulangsu with so many Americans and Europeans living here.

"That argument sounded better when your husband was with us and the Japanese were not on our doorstep. It's not too late to arrange for passage to Hong Kong or Manila."

"Now? With bombers flying over our heads?"

"What better time than in the midst of confusion?" Mother's clock rang the half hour. It was four thirty, still two hours before sunrise. If we chose to, we could leave this all behind, pack a few things, find a ship, and be on our way. I walked between the cluttered shelves and tables, and for a moment I felt the lightness of it... how it would be to let it go—all that love-soaked weightiness of everyone and everything I cared about.

"Would you come with us?" I already sensed my mother's answer. For her, it would be a grueling journey, even if we hired a sedan chair to get her to the ship. More to the point, though, it would take more than the mere possibility of trouble to get her to leave her home.

"No, dear," she answered.

"Then we can't go, either."

Hung-hung-hung. It was a sound I'd heard for the first time last October, lower and heavier than the Zeros. Bombers. Ah Mei slid down from her grandmother's bed and ran to me.

"I'm old and fat," Mother said, raising her voice above the din. "My lily feet are useless. You have the next generation to consider."

I picked up Ah Mei. "No. I'm not leaving you."

"Ah Kwai is here to care for me." She waved her hand impatiently. "Go now so I can get dressed."

She looked rattled. Ready for a cigarette, I supposed. My mother-in-law and Su-lee turned to go. Only Ah Kwai could stay behind. She was the only one who didn't have to pretend she knew nothing about Mother's cigarettes.

We migrated toward the kitchen—as though a cup of tea would solve our problems. I dropped into a chair and motioned for my mother-in-law to sit down. "What do you think?" I asked her. "Should we go or stay?"

She gazed past me, her eyes wandering slowly over an invisible landscape. "Manila is very hot," she said finally. "Nevertheless, one can live there without great discomfort."

Discomfort? Was that what she thought of me, that I was a woman who required comfort? I was a patriot. I could withstand a great deal for the sake of my country and my family. "What about Yu-ming?" I demanded. My husband. Her son. "He'd never find us there."

"Even if we stay here," she said, "it's not going to be easy for him to get through enemy lines, especially not if Amoy falls under Japanese occupation."

"It won't happen that way." Since the moment I jumped out of bed, my mind had been spinning, trying to rearrange the world I knew. I dropped my head on the table and thought.

"Aiya!" Springing up, I knocked over my stool before realizing it was only Su-lee at my shoulder setting the teapot on the table.

"I only told you about Luzon's heat," my mother-in-law continued, "because I have lived there and you haven't. Of course, it was different then, when my husband and my father-in-law were still alive." She slid the tips of her fingers over her cheek as though she were remembering her brief but happy sojourn in Manila as the wife of the Chinese ambassador.

"So, what is your advice?"

She shrugged. "The future contains more surprises than my poor mind can comprehend. But if you want to go to Manila, I'm sure we would be welcomed by the Chinese community there. Many people would still remember my husband. He and his father were highly respected."

"Are you saying we should leave?"

"Only if you want to."

Only if I must. I wasn't a nomad, the kind of person who would simply fold up my tent and ride away at the slightest provocation. Kulangsu was my home. Even Foochew, a few miles up the coast, had been too far away. "How can I leave Kulangsu?" I said. "And what about my mother?"

"It's up to you."

Ah Mei kicked the underside of the table and slid down between my legs. "Besides," I said, "I don't want to put a single unnecessary mile between myself and Yu-ming."

Su-lee pulled Ah Mei out from under the table and set her on the counter. Behind them, the approaching sunrise tinted the fog a dirty scarlet. Su-lee scooped out a spoonful of mango, and then, just as Ah Mei opened her mouth, the sky flashed a sickly shade of pink.

"Su-lee," I shouted. "Take her down. Now."

That was how careful I was in the beginning. I kept Ah Mei downstairs and away from the windows. I turned off lights. I made sure no one went outside. When our congee was ready, I lit a single candle and pushed Mother's breakfast table as far from the window as possible.

Later, my mother-in-law and I sat in the kitchen and drank more tea. You don't get used to the sound of bombing, not in a single day. I flinched with every explosion. I scrunched my shoulders and squinted and clenched my jaw until my head ached. The two of us sat there, drinking tea and trying to guess whether our soldiers, despite our relative lack of equipment and ammunition, would be able to hold the Japanese back. Our officers were more intelligent than the Japanese leaders, weren't they? We had a glorious, centuries-old history of military heroes. Didn't Chuko Liang from the Three Kingdoms period devise strategies to defeat the strongest foe? We sat there recalling famous stories from the past until we tired of the game. Then we stared into our teacups and listened to the exploding shells. Already I was sick of hiding out. I emptied my teacup and pushed back my stool.

"I think the bombing has slowed," I said.

Ah Kwai caught me on my way out the front door. "I need to see what's going on," I whispered.

She didn't hesitate. "I'll go with you," she said.

Before we'd gone ten steps, Old Mr. Lim called to us through the iron bars of his gate. "Tell me what you find out," he said.

I nodded, and we set off down a narrow lane. It was true, the bombing had become less frequent, but it was still going on. From the lane, walls and houses blocked our view on either side. Then, at my old middle school, an expanse of sky opened up. We climbed a little knoll that overlooked the play yard. More than a dozen teachers were gathered on the porch. One of them saw us and pulled the others into a tighter huddle. They seemed to be conspiring about something.

Through the trees I caught sight of planes approaching from the northeast. Then a formation of enemy bombers escorted by fighters flew straight toward us. At the last minute, they curved back toward Taiwan, leaving me panting, my heart pounding as loudly as their engines. Before we left our observation spot on the knoll, we saw two more groups of Japanese airplanes. Always they followed the same path, up and around, ignoring Kulangsu and heading back to the east.

When we returned to our lane, Old Mr. Lim was waiting. He pushed the gate open and limped out to greet us. "Bastards," he shouted, punching the sky and cursing until he fell into a coughing fit. "Tell me," he sputtered finally. "What did you find out?"

"Only that the bombardment is continuing without letup."

"I can hear that from here."

"And it doesn't seem to be getting any closer."

He nodded and we all went back inside.

8

*A*ll day the fighting continued. The sounds—nerve-rattling booms and bangs—were terrible. In the afternoon, the wind changed, and the scorched odor of bombs and destruction fell on us like a poisonous rain, seeping through the roof and walls, choking us with the pulverized remains of buildings and roads, crops and… well, I didn't want to know what else. Surely, I thought, darkness would bring an end to the attack. Surely, at the end of the day, like fishermen hauling in their nets, the soldiers would put down the implements of their bloody work. And yet, the earth turned and the sun sank out of sight, and still they continued to fight. Soon, I thought, tilting back and forth in the bamboo rocking chair, combing my fingers through Ah Mei's hair and rubbing her back. Soon.

When she was sound asleep, I laid her on Mother's bed. I didn't want to put her upstairs in the nursery where she would be four meters closer to any bomb the Japanese might drop on us in the morning. In fact, I decided my mother-in-law and I should sleep downstairs, too. I got Ah Kwai and Su-lee to help me, and we carried our mattresses and bedding down and arranged them in the middle of the sitting room, my mother-in-law's mattress on the floor next to mine.

By the time we lay down, the bombs and guns had finally stopped. But I was still shivering under my quilt, alert to every creak and bump inside the house, every footstep on the lane, every distant echo of a human cry. I listened to my mother-in-law's breathing and watched pale threads of moonlight slip through cracks in the shutters. The light was thicker than usual that night, infused with gunpowder and toxic dust.

"Baby," I whispered to the walnut-sized child inside me. "This is not what I wished for you—to be born in a time of war."

I closed my eyes. I wanted Ah Mei with me. It was cold here on the floor, but she could nestle inside my arms. I rose up on one elbow, and then, changing my mind, eased back down. She was already asleep next to Mother. No need to wake her. Bending my knees, I tucked one cold foot under the other calf and pulled the quilt over my ears. In the distance, I fancied hearing a chorus of white foxes baying at the moon and then an egret sighing as though she were dreaming of migrating geese. The foxes and egret were from a poem, a favorite of my teacher, Dy Yuhua.

I must have dreamed of Teacher Dy, because the next morning, awakened at daybreak by a renewed barrage of whistles and booms, she was still in my mind. A comforting presence. Dy Yuhua had been my teacher of Chinese Literature for three years, sharing with me and all her students not only her love of poetry but also her high ideals.

"Umph." My mother-in-law pushed her covers aside and sat up. Soon both of us were dressed and ready to go on what my mother-in-law called our "reconnaissance mission." Enough of being imprisoned in our own house.

The moment we stepped out the door, I had second thoughts. But my mother-in-law didn't pause. She swept through the gate and out to the lane.

When we reached the beach at Shuzhuang Park, the melon-orange flowers blooming in pots along the wall caught my eye. Seabirds skimmed the surface of the sea, rising into the pale blue sky. Then my eyes refocused and I saw the Japanese ship. It floated long and low in the water. Between two smokestacks, its mast rose beside a central structure that was high and jagged like a child's block tower. We crossed the sand to Nine-Bending Forty-Four Bridge and followed its zigzagging course along the rocky shoreline. Eventually we saw some junks in the cove and a crowd of people with suitcases and bundles piled around them.

"This is where we would come if we changed our minds," my mother-in-law said.

An unlikely occurrence. We wouldn't be so easily scared off.

We leaned on the stone railing for a while, catching a word here and there of the negotiations between the junk owners and the would-be escapees. Their voices rose and fell, panic breaking through then quickly restrained, as though they were afraid the cost would go up in proportion to their desperation.

"I suppose," I said, as we followed the Nine-Bending Bridge back, "that there's no shame in fleeing." I didn't like the way they looked, though. So anxious. Like mice skittering away at the first scent of a cat. Yet only yesterday, we'd been considering doing exactly the same thing. "I suppose," I continued, "that even the bravest general knows when to order his soldiers to withdraw and regroup." My mother-in-law was the daughter of a general. She had to know.

"Are you asking a question?"

I thought of Yu-ming, risking his life for China while these people cared for nothing beyond their own puny lives, and like the child I once was, I blurted out my true feelings. "If flight is honorable, then why do I smell cowardice in that cove?"

A smile flickered on her lips, but she did not answer.

At the top of the hill, we stopped to look back at the sea. For generations, its vivid blue had been the color of hope for Fukienese emigrants.

"Now we will see the other side of the island," my mother-in-law said.

We took the straightest of the curved lanes that cut across the southern third of Kulangsu. My mother-in-law strode ahead on her big feet, her ankle-length skirt flapping against her long legs while I trotted to keep up. The closer we got to the ferry landing, the more people we met going the other way—young people with bundles on their backs, families, peasants, gentlemen, all of them strangers. They stopped us to ask directions to the Municipal Building or the Anglo-Chinese College or to any place at all where they could take refuge. A white-bearded gentleman wearing a fedora and sunglasses asked how to get to Guxin Lu, where he said his second cousin lived. My mother-in-law told him the way. Then she asked for news.

"Yesterday," he said, "two battalion commanders were killed, and Division Commander Tan was wounded. Thus our forces had to fall back to Chang-tou last night. It is only a matter of time before the enemy takes Amoy City." He lifted the little bamboo cage he carried and gazed at his canary. "How many men have been newly turned into ghosts, I cannot say." The poetic phrase brought tears to my eyes and reminded me again of Teacher Dy.

My mother-in-law and I held hands as we fought our way through the crowd of wild-eyed men and women. At the seawall, we had a fuller view of the exodus from Amoy. Junks of every size and description were sailing toward Kulangsu, while on the Amoy side, people pressed down to the shore, struggling for the chance to cross over to the relative safety of the International Settlement.

A formation of enemy fighter planes passed overhead, curving back as usual toward Taiwan. Suddenly one of them broke away and dove toward the helpless boats in mid-passage. Its angle of descent was so steep I half-expected it to dip into the sea and pull up with a wriggling Chinese fish in its beak. Instead, it flattened out and began strafing the little ragtag flotilla, the machinegun bullets stitching a straight seam across the water and into the boats. Then the metallic chatter of the gun and the *plunk* of bullets were gone and the air was filled with the confused screams and splashing of people belatedly jumping overboard.

A jug-eared man beside me raised his fist to the sky. "Death to the dog-shit Japanese bastards!" he shouted. And we all joined in, a chorus of anger and impotence. When the fighter was out of sight, our attention returned to the shattered boats and the bobbing heads. Not far from our shore a small boat was sinking, a family clinging to its sides. A motor launch, in its rush to reach Kulangsu, sailed right past it. As the launch tried to dock, people pushed it away and shouted at the operator to go back and help the family. While they were arguing, the little boat slid below the water's surface, leaving behind six or seven people struggling to stay afloat. Please! I prayed as one small head disappeared and then another. Why in the name of heaven hadn't their mother taught them to swim?

My mother-in-law squeezed my hand. "We've seen enough," she said.

On every side, people were jostling and shoving until I could barely breathe. "This way," I said, pulling my mother-in-law onto a side street. I hadn't meant to stop by Teacher Dy's house, but here we were, on the quiet lane where she and her husband and children lived with his family. Maybe I thought she could find some higher truth in this senseless shooting of innocents. I knocked on the door and waited. From the upper floor, a man's voice rang out. I stepped back, embarrassed. It sounded like her husband, a mathematics teacher at the same school.

"Why must you always be so willful?" he shouted.

"I call it duty," Teacher Dy said.

"You," the man snarled. "You always have to have your own interpretation of everything."

"You knew I was an educated woman before you married me."

"Let's go," my mother-in-law whispered just as the door opened. A young woman stared blankly at us, and when I told her we would come back later, she closed the door without a word.

"Do you think I care nothing for my students?" the man's voice continued as we walked away. "If it were up to me, you know I would stay."

I pictured the lean, wolfish curve of his neck and shoulders. He was intelligent and good-looking, but, well… If someone told him to run, I didn't doubt that he would.

When we got home, Mother was in the sitting room hobbling around on her cane. She listened to our story, and then she called Ah Kwai over. "Get Su-lee to help," she said. "I want you to rearrange the canned goods and sacks of rice in the pantry so the young women, An Lee, Su-lee, and Po-ping, will have a place to hide. We need to be prepared in case the Japanese don't respect the International Settlement. An Lee," she said, turning to me, "I think you've seen enough for now. You should stay inside where it's safer." For a moment, her eyes met my mother-in-law's. Then they both looked away.

* * *

I heard them leaving, or thought I did—though I may have dreamt it, expecting our army would have to withdraw. Maybe what I heard were those left behind—the low, hollow sounds of them wailing, as though enormous holes had been blasted through their chests, leaving them surprised at the emptiness and wondering why it didn't hurt, why all they could feel was a breathless gasp where their hearts and lungs should have been.

Before it happens, it always seems reasonable. You can almost understand it—that a father might die or a husband join the army, that a favorite teacher could disappoint you, that an army would abandon the city. All these things have happened before, and you think you understand that they could happen to you. Afterward, when it actually happens, it doesn't seem reasonable at all anymore, and you realize you didn't have the slightest understanding of what it was like to be abandoned.

During the night, our army retreated. There's an old saying: Of all the thirty-six ways to get out of trouble, the best is—leave. At dawn, the enemy renewed its vicious attack, turning its attention to the opposite side of Amoy where Yu-tze-wei Fortress was still in the hands of our navy. Their bombers stopped looping back toward Taiwan. Now they flew so low over Kulangsu that as I hurried to Teacher Dy's house, I felt the gunners' eyes on me and hid in doorways as they passed overhead. I had to force myself to climb out of the shadows and continue on. It was none of my business, but ... I pushed past a group of glassy-eyed refugees and stepped up to Teacher Dy's door. I needed to know if she was going to stay.

Pushing my hair out of my face, I knocked on her door. "Teacher Dy," I called. "It's Liu An Lee. Are you there?"

The door opened a crack and her father-in-law, a tailor at Neat and Early Tailor Shop, peeked out. "You can't see her," he hissed.

"Why can't I?"

He blinked his watery fish eyes behind his thick glasses. "She's not here."

"Where is she then?"

He couldn't look at me. "I told them to leave," he said, puffing up his chest. "They all went with Principal Chang to Hong Kong."

"Who did?"

"The teachers. All of them."

That couldn't be true. Teacher Chiu wouldn't go. And Meng Yu, my Chinese history teacher, he wasn't the type to let the Japanese drive him away. Why would they leave Kulangsu? It was the safest place.

"Don't be angry, Miss Liu," the old tailor said, changing his tone. "My son promised to hurry back as soon as this is over. In the meantime...?" He lowered his head. "My grandchildren will be safe."

I wanted to pummel him. Why hadn't he done something? Didn't he have any control over his own son? I stepped back from the door, and wished him well—a mechanical courtesy.

On the way home, I chose the lane that led past the school. Perhaps, after all, I would find some of the teachers there. I pushed past a noisy crowd spilling out of the school's main gate and went around to the side. Scrambling up the hill, I braced myself against a low-hanging branch and looked down on what had once been our playground. In the large upper yard where students used to play shuttlecock and volleyball and exercise in rows, hundreds of men and women stood and squatted and leaned against the walls, their children huddled next to them. Below, in the smaller yard and under the roof where we used to play jump rope and marbles, people were lying on the ground and on mats, even on the Ping-Pong tables.

I turned and fled, stumbling as I ran down the hill to the lane. They were refugees. They had no other place to lay their heads. And yet, I couldn't bear the sight of them . . . taking over our school, pushing us out . . . making everything . . . so different.

I must have passed the coal store and Old Yap's pharmacy and the Longtou Street Teahouse. Outside Widow Ng's noodle shop, I greeted someone, but whether it was one or all five of her sons, I couldn't say. I wanted to rest, to lie down on my too-large mattress on the sitting room floor. Yet when I reached our lane, I walked right past our house.

My old tutor lived only a few blocks away, on the south side of the island near the sea. His little bungalow was the last house at the end of a narrow lane. Its mango-yellow paint dulled by years of storms and salty air, its roof mottled with mold and an assortment of cracked tiles, it looked like it had always been there beside the sea. I stopped ten paces from the door. Straining my ears in the lull between bombs, I listened for some sign of life.

The windows were unshuttered, but I couldn't see any movement inside. Maybe he was out, stocking up on vegetables or cigarettes. I moved a few steps closer and paused a spear's length from the door. I didn't know what to expect anymore. Who could guess whether Wei Jing-hai, the kind, upright gentleman who taught me to read and write, still dwelt in this little golden bungalow? I thought of peeking in the window to see if there was any sign of disarray. I couldn't, though. If he, too, had fled, I didn't want to know, not today. I turned and started away. But before I'd walked a dozen steps, I heard the door open.

"An Lee?"

I whirled around, and there he was, his scholar's gown hanging loosely from his broad, bony shoulders. I couldn't stop my tears from flowing as I hurried toward him.

"Here, here, little one. What's wrong?"

"Oh, Teacher Wei, I thought you'd gone."

"Certainly not. No captain would be foolish enough to make room on his junk for a poor tutor like me. Aiya! Look at you—your tears as big as soybeans. Come, come. I'll ask the maid to make us some tea." He handed me a handkerchief and ushered me into the house.

"I hope you don't mind the unconventional arrangement." He gestured toward the sitting room, where his two best chairs were pulled away from the wall to face the window, a small table between. "Mother and I have been drinking our tea by the window these past three days so we could watch the enemy's comings and goings."

The view took my breath away. From one side to the other, his window was filled with Japanese warships. Suddenly four shells leapt like flaming arrows from one of the destroyers. I ducked, although they were aimed at Yu-tze-wei Fortress on the opposite shore. Plumes of black smoke and flames shot up. Our big guns flashed in reply. I looked for smoke on the Japanese ship, but the shells must have fallen short.

"Their guns have a longer range than ours," he said, taking my arm. "Now come and sit down." He poured my tea and offered me biscuits. Then he sat down in the chair beside me. "This morning I've been able to identify three destroyers and eight smaller warships," he said. "Before that, their ships were mainly on the other side of Amoy and Mother and I had to content ourselves with counting airplanes."

I shook my head. How strange our lives had become! "You used to count sea ducks and egrets," I said.

"This is another season, An Lee. A new era. Chinese intellectuals don't retreat from the world to study the classics anymore. We haven't for a long time." He laughed wryly. It was something he never mentioned but sometimes hinted at—the years he'd wasted in his youth studying for the Imperial Examinations only to have them abolished a few months after he passed the first level. He may have won the title of *hsiu-tsai*, but by the time the Republican Revolution of 1911 brought an end to the imperial regime, it didn't mean much to be a mandarin anymore.

Another ship opened fire, and again, smoke and flames went up from a section of the fortress. "We must buy bigger guns."

Teacher Wei stood up. "It takes time to build a modern army. China may be the most ancient of countries, but it is also one of the youngest. Imagine, our Republic is only twenty-seven years old."

Pacing in front of the window, the battle raging behind him like a scene on a giant movie screen, he listed the major rail lines. Our national rail network ran from one end of the country to the other and inland to the northwestern territories and to Lanchow, he said. We had an airline, CNAC, whose Chinese and American pilots were the bravest in the world. We produced our own steel and heavy machinery and electrical equipment. We were even beginning to assemble our own trucks and aircraft.

Teacher Wei had always been like a soldier when he lectured, his back straight, his head high, his feet kicking out with each step. Today, although he was fifty-four years old, the same age my father would have been, he was as straight as ever, his voice as strong and sure. "We have a modern military academy," he said, "and modern universities and technical schools."

Yes, I thought. We have all that, and we have four hundred million Chinese people who know how to survive.

We drank one pot of tea, and then his mother came out to join us for another. When I stood up to leave, she grabbed my hand. "You know, child," she said, "you're still his favorite student."

"And he's my best friend."

Teacher Wei was waiting for me at the door, a Western-style tweed jacket over his Chinese gown. "I'll walk you to the end of the lane," he said.

Before we'd gone ten steps, we were stopped by a huge explosion, and then another, and another. Running back into his house, we stood at the window and watched as great fiery clouds rolled heavenward and the sky over Yu-tze-wei Fortress grew thick with black smoke and hellish fire.

Afterward, when our navy's ammunition dump was thoroughly destroyed, Teacher Wei walked with me again to the end of the lane.

"I feel like I'm falling down a hill," I said, "and each time I think I've reached the bottom, I tumble over and fall some more."

He nodded. "Do you remember, An Lee, when you were a child, about four years old? You were climbing Sunlight Rock with your parents, and we met partway up. I was with my cousin."

"The auntie who pinched cheeks."

"Exactly. That's why you fell. She ran up to you, cooing about your apple cheeks, and as you backed away, you tripped over a row of rocks that marked the edge of the viewing area. What you said a moment ago reminds me of that day. At first I thought you would only fall on your bottom behind the rocks. So I just stood there. I saw your father reaching out for you, and I heard your mother's voice. Catch her, she shouted, and I thought you would be caught, but you rolled head over heels. Even then I thought one somersault would be the end of it, and it was the same all the way down the slope. I could foresee only one tumble at a time, and I always expected that one to be the last. How slow I was to respond!"

"No, teacher. You were the first. I remember."

"I should have been faster."

"You were the one who scrambled down the bank and carried me up to my father."

He sighed. "Sometimes," he said, "it's harder to believe in the evil outcome than in the good one."

Autumn 1938

9

*T*hat autumn, while the Japanese were making their push up the Yangtze toward Wuhan, and eight hundred thousand Chinese troops were gathering to stop them, I was swelling up like a puffer fish. My belly became so large and my ankles so fat that even if I'd wanted to help the national effort, I wouldn't have been able to buckle my shoes, much less strap a belt of bullets around my waist. What was worse, I didn't feel the urge to fight anyone. All those mysterious secretions that course through the bodies of pregnant women had turned me inward, making me hopelessly gentle. Any other time, I would have stomped around the house in a rage when Yu-ming didn't come back after a month as he promised and couldn't even find a way to get a letter to me. It wasn't his fault, I told myself, the tone of my thoughts sounding uncharacteristically sweet. He'd write if he could. I worried about him, though. The gentling influence of pregnancy had no effect on worry and sadness. If anything, it gave rise to more than the usual number of tears.

In September, when we received news that the Nationalist leadership had moved farther up the river to Chungking, abandoning Wuhan, I should have been furious. And I was, but my anger quickly fell away under the onslaught of my craving for cilantro—a simple hunger that had become an obsession after months of shortages and deprivation.

Finally in October, when word came that Wuhan had fallen, I was too involved in my own pushing and straining to care. Such is the lot of women. While heroes were fighting and dying for China, I was lying on my bed, waiting for the next contraction and carrying on a conversation with my unborn baby.

"Sweet one," I crooned, "my precious, what name shall I give you?" I was searching for a name that would remind us of a time before the invasion. In a moment of clarity, I remembered Foochew and the weeks Yu-ming and I spent there, just the two of us, a man and a woman together, everything new and full of promise. "You were conceived in Foochew, my little one, and that will be your baby name: Ah Chew, for the city of your conception."

"Rest," the midwife advised as she smoothed coconut oil over my forehead and massaged my temples.

Later, I thought, when he's ready for school, Yu-ming and I will choose a formal name for him. We'll search history for a Chinese hero. Or, if one should arise in our time, one capable of throwing the Japanese devils into the sea, we will name our son after him. "I swear it," I said, aloud, making my firm intention known to heaven and earth.

"Please, Young Miss," the midwife said, "you must conserve your strength." She touched my eyelids, resting her coconut-scented fingers there until I kept them closed. Then she rubbed my arm and slid her fingers around my shoulders and neck, relaxing the muscles so that I dozed a little. Until...

Oh! Pain! It seemed that some cruel lord of births was commanding my body, forcing it tight like a coiled snake. Ai! The pain! I clenched my fists. Gritted my teeth. "Aiya!"

"Young Miss," the midwife said. "You must keep your distance. Let the pain be where it is. Leave it to do its work while you go elsewhere."

"Elsewhere?"

"Move into your breath, into the wind or the trees. Wherever you choose. You're not needed down below. Not yet. I will keep watch."

How could I go elsewhere? I opened my fingers and stretched them backward while she circled her fingers lightly on my belly. Then I relaxed my closed eyes and tried to move myself to a spot behind my forehead.

"Good," she said from a distance, somewhere near my pain. "Much better."

Breathing long and deeply, I forced myself to concentrate on my forehead.

"You made progress this time," she said when it was over. "But this child appears to be very large."

"Don't worry, Old Wang," I told her. "My baby might be larger than normal, but I'm stronger than the average woman. I promise you this child will be born as quickly as any other child." By now the more energetic secretions of childbirth were pumping through my veins. I was ready.

"We will see," the midwife said, cracking her neck on one side and then the other.

When she straightened up, I could see how incongruous her round face and rosy cheeks looked atop her scrawny, wrinkled neck. "Please, Old Wang," I said. "Rest yourself."

She sat down beside me and closed her eyes. By the time I realized how thirsty I was, she was snoring.

"Oh, baby," I whispered, putting both hands on the bulge of my belly. "Where are you?" He was quiet now—no kicking, no punching. But, oh, how thirsty I was! Where was everyone? *Yu-ming, where are you?*

I squinted at the scroll on the far wall, its chrysanthemums and bamboo now barely visible. Thin strips of moonlight slipped between the shutter slats and fell on the bare floor. What was it tonight, a waxing moon, waning, half, full?

In the distance, another rhythm, the synchronized steps of Chinese policemen. As they approached, the clomping of their leather boots resounded hollowly in the night. Even now, Japanese sailors were patrolling the streets over in Amoy. The footsteps stopped. One of the policemen said something; the other laughed. And then the pain began again, intensifying until nothing existed, nothing except… Yes, it was that small part of me that could watch from afar. In the midst of it, by some ancient female knowledge, I began to understand how to distance myself and at the same time help with the work of giving birth.

The midwife was up immediately, adding another pillow behind my back. She laid her hand on my chest and smiled as it rose and fell with my breathing. Then she walked around and stood between my legs. "Let it happen," she said. "Go somewhere else."

When the contraction was finished, I opened my eyes and Su-lee was standing in the doorway holding a tray. "Would the Young Mistress like some tea or cold boiled water?" she asked. Her eyes were puffy from lack of sleep and bright with fear.

I took the boiled water, sipped it, and closed my eyes. A moment later, dreaming, I found myself standing on the walkway outside our gate, my nightgown silvery in the moonlight. *I have to see what size the moon is,* I told two Japanese sailors. *Half,* one of them said as he swung his rifle up, aiming it at the white half moon. *But where is the other half?* The second soldier cackled and swung his rifle to and fro as though to shoot down a runaway half moon. *No,* I shouted. *Don't!* I grabbed at his arm, and he caught hold of mine. Then I was aware of the midwife patting my hand and rubbing my arm.

"Young Mistress," Ah Kwai said from the doorway, "the Old Mistress told me to bring you this to relieve your pain." She was holding a tray full of the paraphernalia needed for smoking opium. Opium, the source of China's shame and weakness. A poison pushed on us first by the British and now by the Japanese.

"I don't need it," I gasped as the pain started up again, rising and spreading like floodwater. I focused on the spot inside my forehead even while I allowed a passage to open up between my legs.

"Good, good," the midwife said. "You're as supple as a farmer's wife. Before long we will see the child's head."

Soon the pains were coming with hardly any respite between. "Push," Old Wang cried again and again. "I see the head. Push." She needn't have told me, for my body pushed of its own accord.

"Breathe this, my sweet." It was Mother's voice. "Put your mouth around the pipe and breathe deeply. There. Now again."

"Push. Push."

"Again, sweetheart. Again."

I knew it was the opium pipe, but I didn't care. I breathed, and I pushed. Breathed and pushed. Until finally, it was over, and my son cried out in an amazing full-throated bellow.

The midwife held him aloft. Without my glasses, though, he was a blur. "A boy," she said.

"I know. Let me hold him."

"She has to cut the cord and wash him first," Mother said. "Su-lee, add more hot to the cool water and test it with your elbow."

They turned their backs to me and gathered around my son's bathing basin.

I rose up on my elbows. "My glasses. Won't somebody find them for me?"

He was crying and splashing, and they were laughing until the midwife turned around and gave my baby, now tightly wrapped in a blanket, to my mother. She was sitting in her own armchair, although I couldn't imagine how she and the chair got up the stairs. "My little Buddha," she crooned.

"Mother," I said, even though no one was listening, "I'm going to call him Ah Chew."

My mother-in-law stood off to the side, waiting, as I was, to see the baby. By custom, my son was a Han, a member of his father's family. My mother-in-law was the inside grandmother. She was destitute, however, while my mother was rich. "Old Wang," I said. "His father's mother wants to hold him now."

I fumbled on the side table for my glasses until finally Su-lee ran over and helped me. I put them on and watched my mother-in-law smiling down at her grandson. He turned his face toward her and nuzzled her breast. "He's hungry," she said as she walked over and placed him in my arms. "He wants his mama."

*　*　*

Your son was born hungry, I wrote two weeks later. It was the sixth letter I'd written to Yu-ming, one for each month since he left. The others were all folded and stacked in a red lacquer box on top of my desk, each letter one page long. I used the finest brush pen, the thinnest paper, writing characters as small as the eye could see so that a single page could contain a month's thoughts. I hadn't heard from him since he left, but the letters were a testament to my belief that he was still alive.

I dipped my brush in the ink and continued. *The moment I took him in my arms, he started searching for food—sucking air and pushing his little nose into my skin. During his first hour, he drank from both my breasts. His appetite was so great that I had to hire a wet nurse.*

I hoped he would understand that I was different this time. I was up and around almost immediately—cheerful even—my face washed, my hair brushed and parted. If Ah Chew had had a normal appetite, I could have nursed him myself. Caring for him was pleasant and ordinary—despite the enemy across the channel, despite the shortage of food. Not the way it was after Ah Mei's birth when I was so tired, so inexplicably sad and irritated. It seemed inconceivable to me now that I hadn't wanted to hold or nurse her. I'm myself this time, I wanted to write. The other woman, the one who slept such long hours and dreaded caring for her own child, wasn't me.

I put the ink stick down and stared at my brush resting on its white porcelain stand, at the smooth, warm bamboo of its handle and the ink-stained rabbit hairs tapering to a perfect point. How I cared what he thought of me! Yu-ming, only Yu-ming and no one else. A gust of wind rattled the shutters—a cool, salty wind, invisible in the blue November sky.

I picked up my brush. *He brings me such great joy,* I wrote. I wanted to tell him how hard it was to find a wet nurse with enough milk in these days of occupation and how angry our little son became when he was hungry. What a tiger he was! I pretended to scold him for his impatience, but secretly I rejoiced in his spirit. Let the weak and comfortable glory in other virtues: in mildness, obedience, temperance, and prudence. What had all those gentle virtues gained for us—all that prudent kowtowing, that obedient fetching and carrying, those pasted smiles and newly cut sun flags? The examples set by Chinese collaborators had turned those virtues into dog shit as far as I was concerned. All that mattered now was courage and faithfulness, justice, hope, and strength.

His neck is unusually strong. Already he can hold his head up without the support of my . . .

"Mama." Ah Mei pushed open my door and ran in.

I looked over my shoulder. "Mama's writing a letter, dumpling."

"I wanna paint, too," she said, bumping my arm.

"I'm writing, not painting. Where's your nurse?"

"Nurse with my brother." Her plump, rosebud mouth drooped at the corners as it had all too frequently since Ah Chew's birth.

"Here, I'll lift you up on Mama's bed. You can watch." I'd meant to prepare her better for losing her amah, and I would have if Po-ping had stayed until the end of the month. But with her mother getting sick and her leaving in such a rush—even before the wet nurse started—how could I? "Sing me a song," I suggested.

She stood up on the bed, raised one fat hand, and gazed sadly at the ceiling. "Drop the string . . ." she sang, her voice trembling with childish vibrato, ". . . and the kite flies away."

I dipped my brush in the ink and wiped it against the edge of the stone.

"Mama? You not listen!"

"Yes, dumpling, I'm listening. Sing it again."

She made praying hands in front of her chest and took a deep breath. "Drop the string..."

I picked up my brush.

"Mama." She dropped to her knees and moaned.

"Okay," I said. I swished my brush in water and laid it aside. Then I ran toward her, pretending to bark. "Au-au. Au-au."

She shrieked and scuttled across the bed. Then she rolled over and looked up at me, her eyes wide with anticipation. "No, no."

"I'm going to bite you," I said, climbing onto the bed.

"No!" she screamed, squirming and squealing as I nibbled her leg. "You bad dog."

"Yum! What a tasty morsel! Now, where are those little oxen?"

She pulled off her sock and presented a dainty foot.

"This little ox eats grass," I said, wiggling her big toe. "This little ox eats hay." I shook her second toe and then each of the others in turn.

This little ox drinks water,
This little ox runs away,
And this little ox does nothing
But lie in our field all day.

I repeated the game with her other foot.

"Again, Mama."

"Wait. Listen." I stood up. "There's someone at our gate. Do you hear the bell?"

She kicked her bare feet in the air.

"Look. Do you see the big white chicken with black feet the lady's maid is carrying?"

She slid down from the bed and ran to the window in time to see two women step inside, the chicken flopping against the maid's leg. Another silky. I was so tired of drinking black-skinned chicken broth. The first bowlful always tasted good—the broth fragrant, the female medicinal herbs, still fresh—on the second day, though, the leftover soup turned pungent and bitter, and choking it down on the third was pure torture. Thank goodness the other postpartum dish was appetizing—the kidney, chicken livers, and hearts stewed in soy sauce, sugar, ginger, and garlic and served over rice.

I lifted Ah Mei onto my dressing table stool. "Let Mama brush your hair before we go down." She puckered her lips and stared at her reflection as I parted out a section of her fine, shiny hair and tied it with a red ribbon. Then I brushed my own hair, the brush sliding through the wavy bottom half as easily as through the straight hair nearer my scalp. I liked the permanent wave now that the curls were tamed a little. If Yu-ming could see it, I was sure he would, too. I took Ah Mei's hand, and as we left my room, I looked back at the half-finished page. The mail boat from Amoy had been back in service for several weeks now. Maybe today it would bring me a letter.

"An Lee, dear." Mrs. Ma jumped up when she saw me. "You shouldn't have come downstairs on my account. You're still in your confinement."

"Please, Auntie, take your seat. You're the one who shouldn't be going out of your way on these wartime streets. Didn't you hear the strafing a few minutes ago?" She lowered her eyes, reminding me how discourteous it was to discuss war before dispensing with the ordinary courtesies. "Ah Kwai," I called, "Su-lee, bring some tea and snacks for our guest." Su-lee rounded the corner, her tray laden with tea and snacks. "Cut some oranges, too," I whispered.

"I hope you're getting enough rest," Mrs. Ma said, taking my hand.

"Thank you, Auntie. I'm two weeks through my month of confinement, and already I'm more than halfway recovered."

She looked down at Ah Mei, who was holding her skirt out as though she were about to curtsy. "And who's this pretty girl with a red bow in her hair?" she asked.

Ah Mei stuck her finger in her mouth.

"Ah Mei, isn't it?"

There was a rustling in the hall and the flat, hobbling *pom-pom-pom* of a large person walking on tiny feet before my mother appeared in the doorway leaning on her cane. "Ma Yi-hun!"she said, dropping her cane and placing her palms together in greeting. "I thought I heard your voice. Have you eaten? Su-lee, bring some oranges."

Mrs. Ma and I helped Mother to a chair, and while I picked up her cane, she stretched her underdeveloped lower legs stiffly out in front of her and sighed.

"How are your feet, Ling-chu?" Mrs. Ma asked. Even after all these years the former members of the now-defunct Natural Foot

Society continued to be concerned for each other. Mrs. Ma, who'd been among those least in need of the Society's aid, was as dedicated as anyone. Like Mother, she favored cloth shoes, but from the size and shape of her feet, you could hardly tell they'd ever been bound. Her mother had been one of those progressive ladies who turned against foot binding early. She must have thrown her daughter's bandages away years before the Empress Dowager's 1912 edict banning the practice.

"Oh, these old feet," Mother said.

"You must continue to have them massaged with oil."

Mother nodded. "Between them, An Lee, Ah Kwai, and Su-lee massage these useless old feet twice a day. But, Yi-hun, what are you doing out on a chilly day like this? You should be resting in the comfort of your home."

"To tell the truth," Mrs. Ma said, "I look for any excuse to step out. These days, with fifteen people coming and going, six of them small children, my house is like the temple steps on a festival day."

"Your daughters?" my mother-in-law asked.

"Yes. And their husbands and children."

During the invasion of Amoy, every household in Kulangsu had added to its numbers—we fewer than most, taking in only Ah Kwai's young nephew, Yun-yun. Everyone had stories of relatives who escaped Amoy ahead of the invasion, or failed to do so. Mrs. Ma related how her husband, Kulangsu's police chief, had gone to collect their daughters and their families on the morning of May tenth. Somehow, she said, even on that first day, when everyone else still believed the enemy could be held back, he knew Amoy would fall.

My mother-in-law nodded. "Police intelligence."

Mrs. Ma shrugged. "Whatever information he had, it didn't convince my second son-in-law. He was fearful of losing all those bolts of silk and boxes full of imported goods he keeps at the back of his dry goods store. In the end, my husband sent three policemen to help carry things and left the job of arguing with my second son-in-law to our daughter."

"And your son?" my mother-in-law asked.

"He was living with us already."

I concentrated on the plate of sliced oranges Su-lee had set on the table between us. Obviously, I was happy for the Mas, and yet, thinking of them all safe and together, my eyes began to sting. I focused on the sheen of the oranges and the design the membranes made as they fanned out from a central point.

"Oh, my dear!" Mrs. Ma said. "I'm so sorry. I haven't even asked about Yu-ming. What have you heard from him?"

I took off my glasses and wiped the underside of each eye with my handkerchief.

"Nothing yet," Mother said for me.

Mrs. Ma reached over to pat my mother-in-law's hand. "You shouldn't worry, Kao Ping," she said. "That's not unusual. I'm sure you'll hear from him soon."

She was a good friend. I couldn't begrudge her her good fortune. Besides, her husband and her first son-in-law, who was also in the police force, were needed here at home. The second one, though, with his pretentious dry goods store... It just wasn't fair that a gentle person like Yu-ming should have to fight for his country while that one was allowed to stay home with his family. "Please, have some oranges," I offered.

"Oh, no thank you."

"Please."

They weren't very sweet, but Mrs. Ma praised us for being able to find fresh fruit at all and for being so generous in sharing it.

Then the wet nurse appeared with my baby. He was wide awake, kicking and waving his arms and smelling of breast milk and baby powder.

"Look at those big dark eyes!" Mrs. Ma exclaimed.

"Would you like to hold him?" I took him from the wet nurse and brought him to Mrs. Ma.

"How strong he is!" she said. "Truly a tiger, like the year of his birth."

"My baby brother," Ah Mei said. "I his big sister."

*   *   *

That afternoon, while Ah Kwai and Su-lee were outside killing and plucking the chicken, one of its silky white feathers floated past the nursery window. Perhaps, I thought, since only two weeks remained of my monthlong confinement, this black-skinned chicken would be the last one killed for my soup.

"This little ox eats grass," I said, wiggling Ah Chew's tiny toe. "This little ox eats hay." His straight dark eyes watched me with fierce concentration, as though he were trying to memorize the sounds.

This little ox drinks water,

This little ox runs away...

10

Queues. How ubiquitous they'd become: queues for rice and firewood, queues at the pharmacy, even at the stationery store. I shifted my weight. A few minutes earlier, leaving our house for the first time after my monthlong confinement, I'd felt as though I could fly. Now I was a prisoner in a one-foot-square cell, people blocking the way in front and behind. As queues went, it wasn't a long one—a few people in front of me, a few people behind. Still. I tapped my toe. I crossed my arms. I sucked air through my teeth. Finally I stepped through the door into the tiny store. There were two glasses stuffed with fountain pens on the counter—no brush pens or ink sticks in sight. How hemmed in I was here, a dragon born in the Year of the Dragon, stuck in a one-foot-square cave. I inhaled a great gulp of air and spit it back out. We dragons needed freedom, a whole countryside to run through and ravage.

"What?" The young man in front of me glared over his shoulder. "Don't huff and puff at me!" He clenched his grassy eyebrows, oblivious to the fire I was about to breathe in his face. "What do you expect me to do, climb over this old lady's back?"

"Hey, young squirt. Who are you calling an old lady?" The woman in front of him, the second person in our queue, turned around. She was, in fact, no more than twenty-five years old. I knew because she was the older sister of my classmate.

"An Lee," she said, smiling. "I didn't see you."

I swallowed my fire and smiled. "Pei-li. How are you? How's your family?"

"Fine." She looked at the young man between us. "So, what should we do about this turtle's egg who called me an old lady?"

71

"I'm sorry, miss. I wasn't paying attention. My nerves are on edge these days."

"Hmph," I said, slapping his arm. "You're too young for nerves."

"What about you?" he shot back. "All your sighing."

"Let's save our anger for the enemy," Pei-li suggested. And we agreed, although we had enjoyed shouting at each other.

"This afternoon," Pei-li said over the boy's head, "we're playing mahjong at Mother's house. We need a fourth at our second table."

"Sure." What could be better? Chattering women, clicking tiles. Becoming the east wind, the west, north, or south, depending on a throw of the dice. Building a perfectly square wall and then breaching it.

"Hey, miss." The young man tapped Pei-li on the shoulder. "Your turn."

"Bring your baby and his nurse along," she said over her shoulder. "I'll see you at two o'clock."

When it was his turn, the young man stepped eagerly up to the counter, only to rush out a moment later, his face red as a pomegranate.

"They always get mad at *me*," the shopkeeper said. "How can I sell him scissors I don't have? Oh! Miss Liu," he said. "It's you. Please tell your mother I'll pay the rent as soon as I can."

"No, no, Old Yao. That's not why I'm here. I need an ink stick."

"Oh, good, good," he said, tittering as he opened a drawer. "I do have a few, not the best quality." He took out the kind of ink stick school children used. "Look at this," he said. "No box, just a cellophane wrapper."

I opened my purse.

"No, no. It's a gift."

"Then I can't take it. I pushed the ink stick across the counter and he pushed it back. We went back and forth a few times until finally I ran out, leaving my money on the end of the counter.

It was still early, so instead of heading home, I turned toward the waterfront. Before Ah Chew's birth, in the days after the invasion, I went there almost every day. The chaos playing out in the harbor and over on the Amoy side was near enough to be seen with the naked eye, and some of us felt obliged to look. It started as curiosity. As we watched, though—others must have felt as I did—we became witnesses not only to the brutality of the enemy, but also to the suffering and the courage of our countrymen. I felt duty-bound to show up, even on those days immediately after the invasion when the sight of bodies piling up on Amoy's beaches tore at my heart. Now, nearly six months later, I was back.

Before the invasion, the walkway along Kulangsu's municipal seawall was a favorite place for an afternoon stroll. It was a beautiful wall, the bottom portion made from thick, perfectly cut blocks of granite on top of which stood an ornately carved white stone wall with orb-topped pillars like one might find in any great city in the country. Now, the walkway behind the seawall was a viewing post. This morning, the same two battleships I'd seen in the harbor before Ah Chew was born were still there. They were big—as long as eight or ten junks, tall at the center like a block tower. Floatplanes looking like overgrown dragonflies were parked on the flight deck. Above it all flew the Japanese Navy flag, a rising red sun with sixteen rays shooting from it. "Still here," I hissed, releasing a puff of dragon fire.

The man beside me turned his head. "The battleship *Kirishima*," he said, lifting his top lip to reveal a glinting gold tooth. "And the *Ise*."

A tall man in gentleman's attire swung around. "How do you know their names?"

"What do you think? I know how to read Japanese."

"You admit it?"

"Why not?"

The tall man spit. I knew him. Ding Beng-hui, an investor my father had dealt with. He still wore the traditional long blue gown and short waistcoat, white cuffs rolled up outside the sleeves. "Where is your patriotism?" he snarled. "You wouldn't work for the devil pirates, would you?"

"Most assuredly. I'd be an excellent spy, don't you think?"

I saw Ding Beng-hui make a quick appraisal of the younger man, taking in his smirk, his rumpled cotton jacket, and the checkered British-style shooting cap he wore jauntily over one eyebrow. "Hm. So you would," he said.

When the would-be spy turned away to share his knowledge with someone else, I stepped forward and introduced myself to the old investor. It had been three years since my father's death, but saying his name out loud still brought tears to my eyes.

Mr. Ding didn't seem to notice. "Your father was an honest man," he said. "He had good instincts. Whether it was opening up a new market for birds' nests or expanding the rubber trade, his judgment was always spot-on."

We stood side by side, gazing across the five hundred meters of water that separated Kulangsu from Amoy. The basic shape of the Amoy skyline hadn't changed. The buildings were blackened, though, the beach was scarred, and the normal bustle of that waterfront was gone. Mr. Ding reached under the hem of his waistcoat and took out a small notebook bound in leather. "I come here every morning," he said. "Any troop activity, any change in the number of ships, boats, or airplanes—anything that can be seen from our waterfront, I jot down. It's all there in my journal, noted and dated." He slipped the notebook back inside his waistcoat.

"What will you do with the information?"

"As with any investment of time or money, the exact future value cannot be predicted." He reached into his waistcoat and took out an expensive pair of binoculars. "Do you know how many people were killed during those three days in May?"

I shook my head.

"Nobody knows." He leaned close and spoke in a low tone. "I can tell you, however, the number of bodies observable from this spot that were left to rot on the beach: one thousand, one hundred sixty-eight. Not a pleasant business, counting them." He touched his nose and grimaced. "Most people couldn't stand the smell."

"I was one of them," I admitted, remembering how I stood behind the seawall with a handkerchief over my nose and mouth.

"Those innocent dead deserve our regard," he said. "At the very least they deserve to be numbered." He fell silent, gazing at the beach where the corpses had lain baking in the sun, the food of crabs and vultures. The Japanese authorities had waited so long to give permission for the bodies to be taken away and buried that by the time they did, they were unrecognizable.

"Look," he said, pointing at a motor launch flying a small postal banner below the Japanese flag. "The weekly mail boat." Some time ago, amidst loud proclamations of a return to normalcy, the Japanese had restored our mail service. We might not have enough food or coal and charcoal, half our factories may have been shut down or placed under the control of Japanese stooges, but we did have regular mail service. It was all part of the fiction of "younger brothers" liberating "older brothers," of a New Order in East Asia. Why, didn't mail even pass between Free China and the occupied territories? Mail from other people's husbands, that was. Not from mine.

A spark of sunshine reflected off the battleship *Kirishima*, glinting as brightly as the gold tooth of the man who knew its name. I rubbed my hands together, glad I'd worn my padded jacket. A breeze fragrant with seaweed blew across my face. Suddenly an egret from some hidden spot on the beach below rose up in a soft *whoosh*. When I looked back at the mail boat, sea spray was blossoming on both sides of its bow. And from nowhere at all, the knowledge came to me that today would be different. Today, somehow, I would hear from him.

All the way home, the feeling stayed with me—walking past the theater and the public bathhouse, my feet barely seeming to touch the cobblestones, and then into the twisting lanes lined with houses and shops. Piano music danced out an open window, and I pictured Yu-ming's calligraphy, his graceful, sure pen strokes inside his engineer-careful numbered paragraphs.

Soon, I thought as I dressed for the mahjong party. Soon I will hear from him. I took out the powder pink dress I'd had made before he left. It was beautiful. I slid my fingers over the silk and put it back. When he returned, then I would wear it. Today, the green brocade *cheongsam* lined with rabbit fur would have to do. I pulled it on over my head and fastened the hidden metal clasps along the side, smiling to myself that it came together with so little effort only a month after Ah Chew's birth.

It was Pei-li's idea that I bring my baby and his amah. But I also wanted to bring my mother-in-law. She was brilliant at mahjong and Chinese chess, but she seldom had a chance to play. I didn't think anyone would mind.

"Remember," I told Ah Kwai before we left, "if a letter comes, send Su-lee right away to get me. I'll be at the Hungs' house."

"Chamber of Commerce President, Hung Li-son?"

"Yes, the father of my friend Pei-lu and her sister. Send Su-lee as soon as it comes."

*   *   *

In the Hungs' back parlor, all the accoutrements of a ladies' party in a prosperous home were present—the lucky jade plant by the window, the black lacquer screen with its peacocks, and plum blossoms accented with mother-of-pearl and semiprecious stones, the melon seeds, spiced peanuts, and salty-sour preserved plums set out on the mahjong tables. A set of peony-design teacups in apricot, yellow, and white waited for us on the sideboard along with a large bouquet of fresh gold and crimson chrysanthemums mixed with heavenly bamboo.

I was glad to sit down with them and forget the invaders for a while. As we stirred the tiles, a muted clatter like broken shells in an outgoing wave filled my mind with memories of sea and sand and a thousand other mahjong games. Someone laughed. The window jalousies tinkled in the breeze like ice in a water glass. Yes, it was good to be here with my friends. I hadn't seen Ling and her sister, Chi-chi, in ages. We spoke in the beauty parlor, of course, but that was months ago. Ling stopped stirring the tiles and slid her fingers over her raven-black hair. "Your permanent wave still looks so good, An Lee," she said. "Mine is almost gone."

"You put too much oil on it," Chi-chi said. "What do you expect?"

I looked across at Pei-lu. With Ling and Chi-chi on either side, Pei-lu's dark face and straight bob looked plain. Too serious, I thought, remembering how the beauty operator had said the very same thing about me. It had been too long since I'd spent time like this with Pei-lu, and she was my best friend.

We stirred the tiles and built our walls in perfect rows of eighteen tiles with another eighteen stacked on top. Breathing in the secret promise of the tiles' hidden undersides, we pushed our walls forward to form a four-sided city wall.

"He's so handsome," Pei-lu said, glancing at Ah Chew as she shook the dice.

"Before long you, too, will have a handsome son," I said.

"Or a beautiful daughter," Ling added.

Pei-lu blushed. "Oh Ling. Your daughter is truly beautiful."

"That's her nickname. Beautiful," Ling said.

I shouldn't have brought up the subject of sons. How could I have forgotten the conversation between Ling and Chi-chi in the beauty parlor? All that desperate talk about fortune-tellers and dreams and how much Ling wanted to give Ben-hui a son. I wondered if she'd gone to the Chang Chou Monastery and told the old abbot about her dreams.

She took her turn with the dice and threw a five and a four, which brought her around to her own wall, the wall of the east wind. Then she threw again to determine exactly where she would breach it. "It's still all a matter of luck," she said as she placed two tiles atop her wall.

My mind strayed from our cozy room to other breached city walls and back again to our own still lucky island. I preferred to trust Yu-ming's survival to intelligence and skill, but luck could never be discounted. I heard a sound and turned, expecting to see Su-lee with a letter for me. Instead, I saw the Hungs' maid, coming through the doorway, her tray heavy with glasses of lemonade. While she served the table where Pei-lu's older sister sat, we drew our hands and ate up part of the east and north walls in four-tile bites. Then, having received our own glasses, we sipped the sour-sweet juice and took one last tile, our thirteenth, and one more for Ling.

When I was young, my parents played mahjong. They'd set up one table for the women in the sitting room, one for the men in the library. In the summer they played on the patio, mosquito coils burning at their feet. I'd sit around the corner and listen to the sounds, first the chattering of the stirred tiles, then the more orderly *click* of the draw and discard, and all the while the sounds of eating and drinking—glasses tinkling, walnut shells and watermelon seeds cracking, and, later in the night, the clatter of chopsticks and soup spoons, crab shells and chicken bones. What I liked best were the voices calling out their discards and the tiles they claimed—red dragon, west wind, six bamboos. At first I made up stories full of red, white, and green dragons. Later, I started memorizing the players—where they sat, the sounds of their voices, their discards and claims, and I tried to guess what kind of hand each was building and who would win.

Today, as we nibbled peanuts and sipped lemonade, I assessed each of the women's playing style. Ling was enthusiastic but easily distracted. Chi-chi kept her wits about her, but she lacked the ability to plan ahead. Pei-lu was my only real competition—just as she had been all the way through school. During the first round, the round of the east wind, Pei-lu and I easily took more hands than Ling and her sister did. I opened a watermelon seed between my front teeth and held the shell in my mouth for a moment to savor the taste of salt and star anise. Even though there was barely enough nourishment in a watermelon seed for a moment of life, I was glad we had our stores of snacks. I didn't suppose the army would waste space on watermelon seeds, but I hoped Yu-ming had something good to eat. He wouldn't think to mention it in a letter. I wished he would. My mother-in-law saw me glance at the doorway, and shook her head.

Now it was my turn to be the east wind. I called my second mahjong in a row, and Ling groaned. "Aiya, another double score for An Lee." We counted up our points and settled with each other, then Pei-lu rang her little silver bell, and the maid took away our glasses, replacing them with teacups.

"You should wear rouge," Ling said, cocking her head in appraisal of Pei-lu. "And a brighter shade of lipstick. Your husband would like it."

Pei-lu signaled for the maid to pour our tea. "He's too busy to worry about my lipstick." Her husband's family owned a pickle factory, which, as everyone in Kulangsu knew, had been running day and night since the invasion. They still pickled radishes, turnips, and lettuce—everyone needs pickles—but most of their time was spent steaming rice porridge for the refugees, four bowls a day for each one. Many of us contributed money, but without the steamers at their pickle factory and the new petrol tins Standard Oil Company donated for steaming the rice, the refugees from Amoy would have starved.

Ling blew on her tea. "My husband always notices me," she said, "no matter what time he gets home from work."

"Or from gambling," her sister added.

We turned to the remains of the wall, dismantling it, and then stirring the tiles. "Pei-lu's husband is a hero of the people," Ling said. "But my poor Ben-hui…" Her chin trembled. "He's worried out of his mind. His business in China is dead, and he can't visit his concerns in Luzon and Jakarta." She slid two fingers into her sleeve and pulled out a handkerchief.

"An Lee's husband is risking his life for us," Pei-lu said. "He's the real hero."

Ling's and Chi-chi's lacquered fingernails swirled over the soft ivory tiles—celebration red, good-luck-envelope red, blood red. "You must be pleased that we have mail service again," Ling said, her ruby ring catching the light.

My hand hesitated over the tiles. Mail service but no mail. I glanced over Ling's shoulder at the jade plant. Ah Chew was whimpering, his amah dancing and bouncing him on her shoulder. Finally she gave him her little finger to suck.

I watched my baby suck and squirm as Ling licked the salt and garlic off her red-tipped fingers. The amah bounced him faster, to no effect.

I shook the dice, but just as I was about to throw, Ah Chew screamed. I let the dice fall through my fingers and pushed back my chair. Enough!

"An Lee," Ling and Chi-chi whined in unison. "Let his amah take care of him."

I took him in my arms and kissed his salty cheek. "Would you play for me?" I asked my mother-in-law. "I'd like to take him home so he can nurse in his own room."

"Of course," she said.

Pei-lu's mother walked me to the gate. "You can come back later," she said.

"Thank you, but I don't think I will."

It was cold, the sun low in the sky. There was still time for a letter. I pulled Ah Chew's blanket over his head. Old Madam Hung closed the gate, and for a long moment, the vibrations hovered, hollow and metallic under the darkening limbs of a leafless tree. Then everything was silent, and we were alone under a vast array of not-yet-visible stars, each one irredeemably separated from every other as they looked down on us from an indifferent heaven.

11

*I*f he was coming, the postman would have to hurry. The sky was fading fast. I stood at my window, watching the lane through dun-colored tree branches, tangled and dull as the lichen on the tree's lower limbs. The children in the street below jostled each other and leaned against the neighbor's wall. Six short months ago our lane would have been filled with children on their way home from school. Now most of the schools were closed, their teachers gone, their rooms and playgrounds turned into refugee shelters. A group of students wearing the uniform of the missionary school near the American Consulate rounded the corner, and the others stopped playing. They stared, and the students from the missionary school, embarrassed perhaps by their privilege, averted their eyes and walked silently past.

Where in the world was that postman? My glance strayed from the lane to the dark space between our wall and the neighbors'. A short, narrow alleyway that led to our back gate, it was seldom noticed or used. It occurred to me that someone could easily hide there.

By now, the tree branches had lost all hint of color, and the children were beginning to wander home. My mother-in-law would need someone to walk her back after the mahjong game.

I found Su-lee in the kitchen. She and Ah Kwai's nephew, Yun-yun, were leaning against the western window, squinting over a comic book. "You'll ruin your eyes," I said. "I don't know how you can even see the characters. Why don't you light a candle?"

"Ah Kwai says we have to conserve."

"You also have to preserve your eyesight. Save your reading for the daytime."

"Yes, Young Mistress."

She didn't sound convinced. I couldn't blame her. Once a person learns to read, it's hard to stop, and Su-lee—though she'd never been to school—could read as well as any middle school student. We'd started playing school when she was a child not more than three years old. It was magic, I told her. Learn the code, and the stories captured on this page will be yours. Her round black eyes never strayed as she followed my pointer.

"Put your comic book away. My mother-in-law needs someone to walk her home from Mrs. Hung's house."

Yun-yun clapped his hands. "May I go, too?"

"Ask your aunt."

"If you behave," she said. "Stay out of the way, be quiet, and don't gawk at the ladies."

"Yes, Auntie."

She ran her hand over his short-cut hair. "Now, go change your shirt."

It was still light enough for them to walk to the Hungs' house, and my mother-in-law had an electric torch to light their way home. I supposed the postman also had one. He ought to. In wartime, a letter from a husband or son couldn't wait until morning.

Mother and Ah Kwai had gone to bed by the time my mother-in-law returned. Su-lee's eyes were drooping and Yun-yun was yawning. They revived, though, the moment they saw me. "Listen," Su-lee said. She took hold of my mother-in-law's gown and shook it until the coins in her pocket clattered and clinked.

"And look." Yun-yun held out his hand. "Second Mistress gave me this coin."

"She won all their money," Su-lee declared.

"Don't exaggerate," my mother-in-law said. "Young Mistress Pei-lu won almost as much as I did. Now, you two, off to bed." She broke into a smile as she started up the stairs. "I did surprise them, though, didn't I?" The clock began to strike and she stopped to count the chimes. "Goodness! Twelve o'clock. You shouldn't have waited up, An Lee. I had my key."

"I couldn't sleep."

In a breath, her look of exhilaration vanished. "My poor dear," she said sadly.

I hadn't meant to remind her of Yu-ming's absence. Besides, it wasn't from pining over him that I was still awake; it was, more precisely, because I was expecting something—not a distinction that was likely to console her.

I waited until she closed her door. Then I slipped into the nursery. Ah Chew was in his crib, Ah Mei in her little bed, both of them sound asleep. I kissed their cheeks and pulled Ah Mei's quilt up under her chin. Across the room, the amah breathed a delicate female snore. She'd left their shutters open a few inches for air, and I padded over to peer through the crack. The day wasn't over yet.

Without a moon, I had to wait for my eyes to adjust to the darkness so I could distinguish between the various shades of black that defined the form of things—the tree, the neighbors' roofs, the wall around our house. Gradually I was able to pick out the features of our wall, the stone blocks of its foundation, the bricks on which the concrete posts rested, the railing at its top. Beyond the wall, the deeper darkness of the alleyway was a weight I felt more than saw.

Technically, the day was over, but the feeling of expectation remained. I felt my way back to my room. To *our* room. No, this day wasn't over yet—not in *my* mind—not until sunrise tomorrow. I still had plenty of time to hear from Yu-ming, and I would. No matter how unlikely it might seem, I knew that I would.

I couldn't understand why people wouldn't accept knowledge without an obvious source. Everything in the universe came out of nothing, didn't it? Yu-ming was the worst—my beloved Yu-ming, my sweetheart—always asking how I knew something. Where did I read it? Who told me? Never accepting the true answer. Mother understood. She seldom mentioned it, but she had a sixth sense about things. It's better, she told me once, not to talk about what others haven't experienced. And yet, I wanted to tell Yu-ming everything, even if sometimes I had to make up explanations geared to his way of thinking.

I hung my robe over the back of a chair. Then, climbing into our bed, I pulled the comforter up to my chin and closed my eyes. It wouldn't hurt to close my eyes, or even to fall asleep. Awake or asleep, either way I would hear from him tonight.

Somewhere between imagining and dreaming, I saw a small pond, narrow in the middle where a red bridge arched over it. Yu-ming and I leaned on the bridge's rail. We threw rice crackers into the water and watched the carp—their smacking lips, their translucent tails billowing out behind, swishing and turning and brushing up against each other.

Wait!

I sat up. What if the communication I'd been waiting for turned out to be nothing but a dream? I snatched my glasses and jumped out of bed, hitting the floor as hard as my ninety-nine pounds would allow. No, not a dream. That wouldn't do. Not at all. I stomped across the floor. I needed something I could hold in my hands. I opened the shutter and slammed it shut again. I was sick and tired of dreams and blind knowledge and imagination. I wanted.... At least I wanted a letter.

I paced until the room was too small, and then I paced in the hallway. I'd tried before to construct him in my mind—the shine of his hair, its part, left of center, his high forehead, the shape of his ears and eyebrows, the shade of his eyes, the length of his nose—everything, in meticulous detail, all the way to his toes. I'd tried to picture a part of him and I'd tried to see him whole. Neither brought satisfaction.

Stopping outside the children's room, I began to doubt that I would actually hear from him today. Maybe all this belief and joy I'd been carrying around was nothing more than wishful thinking. I opened the nursery door and walked past the sleeping children to the window.

Cold seeped into the room, flowing under my nightgown and up my legs to the small of my back. I recognized all the forms in the yard and alleyway I'd been able to make out earlier. Then I saw something move. A man. He was in the alley looking over our wall. I saw his hands on the concrete railing. Then, in a heartbeat, he was over the top, his feet on the ground, running to the other side of the house.

A thief. I thought of the flimsy lock on the door to the veranda and all the food we had stored in the pantry. I should wake someone. Instead, I ran back to my room. I peeked through the closed shutters. He was just coming around from the side, walking now, looking up at the house. I held my breath. If he took one step closer to the veranda, I'd run down and get Ah Kwai and Su-lee. He didn't seem to notice the veranda, though. He walked on past and stopped below my window. Even though I doubted he could have seen me, I stepped back.

Pok, pok.

I frowned.

Pok, pok, pok.

Rocks. He was throwing rocks at my shutters. I waited for it to stop. Then I pushed the shutters open a crack.

He was squatting, feeling for more pebbles. Suddenly, he straightened up, a soldier's posture inside fisherman's clothes. "Madam Han?"

I poked my head out. "What do you want?"

"Are you Madam Han, wife of Lieutenant Han Yu-ming?"

I was startled to hear Yu-ming's rank. "And who are you? Why are you sneaking around my property in the middle of the night?"

"I was sent by Lieutenant Han, madam." He bowed his head.

I pushed the shutter all the way out and stepped onto the balcony for a better look. Could it be that this man was what I'd been waiting for all day?

"Go around to the back door." Yes, I thought as I grabbed my robe. I was right. Tonight I would hear from Yu-ming. I threw on my robe, tying the belt as I ran down the stairs. He was alive, and this man was his messenger. In the dark, touching walls and the backs of chairs, I hurried through the hall and dining room and into the kitchen.

When I opened the door, the man snapped to attention. "Private Huang Ying-san, at your service," he said, speaking our dialect with the local accent.

"Please, step inside." While he was kicking off his fisherman's sandals, I lit a candle. "You have something for me?"

He opened a panel inside his jacket and took out two ordinary light blue aerogrammes. I thought my heart would explode when I saw my name: *Madam Han An Lee.* I held out my hand, and he gave me one of the letters.

"The other?"

"I'm sorry, ma'am. This is for the elder Madam Han. My instructions are to deliver the letters directly to the two ladies, without any intermediaries."

"My mother-in-law is upstairs sleeping," I said, suppressing a desire to shout at him. After all the ups and downs of the day and night, my emotions were bouncing from high to low like a child's rubber ball. "My husband will be pleased to know how diligent you've been in carrying out your orders," I said with a forced evenness of tone, "but let me assure you, Private Huang, I am not what he meant by an intermediary."

His eyes wandered for a moment, then he handed me the other letter.

"Is my husband well?"

"Yes, ma'am."

I pulled out a stool for him and placed the teakettle on the burner.

"Lieutenant Han instructed me to ask if there would be a reply."

"Yes. I have letters. I'll get them." I dropped some tea leaves into a cup and put a couple of buns on a plate. "Please, Private Huang, have some *shao bao* before you go." I looked at my left hand to be sure the letters were still there. "The hot water will be ready in a minute. Feel free to make your own tea when it boils."

"Please hurry, ma'am. I can't stay long."

I raced up the stairs to my room. Kissing Yu-ming's letter, I placed it on my pillow. I opened the red lacquer box and took out the seven letters I'd written during the seven months he'd been gone. Then I pulled out a green silk ribbon, the exact color chosen long ago: a soft lotus-leaf green for the wind-skirts and water-pads of a lotus pond. Seeing the ribbon, he would think of mandarin ducks swimming in pairs among white lotus flowers blooming pure and untouched above the muck. I wrapped the ribbon around the letters and tied it.

My mother-in-law also had letters to send. I spoke her name from the doorway, and she sat straight up. She took Yu-ming's letter, as though it were an ordinary thing to receive mail in the middle of the night. Then she climbed down from her bed, opened her large camphor chest, and took out her letters, already bound with a ribbon. She handed them to me and reached back into the chest for a hand-knit neck scarf. I started to leave, but she took my arm. "I want to see this soldier," she said. So I waited while she put on her robe and slippers.

He was standing, holding the teacup in both hands, when we entered. "Please be seated, private," my mother-in-law said, frowning down at him like the commanding general her father had once been. "Why did my son send you?"

"Only to deliver the letters, ma'am." He lifted the toes on one foot and then the other, as though they didn't belong on the white tile floor.

"He must have told you not to reveal any information of a sensitive nature."

"That's right, ma'am."

"I don't care about your military secrets. I only want to know if my son is well."

"Yes, ma'am, he's in good health."

"What else can you tell me about him?"

He paused to think. At the edge of our sleeping island, I could hear waves breaking against the reef, the very sound that had given Kulangsu its name: Drum Surf Isle. "I can only tell you, ma'am," he said finally, "that Lieutenant Han's men respect him. He is brave and fair, and he knows everything about . . . well, I mean, about the work we do. Now I have to get back, ma'am." He opened the panel in his jacket, slid our letters and the scarf inside, and then pushed back his stool.

"Is he still in Fukien Province?" my mother-in-law asked.

"Yes, ma'am. For now. I mean, engineering units can be sent anywhere at a moment's notice."

I handed him some buns hurriedly wrapped in white paper. "Thank you so much, private."

"I'll deliver the buns to Lieutenant Han, ma'am."

"No, they're for you. But I still don't understand. Why would my husband send his letters with you and not by mail?"

"I don't know, ma'am. All the lieutenant said was that we needed to test the Japanese defenses." He edged toward the door, and since by now my mother-in-law and I were as eager for him to go as he was, we nodded and thanked him. Then I latched the door behind him, blew out the candles, and bounded up the stairs, passing my mother-in-law on the landing.

Yu-ming's salutation was like a bolt of lightning—*My dearest An Lee*—as though his very lips had uttered my name, as though the words had brought back into existence one who'd faded phantom-thin without my even realizing it. My tears came so fast I didn't have time to protect the letter. I groped for a handkerchief to blot the smeared ink. Wiping my eyes, I scanned the closely written columns of characters. At the end I found what I was looking for.

Darling, it said. The word was at the top of the page, second column from the left. *My heart is filled with a soldier's longing for home— for my mother and for the children. But most of all for you, my beloved wife.*

Dearest An Lee, I miss you more than I can say. Your faithful husband, Yu-ming. I read the words a second time, and yet a third before I went back to the beginning of his letter.

It was written with a fine-tipped blue fountain pen, the characters evenly formed, his style perfectly fluid. I was pleased to think that he must have had a desk or table to write on. As was his custom, each of the paragraphs was numbered with Arabic numerals enclosed in parentheses. In the first paragraph he asked about our health and apologized for having left us alone. In the second, he said he realized we might have fled to Hong Kong or Manila, but if we were still here, we shouldn't worry. Kulangsu was relatively safe. Unless they were willing to take on the Western powers, the Japanese would have to leave it alone.

Do I have a son or a daughter? he asked. (It was his third point. *How are you and the child? Near the end of last month I constantly thought about you and the upcoming birth of our second child. Please have separate photographs taken of you and of the baby, and also of you with both children and of my mother and yours with the children.*

I chuckled. It was his way—still was—to tell me exactly what to do.

I have been a soldier now for seven months, he wrote in paragraph number four. *My ear has become attuned to the lightest footstep, even when I'm asleep; the click of a rifle is like a temple gong. I've traveled countless miles in sun and rain. My skin has turned as brown as any peasant's, and my feet have become best friends with their blisters. It's all part of a soldier's life, of little consequence. My main concern is the heavy responsibilities I bear in securing the survival of our country. The enemy advance has been swift and merciless. I am only a simple lieutenant, hastily trained, and yet every day I'm called upon to lead men in battle or to oversee building and demolition projects in a variety of unusual circumstances. Our unit is constantly being pulled in two directions at once. We have to fight and at the same time try to salvage what we can of our industries. Part by part, we move factories inland—on boats and lorries, even by donkey cart or on the backs of our soldiers. It is undeniably the Great Migration people say it is. Truly our countrymen are brave and long-suffering, the most resourceful people on earth. It makes me proud to be Chinese.*

It was his longest paragraph, followed closely by number five, in which he discussed Japan's advantage over China regarding weapons of all kinds and military supplies. He complained that a supposedly friendly nation like the United States had no qualms about supplying Japan with all the fuel and scrap iron it needed. I paused a moment to admire the elegant slant and curve of his writing. Even with a fountain pen, his calligraphy revealed his soul, strong and confident, and at the same time sensitive and refined.

The sixth paragraph contained an address where I could send my letters from now on, a distribution center for the Chinese military.

I read once more his words of love. Then I folded the aerogramme and placed it inside the top left drawer of my desk. In his next letter he would answer my questions about what he ate and whether he was warm enough and if he got enough sleep. He would answer them first, out of courtesy. But now I had other questions, as well. Why hadn't he fled into the interior with the bulk of Chiang Kai-shek's army? And how would they get supplies from the outside now that the entire coast of China was in enemy hands?

I climbed into bed and pulled the goose-down quilt up to my neck. Did soldiers still sit around fires at night? Did they still train pigeons in case they couldn't get through on the wireless? When I saw Yu-ming again, I would ask him. For a moment I *did* see him, perfectly, inside and out, almost as though he were present. He smiled and welcomed me, even as he slipped away.

Winter and Spring 1939

12

*I*t was February, cool and clear. I joined the early morning crowd at the newsstand and waited. Kulangsu had its own little newspaper, a so-called foreign-published rag that evaded censorship by hiring a Scotsman as its nominal publisher. It only came out on Saturday, though, so if we wanted something in the middle of the week, we had to buy a days-old copy of *Shih tai wan pao*, the occupation version of Amoy's evening edition. They sent us their leftovers, when there were some, and there hadn't been many these past few days.

While we waited, the men threw good-natured insults back and forth.

"Hey, Old Pan, what are you doing down here wasting good money on bad news?"

"And what about you? Too much fun in the bedroom? You need a dose of bitter with the sweet?"

They kept it up until the newspapers arrived—a large stack of them, which may have been a bad sign. I paid my coins and glanced at the headline: "Hainan Island Extends Joyful Welcome." The article that followed began in a flowery, mendacious tone I was becoming all too familiar with:

The bright sun above and beaming countenances below gave the Imperial Navy a prodigious welcome to Hainan Island today. Vast herds of Chinese citizens lined the streets, kneeling respect-fully in joyful thanks as the Japanese officers and men marched past. Later, these same officers and men sheathed their bayonets and stretched out merciful hands to the sick and hungry. Their compassion inspired thousands of grateful Chinese people to cast

*off their former absurd attitude of opposing Japan. Those who
had been healed or received sustenance crowded around the Rising Sun flag, tears in their eyes, to express their heartfelt thanks.
And from their midst a cry of "Banzai" rose to the heavens.*

Bile rose in my throat. "Heartfelt thanks." "Cries of 'Banzai'." It
sickened me to think that a Chinese had written that dog shit. Hainan
Island was China's southern-most point. Where would the Japanese
set their sights next?

Behind me and in front, buyers of *Shih tai wan pao* cursed and
sighed and shook their newspapers. One man threw his on the
ground and then quickly picked it up before someone snatched it.
There were, after all, other articles to be read. I opened to an inside
page and bypassed the international and local news so I could read
the fiction segment on my way home. It was from the "Spring and
Autumn" column of a Shanghai paper. A serialized novel written in
the "mandarin ducks and butterfly" style, it had the usual love triangle—the sensitive hero; the modern, educated city girl; and the virtu-
ous, unassuming traditional woman.

By the time I reached our lane, I was lost in the story, my sympathies hopelessly divided between the women. I looked up to see Su-
lee outside our gate talking to the boy who sold us milk. She tossed a
copper coin in the air and caught it with a flourish, showing her dim-
ples as she handed the goatherd a glass jar. He was a good-looking
young man, lithe and clear-eyed, but very young. He squatted beside
one of the goats and squeezed milk into our wide-mouthed jar. Then
he said something and Su-lee laughed.

I folded the newspaper under my arm, and as I stepped around
the goat droppings, the boy jumped up, leaving his goat's udders still
squirting milk.

"Ma'am," Su-lee said, her cheeks as red as lichees. "Good morning, ma'am."

Oh dear! I thought. It really was time to think about a husband
for her. Returning her greeting, I hurried through the gate, giving the
good-looking young goatherd a perfunctory nod.

Cut off from the rest of China, surrounded by this despicable
enemy, how could we get on with our lives? Under ordinary circumstances, we would have found a match for Su-lee in Mother's family
village. But now ... We couldn't even get to the mainland. And even if

we could, there probably wouldn't be any young men left in the village. That was assuming the village itself was still standing. Besides, who wanted to be married in these days of husbands marching off to war? I thought of Hsiang-mei, our amah, whose husband was drafted before their first child was born. No, this was definitely not the time for marrying.

I brewed a pot of tea in the kitchen and took it to Mother's room.

"Good," she said when she saw the newspaper on the tea tray. "Why don't you invite your mother-in-law in and we'll read it together."

"I'll pour your tea first, before it gets too strong."

"I can do that, dear."

From long experience I knew when to let Mother do things for herself. She'd let people wait on her for just so long, and then she'd rebel. As a child, I used to imagine there was a sprite inside her tied up with a smaller version of her foot-binding cloth. It was the sprite's nature to be lively, but most of the time, it couldn't move. On those rare occasions when it was able to break free, its enthusiasm was extraordinary. I'd seen that same zeal in other women of Mother's generation—the ones who had vowed not to let the bindings that destroyed their feet break their spirits, as well.

Mother rubbed her arthritic fingers in preparation for pouring the tea. "Joyful welcome?" she said, referring to the headline.

I nodded. "I'll be right back."

I found my mother-in-law outside, tending her vegetables. "Something got into my bok choy last night," she said, sighing as gardeners do—exasperation on a field of pleasure. "Just look at these carrots. Almost ready to be thinned." She skimmed her palm over their lacy tops.

"I bought a copy of *Shih tai wan pao*. Mother thought you might like to join us so we can read it together."

She hesitated before putting her trowel in the bucket and removing her gloves.

Most of the time the two women kept to their own sides of the house, Mother staying in her room, my mother-in-law in the garden, the kitchen, or her bedroom. It was only natural. Still, I wished my mother-in-law could feel more at ease here.

"I have to wash my hands," she said.

I waited for her, and we walked to Mother's room together.

"You read, An Lee," Mother said when we were all seated around her tea table.

"Yes," my mother-in-law agreed.

They were both literate, my mother-in-law having learned from one of the emperor's own tutors in his off-hours, my mother from her older brother. They grew up, though, in a time when women didn't read in public. Besides, I loved to read aloud.

I skipped the lead story. "The Japanese navy has taken over Hainan Island," I said. "Beyond that simple fact, the rest of this story is useless."

"I agree," Mother said.

I read another article from the front page about a failed attempt by Chiang Kai-shek's secret agents to assassinate Wang Ching-wei, the newly appointed leader of the Japanese puppet government in Nanking.

Mother held up her hand. "Enough," she said quietly. "Wang Ching-wei might believe in his course, but—"

"He's an opportunist," my mother-in-law snapped. "He has no faith in the War of Resistance."

"Exactly," Mother said. "Chiang is correct. China must not follow the path of despair. Turn the page, An Lee. See what else you can find."

I opened to page two and read a short article about a hailstorm that damaged seventeen villages in Hyderabad, India.

"What is this hail?" Mother asked.

My mother-in-law leaned forward. "Round bits of ice-rain. I experienced it when I was a child in Mongolia. It stings your skin, and when it hits the earth, it bounces."

"Were you harmed?"

"No, of course not. Perhaps they have flimsy houses in India."

Mother frowned. India, after all, was the Buddha's homeland. "The hailstones must have been exceptionally large," she said. "Read on, An Lee."

"You were right, Ling-chu," my mother-in-law admitted when I was finished reading. "It's amazing. Such enormous hailstones!"

"A lucky guess," Mother said, and they both smiled and nodded.

A moment of genuine harmony—all too rare in a period marked by discord between neighbors and family, friends and acquaintances. Was it any wonder? We were trapped on our small cage of an island.

The Japanese and the Chinese collaborators were feeding us a steady diet of lies. Violence and uncertainty were all around us.

All through the winter, I continued wasting my money on that printed messenger of bad news, *Shih tai wan bao*, when the only news I really wanted was from my husband. After Private Huang's visit, I did start hearing from Yu-ming, but not nearly as often as I would have liked. I hungered for his letters, and yet, like a piece of European pastry, they filled me with a momentary delight and then left me feeling more ravenous than when I started.

I had my children, however—my sweet little girl and my tiger baby. Each day was something new for Ah Chew, a new sound or facial expression, a grip held tighter, a head held higher. He learned to roll over and to sit up. By the end of March, he was crawling on his belly, rocking on his hands and knees and eating everything he could get his hands on. A happy, healthy child. I never dreamed anything could happen to him.

Then one sunny morning while Hsiang-mei was watching him, she left him outside on a blanket and came inside to do who knows what. I was upstairs practicing my calligraphy. I heard a commotion and put my brush down.

"What's wrong?" I called down from my balcony.

Su-lee's eyes were wide with fear. "It's Ah Chew, ma'am. He's gone. Hsiang-mei lost him."

"Lost him?" I nearly choked on my heart, which had grown to the size of a water buffalo's. "What do you mean?"

"They were outside, right here."

But I was already running toward the stairs, taking them three at a time, flying through the kitchen and out the door.

"I was gone only a short time," Hsiang-mei wailed before I could ask.

"Where did you leave him?"

"On the blanket."

My mind was racing. My baby. Where was he? My first thought was that some woman must have taken him to replace the child she lost in the invasion. "He can't just walk away," I screamed. "He's a baby. Someone must have jumped over the wall with him. Look for footprints."

I dashed along the wall ahead of Hsiang Mei, looking for disturbed earth and broken branches. Japanese *ronin* could have climbed over and taken him for ransom. A picture flooded my mind of a leering, bow-legged invader.

"Ah Chew," I called. "Ah Chew, where are you?"

"Ma," I imagined I heard him answer. I ran around the side of the house, and... Oh, dear Ma-tsu, Goddess. The front gate was wide open! "Ah Chew," I cried as I ran into the street. I looked to the far end of the lane before I looked down.

And there he was, alone on his belly, one suspiciously dirty hand in his mouth and goat droppings all around him. I scooped him up and wiped his face with the back of my hand.

"Dirty!" I shouted, sweeping the hard little balls out of his mouth with my finger. "That's dirty. Don't put those things in your mouth. What's wrong with you? That's disgusting. Now spit."

He looked up at me and cried.

"Like this," I said, demonstrating. "Now spit. Look, Hsiang Mei, he's been eating goat droppings."

"You found him," Ah Kwai said, clutching her heart. "Thank Heaven."

"Aiya!" Su-lee cried. "I thought he was too young to scoot that far."

"No one could have foreseen such a thing," Hsiang-mei agreed. "How was I to know?"

A stupid excuse. She was his nursemaid. She knew how strong and energetic he was. You don't leave a tiger baby alone on a blanket. I was one blink away from firing her on the spot. Su-lee wasn't blameless, either. She must have left the gate open after her goatherd left. Both of them deserved a good scolding. If Ah Kwai hadn't convinced me to come inside and close the gate, I would have rebuked them right there in front of the neighbors' servants, who were already peering out from their gates and windows.

"Do you realize how many refugees there are on this island?" I demanded the moment the gate was closed. "Eighty thousand. Twice as many refugees as our normal population."

Ah Kwai took my arm, but I pulled away. "Do you think the refugees are all good people? Do you think there's not one of them who would like to steal a beautiful baby like this?" I held Ah Chew in the air. He cried, and Hsiang-mei held out her arms for him. As though I would let him go to her. "Do you think just because we have sympathy for the refugees and give money for their food that we believe every single one of them can be trusted?"

Su-lee wailed out loud, and Hsiang-mei—a refugee herself—glared at me.

"An Lee." My mother was standing in the doorway, leaning on her cane. "Come inside," she said. "It's all right, girls. My grandson is safe."

Was it the invasion? Our occupation, the uncertainty, a mother's loving fear? Was there any excuse for my behavior? The only thing I can say in my defense is that I wasn't the only one on edge during that time. In their impotence and fear, my fellow residents of Kulangsu were easy prey for melancholy and rage. Fortunately, we also had carriers of hope and courage in our midst. Wei Yi-men, the cousin of my old tutor, was one of them.

It wasn't more than a day or two after Ah Chew crawled out the gate that I ran into Mr. Wei. I'd gone down to the waterfront, hoping to buy another copy of *Shih tai wan pao*. It was raining, and as I looked down on the quay, all I could see were slick, black umbrellas, clustered like mushrooms that had sprouted from the cobblestones during the night. I joined them and waited, listening to the rain on my umbrella and watching for a boat. When none came, people began to head back up Long-tou Lu, some of them stopping at a stall with a blue awning over its rough wooden table.

By the time I got there, every stool but one was taken. The proprietress, standing behind a large aluminum kettle filled with steaming soy milk, motioned for me to sit down. She handed me a chipped porcelain spoon and a pair of chopsticks. Then she ladled out a bowl of the sweetened soy milk, broke an egg into it, and handed it to me. Her husband, who was dropping lengths of dough into his pot of hot oil, lifted one out with his chopsticks. He held it, sparkling in the air for a moment. Then he placed it on his chopping board, chopped it crosswise with a cleaver, and passed the slices to me on a saucer. "Fried ghosts," we called them. This one was airy enough to deserve the name.

At the far end of the table, Wei Yi-men sat across from Yu-ming's skinny half brother, Fen. Mr. Wei and I greeted each other warmly while Fen merely nodded and slurped his soy milk. His mother, Watermelon Head, had spent so many years trying to keep him away from Yu-ming that she'd poisoned Fen's attitude toward us all.

I beat the raw egg into the soy milk with my chopsticks and dropped a few slices of "fried ghost" on top. The rain was falling from both sides of the awning, water collecting in a low spot over the hot oil. The husband glanced up nervously as the awning drooped lower and lower over the hot oil. He lifted it with his free hand, and some water splashed over the side.

"Hey! Watch it!" Fen shouted. "What do you think you're doing?" Fen had taken his hat off earlier, and now his hair stuck up in the center like a cock's comb. Jerking like a chicken with a worm, he brushed at the wet spot on his shoulder.

"I'm sorry, sir," the vendor said.

"Now, now. Don't be so hard on him, young man," Mr. Wei said to Fen. "If you'd wanted to stay perfectly dry, you could have eaten at home."

"With my wife?" Fen put on a pained expression for the two or three people who laughed. "As if we didn't already have enough trouble, heaven has to drop all this rain on us."

Several heads nodded. "Too much rain for April. It shouldn't be this cold."

"What are you talking about?" an old woman piped up. "We always get enough rain in April to drown a fish."

"Dog farts!" Fen said. "If this is a normal spring, then I'm a monkey's tail."

Mr. Wei stood up. He put his money on the table and picked up his umbrella. Like his cousin, my tutor, Mr. Wei was tall. He had flecks of white at his temples and a hero's square face. "Hope for spring," he said. It was a symbolic phrase, the sort of code we spoke in, even here in the neutral zone of an international settlement.

"Wait for the dawn," the stall owner replied solemnly.

"Flowers will blossom soon," I said, adding a third image.

After Mr. Wei left, no one spoke. We blew on our hot milk, and as we stared at its surface, we seemed to be looking into our souls, for the phrases meant more to us than a simple exhortation to wait and hope. They meant we should wait without cooperating and hope without losing our integrity. If we wanted to see the flowers bloom, we had to remain pure and defiant.

Walking home, rain falling like a veil around my umbrella, I compared myself with the great men and women of Chinese history—the warriors and scholars, those who fought the enemy and those who beat war drums from the sidelines. I remembered officials who became hermits, taking refuge in the mountains in order to live without compromising their principles. I thought of the loyal ministers and faithful women who died for their emperors and husbands. And I resolved to be strong. Our isolation here on Kulangsu, my loneliness, these were nothing in comparison to what others had faced. And the rain? Only someone as shallow as Fen would complain about the rain.

13

*I*t continued raining all day long, and the next day and the next. Walls grew slimy with mildew, trees fuzzy with moss. Remembering my resolution to be strong, I tried to ignore it. I guarded my tongue for words of complaint and dismissed each dreary thought the moment I recognized it. I was determined not to follow the example of Fen, my ignoble half-brother-in-law. Despite my best efforts, though, by the fourth gray day my soul felt as heavy as the rain-soaked earth.

Then, on the morning of April fifth, I awoke to sunlight. Blessed sunlight. It entered through the cracks in my shutters and fell across my coverlet. Pure, bright sunshine for Ching Ming, the Festival of Clear Brightness. I threw back my coverlet and ran to the window. Pushing open the shutters, I stepped out onto the balcony. It was a rain-washed world, fragrant with jasmine, birds chirping from every tree.

I went back inside and grabbed my toothbrush and tooth powder. Then I draped a clean wash towel over my arm and headed for the bathroom. I finished my toilet quickly and dressed in a simple housedress. Our family graves were in occupied territory, on Amoy Island or on the mainland, so we couldn't sweep them or make offerings beside them today. But that wouldn't stop us from honoring our dead.

My mother-in-law was already in the kitchen, a bunch of shallots in one hand, a cabbage in the other. Thanks to the smugglers, some judicious bartering with our neighbors, and the items still remaining in our pantry, we had enough ingredients to prepare most of the favorite dishes of our beloved dead. We had the makings of bird's nest soup and steamed sea bass with black beans for my father. We had prawns to deep-fry for Yu-ming's father, lion's head pork balls for his grandfather, and tofu, vegetables, rice, and noodles for all the other ancestors whose favorites we couldn't remember.

"Oh, Young Mistress," Su-lee cried when she saw me. "Who's going to sweep the graves and pull the weeds and cut the tall grass?" Her worries were for my father, not for her own blood ancestors. In all likelihood, her parents were dead. No one would ever know where her ancestors lay.

"Don't worry," I told her. "They understand our situation. As soon as we throw out the Japanese pirates, whether it's Ching Ming or not, we'll go out and sweep the graves." How easily I said it, as though the invaders were just a bowl of spoiled fruit to be tipped into the garbage bucket.

Su-lee must have been convinced by my tone, because she wiped her eyes on her arm and turned back to the pile of garlic she was peeling.

The burial ground for my father's family was in what had always been a peaceful spot. It was just beyond Amoy, at the foot of a hill, cows grazing nearby. In the springtime, vegetables sprouted on the terraces and rhododendrons bloomed on the hilltop. Pink rhododendrons. My eyes stung to think of them. Yu-ming's father and grandparents were buried beside another hill. Each year on Ching Ming we left small offerings at the graves. Then we ate a picnic lunch of crispy chicken, boiled tea eggs, and fried noodles, sometimes at one gravesite, sometimes at the other. If it rained, we took shelter in one of the pavilions; on clear days we spread our blankets out on the grass. For dessert, we ate fresh lichees or watermelon, spitting the seeds wherever we liked. Afterward we brought out our kites. Last year Yu-ming and I flew a kite beside his father's grave, and ate lichees under an ancient acacia. I held the bowl and he peeled the lichees for Ah Mei and me. It was two days before he left on his final business trip for Siemens. I could still see his hands, the way he split the lichees' red skin from the top, and then held the translucent white fruit up to my lips.

"Enough?" Su-lee asked, patting her pile of garlic.

Ah Kwai nodded. "For now." She slid her finger down the slick side of a sea bass. "Fresh," she said, holding it up so we could see how clear its eyes still were. She opened a gill to check the color of its blood. Then she took up the de-scaler and set to work.

We spent the morning cleaning and peeling, slicing and chopping. We stewed pork hocks in soy sauce and wine with spring onions, sugar, and star anise. We soaked the rice and the bird's nest and prepared to steam the sea bass. We stir-fried the vegetables and deep-fried the prawns. By noon we had prepared a feast delicious enough to satisfy anyone, living or dead. Ah Kwai covered the offering table with a long white cloth, and after we'd set out the food and lit the candles and incense, we invited our dead to eat their fill. Then we left the table, trusting they would extract the banquet's essence and leave the rest for us.

"Time for us all to take a nap," I said, taking Ah Chew from his amah. "Come on, Ah Mei."

While I napped, my father's spirit, which should have been feasting on steamed sea bass and bird's nest soup, entered my dream. He wore a merchant sailor's jacket, as though he were about to leave for Singapore, Pinang, Kota Baharu, or any one of the many places he'd promised to show me one day.

When I was a child, he promised me starry nights at sea and pirates who carried swords and guns. "If you keep your head down," he would tell me, "there's nothing to fear. We Amoy people know how to deal with pirates."

He promised to show me the cliffs along the Malayan coast where the precious birds' nests for soup were found. "If you can climb to the top of Sunlight Rock in your bare feet without using the trail," he told me once, "I might let you climb the cliffs with the men I hire. For every nest you bring down, I'll pay you handsomely." On warm spring days I would kick off my shoes and practice climbing the rocks along the beach. Even when I came to realize he was joking, that he would never allow me to climb the dangerous Malayan cliffs, I continued to yearn for all the adventures they came to symbolize.

Father had entered my dream in his traveling clothes, as though at last he would take me on our long-promised sea voyage where I would prove myself as capable as any son.

"The sea bass was excellent," he said. "Be sure to try some."

*   *   *

He was right. The sea bass *was* excellent.

"Yum-yum, goody-goody," Ah Mei sang, bouncing on her knees and looking at the next platter as I dished up her sea bass. "Yum. I like prawn."

I turned the lazy Susan and put two prawns on her plate.

"Give her more," Mother said.

"She's such a good eater," my mother-in-law agreed, nodding and smiling.

Looking from one grandmother to the other, Ah Mei took a prawn by its tail, held it up dramatically, then bit into it. "Uhm," she said, and both her grandmothers laughed.

"Your *yeh-yeh* loved prawns," my mother-in-law said to Ah Mei. "He could eat a whole plateful of them. No, no, dumpling. Don't eat the tail. Do you know what your *yeh-yeh* did? He always lined his prawns' tails up around the edge of his plate."

Ah Mei pulled the tail out of her mouth. She waved it in the air and then carefully placed it on the edge of her plate.

Ah Chew bounced on Hsiang-mei's lap. Suddenly he threw himself on the table, grabbed a prawn, and stuck it in his mouth.

"Quick!" Mother said. "Take it away from him. Here." She ladled some bird's nest soup into a bowl. "Give him this. He's too young to eat prawns."

Mother was too protective, I thought afterward when we were sitting on the veranda. If he wanted prawns, why couldn't he have them? Yu-ming wouldn't have minded. Or maybe he would. I was debating whether to write and ask his opinion when the bell rang.

It was two monks from Chang Chou Monastery, Ah Kwai reported. "They've come with a gift. A dragonfly kite."

"Invite them in," Mother said. "Su-lee, make fresh tea."

It was a large kite. Like a real dragonfly, it had two sets of wings that changed from blue to green to purple when they moved in relation to each other, one tissue-thin wing lending its hue to the other. "For your children," the young monk said, bobbing it up and down to demonstrate how smoothly the wings fluttered before handing it to me.

I thanked him and gave the kite to Ah Kwai to take inside for safekeeping. "How did you get permission to leave occupied territory?" I asked.

The young monk snorted. "The puppet soldiers will allow anything for the right price."

If, as I assumed, the main purpose of their visit was to deliver the abbot's response to my letter regarding Ah Chew's birth signs, why would he want to pay a bribe instead of sending his response by mail?

"What news can you give us?" Mother asked.

The young monk leaned forward. "The foreigners are having their own troubles with the Japs," he said. "On our way to Kulangsu we saw a Japanese warship pull up beside a British merchantman. They were yelling at each other in their two different languages. The Japanese officer shouted his commands while the British first mate moved his lips and made himself red in the face, English words having a tendency to fall apart over the sea."

Everyone nodded, except the square-faced monk, who blew across the surface of his tea and stared at my son.

"Then they sent a landing party aboard. The British were powerless to resist."

"Aiya!" my mother-in-law said. "Why don't the British put military guards on their merchant ships?"

"I expect they will after this, especially if the Japanese confiscate the ship's cargo."

Wait, I thought. Weren't we missing something? Before I could figure it out, the older monk put his teacup down and walked over to Ah Chew. Without explanation or permission, he circled him, examining, it seemed, the top of his head. Then, stopping in front of him, he gazed into my child's eyes, and Ah Chew returned his stare without flinching.

"It's true," this strange monk said, his voice reverberating like thunder in my chest. "The *Buddha's crown* aura emanating from the child's head is extraordinary."

Who was this monk with an unnatural interest in my son? Now I was sorry I'd ever taken my tiger dreams to the abbot. After all, hadn't my own interpretation of them been basically the same as his?

Mother scowled. "What are you trying to say?" she demanded.

The monk, no longer ashamed to show his phoenix eyes, approached her. "The abbot directed me to come here," he said, "so that I might verify what the signs of the child's birth together with the dreams of the mother have revealed about him."

"Brother Hu has the gift of spiritual sight," the young monk added.

"And I can confirm that the abbot's conclusions were correct." He reached inside his robe and took out two letters, one sealed with red wax, the other unsealed. "The abbot instructed me to give Young Mistress Liu one of these two letters. He said if I felt any uncertainty

about the identity of the child, I was to give her the unsealed letter."
He turned it in the air, showing us both sides as though he were a
magician about to perform a trick. Then he put it back inside his robe
and turned to me, holding out the other letter.

I took it and broke the seal. After a brief greeting, the abbot
named the Heavenly Stems and Earthly Branches that symbolized the
hour, day, month, and year of Ah Chew's birth and the Eight Characters that were the result of their combination. On the whole, his predictions corresponded with what he told me before. My son would
hold a high position, and there was a strong connection between him
and Ch'i Kung. Not only was Ah Chew born in the Year of the Tiger,
the animal with which Ch'i Kung was most closely associated, but he
was also born on Ch'i Kung's feast day. Even more remarkable,
though, were the strong indications in the abbot's reading of the I
Ching that Ah Chew was Ch'i Kung's reincarnation.

That was going too far, I thought. I didn't want my son to be the
reincarnation of anyone. How foolish we were, all of us, to take such
stock in a fortune-teller, even one as famous as the Abbot of Chang
Chou Monastery! It was nineteen thirty-nine, after all. We were modern people.

"Please, drink your tea," I said. "Su-lee, pass the biscuits around."

On the second page, the abbot explained that the time and place
of my son's birth clearly revealed that Ah Chew had been given extraordinary spiritual abilities. It was his responsibility, he said, to nurture
the child's gifts. In all humility, and yet with the firmest of intentions,
he would like to suggest . . .

I clapped a hand over my mouth. "He wants us to give them Ah
Chew to be raised in their monastery."

My mother-in-law glared at the monks. "I have only one grandson," she said.

"This child cannot escape his destiny," the square-faced monk
said in a strange voice that barely shook my ear hairs but rattled the
bones in my spine. "Old Mistress," he said to my mother, "never have
I seen such a *Buddha's crown* aura in a child. The light reaches a full six
inches above the top of his head."

Why was he speaking to her? I was Ah Chew's mother. I carried
his flesh in mine for nine months. If anyone should decide how his
spiritual gifts would be nurtured, it would be Yu-ming and I.
"Mother," I said, jumping up. This was the twenty-eighth year of the

Modern Era. Emperors and Old Mistresses no longer decreed what would happen to the rest of us.

"Just a minute, An Lee," Mother said. "I have something to say. Abbot Zhang has reminded us today about the precious spirit of our infant grandson. He has read his birth signs and seen in them unusual abilities that should be nurtured with special care. It goes without saying that Chang Chou Monastery, renowned for a thousand years for its holiness and learning, can be trusted to impart proper values to those who reside within its walls. I am honored that the abbot has shown such respect for our family and such regard for this small boy, and I am truly grateful for his most generous offer."

"Mother, please!"

"Let me finish."

Okay, I thought, say what you want. I took Ah Chew from his amah and stood in the doorway.

"As a devout Buddhist," Mother continued, "my foremost desire is to do the will of heaven."

The square-faced monk nodded.

"But," she said, "I have only one child, and she has only one son. This small boy you see here is the sole male heir of two families. We cannot let you take him."

Smirking, I sat down, and while the monk made one last plea, I let Ah Chew grab my index fingers. He pulled himself up and bounced on my knees. I didn't need a prophet to tell me that he would be walking before his first birthday.

The young monk was the first to stand.

"Be careful," Mother warned them. "If even a British ship can be boarded, how much more a Chinese one."

And if British ships are no longer off-limits, what about American and French ships? And what about Kulangsu, whose only protection was the presence of the foreign settlement? Now I knew what we'd been missing earlier with our talk of whether or not English words fell apart over the sea. The salient point of the monk's story was that the Japanese were beginning to lose their fear of the Western powers. And without that, our island would no longer be safe.

In the meantime, the sun was high and we had a new kite. We decided to go to the beach.

*   *   *

Other people had the same idea. When we got to the beach, it was crowded. People were sitting on the rocks and wading and swimming. Little girls with pink and yellow ribbons in their hair tugged on kite strings while little boys chased each other and dug in the sand. An idyllic scene if only our world had stopped at the water's edge. Ordinarily I wasn't afraid to look straight at the enemy ships. But that afternoon, still shaken from the monks' visit, I wanted some time off from reality, so I put my glasses in my pocket and forgot all about the blurry gray shapes beyond the line of surf.

"Look, sweetie," I said, directing Ah Chew's attention upward where the kites bobbed and swayed in the blue Ching Ming sky. "Kites," I said in his ear. I sniffed his neck. No one in the world loved him the way I did.

Mother loved him, of course. But love was no guarantee. You could never tell what pious people like her might do when they were about to abandon earthly reason for heavenly logic. That was what frightened me when she started talking to the square-faced monk.

What a relief it was to be rid of him! "We'll stop by again," he'd insisted at the door. "You may change your mind. Maybe when the child is older ..." I saw Mother's nostrils flare, but she persevered in her courtesy. Before they left, she presented the monks with a generous donation, more than enough to cover their trip, including the money they'd paid to bribe the puppet soldiers.

We hadn't stepped off the veranda before Mother started scolding. "You should trust me, An Lee. Do you think I don't love my own grandson? Would I give my son-in-law's child away without consulting him?" She shook her head and sighed. "You don't even know your own mother."

Thinking now of her rebuke, I felt tired, condemned by my failure of filial piety. If any mother was worthy of trust, mine was. And yet... Something inside me simply wouldn't go along. I had to follow my own instincts. I stopped walking. Running my fingers through Ah Chew's hair, I wished for a poem, one that would contain my guilt and at the same time hold the anguish of this scene, children juxtaposed against warships.

"Mama, look at me." Ah Mei was holding the kite string while Hsiang-mei squatted behind her. The kite rose, the dragonfly's wings fluttering in the air currents.

"Kaa…" Ah Chew said, kicking and waving his arms as though to swim through the air to the kite. "Ka. Ka."

My mother-in-law patted his arm and began reciting a short verse that she seemed to have composed on the spot.

Dragonfly, dragonfly,
Up in the sky,
Turned into a dragon
For going too high,
Don't drop your bombs.
Don't breathe your fire.
Your bombs are too smelly.
Ah Chew says, go higher.

She pinched Ah Chew's cheek and recited it again.

"That's as high as the kite can go," Hsiang-mei said, showing Ah Mei the stick with its last loop of string. "We have to pull it against the breeze now."

Gangzihou Beach was a large crescent, the ends curving so far outward that soon, following the kite, we were walking directly toward the blurry warships. My mother-in-law shook her head. "Sometimes I wonder how they can float. All that steel."

I put my glasses back on and looked at them. We'd been watching the buildup for weeks. By now there were almost twenty Japanese ships in our harbor—battleships, cruisers, minelayers. Destroyers sometimes. On the waterfront and in teahouses people counted and named them. They gossiped about them over chess and dominos, as though the ships were playboys or loose women. Those of us who were interested learned to identify them—not only the *Kirishima* and the *Ise*, but other battleships, as well: *Hyuga, Nagato, Mutsu, Fuso, Kongo.* We knew the cruisers and minelayers, too: *Chokai, Natori, Suzuya, Myoko.*

It was my mother-in-law's idea to make up a poem as we walked backward down the beach watching our kite swoop and dip above the water and sand. She provided the first line, "Dragonfly hovers over lotus pond."

"Wings fragile as spider's silk," I added.

"Tigers and wolves crouch at water's edge," she said, taking her turn.

"Loath to get wet for a mere bug."

As we walked backward adding more verses, it became a poem about Kulangsu and the Japanese wolves waiting for an excuse to pounce. When the opportunity presented itself, I reintroduced the dragonflies, kites, and children, thinking how good it would be to have this poem to commemorate our day at the beach. Tomorrow I would write two copies of it during my calligraphy practice and give one to my mother-in-law.

"Hey, Young Miss, watch out! You're about to collide with an old man."

My old tutor. I recognized his voice. Laughing, I swung around. "Teacher Wei. Imagine, nearly bumping into you today when my mother-in-law and I have just composed a poem." I stopped. Teacher Wei had a young man with him, a gangly fellow with round glasses, a rumpled Western-style suit, and an unattractive green-and-brown print tie that clashed with his blue-and-white striped shirt. The amusement in his eyes told me how foolish I sounded—a schoolgirl trying to please her teacher.

"Chang Ti is a friend of my nephew," Teacher Wei said. "You may know him by his pen name, Yeh Shu-li."

Now I really was embarrassed. Yeh Shu-li was a well-known writer. I'd seen his stories and poems in the Shanghai magazine *Century Wind*. I was about to say a word or two of praise when Ah Mei pulled away from Hsiang-mei and ran over to him.

"You soldier?" she asked.

He laughed.

She cocked her head and looked at him sideways. "You not my daddy?"

This time we all laughed, even as she ran from us crying. My poor, sweet girl. She couldn't even remember what her own father looked like.

"Come here, dumpling," I said. I gave Ah Chew to my mother-in-law and held out my arms.

"I shouldn't have laughed," Chang Ti said. He snapped his fingers to attract a passing hawker of candied crab apples. "For the little girl," he said, handing it to me. "My apologies."

Ah Mei clung to her amah just long enough to salvage her two-year-old pride. Then, her eyes fixed on the deep red, sugar-glazed fruit, she reached out for it. "Mine," she whispered.

Before we parted, Teacher Wei embarrassed me further by inviting us to bring our poem and join them the following week for a gathering of writers and friends of literature at the Moon Palace Restaurant. With Ah Mei waving her sticky hand an inch from my hair, I tried to explain that our little impromptu verse-making could hardly qualify as real poetry. "Thank you, teacher, but really we couldn't." I grabbed Ah Mei's wrist and waved for my mother-in-law to hand me a wet towel.

"On the contrary," Chang Ti objected, "you must. Professor Wei has been too modest to mention the main purpose of our luncheon. It's to honor him on his fifty-fifth birthday."

"No, no, no," Teacher Wei said. "That's only the excuse." He bent down and spoke in a low voice. "Some of us get together on a regular basis so we can discuss literary matters, and other things."

Immediately I had in mind what he meant by "other things," and my earlier escapist desire evaporated. I wanted to hear what my old tutor and his trusted friends had to say about the big issues of the day. Intellectuals in China had a duty to struggle for truth, and I was eager to take part in their truth-telling.

We said good-bye, and as the two men walked away, my mother-in-law and I smiled at each other. "The young poet walks like a Shanghainese," she whispered. "See. His toes pointing outward."

Ah Chew was asleep by the time we got home. I carried him up to bed and then joined the rest for a simple supper of leftover lion's head and cold noodles. Afterward, as Yu-ming and I had done so many times before, I went up to the roof to watch the sunset.

The sky was faded now to a pale blue, violet near the earth, a smear of red where the sun dipped into the sea. Our house had a pitched roof in the center, leaving the whole outer edge for a sun terrace. When the weather was good, we dried our wash on it on bamboo poles; when the seasons changed, we brought our clothes and bedding up to air. I rested my hands on the still-warm balustrade and listened to the seagulls in the distance. *Come home*, they'd been crying for a year now, calling my love home to no avail.

Then the sun was gone, swallowed by the sea. An electric light turned on, and then another. Suddenly I became aware of an eerie stillness. I leaned over the balustrade, looking for some movement. Not a leaf stirred, either on our sandalwood tree or on the hibiscus or jasmine bushes. I ran to the other side of the terrace, and though my slippers padded softly on the tile and my dress swished against my legs, the sounds only served to separate me further from the unmoving, silent world.

I'd been getting these strange feelings ever since Yu-ming left—mainly at night. I'd find myself in my room, surrounded by walls, unseen by anyone, unknown. And I'd feel—not exactly that I didn't exist—but that my existence wasn't quite solid, that I was too light, transparent maybe, or invisible. Now the world seemed to have stopped, and I was left alone to shuffle around this rooftop sun terrace.

I ran back to the front and looked and looked until finally I saw a man and woman coming down the lane. As they passed below me, the woman poked the man in the ribs. "You're talking dog farts," she told him, and he snickered and warned her she'd better not "tweak the tiger's whiskers." They laughed and continued chattering until they were out of sight and everything was still and eerie again.

Feelings about the strangeness of existence come and go—if you don't indulge them, that is. And this was no time to indulge strange feelings, not there in the darkness, alone as I was and still feeling—despite the passage of the bantering couple—so tenuous and apart. I forced myself to focus on the hazy reality of the here-and-now by counting the stairs as I made my way down from the roof. Then, back in my room, I whispered each thing I had to do: *Open door. Turn on lamp. Close door. Open bureau drawer. Take out nightgown. Unbutton blouse.* When I was ready for bed, I told myself to turn back the comforter and to climb up and turn off the lamp. Finally, I told myself to go to sleep.

14

*T*he raucous sounds coming from the private room at the back of the restaurant took me by surprise. I'd been expecting something more sober from Teacher Wei's fellow intellectuals. Above the din, a booming voice was teasing him about being ancient but still not any closer to becoming a sage, at which everyone laughed uproariously. My mother-in-law and I waited for the laughter (and one old man's coughing fit) to subside. Then I took her hand, and we went in.

The four old men on either side of Teacher Wei looked at least as ancient as he was. The only woman at the table was somewhat younger. Teacher Wei introduced her as Ho Song, a literature professor from Amoy University. She'd stayed behind to take care of her in-laws when the university relocated to central Fukien ahead of the Japanese invasion. Two of the old men moved so we could sit between Teacher Wei and Ho Song while Teacher Wei poured our tea and turned the lazy Susan to offer us peanuts and melon seeds. "The elder Madam Han is the widow of Han Gang, ambassador to the Philippines and all the colonies of Spain," he said with a grand swing of his arm.

A bearded gentleman had set out two glasses for us and was tilting a fat brown wine bottle with a red ribbon around its "waist" over them. "I knew your late husband," he said to my mother-in-law. "He was my competitor in the Imperial Examinations."

One of the old intellectuals snickered. "You mean he bested you."

"Is that true, Old Kao?" another asked with an exaggerated "huh?" that made the others chuckle.

"Most assuredly. I didn't mean to infer that Ambassador Han Gang and I were competitors on an equal footing. He was the champion at every level, I, a poor second." He put a hand on his chest and bowed his head.

"Second to none in the brilliance of your poetry," my mother-in-law replied.

"Yes, indeed." Teacher Wei raised his glass. "A toast to Ambassador Han Gang's brilliance and to Old Kao's poetry."

"Wait." Lifting the bottle of Shao-hsing wine, Old Kao finished filling the glasses with apricot-colored liquid and then, spinning the lazy Susan, sent them around to my mother-in-law and me.

"To Han Gang and Old Kao," Teacher Wei said. "*Gang bei.*"

Raising my glass, I glanced at my mother-in-law's smiling profile. Something in it reminded me of the way she looked the first time I saw her—when her husband was still alive and she was a "princess" dressed in yellow silk.

"What poem do you have for us today?" Teacher Wei asked Old Kao.

"Nothing much. An insignificant poem or two."

"Then you won't mind reading one now while we're waiting for Chang Ti and Mr. Fan," Ho Song said, and everyone laughed, knowing, I supposed, that he'd prefer to save his poems until everyone was present to hear them.

"Not at all." Old Kao's mouth curved into a smile. "But here they are now."

The waiter swung the serving platter to the side as two men hurried past. They were flushed and sweating, Chang Ti's hair falling in damp curls over one eye. "Sorry we're late," he said, pulling one of the empty chairs out without waiting to be invited. "We went for a walk."

"Didn't think it would take so long." The other young man slid into the chair beside him. "Thought we'd climb Sunlight Rock, take in the sights, write a poem or two, and then come right back down." Chang Ti's friend had intelligent eyes, but his dark skin and compact, muscular body seemed to belong more to a fisherman or a dockworker than to a poet.

"We had no idea," Chang Ti said, "that such a fascinating drama would play itself out before our eyes this morning."

Old Kao shook his head. "These young writers always overdramatize. No sense of subtlety."

"It's a modern tale," the suntanned poet said. "Doesn't lend itself to the classical mode." He reached for a paper napkin and wiped his sweaty face.

"Nonsense!" Old Kao exclaimed. "In the hands of a skilled practitioner, the traditional structures are infinitely flexible, absolutely precise, capable of being used for every conceivable action of man, woman, or beast."

"Pipe down," someone said. "Let them continue their story."

"Well," Chang Ti said, "we made good time going up. I would have preferred to savor the beauty of nature, but Ho-fu insisted on bounding up the path. You'd think he was a sedan-chair carrier paid by the trip instead of a mediocre story writer."

"Story writer, poet, calligrapher, and landscape artist." His friend smiled slyly. And then—even though we hadn't been introduced and he didn't know whether I was married or not—he winked at me. Like a longshoreman, I thought.

"When we reached the summit," Chang Ti said, "I was so out of breath I had to lie down and rest before I could look at the view. This so-called friend of mine," he said, crossing chopsticks with his friend over the cold plate, "let me sleep through the drama's prelude."

"Slow-moving preliminary action, totally extraneous."

"But essential for building suspense and for the overall dramatic effect."

I was beginning to lose patience with both of them. I could only speculate about the event they'd witnessed. Presumably it had some meaning beyond the perspective of the two onlookers. "Can't you just tell us what happened?" I said.

Surprisingly, the friend took me seriously. He put his chopsticks down and began to describe exactly what they'd seen. "Picture this," he said. "Seven Japanese battleships, eight cruisers, two minelayers, and three destroyers at anchor in Amoy Harbor, all of them lined up in four well-spaced rows, arranged like a fleet of dragon boats waiting for the race to start. They love regimentation, these Japanese. It's their strength and their weakness. Suddenly a British cruiser, the *Birmingham*, comes into view. Why, you're wondering, would the British, who are neither an ally of the Japanese nor at war with them, be heading straight toward a large array of Japanese navy ships? By the time I woke Chang Ti, they were already passing between the first two columns, British sailors lined up along the rails, each one holding something. Luckily, I brought binoculars, and when I got them adjusted, I realized that the British sailors were holding cameras and sketchpads and snapping and sketching as rapidly as they could."

"The Jap armaments were all uncovered," Chang Ti added.

"On that first pass, at least."

"Exactly. When they realized what was happening, the Japs started rushing around, trying to cover their secret equipment with tarpaulins. We thought at first they were mainly interested in hiding their big guns."

"The British would also be interested in the ships' silhouettes," Teacher Wei said.

Chang Ti's friend nodded. "And there was something else. The Jap aerials. Quite unusual."

While the men discussed aerials and their possible uses, the waiter brought in the first two hot dishes: whole crabs roasted in sea salt and deep-fried prawn balls. Both were rarities these days, but if anyone could find fresh seafood, it would be the cooks at Moon Palace. They'd been in business for a hundred years, and they knew all the fishermen in the area. The waiter cracked the biggest crab claw and offered it along with the dipping sauce to Teacher Wei, who tried to give it to me and then to Old Kao, but both of us snatched our bowls away. Finally Old Kao broke the claw in half and gave the bigger chunk to Teacher Wei. Then we all settled down to eating and talking about food.

Who could think of anything else, with sea salt on our lips and sweet, pure-white crabmeat dipped in ginger-laced black vinegar on our tongues? Eating, everyone remembered another bite of crab or lobster or sea turtle and described for the rest how fresh it had been and how it had been cooked and where. And so, memories of past pleasures added another dimension to those of the present.

During the third course—a large grouper steamed in a clear sauce—the focus of Teacher Wei's birthday party shifted from food to talk. Old Kao was the one who started it off. He sat back in his chair and belched. Then, while the others were still picking at the grouper's bones, he moaned and shook his head. "A conquered people in a conquered land," he sighed.

Chang Ti's friend—his name was Fan Ho-fu—slapped his chopsticks on the table. "Who says so? Points and lines, that's all they have. Some eastern cities and some railway lines."

"Yes," one of the old men argued back, "but without those coastal cities and railway lines, we're paralyzed."

"The Chinese people? Paralyzed?" Ho Song laughed. She looked around the table, and when she spoke again her voice took on the heightened, formal tones of an orator. "Only in times like these do the people manifest the full extent of their capability. Did any of us suspect that a whole university could pick up and move on a moment's notice, that Chinese teachers and students could carry textbooks and laboratory equipment and whole libraries on their backs across the mountains to Changting County? And who could have predicted that when they got there, they would continue teaching and studying with all their previous enthusiasm in spite of the primitive and crowded conditions of their classrooms and dormitories, in spite of being separated from their homes and families?" Her eyes shone with the great deed she'd been denied when she chose to stay home with her in-laws while her students and colleagues became heroes for China.

By the time the crispy pigeons arrived, the discussion was in full swing. As the waiter placed the platter on the lazy Susan, Teacher Wei tried to say a few words about the historical dilemma writers faced in times of war. He was beginning to explain the various ways famous literati of the past had responded, but everyone had his or her own passionately held view, and they interrupted before he could make a single point. It made me want to cry for my old tutor, even though I myself had interrupted him many times when I was a child. Never so rudely, though, and certainly not in the presence of his peers.

Fan Ho-fu was the loudest. "We have only one duty," he insisted. "Inspire the people to resistance. Beat war drums from the sidelines."

"And what if all men of letters are wiped out?" one of the older men asked as he ripped a leg from his pigeon. "What would become of our nation's culture then?"

"As intellectuals," Old Kao said, throwing a small clean bone on his plate, "it is our responsibility to perpetuate the nation's cultural life."

"And how does a collaborator do that?" Fan Ho-fu demanded.

"Now, now," Teacher Wei said, holding his hands up. "No one is talking about becoming a collaborator. We have many models from the past of men who remained pure in the midst of war, who found ways to preserve both their integrity and their lives."

I watched their greasy lips and tried to think what I would do if I were an intellectual, someone the people looked to for guidance. They made their points, waving wings and chunks of breast meat in the air, Ho Song daintily raising her pinkie fingers as she extracted meat from the pigeon's bones. I followed their arguments word for word at first. After a while, though, I found myself just sitting back and soaking up the pure energy of their poet's passion—a heartfelt devotion to China that was immeasurably more satisfying than the unreasoning fear and anger I often felt.

Finally the waiter brought our fingerbowls, and we added lemon and swished our fingers around. We dipped our napkins in the water and wiped our mouths. "What a sight that was!" Chang Ti said, throwing down his napkin and laughing. "Those little bow-legged Jap sailors scurrying around like so many mice. They didn't have the slightest idea which piece of equipment they should hide first."

"Their officers didn't know, either," Fan Ho-fu said. "But that won't stop them from punishing their underlings."

Everyone nodded. It was common knowledge that the Japanese were also cruel to each other. I looked into my fingerbowl, imagining the officers and sailors scrambling around the decks to hide things, their faces red with rage, and humiliation. It wouldn't be enough for the officers to punish their men, though, I realized. Someone else would have to pay. And since the British were protected by their neutrality and by the strength of their navy, it was the Chinese who would suffer.

After the pigeons, we had fried noodles and then a simple seaweed soup. As the waiter filled our bowls and passed them around, the room became quiet, except for the slurping and blowing and the clattering of spoons as we tried to hurry the hot soup cool. Unlike the hungry silence that falls over a banquet table when the first course arrives, our silence now was prompted by an eagerness to be done with eating. Everyone was ready to hear the poems.

Teacher Wei was extended the honor of reading first. As always, he followed the classical form, making frequent references to historical events as a means of commenting on the present. With soup bowls and half-eaten plates of noodles still cluttering the table, he pushed back his chair, clasped his hands at his waist, and began reciting from memory his new composition.

Willow blossoms,
your gift
at Saying-Good-bye Bridge

The opening lines brought to mind a famous bridge outside the ancient capital of Chang'an, and right away everyone pictured, not a soldier's leave-taking, but that of a man who would shake off the red dust of the city for a solitary life in the mountains. I watched the river-veins on the backs of my old tutor's hands and listened to the images he evoked—rocky northern mountains, a lonely pine, and a cave where courage could grow unimpeded.

Each in turn, the old men and then Ho Song recited their poems. All were in the classical mode and each reflected the author's stance toward the war. Hearing them, one after the other, I couldn't help comparing, trying to choose a favorite. Teacher Wei's seemed the best to me, although Old Kao's poem couldn't in any way be faulted.

Then Chang Ti stood up. He fixed his gaze over our heads, somewhere beyond the white wall at our backs, and began to recite, not in the normal phrases of classical poetry, but in the vernacular. His poem brought us back from the mountains and lakes to the city, to Shanghai, where the foggy pre-dawn streets in the French Concession were lit by electric yellow bulbs atop rows of black iron posts. The lampposts were gracefully shaped with curling wrought-iron extensions from which a hat, a cane, or an umbrella could be hung. On the morning of his poem, however, what hung from the lamppost in front of the police station was nothing so innocent. In a voice shaking with emotion, Chang Ti painted a detailed picture of a man's head—the congealed blood, the exposed flesh and shattered bone of its severed stump, the wide-open eyes and mouth and the purple tongue that had belonged, only hours earlier, to a young man, Chou Wen-ru, the editor of a Shanghai tabloid.

We were silent, stunned by the conjunction of poem and raw reality, the head as real as though we held it in our hands. Chang Ti sank into his chair, sobbing. "Wen-ru, my dear friend." I patted my mother-in-law's hand. I hoped she wasn't thinking of her father's head rolling in the dust under the hooves of his soldiers' horses. As a child, she must have wondered, as I had, how long his head had continued thinking and feeling after being separated from his body. I tried not to think of Yu-ming. How easily a man's head could be sliced from his body, how quickly his life brought to an end! Chang

Ti lifted his curls out of his soup bowl and raised his wine cup. "To China and her heroes," he said.

"To China and her heroes," we replied.

Fan Ho-fu was the last to recite. He stood up, slowly and with such a soft look on his face that I wondered if the wine had made him sleepy.

Moss spreads
where once we stood

he began, and for a moment I was surprised by the sweet tenderness in his voice.

your soldier's boots
as yet unscuffed.

Then I understood. It was a woman's poem. I recognized every word, every phrase, as though they had passed through my body before forming themselves on his lips. He was describing my life—the way Yu-ming's image faded for me as the days and miles between us multiplied, the way watching the moon wax and wane made my pain all the more unbearable for the indifference of that heavenly light. Fan Ho-fu saw my tears and it seemed to please him, which made me hate him even more than when he winked at me.

"Let us drink to those who get left behind," he said solemnly.

I raised my cup. My cheeks were burning. Who had given him permission to see into my heart? And now to see on my face the recognition of it. It was better, I decided, not to meet a modern author face-to-face, better not to be exposed to his prying mind.

As we left, my mother-in-law stopped to compliment Fan Ho-fu on his poem.

"I'm glad you liked it," he said, his glance sliding smoothly over to my face.

"Good-bye, Mr. Fan," I said, which was more than enough to say to a man who knew too much already.

15

*S*eeing what is strange, consider it not strange.

Mother had a whole collection of Buddhist and Taoist sayings. This one had to do with a holy state of mind achieved through meditation, one that prepared you for the unexpected, whether it was enlightenment or a ghostly visitation. Or so I'd always thought. Now I understood it differently. Now I knew that, even though our situation on Kulangsu was indeed extraordinary, I didn't need to achieve a holy state of mind in order to consider it not strange. All I had to do was wait.

Weeks went by, and eventually the idea of living on a solitary island surrounded by an occupied land began to seem ordinary. Warships a stone's throw from our beaches became a normal part of the scenery. Food prices higher than anyone previously could have imagined became the new standard. Yu-ming's absence, the more-or-less regular arrival of his letters, who could have predicted I would ever get used to that? But I did. And, like everyone else, I started to feel entitled to remain exactly as I was, marking time on the fringes of the war around us.

The Japanese, of course, were only waiting for an excuse to relieve us of our privileged status and to humiliate the foreign powers whose citizens lived beside us. On the first anniversary of the Battle for Amoy, with the assassination of Hung Li-son—a tragedy in its own right—they found their excuse.

The morning when the news came out, I was in my bedroom, reading aloud to Ah Chew from *Romance of the Three Kingdoms*. Even though he was barely seven months old, he sat like a miniature student in his child-sized upholstered chair, following me with his eyes as I paced in front of him. I gestured with my free hand and read in the declamatory tones of an actor. I wanted the melody of the ancient words to sink deep into his consciousness. He looked down at the little gourd he was turning over in his hands. I waited for him to look up. My favorite part of *Romance of the Three Kingdoms* was the couplet at the end of each chapter. I read it, and he joined in, babbling to mimic my tone.

Suddenly he looked away and I lowered my book. Something was wrong. The screen door slammed. Footsteps slapped through the kitchen and pounded up the stairs.

"Young Mistress, Young Mistress!" Su-lee stopped in my doorway, panting. "Your classmate, Hung Pei-lu."

"What about her?"

"It's her father." She put her hands over her mouth and blinked furiously. "Someone killed him, Young Mistress."

"No. Who told you that?"

"The maids next door. Shot dead. That's what they said."

"How would they know?" I scooped up Ah Chew. Pushing past her, I hurried down the stairs, through the kitchen, and out the open door, past the basins of soaking clothes and the towels and rags fluttering on the clothesline.

A crowd was gathering in the street. My mother-in-law, Ah Kwai, and her nephew Yun-yun were already there. Even old Mr. Lim from across the street had come out from behind the wrought-iron bars of his gate. In the middle of it all stood the next-door maids.

"...late at night," one of them was saying, "right outside the Hungs' gate."

"How do you know?" I pushed my way into the crowd and faced my neighbor's old kitchen amah.

"My cousin told me," she said proudly. "He's the head cook at the great house across the street from Chamber of Commerce President Hung Li-son. His master is Ding Beng-hui." She looked around at her audience. "My cousin heard the shots with his own ears. He saw the pool of blood on the cobblestones after they carried President Hung inside." Clearly reveling in the attention, she closed her eyes halfway and frowned at the gasps her words elicited.

"How do you know he didn't survive?" I argued. "Did your cousin see his dead body?"

"He died," she said, clamping her mouth decisively shut, even though she didn't have a shred of proof.

I wanted to shake her. This wasn't the sort of thing to be spreading rumors about. The Kulangsu Chamber of Commerce, to which all influential Chinese and foreign businessmen belonged, was the most powerful organization on the island. I couldn't believe someone would kill its president.

"Who would do such a thing?" Su-lee blubbered.

Old Mr. Lim shook his cane at her. "Who else? The bow-legged devils and their running dogs."

I hoped he was right. It was easier to aim our hatred in a single direction.

"It might have been a thief," the neighbor lady suggested.

"Or the goons of one of his rivals," my mother-in-law said.

We threw our theories back and forth for a while, trying to squeeze another drop of information out of our ignorance. I fanned myself and wiped the sweat off my forehead. Where had Hung Li-son's Sikh bodyguard been?

Several people stepped back, and the tall American lady who lived on the corner moved into the space that had been cleared for her. "What?" she asked, waving her hands and trying to say something none of us could understand. She was a piano teacher, and her fingers were very long.

"She wants to know what happened," her maid explained.

"A man killed," I told her in English. And Old Mr. Lim, who spoke English fluently, explained the rest. Mrs. Bradley didn't cry out at the news, but her white face became whiter still, and she pressed her lips together so tightly they almost disappeared.

"Very bad, very bad," she said in her strangely accented Chinese, nodding her head each time. "Very bad."

Two days later, on May thirteenth, Mrs. Bradley experienced personally one of the "very bad" results of Hung Li-son's assassination. It was morning, and Mr. Bradley, who worked for the Standard Oil Company, was at his office. Mother and I were eating breakfast. We didn't know yet that two hundred troops from the Japanese Imperial Navy had landed on Kulangsu at daybreak to investigate Hung Li-son's assassination. Nor did we hear the sailors banging on the Bradleys' gate. We wouldn't have noticed if I hadn't heard the postman and run outside to get my letter.

"Letter. Letter for Madam Han Yu-ming," he called.

In my excitement, I failed to hear the anxiety in his voice. He gave me Yu-ming's letter and hurried off without a word. When I looked up, I saw two Japanese sailors outside Mrs. Bradley's open gate. One leaned against the wall smoking a cigarette; the other stood at attention, his bayonet gleaming in the sunlight. I ducked back inside, quietly pulled the gate shut, and slid the bolt into place.

This was what we'd been preparing for, the day the enemy would force their way into our house. We knew we couldn't deny them entry. All we could do was to hide the children and the young women from them. The hiding place for me and Ah Chew and his amah was behind a false wall in the back of my closet. A stuffy, hot little enclosure with only enough room to crouch. Su-lee and Ah Mei hid in my mother-in-law's closet.

I left the wall open a crack and listened for the Japanese while the amah nursed Ah Chew. After he fell asleep, I took out Yu-ming's letter. I breathed on the aerogramme's flaps one by one until they were soft enough to open. Moving a few inches away from Hsiang-mei and Ah Chew, I switched on the electric torch I'd grabbed on my way into the closet. It was becoming a familiar routine, this letter reading. How pitiful that I'd begun to consider it "not strange" to have a husband I couldn't talk to or touch, one who came to me only in the form of airmail paper and blue ink! The light from my torch moved down the page and then down again and again.

And all the while, crouching in the back of a closet like a rat in a hole, the air thick with my body odors, I listened for the Japanese. Maybe I should have saved Yu-ming's letter until later. Maybe if I'd been sitting at my desk when I read it, sunlight and a roomful of air around me, maybe then I would have felt differently about the sweet-voiced woman on the riverbank. Instead, I was crouching, my mouth dry and my bladder full. Who can say what caused jealousy's noxious seed to plant itself in my belly? I'm sure the whole thing with Fan Ho-fu had nothing to do with it—his winking or the way he put into words everything I felt. It might have predisposed me, but… No. I don't think so. It was the indignity of hiding in that cramped little closet that distorted my mind.

Yu-ming wrote to me from what he called *a blessed moment of peace* when *all the world was beautiful.* He described the riverbank, the willows overhead, the green water flowing smoothly past. In his previous letter he'd written about a donkey wounded in the crossfire of battle and stranded between his men and the Japanese. All night long it brayed, drowning out the moans of the wounded soldiers caught in the same no-man's-land. In this letter, instead, he wrote of a young woman's sweet songs. Wiping my forehead with an already wet handkerchief, I imagined her slender fingers plucking the strings of a zither. There must be beautiful women everywhere he goes, I thought.

That was when I should have stopped. Instead, I kept right on reading, the beam of my electric torch moving down the page like Sherlock Holmes's magnifying glass, focusing my attention—and my suspicions—on each of Yu-ming's words, one circle of characters at a time. Wasn't it unusual, I wondered, for him to write about the apricot orchard and the unripe fruit that he and his soldiers couldn't resist eating? And why did he write so little this time about economic and political affairs? He did mention one of Chiang Kai-shek's speeches and also the small private plants that were producing motor fuel by distilling native wine. But mostly he wrote about other things—a flower floating down the river, melon vines growing up its banks. Someone must have inspired his poetic turn of mind.

Even his concluding words aroused my suspicions. *I want to be with you,* he said. *My resolve is firm. Come what may, I will find a way to roll up the ground and return to you.* It was precisely what I'd wanted to hear. And yet, perversely, I found myself wondering if it was because of some other woman that he had become more attuned to his romantic feelings.

Ah Chew began to whimper, and finally I put the letter down and took him from his amah. *Don't forget, Yu-ming,* I said with thoughts powerful enough to travel the miles. *Don't forget. You have a son here at home. You have a wife and son and daughter back here in Kulangsu.*

It was midday before we came out of our closets. Then we waited another couple of hours before venturing into the street. It looked safe enough, so I took Ah Kwai with me and went to the house on the corner to see if everyone was all right.

Mrs. Bradley was playing the piano as we approached, the same sort of music we often heard when we passed her house. Her younger maid opened the gate. "We weren't violated," she said without being asked.

Mrs. Bradley motioned for us to come in. Then she said something unintelligible to the maid, who didn't need to be told to bring drinks.

"You okay?" I asked in English.

"Yes, yes." She held out her arms and turned her hands over and back to show me she was just fine.

"House okay?"

She nodded and swung her arm broadly to indicate the room. Every time I looked at her hands, her fingers grew longer, sticking out like spokes on a wheel. Suddenly she frowned. She pointed at a low table, then at the top of a bookshelf and a spot on the floor, and she spoke so many English words that even those I caught flew away from me before I could put them together.

I shook my head. "I not understand."

"The Japanese," she said very slowly, "they took my ivory Kwanyin statue." She indicated its height and pointed at the bookcase where it used to sit. The young maid came in with a tray set with glasses and a pitcher of lemonade and put it on a carved rosewood side table.

"They took the Kwanyin statue and Master's silver cigarette box," the older maid said. She was leaning against the door frame holding her side.

Mrs. Bradley jumped up. "Please, you rest. Doctor..."

"One of them broke Madam's Ming vase," the maid said, tears forming in her eyes. "He kicked it with his boot, and then he laughed."

"Now, now." Mrs. Bradley patted the maid's hand. "Only a vase."

"When I dusted it, I was always so careful. Madam said it was very precious. I would have stopped that accursed Jap if he hadn't knocked me down with his rifle butt."

"Please," Mrs. Bradley said. "Please sit down."

"She thinks my rib is broken."

"What did they think they would find in our house?" Mrs. Bradley asked. At least I think that's what she asked. "What would we know about Mr. Hung's murder?"

I had no answer.

Nor could I supply any logical reason why, for the next three days, the Japanese searched hundreds of Chinese and foreign residences and carried off thousands of refugees. No one believed they cared about justice for Hung Li-son. And no one came to our aid. There were two American destroyers lying off our shore, but all they did was watch.

It was a police action, not an invasion. Still, we had no idea what to expect. We'd heard the stories from Nanking and Hsuchow and Amoy—any place the Imperial Army or Navy had entered victorious. Our heads were full of accounts of rape and wanton murder. Most days I pushed them aside as best I could. Sometimes, though, at night, the worst of them rose up. The whole scene could present itself in a mere instant—unarmed men beside a pit destined to be their grave staring empty-eyed at the bayonets that would send them there, a pregnant woman or a little girl between the thighs of a dirty Japanese while her husband or father looked on and other Japanese animals waited their turns. Worst of all were the dogs. I tried never to think of them, but my very efforts strengthened the image. When it flashed into my mind, I was always one of the people in the walled courtyard, herded in by leering enemy soldiers eager to release on us the sharp-toothed military dogs that would tear us to bits.

In the daytime, I was rational enough to remember that the house-to-house searches were only part of a police action. I convinced Mother that we didn't need to spend our days in hiding. If the Japanese came to our house, Su-lee, Hsiang-mei, and I would stay in the background as much as possible. In the meantime, anything of value would be put away while the cheapest, gaudiest objects would be placed in plain view.

Besides, the equation was beginning to change. The British sent two ships into Amoy Bay, one a cruiser flying the flag of the admiral. That still made only four Western ships to the Japanese twenty, but by the following morning, there were eleven British, American, and French warships. Unfortunately, their presence didn't put a stop to Japanese arrogance. They still had the audacity to ask the Kulangsu Council to appoint a Japanese chief of police and a Japanese chairman and secretary of the council. The council steadfastly refused their demands, but discussions continued on board a British cruiser, and the two hundred Japanese troops stayed, continuing their searches and interrogations. If the council did give in, we would become a de facto colony of Japan, and then Yu-ming and I would be separated even more conclusively than we were now.

"If the Japanese take control here and the Western powers don't fight back," Mother said at breakfast one morning, "they will go on to seize power in the Western-administered areas of Shanghai. We are their test case."

I was stirring pork *sung* into my *congee* as she spoke. "The Japanese are still afraid of the Europeans and Americans," I said. "They won't risk bringing the Western powers into their war."

Mother shook her head. "This isn't a game of Chinese chess, An Lee. The Japanese, like all men, live inside a red cloud of pride and desire. They're obsessed with being bigger than they are."

I smiled as I poured our tea. "Maybe if the Japanese weren't so small, they wouldn't need to be so belligerent." I rolled the idea around with my tea, enjoying the taste of them both, ignoring the fact that I, too, was short.

We were still discussing the Japanese, turning them into ideas that fit comfortably inside our heads, when the dwarf pirates themselves rang at our gate. Ah Kwai, who was older and less attractive than Su-lee, ran ahead to open it. The rest of us held our breaths and strained our ears, listening for something understandable in the low-toned bark of Japanese arrogance. At last they were here. Blood raced through my body. I wanted to run out and confront them—these intruders, these...

"Old Mistress, Young Mistress." Su-lee burst into the room. "They said we must assemble in the sitting room. Immediately."

"Stay calm," Mother cautioned. "Here. Help me up."

Those sons of turtles had better not lay a hand on my children or any of us women.

Despite the fire burning in my chest, I approached the sitting room with a show of humility. A chicken approaching the foxes. As we stepped inside, two sailors whipped around, training their rifles and their cold black eyes on us.

"There! There!" the third sailor shouted, motioning for us to stand in front of the window.

We hurried to comply and then turned to face them: three frowning bluejackets who looked shockingly out of place within the familiar walls of our sitting room. They wore naval blue uniforms edged with white braid with puttees wound around their lower legs. The canteens and bags tied to their belts stuck out clumsily from their hips. I couldn't help noticing how incongruous their steel helmets and rifles looked next to the embroidered pillows on our wicker love seat.

"Where your men?" the one with the mustache asked.

"No men," Mother said. "Our men are dead."

"Hmph." He looked around, frowning. "*Her* man," he said, pointing at me.

"Gone," I replied.

"Your man hiding?"

"No. My husband is in Chungking." My heart was pounding, but my mind was unnaturally clear. Chungking was as plausible a place as any, and as far away.

"Mm," he growled. Then he shouted an order that his men acknowledged with a bow. Their rifles and canteens bumping against the furniture, they opened drawers and looked under cushions. I forced myself not to frown or laugh at the way they were trying to keep up the fiction of authorities investigating a murder case. I didn't want to give them an excuse to slash our cushions or throw our vases against the wall. They might urinate on our carpets or …

The sailor in charge, who was only slightly older than the other two, took a notebook and pen from the bag on his hip and sat down. He put his steel helmet on the floor and crossed his leg like a school-teacher. "Names," he said. "Most old first."

"My name is Liu Ling-chu," Mother said in a clear voice.

He leaned over his notebook and frowned. "Which way write *Liu?*"

Mother drew the character with one finger on her palm.

"Ah," he said and wrote it down. "Which Ling?"

Mother held up her palm again and wrote the character for *Ling* on it.

He blinked as his men opened the drawers in our medicine chest and banged them shut. Suddenly he swung his arm in an abrupt gesture and shouted something in Japanese that caused the younger sailors to leave the room.

"You," he said, pointing at me. "You write." Giving me his notebook, he made me sit next to him and write down our names and ages. Then he took the notebook back and ordered me to stand with the others again while he finished questioning us. Did we hate Hung Li-son? Who hated him? Did we know anyone who was jealous of him? Who wanted his position? Did we know where he lived? Had we ever been to his house? When?

When I said I'd been to his house to play mahjong last November, he grilled me on the other guests and what they had said about Hung Li-son. When I said they didn't say anything, he pounded his fist on the arm of the love seat. "You lie," he shouted. "You in house of commerce president. You talk something about him."

"We spoke only about women's matters," I said, "about children, food, and our game of mahjong."

"What else?" He was working himself into a frenzy.

"Hairstyles and lip coloring."

"What other thing?" He raised his fist. Then, seeming to remember the unsatisfactory sound it made on the wicker arm, he jumped to his feet instead.

"Babies. That's all." On my way to the sitting room, I'd told myself we were lucky. It was morning so they wouldn't be drunk yet. But this edginess was something else. He was like a stopped-up water kettle on a high flame.

Upstairs, the other men seemed to be moving furniture. I thought of the Swiss clock I'd wrapped in a baby blanket and hidden in the bottom of my camphor chest. I was afraid that if they found it, this little man with his neatly trimmed mustache and stopped-up desire to run wild would consider what I'd done an act of subterfuge and reason enough to punish us all.

"Mmrr." That deep-throated growl again. It came from his abdomen—*chi* gathered in his *dan tien* and then thrown out at us.

"Ma."

"It's all right, dumpling," I whispered to Ah Mei. "It's all right." If he growled again, she was bound to cry. I rubbed her hand, frantically trying to think how I could calm her, or at least placate this high-strung sailor, when, suddenly, his countrymen came tripping down the stairs with some of the decoys we'd set out for them—some ceramic figurines, a flute with red and gold tassels, and a bronze bell. One of them had our electric torch. He twisted his wrist, throwing the beam of yellow light from wall to wall. Then he shined it on our faces and laughed. The older sailor grabbed it from him.

"Why you need this?" he demanded. "Women don't walk about at night."

What was he getting at?

"Oh. So man live in house."

It didn't make sense. If they wanted some reason to believe a man was here, why didn't they just bring down some of Yu-ming's clothes?

"Evidence," he said. "I take."

He left us lined up against the window as they searched for other "evidence" to carry away. They didn't bother to explain the relevance of a tin of English biscuits and a *tiao chi* board and bag of marbles. They thumbed through a stack of comic books, choosing their favorites. Then, abruptly, their frenzied leader raised his arm and put an end to it. "We go now," he said.

"They have other so-called evidence to gather," my mother-in-law whispered when they were out of sight.

I laughed under my breath. Su-lee pinched her mouth and laughed through her nose, and even Ah Kwai and Hsiang-mei chuckled.

"Quiet down," Mother said. "All of you. We don't want them to come back."

"They'd better hurry, before the white men decide to push them off the island." Su-lee's laughter was turning to giddiness.

I couldn't help joining her, even though I knew the Western powers weren't about to come to our aid. Even the invasion of the Chinese section of Shanghai hadn't roused them.

All that day conferences continued on the British ship. Finally the Japanese withdrew some of their forces, leaving behind, it was later determined, a total of forty-two men. The British, American, and French counted them precisely, and then each country sent ashore a landing party of exactly the same number.

The following night the Japanese tried again to put reinforcements ashore and were caught in the act. After that, they pulled out most of their men, leaving behind only those needed to guard their consulate.

This wasn't war. It was a chess game.

16

*H*aving lost face when they failed to take control of Kulangsu, the Japanese were more determined than ever to occupy it. They started by tightening controls on trade. Every ship that entered the harbor was required to hold a permit from Japanese authorities, even though they rarely issued one. At first, we thought it was just a bureaucratic power play. We didn't realize how quickly the de-facto blockade would result in food shortages.

The commander-in-chief of the British Asiatic Fleet sailed in from Hong Kong to join Admiral Sir Percy Noble in delivering an official protest. And still the siege continued. Yu-ming could roll up the ground all the way to the edge of the sea, but unless he could devise a way to evade the Japanese sea wolves and get across the water, I'd never see him. Some nights I dreamed of ships, sometimes of wolves. Sailing, pacing, they circled our island, firing their guns, snarling. And always, Yu-ming was somewhere on the other side.

Waking from such a dream, I'd find myself engulfed in a great wave of loneliness. An expanding ball of nothing, a vacuum that couldn't be quelled. At some point, this thing would become so large or I would become so weak that . . . I didn't know what. I only knew it would be something I wouldn't be able to bear. "Please come home," I'd whisper. "I need you." And lying there, in the dampness of my pillow, I'd feel too exhausted to think or move. After a while, though, even sadness becomes tiresome. I'd roll out of bed, stumble over to the closet, and choose a dress, one that was neither new nor old, bright nor dull.

Because of this war, Yu-ming and I had been apart for almost four hundred days with no end in sight. I brushed my hair a few strokes and put the brush down. Time to start my day.

Passing the nursery, I looked in at the three beds—the small bed, and the crib, and Hsiang-mei's long, narrow bed set apart against the wall.

Ah Kwai was in the pantry. Su-lee was out in the breezeway, humming over a washtub. As I opened the screen door, she wished me a good morning and went back to sloshing the clothes against the washboard. Everyone was alone, it seemed—Ah Kwai, Su-lee, my mother-in-law across the garden with her watering can, Yun-yun under the tree throwing nuts against the wall. And Mother, especially my mother, always, for as long as I could remember waiting in her room for my father, and then, no husband to wait for.

It didn't take long for people to realize what the new Japanese regulations meant for our supply of food and fuel. If the blockade continued much longer, the reserves in our pantry would soon be gone. Each morning Ah Kwai left for the market a little earlier than the day before.

One day my mother-in-law and I were in the kitchen shelling walnuts when she returned. "Look at this," she said as she walked through the door. She raised a nearly empty shopping bag for Su-lee to see. Her normally smooth brown face was flushed and a few hairs had come loose from her bun. Then she saw us. "Oh, Madam, Young Mistress, I'm sorry."

"Ah Kwai, what's wrong?"

"It's all right, Young Mistress." She lowered the bag and looked at me with that expression of absolute calm I'd known and depended on all my life.

"Tell me, Ah Kwai," my mother-in-law said in her no-nonsense voice. "What happened?"

"Nothing, Madam. Except . . . it's not so easy these days." She leaned her bags against the cupboard and smoothed her stray hairs. "I left home early. When I got to the market, other shoppers were already there, but nothing to buy. These days the vendors know they can sleep late and still sell everything at a high price. I put myself second in line at the vegetable vendor's stall and waited." She turned to me. "You have to be first or second, otherwise you don't get anything. The woman in front of me had only one bag, and she looked reasonable. She said she came to buy cabbages and carrots. Well, I thought to myself, even if she bought all the carrots and cabbages, I could still buy onions and green beans. Maybe I'll be lucky enough to buy some *won soy*, I thought—though I hadn't seen any for many days."

"So what happened?" my mother-in-law prodded. "Didn't the vendor come?"

"He came all right. He and his wife had two baskets full of vegetables. The other woman and I thought it was our lucky day. We didn't see the kitchen amah behind us with her thugs. As soon as the vendors had things set up, she pushed to the front of the line and started choosing vegetables. We told her to wait her turn, but she wouldn't listen. 'Aunties,' the thugs said, rolling up their sleeves to show their muscles, 'don't you remember? We were already here.' We continued to protest, but they turned their backs on us and helped the kitchen amah fill up her many bags. These days no one buys just two or three onions. They want two or three catties instead."

"Whose amah was she?" I asked. It was one thing to be pushed around by the dwarf pirates, another to be abused by our own people.

"She works for Goh Dang-ben. His old cook quit last month."

"I'm not surprised." My mother-in-law sniffed. She still had bad feelings toward the Goh household, even though the thought of marrying Goh Dang-ben's fool of a son had never crossed my mind.

"Tomorrow I'll go with you," I said.

"Absolutely not, Young Mistress. I'm ashamed you even thought of it. Don't worry. As long as there's food available, you can trust me to bring some home."

I nodded, reluctant to make her lose face.

She reached into her bags and took out a small cabbage. Then she turned back to me. "If you can give me more money tomorrow and send Su-lee and Yun-yun with me," she said, "we will show our determination and return with our bags full."

"I'll ask the Old Mistress."

"Of course," Mother agreed when I told her Ah Kwai's request. "If we really need it."

I opened the jar of oil I used to massage her feet and sat down across from her so we could discuss it. "If they keep stopping boats," I said, removing her slipper and putting her foot on my knee, "soon there will be nothing left in the market." I rolled her white stocking down to her toes, shook it in the air, and laid it across the arm of my chair.

"All we can do is listen to heaven and follow fate," she said. She flexed her foot and wiggled her deformed toes while I poured the oil into my palm. Mother always started by proclaiming her trust and obedience to the will of heaven. But it was her nature to weigh and count, to choose a course of action and see that it was acted upon. While I massaged her feet, we talked about the Japanese and their intentions. We considered the contributions from smugglers and black-marketeers. And we discussed where in our house we might store more food and fuel. In the end, we decided on a sum of extra money to give Ah Kwai.

The next day she succeeded in buying a bunch of ripe bananas, a live chicken, and some vegetables for dinner along with some dried mangoes, preserved vegetables, and salted eggs to add to our stock. She and Su-lee and Yun-yun were smiling when I met them at the gate, Yun-yun especially. "Su-lee made us take the long way home," he proclaimed with a naughty smile as he squeezed through the gate ahead of his aunt. "Past the American consulate so she could ogle the sailors," he shouted over his shoulder as he sprinted away.

Su-lee dropped the chicken and took off after him. "You little smelly egg."

"Su-lee loves a white-faced sailor," Yun-yun sang. A moment later they were back, racing through the breezeway that separated the maids' quarters from the house. "Auntie," Yun-yun cried, "she pinched me."

"Enough. Both of you. Come inside. Su-lee, put some water to boil. When it's ready, you two worthless children can kill and pluck the chicken."

"I'm not a child," Su-lee objected.

"Children act like children," Ah Kwai recited without looking up. "Young ladies act like young ladies."

*   *   *

I had no intention of ogling the American sailors, but a couple of days later as I passed that same consulate, I noticed a crowd of onlookers clustered around the barred gate. The solid brick wall that surrounded the American compound was high, so if I wanted to see what was going on, I had to push through the crowd at the gate. Over the tops of their heads, all I could see was the familiar two-story brick structure. Edging forward, I saw that there were enough tents pitched in the backyard and along one side to house what must have been forty-two sailors. American military personnel were not a novelty on Kulangsu, but this many sailors relaxing and playing on the consulate lawn was. They were playing cards under trees, throwing balls, and playing tennis.

Someone called for the crowd to make way. We started moving aside, but we weren't fast enough. The Yankee sailors who were marching up the lane with a parade of coolies shoved us out of the way and formed a barrier for the men with their enormous, shiny pots and kettles smelling of roasted beef and onions and garlic.

"That's what they eat?" the woman next to me asked, turning up her nose. "I don't like the smell."

"It's so much food!" someone else said. "Enough for a whole battalion."

"No, it's not," the woman replied. "You don't even know how many men are in a battalion."

I was about to enlighten them when someone came up behind me, so close I could almost feel his breath on my neck. "They cook on their ships," he said in my ear, "carry their food here three times a day." I recognized the voice. It was the impudent young man of letters from Teacher Wei's birthday party, Fan Ho-fu.

"Mr. Fan," I said, stepping away from him. "I see you're still here in Kulangsu."

"And you, Madam Han, I see you are out and about all by yourself."

I raised my chin and glared at him. How dare he? My mother and mother-in-law, even my maids, could scold me for going out alone, but what business was it of his? His eyes sparkled, as though he enjoyed goading me. I was tempted to lash out, but that was exactly what he would have liked. "I'm surprised," I said. "I would have thought a writer like yourself would have found a way to get back to Shanghai or escape to some place with more publishers and printing presses."

He smiled and raised his eyebrows. "Hairy legs, huh?" he said, motioning with his chin toward the Americans on the tennis court. "Maybe I'll put a hairy-legged American in my next story."

I concentrated on the back-and-forth of the tennis ball. "The image is too bizarre."

"Exactly. It's a time-honored technique. Point to the bizarre to glorify the commonplace."

I thought of Yu-ming's smooth legs. Here on the street were dozens of honey-colored legs, some of them too thin but none of them too hairy. Just then, the tennis ball flew over the wall. Fan Ho-fu caught it with one hand and in the same motion tossed it behind him to a child who disappeared into the crowd.

"Hey!" A sweaty, red-faced sailor leaned his head over the wall. "Hey!" he yelled again. "Who's got our ball?"

Fan Ho-fu pointed down the street. "It went thatta way," he said in the sailor's own language. Then he turned to the crowd. "His ball ran away," he told them. Everyone laughed, and the sailor shrugged and went back to his game.

"They have plenty of balls," Fan Ho-fu said. "Now, where were we?"

"Your image of the American's legs. It lacks subtlety." I should have started home. I don't know why I continued arguing with him.

He smiled. "Tell me, what image would you choose from this scene?"

"Those huge pots of food. The way the Americans don't even bother to look up as they're carried through the gate. Only we on the outside look."

He smiled again. Then he crossed his arms over his chest and looked at me sideways. "You ought to join our group."

"Me? I'm not a poet."

He laughed. "We poets are not in the habit of recruiting our competition."

I blushed and started to back away.

"The Kulangsu Cultural Circle has more than enough poets," he said. "That's why some of us have broken away to form our own group." He stepped closer. "The Kulangsu Cultural and Resistance League," he said in a low voice. "Poets and merchants, playwrights and students. All of us devoted to literature and national salvation."

Yes, I thought in a rush of enthusiasm. I can be one of those women.

"Think about it," he said, raising his eyebrows. "I'll contact you." His black eyes appraised me. Then he shoved his hands into the pockets of his Western-style trousers and walked away.

I watched him disappear around a corner. I wanted with all my heart to serve China. I had my children to think about, though, and my mother and mother-in-law. Besides, what would Yu-ming think? I started down the lane, past the pharmacy and the rice store. It wasn't fair. Men could fight or stay home, but we had no choice in the matter. I hurried past the coffin shop and the public bathhouse. Anger and confusion raged in my chest as I walked faster and faster. Finally I pulled my skirt above my knees and raced down the lanes like a child. I stopped to catch my breath in front of the Widow Ng's noodle shop. Her third son was out front smoking a cigarette. "Still fast as the wind," he said with a crooked smile.

I tossed my head. "That I am." I could see he was remembering the foot race I challenged him to when we were children. A race I easily won. Now, though, his legs were longer and stronger. If I dared to challenge him today, I wouldn't have a chance of winning.

*   *   *

For the next several days, I considered what might be involved in joining Fan Ho-fu's group. Wavering between my obligations and the yearnings of my heart, I was more confused than ever by the time he contacted me.

The young woman he sent was a student. She wouldn't tell Ah Kwai what her name was. When I met her at the gate, she still declined to identify herself. "Madam Han?" she asked.

I nodded.

"Mr. Fan wants to know if you are going to join the KCRL."

It took me a moment to realize that she was referring to Fan Ho-fu and the Kulangsu Cultural and Resistance League. "Oh," I said. "I don't know…"

She frowned and lowered her eyes. "Well," she said, "if you don't know, then how will I know if I can trust you?"

It occurred to me that I could just let her go. It wouldn't be my fault for not joining them. Fan Ho-fu hadn't given me enough information. The girl looked at me through her straight-cut bangs. Then she turned away.

"Wait," I said. "You can trust me. But can't you tell me more about…"

"Two thirty tomorrow. Gu-sheng Lu. Number forty-six, apartment seven."

17

*G*u-sheng Lu was a quiet lane on the northwest corner of the island. It ran for a kilometer or so along the shoreline, where it rose to a rocky hillside and then turned inland into an unremarkable neighborhood of drab three-story buildings. That was where I found number forty-six, wedged tightly against other flat-faced concrete and brick structures. The outer door was unlocked, so I stepped unannounced into the lobby, a small, dark space with closed doors on either side and a set of buzzers in the middle. I pushed the buzzer for apartment seven and waited. I was right on time. I looked over my shoulder at the door to the street. Maybe people came early to this kind of meeting. Or maybe late. Somewhere beyond one of the closed inner doors, a door hinge creaked and then a latch snapped back into place. Someone with a light, confident step approached the door and opened it halfway. "Yes?" he asked.

All I could see was his general shape, a glimpse of teeth, and a jagged white scar running from his hairline to his eyebrow. "I'm looking for Mr. Fan Ho-fu," I said.

"And you are?'

"Han An Lee."

"You'll have to choose a nom de guerre, miss. No real names here." He pointed at his scar. "I'm Lightning."

Oh dear, I thought as I followed him down a hallway lined with bookshelves and cabinets. Suppose they want me to choose a name on the spot. A list of unsuitable choices ran through my head—Tiger, Dragon, Avenging Sword, Faithful Pine. We passed apartment five and apartment six. Stopping at number seven, Lightning knocked three times. The door opened, and there I was, about to join my first meeting of the Kulangsu Cultural and Resistance League. My heart skipped a beat. The schoolgirl I met the day before closed the door behind us and hurried back to her seat on the floor. The others—eight or nine men and women sitting on the floor and in straight-backed chairs—looked at me.

"Have a seat," Fan Ho-fu said.

There was an empty chair, but sitting on the floor seemed a better choice since this was my first meeting. Still trying to come up with a good *nom de guerre*, I found a spot beside the schoolgirl and settled into a cross-legged pose.

"You've met Lightning," Fan Ho-fu said. "And I believe you already know Black Boulder."

Chang Ti, a.k.a. Black Boulder, raised his chin in acknowledgment.

"This is Hermit." A balding man with large bags under his eyes placed his palms together and nodded.

In such a dimly lit room—heavy velvet draperies across the window, glaring light from a single lamp casting long, distorting shadows—I had to squint through the cigarette smoke to get a good look at their faces. Still, I don't know why I didn't see Pei-lu sooner. Willow, Fan Ho-fu called her. She was wearing a cap, and when he said her name, she pushed it back and smiled.

My God! What was she doing here? She was in mourning for her father. I couldn't believe that mild, intelligent Pei-lu would... She was a wife and mother after all. Of course, so was I. I turned my attention back to Fan Ho-fu.

"This is Cricket," he said, nudging the schoolgirl with the straight bangs and pony tail. "My right-hand girl."

Cricket blinked in my direction.

"I'm known as Storm," he said when he'd finished introducing the others. "And what shall we call you?"

"You may call me..." East Wind, I thought, Barracuda, Shark. "Sand Shark," I said suddenly, remembering the silent, menacing fish that swam beside me one day at Gangzihou Beach. I drew up my knees and hugged them. Not bad. Sand Shark. In fact, I rather liked it.

"All right," Fan Ho-fu said. "Let's get back to business."

Black Boulder stood up. "As I was saying?" He squared his shoulders and straightened his glasses.

I couldn't help thinking that Willow would have been a name that suited Chang Ti better. You'd think a poet could have chosen a more appropriate name for himself.

"Distributing propaganda leaflets is a waste of time," he declared. "Slogans on a page don't touch people's hearts. Theater, on the other hand, is immediate and alive. It strikes the deepest chords of sentiment."

"Yes, but where would we find patriotic dramas?" Lightning asked.

"We'll write them."

"What about the censors?"

Chang Ti was pacing now. "We can obscure the meaning by using Chinese symbols and historical references."

Lightning shook his head. "I say this is no time for obscurity. The wolves are at the gate. Better to take up our swords and slice off their heads."

Hermit shook his head. "They'll only send more wolves. If we want to serve the cause of National Salvation, we must be more cunning."

That morning I'd been filled with enthusiasm. After an evening of indecision, it felt wonderful to have finally made up my mind, to know that I was about to become part of the anti-Japanese struggle. Well, here I was. I tapped my fingers on my legs, and the convoluted argument about the comparative benefits of different types of patriotic dramas continued.

Hermit's baggy eyes bugged out as he made his argument. "People are used to watching costume drama," he said. "They like it. You can't expect them to come out to see a modern political play."

The schoolgirl jumped up. "What are you talking about? This is nineteen thirty-nine. The whole world has changed. Dwarf pirates are crawling across the land like a plague of locusts. We cannot go back to the old ways."

Fan Ho-fu lit a cigarette and let a trail of smoke escape from his lips. Why didn't he break in? This was supposed to be a resistance league, not a theater circle. I caught Pei-lu's eye, and she shrugged. Was this what the KCRL did?

Lightning cleared his throat, and when no one seemed to notice him, he tipped his chair against the wall and crossed his arms over his chest.

Who could say which side had the better argument? I didn't really like either one. Any theatrical show, be it modern or historical, would take too long to produce, it seemed to me. It would cost too much. Then there was the question of where to perform it. And how could we be assured of attracting an audience?

Chang Ti punched his fist in the air to make his point about the superiority of producing a modern play. "One that speaks directly to the people," he said, spinning around. "In their own language."

"Yes," I said. He had a point. Street performers—magicians, acrobats, jugglers, fortune-tellers—they all spoke directly to the people. In their own language or even in no language at all. "Not in a theater, though. We could perform it on the street. No fancy costumes, no expense for renting a theater."

Fan Ho-fu smiled. "Street theater," he said as though he'd been waiting all along for me to propose it.

"Exactly," Willow agreed. "Short, realistic skits."

"Wait," Chang Ti objected. "Anyone can do street theater. Anyone can write it."

Lightning tipped his chair forward with a bang. "So what? I like Sand Shark's idea. We're not here for a literary contest. Our country's at war. If we want to mobilize the masses, we have to take our message to the streets."

Mobilize the masses? That was a favorite phrase of the Communists. I hoped this wasn't a CCP-sponsored group. I looked around the circle. Certainly my friend, Pei-lu, wasn't a Communist. And Chang Ti... No. His sympathies were too firmly allied with the educated class. I glanced at Fan Ho-fu. Who could say? Anything he did or thought wouldn't surprise me.

As the squabbling continued, I stopped worrying. Even if the CCP wanted to, it wouldn't be able to control a group like this. They couldn't agree on anything. And now, thanks to my suggestion, we had three proposals to argue over, four if you wanted to count the printing and distribution of propaganda leaflets. Supporters of each stood up and argued its merits. Lightning, Cricket, and some of the others kept shouting and interrupting, becoming more and more emotional as time went by. Since I was the newcomer, I tried to keep my mouth shut, but before long I, too, was shouting and interrupting.

When it seemed that we were all worn down from arguing, Fan Ho-fu, who hadn't joined the discussion at all, stood up. "Regrettably, we don't have enough members to accomplish all these goals," he said. "So, I propose that we decide what we're going to do by taking a vote."

There was some grumbling, but eventually everyone agreed. We went around the room, each person expressing his preference, and although, when we finished, street theater was the clear winner, Hermit still objected. "This was just a preliminary vote," he said. "Now that we have narrowed it down to the top two choices, we should vote again."

Over a chorus of sighs, we voted again. Street theater was still the winner.

"I don't understand," I said to Pei-lu on the way home. "Is Fan Ho-fu the leader of the group or isn't he?"

"There is no leader, not officially anyway. Chang Ti, Hermit, Fan Ho-fu, and several others who used to belong to the same literary circle got things started. I think no one wants to upstage the others, or to be upstaged. But, you know, a leader always emerges."

We were walking down the portion of Gu-sheng Lu that led toward the sea, our heads close together to keep our conversation private. "Are the meetings always this contentious?" I asked.

"This is only the second meeting."

"Oh, I didn't realize."

"As soon as we settle on a purpose, we won't have time for all this arguing. I was so disappointed after the first meeting. I'd expected to get right to work writing slogans. It's frustrating to get a slow start when there's so much to be done."

Yes. That was exactly how I felt—frustrated. "It's still early," I said. "Why don't we go climb Sunlight Rock?" It was a beautiful spring day, and after all that wrangling in a dreary, smoke-filled room, the prospect of sunshine and fresh air and a scramble up Sunlight Rock was irresistible.

The trail started out in a wooded area. Making small talk, we walked under a canopy of leaves for a time. Then, going single file up the narrow steps, we devoted our full efforts to the climb. At Lotus Flower Convent we stopped to wonder, as we had so many times before, at the huge slab of rock balanced precariously on a small neck. Every child believes that the rock is poised to fall at any moment. And yet, nearly every child and adult who climbs Sunlight Rock steps into the hall formed by this quirk of nature. Pei-lu and I were no exception. We paused for a moment—two flesh-and-blood women under tons of granite, and then we proceeded on our way. Without stopping at The Dragon's Cave or The Platform for Directing the Rain or any of the other scenic spots along the way, we walked steadily up the steep, winding trail.

When we reached the summit, both of us were panting. We held hands and silently looked out at the view. It could have been any day, any year. As far as the eye could see, the world was still all blue and green and beautiful. We let the peace soak through the crust of our skin. Then we found a flat rock, hot from the day's sunshine, and sat down. Pei-lu, who was wearing mourning from head to foot, paused to place a handkerchief on the rock before sitting down. "Who told you about the League?" she asked.

"Storm," I said, using Fan Ho-fu's nom de guerre. "I don't know why he chose me."

"He must have seen something he liked. Besides, there's no reason we women should be kept in the house, cooking and caring for children. Especially at a time like this."

I was surprised to hear her talk that way. I was the one who chafed under a woman's limitations, not Pei-lu. "Why did you decide to join?" I asked.

"I know, you must be wondering. I'm in mourning. I should be at home, grieving for my father and comforting my mother and sister." Her lips trembled briefly. "But, An Lee, my father did not die in an accident or from a heart attack. He was murdered in cold blood. And, as anyone can tell you, the Japanese instigated it. I don't care who pulled the trigger. They were behind it. It was their pretext for sending more men ashore. Their vain hope for taking over the Municipal Council." Her words came as angry and fast as a machinegun.

She turned her head from side to side, looking for other climbers, and when she was assured we were still alone, she continued. "I wept inside my house," she said, "and in my sister's and my parents' houses. I received well-wishers, including you. I arranged for my father's funeral, and I followed the phony investigation of his murder. None of it seemed to make any sense. I thought I was going to explode. I wanted to kill someone. But no single person was responsible. Cricket must have seen how frustrated I was. She was often there in my sister's house, tutoring my nephew in mathematics. She was a student at Amoy University before it was moved inland ahead of the occupation. One afternoon, she asked if I would walk her home after her tutoring session. As we walked, without mentioning any details, she broached the subject of the Kulangsu Cultural and Resistance League. You know, An Lee, it was the first positive thing that happened to me since before my father's assassination."

I usually had a mouth full of opinions, but I couldn't think of any words to comfort my friend. I patted her arm and forced my lips into a smile.

"The league is not what I expected," she said. "Sometimes I want to pummel the lot of them. Then I tell myself to be patient. At least for now, the work of the League is my best chance to avenge my father's murder."

I put my arms around her. "Dear Pei-lu," I whispered. "Together you and I will avenge your father's murder."

A gull rising on a current of cooling air looked at us, two women at the very summit of the island, vowing to be sisters in vengeance. Then he flapped his wings and dropped out of sight.

August 1939

18

*S*treet theater wasn't exactly vengeance, but it was exciting. We were undercover actors playing ordinary people, splashing our dramas down in unexpected places, quickly making our point, engaging the crowd, and then disappearing. I loved taking part in the performances. When a drama was successful and the crowd took up our slogan of resistance, it was like being caught up in a tidal wave of hope and solidarity.

Then we had to go home and write another drama. Kulangsu was too small for repeat performances. The whole effect of one of our plays depended on convincing onlookers that the incident they were witnessing was real and then drawing them into it. And now that Chang Ti, Hermit, and some of the others were concentrating on their full-length play, that left it to Pei-lu, Fan Ho-fu, and me to continually invent new incidents for Cricket and Lightning and the friends they'd brought in to perform.

Sitting at my desk, the rain clattering on the roof like a troupe of musicians at a temple fair, I rolled a ballpoint pen between my fingers and thumb. I leaned on my hand and stared at the French doors. My eyes were beginning to droop. I wasn't at my best late at night, but at least I could work without being seen. So far, no one in my household knew what I was doing. I circled my pen at the top of the page, making spirals and then crossing them out.

This new drama, like all the others, had to be about an ordinary person performing a heroic deed, something that would inspire the people. I thought of the time Yu-ming braved the schoolyard bullies to rescue a little harelipped boy. For the sake of street theater, the person rescued could be blind perhaps, or crippled. I put my pen down.

The wind couldn't possibly make that kind of sound, could it? I walked over to the French doors. When I opened the doors, the knocking stopped.

"Madam Han," a voice said through the shutters. "I'm Private Huang."

Yes. I recognized the voice. It was the young soldier who had brought letters from Yu-ming so many months ago. I unlatched the shutters and pushed them open.

"Good evening, Madam." He was standing on my balcony, holding on to the rail as the rain pelted his back. "I've been instructed by your husband to fetch you," he said. He handed me what looked like a fisherman's rain jacket. "Here, wear this over your clothes. And wear something dark. I'll wait for you here." I opened my mouth to object, but he waved me away. "Hurry," he said.

Yu-ming, my heart sang as I ran to the closet. I'm going to see Yu-ming. I could hardly believe it. I found a black blouse and a pair of loose black pants. Leaving my nightgown where it fell, I quickly put them on. I grabbed a dark blue sweater and returned to the French doors. "We can go out through the kitchen," I whispered.

He shook his head. "Someone might wake up. No one should know where you're going."

It was a different world he and my husband lived in. And yet, instinctively, I fell into its ways. I pulled on my rubber boots and attached the clasps on the rain jacket. He gestured toward the balcony railing, and I climbed up and over. He held out his hands, and I grabbed them and let him lower me halfway to the ground. He let go, and I landed, remembering to bend my knees. Then he was beside me and we were climbing over the outer wall.

We dashed up the narrow alley beside our house and continued on, staying on the loneliest lanes, hugging the walls, avoiding puddles and loose stones. Two shadows in the ink-black night. I'd played this role before in dreams, and it felt as natural as anything I'd ever done.

At the end of a quiet lane, we climbed over a wall and headed into the trees, following a path made by dogs and children. Our footsteps on the rocks and mud and the sounds of our jackets brushing against the bushes were drowned in a soggy world of rain-battered foliage. Branches and leaves scratched our faces; jutting rocks and fallen trees threatened to trip us. Finally Private Huang stopped. We were at the edge of the woods. Taking another step, I saw in front of me the pure black of open space, and heard the crash of waves striking the rocks below.

"There's a trail," he said. "Stay close to me." He squeezed between two boulders and started down.

Keeping close, I dug my fingers into crevices and felt for footholds with my toes. Just above the water, I turned and backed down a series of slippery, moss-covered steps cut into the rock. When we were close enough, I followed Private Huang's lead and jumped.

A small boat was waiting for us. We got in and settled ourselves in the bow as the boatman pushed us away from the rocks. He climbed aboard, and, working his long sculling oar, maneuvered us through the breaking waves and into open water. We seemed to be heading east, into the wind, meeting the waves head-on. As the child of a merchant mariner, I easily fell in with the boat's movement. Tonight, my heart sang with every dip and rise, tonight I'm sailing out to meet Yu-ming.

Then the boatman stopped sculling and hooted like a loon. I squinted into the rain-streaked darkness, and gradually the bulky, rolling shape of a junk emerged. We bumped against its side, and hands reached down to lift me up.

"Madam," one of the men said as my feet touched the deck, "welcome to my humble ship."

"I'm honored to be invited aboard such a fine vessel," I said, although I could see nothing of it.

"Please," he said, "go inside the deckhouse where it's dry."

I felt someone beside me, taking my arm. He guided me across the slippery deck and up some steps. Someone opened a door, and we stepped into a musty cabin smelling of tobacco, garlic, and fish. I reached out for him, but he was gone.

"Where are you?"

He laughed and lit a match. "Here."

Here. His own voice. It was astonishing in its familiarity. My legs felt soft as tofu in warm soup. A candle flared and he took shape—Yu-ming in fishermen's clothes.

"You're soaking wet," he said, touching my hair.

I let him undo the clasps on my rain jacket and slide it off my shoulders. Holding the door frame to steady myself, I watched him hang my jacket on a peg and remove his own. "How long can I stay?"

"Only a few hours. We have to be gone before sunrise." He smoothed a towel over the top of my hair. "An," he said, holding me against his chest. "My dear An Lee."

The feel of him softened me and held me in such comfort and relief that I could barely whisper his name.

"Is my mother well?" he asked, relaxing his arms.

"A slight cough."

"She's sick?"

"It's almost gone."

He asked about my mother and the children and the maids. "You're still wet," he said, touching the soggy neck of my sweater. "And look at your pants." They were soaked clear through where the jacket hadn't covered. He walked to the door and locked it. "The captain has offered us the use of his cabin and bunk," he said as he turned his back and began to undress.

I glanced at the bunk. A wooden shelf covered with a rice-straw mat. Unbuttoning my sweater, I watched Yu-ming fold his shirt. He took off his undershirt and folded that, too. I threw my wet sweater to the side and raised my shirt over my head.

"Do you have enough food?" he asked, swinging around.

My bare skin tingled. "Yes, fine for now."

"How long will it last?"

"Months." Water dripped off my hair onto my breasts and back. I wanted to say we could talk about this later.

"How many months? This war could go on for years." He started pacing—three steps this way, two steps the other—his belt hanging loose from his still-buttoned pants.

How much longer? The question was always on my mind. *When will it be over? The enemy advance has slowed, hasn't it? Everyone is saying their supply lines are overextended. And if England or France or America joins the war . . .* My body longed to fall into his. Still, I wanted him to reassure me.

Two more steps. He turned, and even in the candlelight I could see the worry in his eyes.

"Don't worry about us," I said quickly. "The smugglers and black marketeers are in full swing now. Anything we can't buy in the market, we can get in the back alleys." I took his hand and drew him close. I unbuttoned his pants, and he untied the string around my waist, his breath warm on my neck. We climbed onto the captain's bunk.

And there, finally, after sixteen months of separation, we came together again. We were like mad bees hungry for nectar. All the love and sadness and longing we'd stored up exploded. When it was over, we collapsed, panting, more exhausted than if we'd climbed to the top of the Great Southern Warrior.

"I can feel your ribs," I whispered. "Aren't you eating enough?" At least, his skin was still smooth—no scars on his shoulders, no boils on his back, no bedbug bites on his buttocks, no rash between his legs. He shivered at my touch.

That night, he finally told me the story of his "enlistment." We cuddled under the captain's blanket—he, stretched out on his back, his head resting on a pillow stuffed with unhusked rice; I, in my favorite position, my head on his shoulder.

"I'm sorry," he said. "I had no intention of joining the army. You know that, An Lee. I was the only man in the house. I thought I could serve my country best through my work as an engineer."

I caressed his belly and listened. Before he went away, we used to talk late into the night, and as we told each other our stories, his story became mine and mine, his. This was one story he'd kept from me until now.

"It was on the third day of my trip," he said. "I didn't have enough data yet to make a clear recommendation to my boss at Siemens. I'd checked out two locations that day along the Jiulong River, the second being the most promising site for a hydroelectric dam. It was getting late, and the road that led down from the ridge and through a forested area was rocky and eroded. The first people I encountered after more than an hour of walking were a couple of Chinese soldiers. They jumped out of the woods and trained their guns on me. My first thought was that they were either Communists or ordinary bandits. Their calves were wrapped in soldiers' khaki, but they wore straw sandals and olive-drab uniforms hidden under non-regulation padded jackets. One of them held a pistol to my head and demanded to see my identification. He probably couldn't read. Nevertheless, he pretended to study the card I gave him. His companion searched me and found my notes, my slide rule, and the book of formulas Siemens field engineers carry."

Yu-ming shook his head. "That manual was almost my undoing. The soldier opened it, and his eyes grew wide. 'Look at this!' he shouted. 'A spy? This stinking mother's a Japanese spy!' They cursed, and the older one waved his pistol in my face. I explained that the foreign print was German, not Japanese, but they would have none of it. Finally, when they'd calmed down a little, I talked them into taking me to their officer-in-charge." Yu-ming chuckled. "I should have just taken their guns away. Of course, I didn't know the techniques then that I know now." He looked away, still smiling. In the flickering light I could see that he was proud of his newly acquired warrior skills, and I, too, was proud of having a husband who knew how to disarm two soldiers at once.

"Their camp must have been at least five kilometers away, and the path through the woods was slow-going, so it was night before we arrived. Their commander was sitting in front of a fire. They told him they'd caught a spy and handed him my field manual. I was confident that the person in charge of these uneducated young men would be literate and reasonable.

"Well, the officer looked up at me, and I couldn't believe my eyes. It was Li Chung-wei, my classmate from Chiao-tung University. 'Old Han,' he said using the Shanghai dialect we used to speak there sometimes, 'my scouts think all your formulas are Japanese code.' He snorted. 'I tell you, Han, it's so hard to train these blockheads!' I glanced at the scouts, whose simple faces registered nothing of the insult. 'Don't worry,' he said, 'they can barely speak their own dialect.' I wondered when he was going to tell them to put their guns down, but out of courtesy I waited for him to make that decision. We chatted for a while about college and our mutual friends. 'So, you went to work for Siemens,' he said. 'And you became a soldier,' I replied. 'Exactly.' He declared that it was the best of decisions, and from his demeanor I could see that he was a patriot, zealous, and eager to serve his country. When he spoke about the need for more engineers, his eyes glowed. 'You wouldn't believe how hard it is to get competent men to join up,' he said. 'It's disgraceful! We dragoon peasants into service, but when it comes to officers, we sit back and wait for them to volunteer.' He was glaring into the fire. 'We should have better methods for recruiting officers, don't you think?'

"I shrugged. That was my big mistake. Li's face twitched, and I had an inkling then that this man across the fire from me was no longer the happy-go-lucky student of our Shanghai days. 'My men still believe you're a spy,' he reminded me, smirking as though he were about to get the better of me in a card game. 'They're just waiting for me to give the word so they can shoot you. I'd be delighted to help an old friend out, but in fairness, don't you think that old friend should do something for me? I'm in desperate need of another officer here.' Despite his expression, I still held out hope that he was only teasing. Suddenly he jumped up. His face was ferocious, all red and black in the light of the fire. 'You have a duty to your country,' he shouted, and a dozen rifles clicked. 'Well, what is it, Han,' he asked without a drop of humor, 'death or life in the army? I have the induction papers in my tent.'

"'Have someone bring them out, then,' I replied. And without further discussion, they brought me the papers and I signed my name." He took me by the shoulders and looked solemnly into my eyes. "Now you know how your husband came to be a lieutenant in the Chinese Army."

"He wouldn't actually have let them shoot you, would he?"

Yu-ming laughed and rolled over on top of me. "I never asked."

19

Our one night together, and it had to be August, a month when the days were long and the nights oh so short. I didn't want to waste a single moment, and yet, without the slightest intent or foreknowledge—who can explain it?—sometime during the night, relaxed and exhausted after experiencing the *clouds and rain*, I fell asleep. When I woke up, Yu-ming's eyes were closed. *My God!* I thought. *How long . . .* Then I saw the candle, which seemed almost as tall as before. Almost. Who could say how many precious minutes we'd squandered while that length of candle wax was being turned to flame and fume?

I put my lips next to his ear. "Tell me about the places you've seen," I whispered.

He blinked his eyes open. "I was assigned to mobile warfare," he said. "I received my orders by radio. So far I haven't come face-to-face with Chiang Kai-shek, but I've encountered many well-known generals and politicians." He told me their names, openly commenting on their reputations for heroism and brilliance, or in other cases, for cowardice and stupidity. I watched the candlelight dancing on the rough-hewn ceiling planks, and imagined the men he described. Yu-ming had a way of opening the world up for me, making it twice as large as it was without him. I'd grown accustomed to that larger world. How I'd missed it!

I leaned on my elbow and watched his face as he told me about the villages and towns he'd passed through, places in our own province whose names I'd never heard. One village was surrounded by rice paddies; another cultivated peanuts and soybeans; one had tangerine trees as far as the eye could see; another had terraces for growing tea. "Those villages were the lucky ones," he said, "the ones the Japanese soldiers didn't have time for. Others were memorable only for the devastation. Their pigs and chickens were gone, their fields and houses burned. Their young men were either dead or hiding in the mountains."

"How do our own soldiers behave?" I asked, suddenly remembering how from ancient times soldiers had been a burden on the lands they passed through and that men separated from their homes were tempted to throw off all restraint and behave like beasts.

"It's the responsibility of our officers to keep them in line. During wartime, military discipline has to be severe. Sometimes there's no other way." He closed his eyes and paused. "Last week, I was forced to shoot two of my own men for raping Chinese women."

His words vibrated hollowly in my ears. How many times I'd read about war, watched operas about it, played at it with my toy soldiers. I couldn't feel shocked at what he'd done. He was a soldier now. Still...

I lay down beside him, and as he caressed my thigh, I tried to get used to the new reality...of him, Yu-ming, a man who had killed other men.

After all that he'd confessed to me, I was on the verge of telling him about my involvement in the Kulangsu Cultural and Resistance League. He'd be angry, though, I was sure of that. He'd order me to stop. I glanced at his face. No. I couldn't possibly ... I smiled and waited for him to resume his narrative.

"Most of my soldiers are peasants," he said. "They come to me as raw recruits, frogs at the bottom of a deep well. I have limited supplies and less time, and yet it's my task to lift them up. By the time I see them, most of my men have already experienced the enemy's savagery. It's the same everywhere. Officers can promise fifty or even a hundred *yuan* for the delivery of prisoners; they can threaten the most severe punishment, and still our soldiers would rather kill their prisoners and make up a story about their dying along the way than let them live another day."

He sat up and looked at me. "Tell me about my son," he said.

My whole body softened into a smile. "Your son is very strong. You can be proud." I climbed between Yu-ming's legs and knelt with my knees almost touching his jade stem. "He's as brave as a tiger and as smart as a monkey."

He laughed. "He's only ten months old, and you've already made him a hero."

"If you could only see him, Yu-ming."

"You say he's intelligent and brave, but how can you know, when he's still too young to speak? As for courage ..." He was teasing me now. "One never knows how brave he is until his courage is put to the test."

"Hmph." I slid my fingers between his legs and held him. It was obvious to anyone who saw our son how alert and courageous he was. But this was no time for long explanations. Instead, I threw out a challenge. "Next time we meet, I'll bring him with me. Then you can see for yourself."

He pulled his hips back, as though he couldn't think with my hands on him. I sensed how much he longed to see his son. Finally, he shook his head. "No, An Lee. It's too dangerous."

We will see, I thought. "When will you send for me again?"

"You're not afraid to come out at night like this?"

"Not at all."

"It won't be for a while," he said. "I'm being sent to the School of Guerrilla Tactics."

"You're not a guerrilla."

"The generalissimo has ordered all his officers to undergo three months of training in partisan warfare. It's a brilliant idea. Guerrilla tactics are extremely effective against an overextended enemy struggling to hold on to conquered territory. We will learn the most up-to-date scientific techniques."

"Up-to-date?" I scoffed. "Sparrow warfare has been around since the days of the Warring Kingdoms. Even earlier."

"Of course, but the old tactics have been upgraded to suit modern times. Professors from our best universities have devised weapons made from readily available materials. Did you know, An Lee, that when a sugar cube is dropped in the gasoline tank of an airplane or armored car, it will dissolve, and deposit carbon in the motor cylinders? Eventually the engine will stop." He sniffed with delight. "It's such a perfect means of sabotage. By the time the engine breaks down, the vehicle is already in use and it's too late to repair it."

He wanted to tell me all about the weapons and methods guerrillas employed. And for my part, I was happy just to lie there beside him and listen to all the scientific jargon I hadn't heard for so long. I

155

slid my knee over his thigh and ran my toes up and down his leg and foot, enjoying the feel of his iron-hard leg bone. For an instant everything became perfect. A moment of perfection that contained everything—his voice (which was part of me), my fingers and toes (which belonged also to him), the narrow bunk, the blanket, our discarded clothes, boots, and jackets. It contained the plink of rain (our background music), the rocking boat (our cradle), the burning candle (our incense). The men sleeping outside and below decks were also part of it, and the skiff that brought me here and the rocky shore that awaited my return, even the enemy's steel-gray ships and the occupied land surrounding Kulangsu. Everything. And together, everything was perfect.

I came back—though the moment was outside of time—to Yu-ming's explanation of guerrilla mail service. Instead of stamps, he was saying, they used feathers, one feather pasted on ordinary letters, two on those of greater importance, three on letters of extreme urgency. "Special delivery." He pulled me close and kissed me. But it was already too late. Someone was knocking and then calling out to us. "Lieutenant Han, Madam, it's time." Yu-ming threw off the blanket and jumped up. And once again, we were soldiers.

I stepped into my pants and tied them. "Are they really fishermen?"

"Yes," he said, his back to me as he pulled up his trousers.

"They're not soldiers?"

"That, too."

Out on the deck, a fisherman/soldier helped me over the side. Private Huang jumped down, and the boatman—also a soldier—took up his long oar and pushed us free. We were all soldiers, I realized as we moved away from the junk and from my husband. Looking into the rain, my backbone effortlessly adjusting to every bounce and sway of our little boat, I thought about guerillas and their tactics. How easy it would be to drop a few cubes of sugar into the gasoline tank of an enemy vehicle!

I could be a guerrilla, I thought as we crashed through the off-shore breakers and slammed into the beach. In a flash I was up, jumping free of the boat beside Private Huang. We scrambled across the sand and rocks and climbed the cliff. Then he went back, and I found my way through the woods alone.

Our mothers would take care of the children, and I would join a guerrilla band, I imagined as I climbed the wall out of the woods. Didn't Mother Chao, the "Mother of Guerrillas," also have children? As I walked down the dark lanes, barely a promise of dawn in the east, I remembered the stories I'd heard about Two Gun Sister Wang. People said she was short and plump and looked like any other forty-year-old peasant woman, but that didn't stop her from killing the puppet police commissioner in his own bedroom and running off with his head. In comparison to her feats, the accomplishments of the KCRL were small indeed.

Back in my own room, I threw my wet clothes on the floor and climbed into bed. I reached out for my absent husband, and then I curled up and fell asleep.

Later, when I awoke, the wet clothes I'd rolled in the fisherman's rain jacket and left on the rug beside my bed were gone. Su-lee must have taken them while I was asleep. Now she and everyone else were probably waiting like ants on a hot cooking pot for me to get dressed and come downstairs. The overnight appearance of wet clothes and a strange rain jacket was not something Su-lee would keep to herself.

It was nearly lunchtime and I was hungry. The moment I entered the kitchen, Ah Kwai jumped up to greet me and Su-lee came running in from outside. The screen door slammed behind her; stray soap bubbles clung to her wrists. Hsiang-mei was close behind with Ah Chew on her hip and Ah Mei holding her skirt.

"I'm sorry, Young Mistress," Su-lee said. "Your clothes were very wet. They soaked through the rug to the wood floor." It was her excuse for taking them away while I was still asleep. At the same time it was a question, a polite accusation.

I sniffed for effect and tried to knit my eyebrows. But I was too full of last night's pleasure and pain, and it sprayed out in a confusion of laughter, spittle, and tears. I bent over and covered my face.

"What, Young Mistress? What is it?" they all asked at once.

Like a schoolgirl with a secret, I couldn't hold back. "I was with Yu-ming."

Su-lee clapped her soapy hands. "He was here?"

"Not here. He sent someone to fetch me."

"Where did you go?"

"I can't tell you." Another delicious secret. There hadn't been any harm in disclosing our tryst, surely not. Yu-ming would be miles away by now. I didn't want to mention the fishing junk, though, in case we met in the same place again next time.

"Is he well?" Ah Kwai asked.

"Is who well? What's all this racket?"

"Oh, Mother-in-law. I meant to tell you first, but these wicked women forced it out of me. I was with Yu-ming last night."

She coughed, and Ah Kwai ran over to rub her back.

"He asked about you, Mother-in-law, and he made me vow to act as your most filial child, to love you and care for you as he longs to do himself."

She stopped coughing and touched her handkerchief to the corners of her eyes. "How is he? Has he lost weight?"

"The same," I lied. I told her about his upcoming course of study at the School for Guerrilla Tactics. And then, noticing a lingering look of discontent, I described the difficulty involved in reaching him. She wouldn't have feared the darkness or the climb up the hillside trail, but she was prone to seasickness, so I told her in detail about the little skiff and the large waves we had to contend with.

"It was good you went instead of me." She pulled out two stools. "Ah Kwai, make some fresh tea and breakfast for the Young Mistress."

I couldn't stay seated. I felt like dancing. "Your daddy wants to see you," I said, throwing Ah Chew in the air. He shrieked with laughter. I threw him up again, and then I held him under the arms and twirled him around while everyone shouted at once that he was too heavy and I would hurt myself, and I should watch out for the pans and knives. Ah Mei begged for a turn, and I twirled her, too, her legs clamped around my waist, her hair flying out like silken feathers.

That night and the night after, I dreamed of Yu-ming, and of war and guerrilla fighting. In a series of dreams, Yu-ming and I led a band of guerrillas against trains that the enemy used to transport their troops and supplies. We sent our men out to dynamite the tracks, and when we ran out of dynamite, we removed iron spikes along the curves. In one dream, I was by his side on a hillside watching an enemy train heavy with men, weapons, and supplies approach. As the locomotive started around the bend, we held our breaths and listened. The first wheel fell off the rail with a *crack*. Then we heard the thunder of cars crashing down the hill in a hellish tumult.

In the daytime, I neglected what now seemed like the more sedate business of writing street drama. Instead, standing at the doors to my balcony watching mist turn to a shower or a downpour gush from the gutters, I dreamed up one guerilla exploit after another.

For those few days, it was as though I had a man's heart inside a woman's body. Then, for some reason, my adventure dreams and daytime imaginings simply stopped. I couldn't say why, but judging by the womanly sentiments that replaced them, I could make a very good guess.

20

Cricket's friend, a tiny girl with a large voice who called herself Dragonfly, was already in place. The way she stood chatting with the refugees, no one would have guessed that she was anything other than a displaced young woman waiting in line with the rest for her daily portion of rice. From my post in front of the bookshop, pretending to be interested in a display of secondhand novels and textbooks, I watched her reflection in the glass. The nausea that started before breakfast was still with me, a queasy, shaky feeling, indistinguishable now from the nervousness I always felt just before one of our dramas. I rubbed my breastbone and swallowed. I felt nauseous, but I doubted I was in danger of vomiting. It was too late in the day for a serious case of morning sickness. This was just a little stage fright. Nothing to worry about.

Our group had performed eight or nine times already and hadn't experienced a single problem. The Japanese on the Municipal Council must have wanted the Kulangsu police to stop us, but they hadn't done anything. Even if the police chief did decide to send some men, they'd never catch us. Our dramas were so realistic and so short that by the time anyone realized that what they were watching was actually a play, we were finished and already disappearing into the crowd.

I moved one step back so I could see Lightning's reflection. He was squatting off to the side, playing checkers with another League member, both of them ready to go. The other principal player in the drama, a skinny young man known as Dagger, was loitering in a doorway, looking suspicious but not too suspicious, as specified by Pei-lu's stage directions. Today Pei-lu was in charge. Fan Ho-fu was busy somewhere else. I had a simple role. I was a bystander, someone who argues with Lightning so he can bring out our main points about resistance to Japanese aggression.

It was almost time to begin. Our "audience" had formed themselves into two fat lines facing the closed doors of the pickle factory at the end of the street. According to Pei-lu, the doors wouldn't open for another twenty minutes. She hadn't told her family about the League, so I was surprised that she'd set her drama here at her husband's factory. It seemed to me she was taking a chance that one of his employees would see her.

I scanned the crowd reflected in the window for anyone who might recognize me. I hadn't told my family, either, and since we didn't wear real costumes, there wasn't much I could do to disguise myself. Today I was wearing my hair in short braids. My face was scrubbed clean, and my clothes—wrinkled cotton pants and a simple blue tunic—were as plain as possible. I turned around and caught Pei-lu's eye.

"Ready?" she mouthed, her eyes burning with the reflection of a red light in the bookstore window.

I nodded. "Ready."

And, in what passed for a raised curtain in street theater, she held her right arm in the air.

Our first actor, Dagger, sauntered out of his doorway. Lightning and the man he was playing checkers with barely raised their eyes as he passed. The girl, Dragonfly, appeared to be too busy chatting with the women around her to notice as he edged up to her and slid his hand in her pocket. Only when he was the agreed-upon ten paces away did she grab her hip.

"My money," she screamed, her voice siren-loud. "Somebody took my money."

In an instant, every face turned and gawked at her, a frantic, red-faced woman, whipping her head from side to side.

"There he is," she shouted, pointing at Dagger, who seemed unable to hide the bright pink cloth of her makeshift purse.

He sprinted away, spilling coins as he went. "Thief, thief," the crowd shouted. "Stop that man." Someone almost did, but the "thief" dodged and the would-be hero, losing his footing on the red and black markers from a spilled checkers board, tripped and fell.

A split second later, Lightning tackled Dagger. "On your feet," he said, grabbing the coin purse from him. He retied the pink cloth and threw it high in the air. "Young miss," he shouted as the purse arced over the crowd. "This money rightfully belongs to you, not to this unlawful usurper."

A low rumble of agreement rose from the crowd.

"How dare you steal from a poor refugee?" Lightning demanded.

The refugees nodded and shook their fingers at Dagger. How dare he?

Dagger hung his head. His eyes brimmed with tears. "What choice do I have?" he asked in a voice that artfully combined indignation and sorrow. "I'm a refugee, too. I have no money. My baby sister is sick. She needs medicine."

"We all have our problems," someone retorted. "Why steal from one of us?"

"Please," Dagger cried. "Have mercy."

Lightning handed Dagger to his friend and jumped up on a low wall. "My friends," he shouted, "I say, let us be merciful to this boy and let him go with a warning." Lightning was our best actor. His voice and bearing always had the effect of quieting the crowd. "This boy you see here is a common thief, forced into crime by our common situation. We can overlook his crime. But..." He raised his arms. His scar shone white in the sunlight. "My friends, I tell you, there are crimes that cannot be overlooked." He closed his hands into two great fists. "There are evil men, enemies of China, who murder and rape in the millions, who pillage our land and send whole populations running for their lives. My friends, those evil men, the ones who would steal the land of our ancestors, are the real criminals. Their guilt can never be washed away."

He went on like that for a while, stirring up the crowd. Then he uttered the words I was waiting for. "We must continue to resist Japanese aggression. We must stand up and save ourselves."

"But how?" I asked, projecting my voice. "How can we save ourselves when the enemy is so strong?'

"What?" Lightning exploded. He seemed to be admonishing the whole crowd. "Do you doubt that the Chinese people are strong? Do you?"

"No," they cried.

"And what makes us strong?"

"Unity. Unite for China." We repeated it until the whole crowd was fired up and shouting along with us.

"Down with Japanese imperialism," we yelled. And they joined in, chanting our slogan and adding their own. "Stand up for China."

As I moved among them, passing out our newest leaflet, my veins pulsed with their fervor. This was the prize, the reason we wrote and rehearsed and performed our dramas. This exhilarating feeling. The power we all had when—

"The doors," someone shouted, and suddenly another energy flashed through the crowd.

They stopped chanting, and as the factory doors swung open, they dropped their leaflets and dashed to get in line.

"Run." It was Pei-lu.

I dropped my remaining leaflets and caught up with her. "What?"

She shook her head and grabbed my hand. "This way."

It was the only way out, away from the pickle factory, which was at the end of the cul-de-sac. Lightning and his friend were ahead of us. I looked over my shoulder for the others. "I don't see Dagger and Dragonfly."

"We'll find them later," Pei-lu said, pulling me along.

Finally, at the corner we slowed to a walk. "I think my husband's employee recognized me," Pei-lu said. "He looked right at me."

I squeezed her hand. I didn't know what to think. The nausea was gone, but my knees were weak. "Isn't that a tea shop?" I pointed down the lane to where some men were sitting around a table on the sidewalk. As we reached the door, I felt someone tap my shoulder. Good. Now Dragonfly was with us.

"Police," she whispered.

I swung around, and there they were, fifty meters behind, six or seven of them, each one holding a club. They turned in to the cul-de-sac, but they were too late. We were already gone.

Dragonfly pulled us to the side. "I told him," she hissed. "Dagger. He wouldn't listen. Stuffed the leaflets in his pants. If he gets caught with them, it's not my fault." She pinched her face into a profound frown, glared at the tea drinkers, and marched off.

Surely she was worrying for nothing, I thought. We'd all had plenty of time to escape. Pei-lu opened the tea shop door and we went in. The sound of the iron chair legs scraping across the concrete screamed our presence as we sat down. I took a paper napkin and wiped some crumbs off the yellow linoleum tabletop. Bits of napkin stuck to the sugary, rust-colored tea stains. Where was the waitress? I just wanted to sit here and drink my tea. I looked at Pei-lu. She was staring into space, her hands folded in her lap. Where was all the energy we felt such a short time ago?

"The play was good," I said. "It really caught the crowd's attention."

"Until the factory opened its doors. I should have planned for that—that they might open early."

"Still, it worked. It achieved its purpose—keeping alive the will to resist the Japanese." I sounded more cheerful than I felt.

Where was that waitress? It looked like she was going to keep picking her teeth behind the cash register until one of us called her over. I tried to catch her eye, but she wouldn't look at me. "Miss," I called, waving my hand. "A pot of tea please. Miss."

She raised her chin in acknowledgment, picked one more tooth, and then, scuffing her slippers across the floor, walked over to the teakettle.

People could be so disappointing, I thought. So fickle. Shouting their solidarity one minute and shoving each other out of the way for a bowl of rice the next.

The waitress sauntered over to our table. "We only have jasmine tea," she said through her blackened teeth. "No other kind."

"That's fine," Pei-lu and I said together.

"Could we have a wet rag?"

"Do you have steamed buns?"

She shook her head and walked away.

"How did the police find out?" Pei-lu asked.

I remembered now that the factory wall had windows as well as doors facing the street. I wasn't about to say anything to Pei-lu, though. She was taking this all too personally. "Don't worry," I said. "Even if Dagger gets himself arrested, he won't be able to implicate us. He doesn't know our real names or where any of us live."

"I know, I know. But what about him?"

I poured her a cup of tea and passed it over. The waitress still hadn't wiped our table. "Even if the police do catch him—and I doubt that very much—what could they do to him? After all, Kulangsu isn't under occupation. Our police aren't taking orders from the *Kempeitai*."

"It's not that simple." Pei-lu sighed and reached for her cup. "Oh well. Let's drink our tea. This kind turns bitter so fast."

I poured another cup and took a sip. Already it was getting bitter. Suddenly I leaned across the table. "I think I'm pregnant," I said.

"What? How?"

I smiled. "I met with Yu-ming. He sent someone to fetch me."

"Oh, An Lee. Why didn't you tell me?"

"Military secret." I smiled again. "You know, I probably shouldn't have said anything yet about being pregnant. I'm not absolutely certain."

"How certain?"

"Ninety-nine point nine percent." The precision of the number I came up with made me laugh. It sounded like something Yu-ming would say. Ninety-nine point nine percent. An almost-baby. A not-quite baby. I couldn't stop giggling.

Pei-lu just smiled and shook her head. "It's not that funny."

Maybe not, but then, another thought struck me that seemed even funnier. "Can you imagine," I sputtered, "a ninety-nine-point-nine-percent baby produced from a one-night chance?"

Not as hilarious as I originally thought, but then laughter contagion is more powerful than the funniest joke, even—or perhaps especially—when the person in question is sunk in a cloud of worry. Every time she stopped laughing, I told her another small detail about my rendezvous with Yu-ming, and somehow everything came out funny—Private Huang on my balcony, the way we hid in shadows and skulked through the woods, my dreary, rain-soaked clothes, the fishy smell of the captain's cabin. The story kept us going through several small cups of tea, the tea becoming progressively more bitter, even as our spirits continued to improve.

When we were finished laughing, we dropped our coins on the table and left. There was no sense talking about Dagger or the employee of Pei-lu's husband. We'd just have to wait and see what happened.

*   *   *

You'd think an organization like the Kulangsu Cultural and Resistance League would be able to gather and disseminate information quickly and efficiently. In reality, though, our little group had always operated in a somewhat chaotic manner. As time went by, it seemed to get worse—members arguing and, some, like Chang Ti and Hermit, breaking off to work on their own projects. Lightning and Cricket complained that they were tired of performing street theater on the little protected island of Kulangsu and threatened to leave. They wanted to go over to Amoy, invade the enemy's own territory. Fan Ho-fu must have felt the same. For some time it had been obvious that he'd lost interest in our dramas and had been just going through the motions at our meetings. And yet, each time Cricket and Lightning proposed moving into occupied territory, he'd shake his head. "No," he'd say quietly without explanation. I might have been imagining things, but it always seemed that he'd glance quickly at me when he refused to go along with them.

Anyway, considering the loosely organized nature of our group and what seemed to be its slow but inevitable disintegration, I suppose it wasn't surprising that I heard about Dagger's arrest from Ah Kwai. Her long-standing friendship with Police Chief Ma's kitchen amah gave her a closer connection to the police than any of our members had. I didn't think to quiz her, though. She was the one who brought it up.

I was in the kitchen, playing cat's cradle with Ah Mei while Ah Kwai cleaned up after lunch.

"Just look at this," she said, holding up a dirty rice bowl. "All this rice wasted. She walked over and handed the bowl to Ah Mei. "How many grains do you count?"

A good lesson, I thought—counting combined with frugality. As it turned out, though, the lesson she had in mind wasn't for Ah Mei. It was for me.

"One, two three," Ah Mei counted, pointing at each wasted rice grain.

Ah Kwai nodded.

"Four, five, six. Six grains of rice."

"Correct." Ah Kwai took the bowl from Ah Mei. "It seems that someone in this house thinks it is all right to waste six grains of rice, even now, in the middle of a war."

"Not me," Ah Mei said. "Must be my brother."

Still holding the bowl, Ah Kwai looked at me while she spoke to Ah Mei. "We all have different jobs," she said. "Your daddy's job is to fight the Japanese. Mine is to find food for us all and cook it. Your mommy's is to take care of you. And your job is to eat so you can grow big and strong."

"What about my brother?"

"His job is the same as yours." Ah Kwai put the bowl in her wash basin. Then she turned back around. "The most important job for all of us, though, is to survive. It is the duty of every Chinese."

"Sur-vive?" Ah Mei asked.

"To live," I said.

Ah Kwai waited for Ah Mei to run off before finishing her lesson. "Mrs. Ma told my friend a strange thing," she said as she swished a plate in the rinse water and stacked it against another on a towel. "She said some young ladies from good families are taking part in anti-Japanese rallies. They don't seem to care that they are putting their families at risk." She kept her back to me, her hands moving rhythmically from soapy water to rinse water to towel.

"How does she know that?"

Ah Kwai wiped her hands on her hips and turned around. Her expression told me she suspected more than she would say. "Mrs. Ma knows because her husband's men arrested a young man at one of those rallies. The police questioned him for six hours." She paused, daring me to ask another question. When I didn't, she told me what I wanted to know. "Lucky for the young man, they let him go. And lucky for those ladies, he didn't know their names." That was all she said, but the look she gave me was not one I would soon forget.

*　　*　　*

"You what?" Two days had passed, and now that I finally had a chance to talk to Pei-lu, I couldn't believe what she was saying. "Why would you tell your husband?"

"Why not? He was going to find out sooner or later."

"You don't know that."

She dusted her fingers over the top of a row of books. The entire inner wall of her family library was covered with books, hundreds of them. "I wasn't going to give in to a blackmailer," she said, turning toward me. "I told you. That snake tried to extort money in payment for keeping his mouth shut. Wouldn't you think he'd have some loyalty to the wife of his boss?"

I threw up my arms in exasperation. "He could have told your husband whatever he wanted. All you'd have to say was that he was lying, or mistaken. You could have said it was a coincidence. You just happened to be there when one refugee stole another's purse. How were you to know it was street theater?"

"No, An Lee, you can't let a snake like that just crawl back down his hole. He'd be sure to slither out and bite you at the very next opportunity. In this case, bite my husband. I had to expose him. It was my duty." She walked to the window. "Anyway, don't worry about me. I'm all right." She pushed one of the wine-red drapes aside, looked through the inch-wide slit, and let it drop back.

She wasn't all right, though. That was plain to see. For the past two days her amah had been turning me away at the gate, telling me her mistress was "indisposed." Now, here we were, meeting in the library with the door closed, the curtains drawn, and only one lamp lit. And still, even in the dim light, I could see that her eyes were swollen and rimmed in red.

"I was wrong," she said, speaking into the closed drapes. "I put his factory at risk by setting my drama there. What kind of wife does that?"

A patriot, I would have replied a few days ago. A faithful daughter, one who is required by filial piety to avenge the murder of her father. Even in my head, the phrases sounded old-fashioned and bookish. Oversimplified. My glance roamed...from the huge collection of books to the armchairs and the desk. So many objects—a lacquer box, a paperweight on a sheaf of paper. Photographs of Pei-lu's family. Of her father, the frame draped with a memorial ribbon. I looked at Pei-lu's back, the unusual droop of her shoulders. What could I tell her?

"You've always been a good wife," I said at last. "A good mother."

She huffed—a little scoffing laugh. "So." She turned around and looked at me, her head cocked. "Still think you're pregnant?"

"Ninety-nine point nine percent sure."

She almost smiled. "I suppose you'd like me to draw the drapes," she said.

"Well, it does feel as though we're locked inside a camphor chest. Without the sweet scent of camphor, that is. You could even open the window a crack."

She raised her eyebrows. "Don't be greedy," she said as she reached up and opened the drapes halfway.

Later, walking home, it occurred to me that we never did get around to discussing the Kulangsu Cultural and Resistance League. With all that had happened, I supposed it would be a good idea to take some time off and think things over.

It was getting late. Knife-sharp shadows fell across the lane, dividing everything into light and darkness. Sculptured patterns atop one wall threw stretched-out replicas of themselves on another. In this neighborhood, the walls were high and the gates recessed. Passing a former classmate's house, I noticed a woman suckling a child on the steps in front of the gate. They were almost hidden in the shadows. Above their heads, the intricately patterned pillars and the arch were suffused with golden light. The beautiful gate with its lights on top shaped like royal egg cups belonged to our past. The woman was our reality now. I searched my pocket for some coins and dropped them in her bowl. Then I hurried past another equally attractive but less ostentatious gate and turned onto a lane lined with shops and modest apartments.

A crow hopped in front of me and stopped. "Ha," I shouted, waving my arms. "Ha. Ha." At the last minute, it spread its wings and rose a few feet to a low-hanging branch, where it stayed, cawing at me until I was out of sight. What was I doing, I wondered, bringing another child into this sad, angry world?

1940

21

ever mind the ever-present danger, the scarcity of food, and Yu-ming's absence. Mother and my mother-in-law were delighted when I told them I was pregnant. The baby, still at that time no more than a dewdrop of life, was already destined to be a boy or a girl, and yet I perceived a scent of supplication in the air. And it was true, even I, a woman born after the revolution, wished for another boy to carry on the names of the two families. Without a second son, the whole burden fell on Ah Chew, who was not only the first and only male descendant of Yu-ming's branch of the Han family, but also, having been formally adopted by my mother, the sole male heir of the Liu family.

Mother doted on Ah Chew. She played finger games with him and let him crawl on her bed. They chanted the Amita Buddha's name together, *a-mi-to-fu*, so that Ah Chew learned the sacred syllables almost as soon as he learned to say mama. Ah Kwai, Su-lee, and Hsiang-mei made much of him, too. All day long it was *Young Master this* and *Young Master that*. The only thing they wouldn't give him—in deference to Mother's wishes—was meat. When there was some, they gave it to me, for the sake of my unborn child. When no one was looking, I would hide a portion in my sleeve and carry Ah Chew outside so they wouldn't hear him smacking his lips. A child with his appetite should have lived in a time of plenty.

Ah Kwai did her best to supplement the preserved food and rice we had in the pantry. Almost every day she was able to bring home some fruit or vegetables, less frequently, a handful of reef fish or a few oysters or crabs. Owing to Su-lee's relationship with the goatherd, we usually had enough goats' milk. But we seldom had meat. Mother didn't seem to mind. She hadn't eaten meat since her vow to T'ien Hou more than twenty years ago. To her mind, tofu and vegetables were good enough. For us mortals, that was. But the feast day of T'ien Hou was approaching, and that concerned her.

The most popular deity along the coast of Fukien, T'ien Hou was also my mother's benefactress. Before I was born, Mother promised to abstain from meat for five years if the goddess would save my father's life during a typhoon. Later, when she was pregnant and came down with a high fever, she prayed to T'ien Hou again. She'd give up meat for the rest of her life, she vowed, if only the goddess would protect her unborn child: me. Once, in annoyance, Mother told me she should have asked T'ien Hou not only to save the child, but also to make it a son. For many years I believed that it was Mother's fault I was a girl.

Then, a week before T'ien Hou's feast day, Ah Kwai, who was always resourceful, talked the goatherd's mother into selling her a live chicken. She kept it in the breezeway during the day, throwing it feed whenever it clucked, and at night, letting it bed down in her room. The chicken was more than we could have hoped for, but Ah Kwai thought she could do better. Otherwise, I don't think she would have invited Fen into our garden, which was exactly where I found him one morning, lazing against our sandalwood tree.

The moment I opened the door, he straightened up, striking a pose with his walking stick, hip out, one black-and-white toe of his spectator shoe flexed. Prosperity had filled out his cheeks, but his protruding chicken neck was as skinny as ever. "I came to you first, sister-in-law," he lied. "All the world knows that your household has a deep devotion to the goddess. Sadly," he said, affecting a frown, "due to the bad karma we're presently experiencing . . ."

"You needn't spout pious words for my benefit, Fen. Just tell me what you have and how much you want for it."

His face twitched. "I have many customers," he said, narrowing his eyes, "regular patrons who are exceedingly grateful for the service I provide." He stepped back.

Go ahead, leave, I thought. Go sell to those people who don't care how you make your dirty deals or how many friends of the Rising Sun you do business with.

Ah Kwai cleared her throat and gave me a look. She wanted what he had to sell, and Mother did, too. If I didn't quickly repair the damage I'd already done, my brother-in-law was bound to double or triple the already exorbitant amount he'd planned to charge us.

"I can see, brother-in-law, why your service is so highly prized." I watched his face, which showed no sign of being insulted by my exaggerated tone. "Your work requires a high degree of cleverness to procure food where no one else can find it." I should have called it intelligence instead of cleverness, but I couldn't control myself to such a degree. "I may have sounded abrupt a few moments ago. I only meant to hurry things along. I know how busy you must be."

"Oh yes. I hardly have time to sleep." He licked his lips. "If not for me, I don't know how many people would have starved to death. They sit at home, waiting for their food to come to them." His white suit and vest was the kind a pimp or a gambler would wear, although Fen would have no need to gamble these days. Bribery and smuggling would have been more than enough to keep him amused. "The important thing," he said, twirling his walking stick, "is contacts. And I have many friends. The Chamber of Commerce has no idea how to negotiate with the authorities in Amoy." He chuckled and snorted through his nose.

I stared at him blankly. I'd had enough of smiling and nodding.

"Well," he said finally. "What is it you need?"

I deferred to Ah Kwai, who named off the list of things we were looking for: prawns, a lotus root, carrots, onions, and snow peas. We didn't need a chicken, she added with a trace of smugness. We already had our own. We haggled for a while before agreeing on a price, one that was contingent on the quality of the food actually delivered.

The next morning Fen's coolies showed up at dawn. Everything they brought was okay, except for the wilted spring onions, which we were able to bargain down.

Once they were gone, I could enjoy the sight of all that food— the bright orange carrots and glossy green snow peas, the prawns and lotus roots and onions. I was as bad as those refugees in front of the pickle factory who threw their leaflets on the ground and ran to get their bowls of rice. I didn't care, though. I picked up a pea pod and ran my thumb over the tiny peas hidden inside. "Remember how we used to ride the ferry over to Amoy City?" I asked. "All those eggs and buns and cakes we brought to lay in front of Ma-tsu's temple."

Su-lee clapped her wet hands. "I remember the puppet shows and the fireworks."

Ah Kwai shook a spring onion at her. "If she could have, this little goose would have stayed watching the fireworks all night long."

"I loved it." Su-lee put her hands around the mango she was washing and held it up like a prayer offering. "Flowering fire. It was so pretty." She sniffed the mango and closed her eyes. "Giant-sized peonies and chrysanthemums. Poof." She put the mango in a basket and frowned. "It's all ruined now. I'll never watch fireworks again. They sound too much like bombs."

"Of course you will," I said. "When this is all over…"

"No. I won't." She was adamant.

"Su-lee…" How could I convince her? Someday this war would be just a memory. We'd go back to our old ways. We'd forget that firecrackers sounded like machineguns and bombs looked like fireworks displays. Wouldn't we?

Later, when the food was all cooked, we set up a low table for T'ien Hou in front of her statue. We covered it with a long white cloth and laid out the food and condiments. Mother and my mother-in-law came out for the prayers. Then I took Ah Mei and Ah Chew upstairs to my bed for a short nap, just long enough to show our respect for the goddess before eating what was, after all, her feast. The children wouldn't settle down, so I put my legs on them to keep them still before closing my eyes.

When I woke up, Ah Chew was gone and the leg that was meant to hold him in place was resting instead on a small pillow. I swung the other leg off Ah Mei's waist and jumped down.

It didn't take us long to find him. T'ien Hou's table was in disarray. A small greasy hand holding tight to a chicken bone was poking out from under the tablecloth. When Ah Kwai lifted it, there he was, lying on his back, sound asleep, his belly bulging grotesquely. All around him were half-finished buns and bones and shrimp tails, and his cheeks were spattered with oil and sauce.

Ah Mei sucked in her breath. "Bad boy!" she said. Then, seeing the amusement on our faces, she giggled and added sweetly, "He's such a naughty little brother."

"Oh well," Mother said. "I suppose Ma-tsu already took what she wanted."

"Undoubtedly," I agreed, thinking that if anyone other than Mother's favorite had profaned the table, she wouldn't have been so tolerant.

175

"He didn't touch the rice," Su-lee said as she cleaned up around it.

My mother-in-law nodded. "You can't make a tiger eat rice and tofu."

"You're absolutely right," Mother said. "From now on, let him eat meat."

*　　*　　*

That was Ah Chew's last opportunity to desecrate such a lavish feast. As winter wore on, food became more and more scarce. Each tangerine, duck egg, or morsel of meat Ah Kwai brought home was an occasion for rejoicing. Still, despite everything, the child inside me grew and quickened. If he did, indeed, reach full term, he would be born in the Year of the Dragon, as I was—two months after my twenty-fourth birthday, two cycles after my birth. And, even though the dragon was known as the lord of the sunrise, I had to hope that this time the Year of the Dragon would favor not the Land of the Rising Sun, but China.

In Yu-ming's letters from the School of Guerrilla Tactics, he sounded hopeful. He wrote about our air force and how the new Russian planes were superior to most of what the Japanese had. Even the season cheered him. *Winter is our friend,* he wrote. *The fog it layers over Chungking is so thick that the enemy bombers won't be able to get off the ground until halfway through the spring.* He was given a promotion even before the training started and then another when he finished.

Now that he was a captain in the Chinese Army, I thought, surely he'd have some control over where he traveled and when. Surely he'd find a way to send for me. In the meantime, I practiced my calligraphy and played with the children. On sunny days I dressed them in padded jackets, and my mother-in-law and I took them to Bright Moon Park or Yu Garden. I cooked and I read. Occasionally a movie came to town—usually a foreign movie since most Chinese film companies had been shut down. My mother-in-law and I went to see *Charlie Chan in Honolulu,* and found it amusing. It couldn't compare, though, to my favorite Chinese film, *New Woman.*

The KCRL had a couple of meetings, but the general level of enthusiasm was less than before, and Fan Ho-fu, Lightning, and Cricket, three of our leading members, seemed to have lost interest altogether.

I didn't talk to Teacher Wei about my association with the Kulangsu Cultural and Resistance League. When I visited him that winter, we talked instead about our army's successes—the Japanese garrison in Kaifeng that our soldiers captured, the bridge they sabotaged, the lines they cut. They were small triumphs, but they gave us hope.

One day, after hearing word of a victory in Fuyang, Teacher Wei was especially enthusiastic. "We're going to grind them down," he exclaimed. Behind him, the gray sea was spotted with warships, but we no longer counted them. "They may win some battles, but we will outlast them."

I nodded. The prospect of outlasting them was an old man's consolation, a historian's long view of victory. Bittersweet at best.

He paced in front of the window, his blue gown swinging, hands clasped behind his back as he named off all the invaders who'd ever tried to conquer China, starting with ancient northern tribesmen who wore the skins of animals and drank blood from the skulls of their enemies. Going down through the ages, he pointed out how every single invader had eventually been pushed out or assimilated—the Tibetans, the Turks, and the Tungus. When he got to the Yuan Dynasty, I objected. Certainly it was no comfort to consider the Mongols who ruled China in whole or in part for more than a century.

"Forgive me," he said. "I talk too much. You're not my little student anymore." He refilled my teacup and picked up a magazine. "Have you seen this?" It was the literary supplement to our newly reestablished "foreign-published newspaper," *The Chinese-Scottish Times*. I wondered about the Scottish businessman under whose name the paper was registered—if he was as ugly as they said he was, and how he'd learned the ways of a gangster well enough to be paid what was said to be a handsome salary for doing nothing.

"No. I haven't seen this one," I said, taking the magazine from him. I scanned the index and found Teacher Wei's pen name. "Teacher, don't you think you should invent another nom de plume? Everyone knows this is you."

He started for the kitchen. "Let me know what you think of it."

On the surface, his poem was about an old man pledging love and loyalty to his wife of many years. Under present circumstances, though, a reader would naturally take it as a patriot's statement of his unwavering loyalty to China. As always, the words Teacher Wei chose were both subtle and precise.

"Excellent!" I said when he returned. "It's very moving."

"No, no. It's nothing special. Here, have something to eat," he said, offering me a steamed bun.

My morning sickness was a thing of the past. Now, every time I saw food, my stomach gave a welcoming growl. "No, thank you, teacher," I said, trying to be polite.

"It's only a mouthful."

"Please, save it for your mother."

Auntie Wei waved from the doorway. "Eat," she said. "We have plenty."

We ate our buns. Then Teacher Wei picked up the literary supplement. "Chang Ti also has something in this issue," he said, turning the pages until he found it. "A remarkable piece."

He handed it to me and then sat on the edge of his chair waiting for me to read it. "Well, what did you think?"

I was about to answer, when the author himself burst into the sitting room.

"Professor," he said. Then, seeing me, he stopped. He half-raised his hand in greeting. Then he sank into a chair, slouching against the back as though he were in his own house. His hair looked like it hadn't been washed or combed, and the shirt he wore under his Western-style tweed jacket was wrinkled and open at the neck. He took the steamed bun Auntie Wei brought him without even the pretense of a polite refusal. Then, leaving it to get cold on the side table, he took out a cigarette. How was it possible, I wondered, that such a boorish person could write such graceful poetry?

"I liked your poem," I said, indicating the literary supplement on the table.

"A sweet little thing, isn't it?" He lit a match, inhaled deeply, and then, tilting his head back, puffed out fat rings of smoke.

"I wouldn't call it sweet. It was far more eloquent than that."

"Hmph."

He was determined to be disagreeable, even with regard to his own poem, which was, as Teacher Wei had said, quite remarkable. The world Chang Ti created in the poem was vivid—the little pavilion on the lake's far shore with its red pillars and flying eaves, the willow branches that hung over the lake holding tightly on to their leaves in deference to the perfect mirror-surface below. The young lovers in their rented boat—his rhythmic rowing, her jade-green hair ribbons. Chang Ti had a way of making you love what he loved, hate what he hated: the airplanes, so small when glimpsed under the flying eaves, so indifferent, and then the glistening blood splattered across the red pillars, the bomb fragments hissing in the cool water. And when the stone with the emperor's poem carved on its surface cracked, you couldn't resist crying out with the author at the hideousness of our enemy.

Chang Ti stared at the tip of his cigarette and then flicked the ashes into a bowl. "It might as well have been written by a pacifist," he said angrily. He took another puff. Then he blew the smoke out in a formless cloud. "Where is the call to arms, the drumbeat for resistance?"

"That's not your style, Ti," Teacher Wei said.

"Not my style!" Chang Ti shouted, jumping up and throwing his half-smoked cigarette into the bowl. "You see? That's the trouble. I have the style of a weakling, a spineless man-woman who knows how to struggle only with ideas and philosophies."

"On the contrary. Everything you write is a testament to your courage. Tell me, Ti, how many times have you risked your life to publish in magazines like this?" Teacher Wei picked up the literary supplement and threw it back down. "Your writing upholds humanitarian values, reason, and individual autonomy."

Chang Ti turned toward the window and knocked his head against the frame. "The time for all those enlightened ideas is past," he said, spinning around. "All that's left is the fighting."

Teacher Wei took his elbow. "What's bothering you, Ti?"

Chang Ti pulled away. He picked his half-smoked cigarette out of the bowl and blew on it. "I'm a worm," he said, his voice breaking. "While Ang Jin and Fan Ho-fu chase the tiger and yank his balls, I'm cowering inside my house, writing pretty little poems and useless plays."

"What do you mean, chase the tiger and ..."

"Fight the Japanese, of course. Shed their blood for China." He stuffed the cigarette into his mouth and puffed hard to relight it. "While their brother hides like a frightened lizard on this foreign-protected island." He threw his cigarette back into the bowl and collapsed over his knees, sobbing.

"You mean they joined the army?" I asked.

He raised his head long enough to give me a warning look. Then he flopped down again.

The KCRL, I thought. But, no. We weren't doing anything you could call "yanking the tiger's balls." I looked at the top of his unwashed head. The room throbbed with his oversized feelings. What was he talking about? What was this more heroic path that Fan Ho-fu and Chang Ti's other friend had chosen?

Suddenly he jumped up. "Resist. Defy. Struggle," he shouted, punching the air with his fist. "Resist," he said again. "De...?" He shook his head and sank back into his chair. "It's no good. I can't. You see? My most deeply felt sentiments, and I can't express them." He sobbed and sniffled without wiping his nose.

"Here," I said, hurrying across the room to give him my handkerchief.

He took it and wiped his nose without so much as a glance or a thank-you.

I crossed my arms and glared at him. "Be realistic," I said. "Can a rooster give milk? Can a goat crow?" It was an inane barnyard allusion, laughable to the ears of a famous writer like Chang Ti. Nevertheless, I continued to take him to task. "None of us can change who we are. Teacher Wei can never return to being a young man. I will never be a battlefield hero. And you, Mr. Chang, you will never be the kind of person you seem to think you ought to be."

He glared at me, and, despite the handkerchief in his hand, wiped his nose on his sleeve. Then he looked away. The sadness on his face made me regret what I'd just said—all my realistic, hopeless "nevers."

There was a long silence. "I'd better go," I said.

Teacher Wei stood up, but when I waved him off, he turned back to Chang Ti and let his mother see me to the door.

Once outside, I swung my arms and shook my hands, trying to throw off all the gloom and melodrama Chang Ti and I had created. He wanted too much. That was his problem. If tomorrow, all the Japanese armies in China were chased into the sea, he still wouldn't be satisfied. No, he'd want to be the advisor who designed the battle plan or the general who executed it. What was the matter with him? Didn't he ever look in the mirror?

And what about Fan Ho-fu? I dug my heels in and swung around to see Teacher Wei's house looking back at me, the same as ever, a little weathered bungalow at the edge of the great gray sea. Where would Fan Ho-fu have gone? What grand and dangerous thing was he planning?

And why did I always get left behind?

22

*T*he next morning the fog moved in. As I walked beside the sea, other beach walkers would step out of the mist without a word and then pad away, back into their own small white worlds, leaving me alone in mine. At first it felt peaceful, listening to the shushing waves and the muffled cries of invisible gulls. Soon, though, I tired of seeing nothing ahead and nothing behind. It was like being blind, stuck in a cloud of unknowing. Why, I wondered, did Fan Ho-fu disappear like that? Not a word…to any of us. Except for Chang Ti. I would have thought that … Well, what did I think? He had no obligation to me. And yet… I kicked the sand and moved closer to the water's edge. Suddenly I wanted to see those shushing waves. To see something. The surf was as white as the fog, movement but no color. It splashed over my feet, and I skipped away. Fog this thick would be perfect weather for going out to meet Yu-ming on a fishing boat.

In April, it warmed up, and the fog began to burn off early. Peach and plum buds grew fat and dropped their pink and white petals on the ground where children kicked them and gathered handfuls to throw in each other's hair. Ah Chew was old enough by then to toddle after his sister. He was beginning to speak. Everyone was surprised by the number of words he could say. As for me, I was already eight months' pregnant. Yu-ming knew about my condition. He must have known that if he didn't send for me soon, I'd be too far along to climb down the cliff and back up again.

At night I tossed and turned, my belly weighing me down, my ankles swelling, my calves seizing up when I pointed my toes. Lying there, awake, I worried that Yu-ming had found another woman. She was taller than I was, with transparent white skin, a perfect oval face.

She was more obedient, a traditional woman in every way. On other nights, she was a free spirit, college-educated, a woman of the world.

The baby was a living stone, pressing down on my bladder and then up on my diaphragm and back on my spine. Every time I started to drop off, one pain or another woke me up. Was it any wonder then that my crazy thoughts grew and fed on each other? Worst of all was the idea that I might be like Watermelon Head, the first wife that Yu-ming's father had stopped loving when he brought his second wife home, and that Ah Chew would be as unloved as Fen had been. The notion didn't make any sense in the light, but there was always the next night …

When I'd almost given up hope of seeing Yu-ming, finally, one night in late April, Private Huang showed up on my balcony. I heard his knock and opened the door. This time it wasn't raining.

"Just a minute, private," I said. "I want to bring my son." Yu-ming needed to see him.

"Captain Han didn't say anything about a child, ma'am."

"It's all right. My husband will be happy to see him."

I left Private Huang on the balcony and ran to the nursery. "You must be very quiet," I whispered, "and do exactly as Mama says." Ah Chew nodded solemnly. He climbed to his feet and held up his arms. "Don't worry," I whispered to Hsiang-mei, who was already on her feet. "We'll be back before dawn. Here." I grabbed Ah Chew's shorts and a pair of suspenders and handed them to her. "Help me dress him. Quickly." I pulled his shirt over his head and stuffed his hands in the sleeves. Hsiang-mei found his stockings and I buckled his sandals. "Don't say anything to anyone," I warned. "Now, go back to sleep."

Private Huang wasn't happy. "Madam," he said, "the captain will be angry."

"I'll take responsibility," I said.

He looked unconvinced.

"Here," I said. "I'll strap him on your back. We'd better go down the stairs and out the back door."

Reluctantly, he agreed.

Following a new route devised by Private Huang, we made our way through the dark streets and down a gently descending path to a different beach. Even though I didn't have to clamber down a cliff this time, still, I felt unstable. I couldn't see my feet, and the weight of my belly put me off balance. When we were in the skiff, Private Huang took Ah Chew off his back, and I put him between my knees. "You must be a good boy now," I reminded him. "Don't be afraid. We're on our way to see your father. Do you remember how to greet him?"

"Yes," he said in a tiny, serious voice.

I sat him down beside me and made him practice the words of greeting. Then I held his hand, and we stared into the night until we reached the junk. As before, someone shined a light down on us. The boatman secured us against the junk, and two men reached down to take my hands. I glanced back at Private Huang, who was strapping Ah Chew to his back, and caught a glimpse of Ah Chew's round black eyes over his shoulder. He was a brave little boy, I thought, and not yet two years old.

Once on deck, Private Huang handed him to me. The captain, whose voice I recognized from before, said a few words of welcome. Then Yu-ming was at my elbow, guiding me across the slippery deck and into the deckhouse. Someone closed the door, and Yu-ming lit a candle. As he turned to face us, a dark silhouette before the candle's glow, I felt Ah Chew's little heart pounding against my chest.

"I told you not to bring him." Yu-ming's voice was soft, but there was no mistaking his anger. "And yet you just go ahead and do whatever you please. I suppose you realize I'll have to punish Private Huang for disobeying my orders."

Ah Chew shivered. I hugged him against my chest and answered his father, returning complaint for complaint. "Is this the way you greet your wife and your only son on this, your first meeting with him?"

He pressed his lips together. "I told you it wasn't safe. That's all I care about, your safety and his."

"I know that." I put Ah Chew down. "Say hello to your father," I said. And he bowed deeply, offering Yu-ming the formal greeting of son to father.

After a brief pause, Yu-ming accepted his greeting with suitable formality. Balancing there on his tiny feet, Ah Chew must look to his father like any other child, I thought. And poor Ah Chew, what must he be thinking of this angry man dressed in loose-fitting fisherman's clothes when all along he'd been expecting an army officer for a father? Whatever he was thinking, Ah Chew maintained his composure and continued to stand in front of his father like a little soldier awaiting his next command.

"How old are you, young man?"

Ah Chew held up two fingers, reckoning his age the Chinese way in which a child is a year old at birth. "Two and half," he said.

"Show Papa how you count your fingers," I prodded.

He put his hand in front of his face and carefully curled up all but his index finger. One," he said in his best counting voice. He unrolled his middle finger and counted "two." Then he carefully brought his index finger back down and placed it under his thumb while he held up the other three fingers. "Three, four, five," he said quickly, raising all five fingers.

"Good," Yu-ming said. "Next you must learn to count in Mandarin."

"Of course," I said, picking him up again. Yu-ming had no idea how unusual it was for a child Ah Chew's age to be able to say more than a handful of words, let alone count to five. But then, even if he had known what other children were capable of, Yu-ming would have expected more of his own son.

"I wanted you to see him," I said. "And I wanted him to meet his father." The boat hit a wave and I staggered a little.

Yu-ming reached out to steady me, and Ah Chew, believing he was being invited, held his hands out to his father.

"Here. You hold him," I said. "He wants his daddy."

Yu-ming lifted him under the arms, and immediately Ah Chew clamped his legs around his waist.

I laughed. This was the moment I'd dreamed of. "Look at him. A child who has known only women, and yet, he has the courage to jump into his father's arms on your first meeting."

"I know, I know." He carried Ah Chew over so he could look at him in the candlelight. "You've told me over and over how brave our son is. So," he said, finally smiling at his son. "You're not even afraid of your father." He studied Ah Chew's features, and Ah Chew looked back in unblinking fascination. "You didn't tell me how much he resembles my father and my grandfather."

"He looks like both our fathers, yours and mine."

The boat was rocking harder now, and to keep my balance, I had to adopt a horse-riding stance, which made the baby press harder than ever on the floor of my abdomen.

"You should sit down," Yu-ming said. He put Ah Chew on the captain's bunk and helped me take off my jacket. He hung it on a peg while I unbuckled Ah Chew's shoes and slipped out of my own. "It's good for him to learn Mandarin early," he said.

"He's already becoming familiar with the sounds. Haven't I told you how I read classical literature aloud to him in Mandarin and how attentive he is?"

He sat down beside us and untied his shoes. "Soon," he said, putting his shoes neatly next to Ah Chew's and mine, "you can start teaching him to recognize some simple characters and hold a pen."

"Yes," I said, even though Ah Chew was still far too young. Even his older sister could only recognize a few basic characters. My imagination raced ahead, though, to the time when he would be able to write a letter to his father. As soon as he gained enough control to make the basic strokes, I could write a phrase or two for him to copy. I glanced down at our future young student. He was sitting up straight, but his eyes were closed. "Ah Chew," I said softly. He sighed and snuggled against my hip.

"Let him sleep. He's only a baby." Yu-ming stood up. "How is my mother?"

I stretched Ah Chew out on the foot of the bunk. "She's fine."

"And your mother and Ah Mei?"

After assuring him that everyone was fine, there wasn't much more to say about our life without him—only that it was going on as before. Everything else that I intended to tell him he knew from my letters. Maybe there were things he could have told me about the war, but I didn't ask. Like those wives whose curiosity extends no further than their gates, I was content there inside our small floating world. We were like the happy family on a wall hanging or a fishing family that lives on their boat. Husband and wife, son and unborn child, together under the roof of our little cabin house.

I held out my hand, and he helped me up. "You smell good." I leaned closer and sniffed the crook of his neck. "I'd know your smell anywhere."

"I took a bath this afternoon."

"You still smell like yourself."

He put his arms around me and laughed. "Sometimes, An Lee, you're exasperating."

"You married me, didn't you?" I slid my hands up under his shirt.

"No other choice."

"Not true, not true. You always liked me."

He laughed again and guided me down to the bunk. "That little boyish girl, always racing and fighting with the boys."

I pulled him down beside me. "Dearest husband, your memory deceives you. That must have been someone else."

Sometime during the night, while Yu-ming and I were teasing and talking and holding each other, Ah Chew woke up. I saw his eyes watching us, wondering. *Look at us, my son,* I thought. *Look at your parents, and see how happy we are together.*

23

*T*hree weeks later, Ah Tou was born. Perfect little fingers and toes, pouty red lips, milk-fat cheeks, and big dark eyes. When I carried him, his body melted into mine—an exact fit. Some would say I loved him so much because he was small and weak, because he entered the world silent, sputtering to life only after the midwife spanked him and even then, continuing to wheeze until she put a straw down his throat and sucked out the mucus.

I don't agree. I don't appreciate weakness. If anything could explain why I loved this baby so much, it was his affectionate nature. And—okay, yes—because of his clear preference for me. He only went to the wet nurse when he was hungry. Then as soon as he'd had his fill, he wanted me to hold him again. During my monthlong confinement, I spent more time rocking him and singing to him than I had with either of the other two. When my confinement was over, I continued to hold him, sing to him, and tell him stories. One of the stories I told him—brought to mind by the rash of tiger attacks we'd been having—was about a boy who had magical tiger shoes.

"Once upon a time," I said, rocking gently in the old wooden rocking chair, "there was a little boy whose mother had died. He missed her so much that he sat for hours each day, gazing at her picture. One day the boy's mother stepped right out of the picture, sat down on a stool, and started embroidering a pair of shoes for him. Before nightfall, she jumped back into the picture. Every day, she came out again and continued embroidering his shoes. They were striped like a tiger with little ears and green tiger eyes. When they were finished, the boy slipped his feet into them, and they fit."

I tickled Ah Tou's feet, and he curled his toes and opened his mouth without laughing.

"One day a jealous official took the picture from the boy's home, and his mother disappeared. After a long search, the boy found her spirit deep in the mountains living with the fairies. She couldn't return to human form, she told him, unless he followed her instructions. 'Go home and put on your tiger shoes,' she said. 'You will find the picture in the official's bedroom. In the presence of the magical shoes, I will be able to step down.' He followed her instructions, and everything happened as she said it would. But when the boy and his mother tried to leave…" I waved my arm, and Ah Tou's eyes fluttered with excitement, "…the official blocked their way. In a flash the shoes jumped off the boy's feet. They turned into two ferocious tigers and pounced on the official."

I growled and tickled Ah Tou's feet so enthusiastically he cried and I had to hold him to my chest and pat his back.

When I was a child, I'd loved that story—the magical shoes, the ferocious tigers. It seemed to me that everyone loved tigers—their beauty and strength, the danger they represented. *Tiger-ness*, that's what I loved, the *idea* of a tiger, the myth. The real thing, on the other hand, was something altogether different—eight feet long, one hundred fifty kilos, jaws strong enough to break a man's neck, and an appetite large enough to finish off thirty catties of meat in a single day.

Fortunately for us, the thousands of tigers who lived in our province usually stayed in the mountains and coastal caves where they preyed on deer, fish, wild pigs, and livestock. Now and then, they killed a hapless farmer or goatherd, but mostly they kept to themselves, allowing us to enjoy *tiger-ness* without having to contend with the actual animal.

Lately, however, that was changing. First a tiger killed a farmer, then a child. A few weeks after I told Ah Tou the story of the magical tiger shoes, a tiger killed a Japanese soldier standing guard at an outpost on Amoy Island.

"Why would they swim across the channel to Amoy?" I wondered aloud a couple of days after the attack on the soldier. Mother and I were in her room, waiting for our tea to steep.

"Hunger," she said. The obvious answer. "The Japanese burn our fields, confiscate our rice, and eat our livestock. What choice do people have but to go deeper into the mountains in search of wild game?

And then, what choice do the tigers have but to look elsewhere when their food source is depleted?" She rubbed her swollen knuckles. The shortage of food had made her arthritis worse, and, although she was still heavy, her skin and muscles had grown limp from inactivity and malnutrition. "Have you forgotten what good swimmers tigers are?" she asked.

I shook my head and poured a little tea in her cup. "Your tea is ready," I said. The thought of real, hungry tigers was beginning to make me nervous. That, and the prospect of my first trip into occupied territory. Tomorrow Pei-lu and I were going to cross over to Amoy City to see *Gone with the Wind*. We wouldn't have considered making the trip for an ordinary movie, but everyone was talking about this one. It was in color. The big hit of 1940. With the Shanghai movie industry in tatters, all we'd seen lately were Hollywood films, things like *Paris Honeymoon* and *Young at Heart*. *Gone with the Wind* was supposed to be ten times better than any of them. Unfortunately, it wasn't playing on Kulangsu. Ling and her sister, Chi-chi, had already seen it twice. They said it was no trouble getting back from Amoy just as long as we brought identification and a few packs of Lucky Strikes—and as long as we didn't forget to bow with sufficient deference to the guards.

I'd been looking forward to an outing with Pei-lu. After confessing to her husband about her participation in the drama in front of his factory, she'd been staying home more than usual. I was sure she didn't tell him about my involvement, but he may have suspected it.

I poured my tea and held the warm cup with both hands. "How is your arthritis today?" I asked, steering the conversation away from man-eating tigers.

Mother rubbed her knees. "The same as always."

The next morning Su-lee greeted me with more tiger news. "Oh, Young Mistress. This time there were two tigers on Amoy Island." She sounded breathless. "Last night they killed a farmer's wife. She was walking to the outdoor toilet. Oh, ma'am, please don't go to Amoy."

"They won't come into the city, Su-lee. Don't worry."

I walked away, but she followed me into the nursery. "The farmer had a gun. He shot and killed the female tiger."

I picked up Ah Tou and held him away from me so we could look at each other.

Su-lee shuffled from side to side and cleared her throat. Obviously, she had more to tell me.

"What else?"

"Oh, Young Mistress, it's a terrible thing."

"What?"

"It was just the farmer's bad luck. The Japanese soldiers heard the gunshot and came running. They took his gun and beat him with it. Then they carried the dead tiger away to eat, but they wouldn't allow anyone to pick up the poor woman's body. It's so terrible, Young Mistress. They're using it for bait so the other tiger will come back."

"Barbarians!" I said, looking away so Ah Tou wouldn't see my face.

*　　*　　*

Gone with the Wind was definitely worth the trip. Not counting the intermission, it was four hours long. Afterward, as Pei-lu and I stumbled past the queue waiting outside for the evening show, I felt stunned, my mind so full of the spectacle, I couldn't say a word.

We stepped off the curb and started down the main street, visions of Scarlett O'Hara and Tara dancing on the gray blocks of buildings on either side. The crimson tint from the sinking sun looked pale compared with the Technicolor flames we'd just seen over the city of Atlanta.

A neon light blinked on, then another. Powder and Fragrance Hall, The Lucky Goose. The air smelled of petrol. Behind us, an engine roared, and we jumped back onto the sidewalk. It was only a truck, but we hadn't seen one in a long time, living as we did on our protected little island, where, even before being designated a haven for international trade and settlement, our own people had made it a sanctuary from the bustle of wheeled vehicles.

Amoy seemed different now. A group of boisterous young men pushed past us. Instinctively, I blamed their behavior on the occupation. They danced toward a sidewalk vendor who was frying garlic-flavored peanuts on a little charcoal brazier. One of them reached down and grabbed a handful of the sizzling hot peanuts. He screamed, and then, dancing in circles, threw them from hand to hand. "Your mama," the vendor shouted after him, shaking his fist. The man made an obscene gesture. Then he threw a peanut in the air and caught it in his mouth.

"It's getting dark," Pei-lu said. "We should catch a pedicab or a rickshaw." We'd already gone half a block, and by now the crowd waiting for a ride in front of the theater was immense.

"There." I pointed at a pedicab on the side street.

"It's parked in front of a nightclub."

"Who cares? We're not going inside."

We started toward The Dancing Phoenix and were halfway down the side street when two Japanese sailors came out. They climbed into the pedicab and rode away. "Oh well," Pei-lu said, turning back.

"Wait. Another one's coming." I grabbed her hand and we ran, barely missing a bargirl and a drunken Japanese sailor. The pedicab pulled up to the nightclub's entrance, and one of its passengers leaned over to pay the fare while his companion swung her silk stockinged, high-heeled feet out over the pavement. "Cabby," I shouted, running around the other side as the man, a dapper fellow in a cream-colored suit and hat, stepped down. He straightened up, his hand on the brim of his hat, and for a split second I was face-to-face with none other than Fan Ho-fu. Then he was walking away, his arm around the woman's shoulder as they strode into the nightclub.

"Wasn't that Cricket?" Pei-lu asked. "It looked like her under all that makeup."

I put a finger to my lips and climbed into the pedicab beside her. "Cricket and Fan Ho-fu," I whispered.

"What are they doing here?"

"I have no idea." I was livid. Fan Ho-fu was the one who had invited me to join the KCRL. It was because of him that I'd imagined I could do something to resist the Japanese. How foolish I'd been. He was nothing more than a dilettante, an actor trying out one role and then another. "Let's talk about it later," I said. Whether or not the KCRL ever got together again to produce another piece of street theater, still, we couldn't speak openly about it or its members.

When we reached the guard post, we paid the driver and got in line behind a white man and woman who looked as though they also had come from the movie. I reached in my pocket to feel for my pass. It wasn't there. A surge of panic flashed up my spine as I stuffed my hand in the other pocket and felt on either side of the pack of Lucky Strikes I'd brought for the guards.

"Pei-lu," I whispered. "I can't find my pass."

"Your vest pocket. Remember?"

I sighed and put the pass back in my vest pocket. When it was my turn, I stepped forward and bowed deeply, careful to keep my eyes lowered as I held out my hand. It had been easy enough to leave

Kulangsu, but now that I was trying to come back, the guard's attitude was different. He looked me up and down, frowning at my pass and then at me.

"Why you want go to Kulangsu?" he asked.

"I live there."

"How long you live there?"

"All my life."

"How long?" he shouted, grasping his rifle.

"Twenty-four years."

He frowned at my pass again. "Hmm," he growled. He looked over my head at the people waiting behind me and smirked. Finally he swung his arm toward the waiting boat. "You go," he said.

I was glad to oblige.

Our ferry was a small motor launch that held no more than a dozen passengers crowded together along the sides. Before the occupation, the ferry between Kulangsu and Amoy carried at least a hundred people, and it ran every ten or fifteen minutes. Now, there was nothing but this launch and a schedule that depended on the whim of an alien usurper. The launch filled up—not an inch to spare—and still we waited. The operator, a flat-faced Japanese sailor with a rifle under his arm, put his finger in his ear and shook it. Then, when he was good and ready, he pulled a cord and the motor grumbled to life. I shivered and hugged my knees as we backed away from the dock and turned out into the narrow stretch of water that separated Amoy and Kulangsu.

As soon as we were on dry land and past the Kulangsu guard station, Pei-lu turned to me. "Are you sure that was Fan Ho-fu?"

"Yes." I put my arm around her shoulder and leaned in close. "I looked right at him. Then he walked away, as though he hadn't seen me at all." I didn't tell her that he winked. It seemed that Fan Ho-fu always had a wink at his disposal.

"It looks like he's traded patriotism for the pleasures of a dissolute life. And dragged poor little Cricket along with him."

I could feel her hot, angry breath on my cheek. Now that I was back home, though—away from the occupation forces and the neon lights, the nightclubs, trucks, and buses—I felt calm enough to give Fan Ho-fu the benefit of the doubt. It was true that he was a joker, a man with unorthodox manners and views, but I wasn't ready to say that he was insincere in his love for China. Besides, I remembered what Chang-ti had said about Fan Ho-fu planning to shed his blood for China. I still didn't know what that meant. "I think we should withhold judgment," I said. "Maybe they were playacting."

"Without telling the rest of us?"

"The rest of us?" Did the Kulangsu Cultural and Resistance League still exist? And if it did, were Pei-lu and I still part of it?

"I know," she said. "I promised my husband I wouldn't have anything more to do with the League. But ..."

She didn't say it, but I knew she was thinking about her murdered father and our promise of vengeance.

"Oh well," she said, squeezing my hand. "I suppose you're right. We can't conclude that Fan Ho-fu has fallen into a life of vice merely because we saw him strutting into a nightclub in a pimp's outfit with a beautiful young girl on his arm, the slit in her dress up to here." She laughed. "Okay, tell me, who did you like better, Ashley Wilkes or Rhett Butler?"

"Me?" I was glad to change the subject. Since Ah Tou's birth, my interest in the KCRL had waned. Yet I couldn't forget that I'd given Pei-lu my word that afternoon on Sunlight Rock.

"Yes, you. Which man would you choose?"

I looked up, past the window lights and the tiled roofs and the fenced-in rooftop patios to the slice of moon above Sunlight Rock. "Ashley Wilkes was a man of honor," I said. "He always wanted to do the right thing."

"So? Was he your favorite?"

I sighed. "Of course not. With that big nose and high, narrow forehead. He was so...." I didn't want to say it.

"Cold?"

"Compared to Rhett Butler."

We giggled like schoolgirls and talked about the movie all the way to my house. It took that long for us to analyze the two men and why the kindhearted rogue appealed to us more than the gentleman of imperfect honor, a discussion that kept us from having to talk about the KCRL and war and hunger and the death of Scarlett's beautiful little girl.

*   *   *

One would have expected my dreams that night to be filled with scenes from *Gone with the Wind*. If I'd been smart, as I closed my eyes

I would have conjured up Scarlett O'Hara running down the stairs in her white dress and sitting on the porch, her petticoats and ruffles all puffed up around her. I would have called to mind Tara's rows of trees or the dancers twirling at Twelve Oakes, Yu-ming and I among them. Instead, I simply climbed into bed and closed my eyes, allowing sleep to drop its net over me and haul my sleeping mind where it would.

Before sunrise, I found myself in a field watching four Japanese soldiers with rifles, the dream as vivid as a vision. The soldiers crawled onto a roof, stopping just short of the ridge. "Go inside," one of them shouted in broken Chinese. "Don't make a sound, or else." He jabbed his bayonet in the air and grunted, and the farmer's family and I ran inside while the farmer's wife lay dead outside. Bait for a tiger.

When I awoke, I jumped out of bed and called out to the maids. "Su-lee, amah, go tell Ah Kwai they're going to sell tiger meat." I ran into the hall and down the stairs. We hadn't seen meat for weeks. Poor little Ah Chew, after getting Mother's permission to eat it, had hardly tasted a bite. Su-lee was alone in the kitchen, drinking her morning cup of tea. "They killed the tiger last night," I said.

She put her cup on the counter and picked up some matches. "Yes, Young Mistress."

"And they're going to sell its meat."

"Yes, Young Mistress." She lit the gas under the teakettle. Sometimes Su-lee could be so infuriating.

"Where's Ah Kwai?"

"She went shopping for tiger meat." She rinsed out the teapot and took a tea canister out of the cupboard.

"How did she know?"

"The aunt of Mrs. Lim's maid said the Japanese sold a portion of the meat when the female tiger was killed. She told Ah Kwai that if we wanted some this time, she'd have to get in line early."

"But how did she know the Japanese would kill the tiger tonight?"

Su-lee giggled, because naturally a tiger would want to return for his kill while it was still fresh, and, obviously, the Japanese would know enough to stay downwind from the corpse and they'd choose their best sharpshooter and also because the only reason I was asking was that I wanted to be the one who knew about the tiger meat.

Su-lee sprinkled some tea leaves in the pot and when the water boiled, filled it halfway up. Then she looked at me, her head tilted to the side. "Young Mistress," she said, "you're in your nightgown."

"Yes, yes. I know. I was in a hurry." I pulled out a stool and sat down. "We shouldn't expect too much. They'll keep all the good meat for themselves. After they give the heart and liver to their commander—probably the tiger's pelt also—there won't be much left to sell." In my dream, what an elegant tiger he was! So close that I could see the golden sheen of his fur and count the perfectly carved pieces of night that were his stripes. Inside the farmer's house, the poor man, battered from the soldiers' beating and leaning on his son's shoulder, stared, expressionless, at the body of his wife. When the tiger was only inches from it, one of the soldiers fired a single shot. Yes, I remembered now. Only one shot. They must have had orders to keep the pelt intact so they could give it to their commander.

It was afternoon before Ah Kwai returned. Gathering around the kitchen table, we watched her peel back layers of paper to reveal, not a pink chunk of flesh or even a bloody rib or a lumpy piece of intestine. No. On the table in front of us was a six-inch length of tiger tail, complete with its golden, black-striped fur.

Yun-yun cheered and hopped in a little circle.

"It's thick," my mother-in-law said, weighing it in her hand. "And heavy."

I had no idea what we might do with our furry portion of tiger, but I, too, was pleased. It seemed a real treasure, as much for its tiger-ness as for its protein content.

Ah Kwai had it all figured out, though. She washed the tail and scalded it with boiling water, plunging it after a few seconds into a basin of cool water. Then she scraped it with a knife chosen for its dullness so as not to damage the skin or scrape any of it away. Last of all, she boiled it with ginger, scallions, and white peppercorns.

That night she served us the broth for dinner. When all the bowls were filled, we picked up our spoons and sipped slowly, savoring the sticky feel and wild flavor. Only Ah Chew rushed through his serving, looking around for more when he was finished.

"Good, good. More, more," he said, grinning.

"Another bowlful for my grandson," Mother announced.

I thought I glimpsed something on her face. A raw sort of hunger. For the soup? I wondered. If so, I didn't want to see it. I was used to my mother as she was, her widowhood, her bound feet, her abstention from meat. All my life she'd been a vegetarian. I didn't want to think about her struggling to keep the vow she took in order to bring me safely into the world. But there it was again. She looked toward the kitchen, waiting for Ah Kwai to bring the broth, and I could see an almost frantic concern that was too personal to be solely on Ah Chew's behalf.

"Here you go, dumpling," she said as Ah Kwai set it down in front of him. "Here's your tiger-tail soup. What does it taste like?" she asked the rest of us.

"Stronger than chicken soup," I mumbled. "Makes my mouth tingle."

"It's a smoother taste than venison, but more powerful than mountain sheep," my mother-in-law said.

Ah Mei bent her little eyebrows and wrinkled her nose.

"That's nothing, child," my mother-in-law said, chuckling. "The Empress Dowager used to eat leopard. And when she had bear paw for dinner, everyone in the Imperial Palace heard about it."

Ah Mei shrieked, and we all laughed. With our tongues a-tingle and our bellies full of tiger-tail energy, it was surprisingly easy to laugh.

24

*I*didn't go back to Amoy again for several months. Then in the fall
I decided I needed to see a fortune-teller, one who knew what he
was talking about. The fortune-tellers in Kulangsu were worthless. I'd
been to every one of them, and none could give me a satisfactory
reading of Ah Tou's birth signs. I kept thinking about the glorious
dreams of the monk and the three white tigers I had before Ah Chew
was born. I wanted something like that for Ah Tou. Lacking a dream,
at least I wanted his fortune told by a qualified seer. I had no other
choice but to go look for one in Amoy.

My mother-in-law didn't see it that way. She hadn't set foot off our
"solitary island" since before the fall of Amoy more than two years ago,
and she didn't like the idea. It wasn't worth the risk, she said.

"Not worth it?" I turned Ah Tou around in my arms so she could
see his face. "Isn't this baby, your grandson, worth any risk?" When it
came to Ah Tou, I had a hard time keeping my feelings in check. I
turned him around and hugged him. "I can't leave it like this, Mother-
in-law. That old wind-mirror told us next to nothing yesterday. It was
as though he couldn't see the future at all." I kissed Ah Tou's ear.

"Fortune-tellers don't make the future happen, An Lee, so what
does it matter?"

"I know, I know." I glanced at Ah Kwai, who was ladling some
vegetable stock into a bowl of noodles for Ah Chew.

Ah Tou squirmed, silently poking his nose into my breast in
search of milk. It might have been true that no astrological reading,
whether good or bad, would have an effect on his life, but I couldn't
leave it like this. "It isn't really a risk," I said. "You show your registration card and they let you through. That's all."

My mother-in-law covered her mouth with a handkerchief and cleared her throat. "Okay, dear," she said finally. "If you're so intent on going, then I'll go with you."

"But Madam Han," Ah Kwai objected. She handed Ah Chew's bowl of noodle soup to the amah. "You can't go with that cough."

"It's nothing," she said. "I'm fine. You and An Lee have already ventured into occupied territory, you several times, Ah Kwai. Now it's my turn."

The following morning as we left the house, I was in high spirits. Amoy in the light of day! I felt like a villager on her way to the provincial capital. Just thinking about it made my heart skip a beat. But as the checkpoint came into view, I began to have second thoughts. What if something happened to my mother-in-law? Yu-ming would blame me, railing against my "superstitious" beliefs. I'd never be able to convince him that it was my responsibility as a mother. I absolutely could not leave Ah Tou without a satisfactory reading of his future. "You should go back," I told my mother-in-law. "Really. I can do this by myself."

"No," she said. "Let's go."

The checkpoint was manned by two Japanese sailors wearing expressions of superiority that were strikingly at odds with their peasant faces. "You. Step up," one of them said, frowning at me through his thick glasses.

I stepped forward and bowed ninety degrees.

"Why you want go Amoy?" he asked. The standard question.

"I have to see a fortune-teller."

"Hmph. Chinese fortunes all good," he said, scowling. "Now China belonging Greater East Asia Co-Prosperity Sphere."

"Yes. So fortunate for us. Nevertheless, my baby needs his eight-character fortune told."

He sucked air through his teeth to impress me with the difficulty of granting my request. Then he growled in the Japanese way and asked for my identification card. When he'd finished taking down my registration number and issuing me a pass, I bowed and moved on through. Not so bad. The second time around, everything was easier.

I looked back at my mother-in-law, who was bowing to the near-sighted guard as his compatriot, a dark-faced sailor with a scar on his cheek, waved another woman forward. In the process of placing her basket on the ground, the woman forgot to bow, and the guard smacked her across the face. "Take off shirt," he demanded.

I sucked in my breath and watched as the woman's fingers fumbled, unable to push a single button through its buttonhole. Just rip it, I thought with a bystander's presence of mind.

"Don't look," my mother-in-law said. "Let's go." We hurried to the motor launch, resisting the urge to look back when we heard the woman's muffled cry and the sound of fabric ripping. As soon as we were aboard, the boatman kicked us away from the dock, and with a roar of the engine, we sped away.

I looked across at Amoy, the big, gritty city to Kulangsu's genteel mansions and picturesque lanes. The massive buildings along the waterfront cast long morning shadows across the street and into the water. Most were six or seven stories high. I shaded my eyes so I could see Amoy's jewel, the Crane River Hotel. It stretched half a block in two directions, its entrance curving around five huge pillars at the corner. When I was a child, I thought it was our hotel because it had the same red bricks as our house and the same blue balustrades on its balconies.

A heavy wind was blowing in from the sea when we landed. If we hadn't been so accustomed to walking, my mother-in-law and I might have taken the tram or a rickshaw up Zhong Shan Lu. I squeezed her hand.

"Yes," she said, smiling for the first time that day. "It's good to get out. Lacking an occasional outing, even an emperor's palace can be a prison."

In the daylight, everything about Amoy was different—no gangs of young men, no neon lights blinking the names of nightclubs and gambling halls. Not that vice and its wartime proliferation weren't still present. Even in the daytime silvery-yellow smoke escaped from the doorways of opium dens, and Chinese bandits alongside Japanese *ronin* swaggered through the business district looking for merchants to prey upon. We didn't pass any "wild flowers," but posters for their "halls of fragrance and powder" invited passersby from every second corner. "You want fun? Please come in." They advertised by nationality—Chinese beauties, Korean or Taiwanese beauties. And they didn't hesitate to give their customers clear directions: "Comfort house at the Third Sino-Japanese Friendship Club, 500 meters ahead."

"I hate the Japanese," I said under my breath.

"Sh."

"And the British." All those imperialist nations that had preyed on China when she was weak, forcing opium down the throats of the Chinese. Now the Japanese were doing the same thing. Even worse. It wasn't long before we came upon a sign with an arrow pointing toward a heroin-dispensing den.

"Hospital," my mother-in-law read aloud, keeping her inflection flat. The shamelessly ironic euphemisms the Japanese employed had long since ceased to surprise us. Still, on this morning of freedom, nothing we saw on our way to the temple could totally extinguish the pleasure I felt at being out in the great world for a few hours.

We followed Zhong Shan Lu uphill from the water, occasionally stepping off the sidewalk to get around slower-moving pedestrians. It was a strenuous climb, but the wind dried our perspiration almost as soon as it formed. We were like Scarlett O'Hara, I thought—strong women. And in wartime, that was what mattered— strength, and the determination to survive. Even as the street flattened out, knots of tortoise-like walkers and leisurely shoppers kept us on the street until the screaming siren of a lorry filled with police forced us back onto the sidewalk.

Finally, we caught sight of the Temple of the Thousand-handed Goddess of Mercy. Its red and blue flying roofs and gold-leaf ornamentation stood out in stark contrast to the drab gray tile roofs of neighboring buildings. The main pavilion had three roofs, one on top of the other, a phoenix on every roof tip. The sight brought tears to my eyes. Despite the war, the temple was still here, everything the same as before—the giant black censor standing on its three sturdy legs, worshippers lighting joss sticks and mumbling prayers, a professional scribe sitting at a rickety table writing love letters and bills for the illiterate. And the fortune-tellers still sat in the temple square plucking their three-stringed instruments to announce themselves.

I would have preferred to take Ah Tou's birth facts to the abbot of the Chang Chou Monastery. But even if I'd had dreams to relate, the monastery would have been too far and the way too dangerous. I looked around the square at the fortune-tellers. One of them, an old man with a wispy white beard, had attracted a small crowd. He sat on a mat, his legs crossed in a position of meditation. His sightless eyes stared at a young woman who sat across from him on a low wooden stool. "Number thirty-five," he said in the bland tone fortune-tellers affect to mask the joy or sorrow in their predictions. The wind was quickly picking up force, howling over the roof tiles and inside the eaves. "Fire above, earth below," the old man said, raising his voice. A gust blew his beard into his face. It sounded like a good hexagram. Better than Ah Tou's, which was mountain over lake—although certainly good and bad could be found in every hexagram. "He will easily attain positions of power," the fortune-teller continued, ignoring the hair caught on his lips.

The woman clasped her hands together, letting go of her skirt just as another gust lifted it up to her shoulders. The fortune-teller, who must truly have been blind, showed no sign of having seen anything. "The child must guard against temptations to corruption," he advised.

A bucket clattered across the paving stones, and everyone looked around nervously. It wasn't too early in the year for a typhoon. "Much admired. Wealthy. Such a lucky child!" Who cared if he was also "conceited" and "sometimes shallow," predictions that rose up in the wind together with the dust and dry leaves. Those stupid fortune-tellers on Kulangsu. I didn't need them to tell me that Ah Tou was calm and kind. In a dangerous world, what use was it to be "balanced" and "selfless"?

The woman moved her stool closer. Roof tiles and shutters were rattling all around us, and since blind people sometimes speak as though their world were smaller and closer than everyone else's, I couldn't hear him now. The woman would remember whatever she chose to anyway. I, on the other hand, recalled everything the stupid fortune-tellers had told me, particularly the things I hadn't wanted to hear. "Yielding," one seer had proclaimed. "Low-energy." Another called Ah Tou "the diminishing one." What in heaven's name was that supposed to mean?

Something was happening in the street, and by the way people scattered, the shouting and horn honking must have been unusual, even under occupation. The woman pushed her stool back, and suddenly the fortune-teller found his loud voice. "Kind lady," he said, "an offering. Lamp oil for the venerable God of Good Sight." The trembling strings on his *san xian* intoned a plaintive accompaniment to his plea. Of the earlier crowd around him, now no one remained except my mother-in-law and me.

As soon as the woman turned to go, I grabbed the little stool, pulled it closer to the fortune-teller, and sat down. "My second son was born this year, nineteen forty, in the month of May," I said. He held his hand up. In the street, a siren screamed. He closed his milky eyes and tilted his head to one side, listening to the cries of "make way, make way." Then, without a word of explanation, he started stuffing his tiles and charts into a cloth bag.

"Sir, what . . ."

He placed his *san xian* on a mat, rolled it up, and secured it. "The stool," he said.

"I came all the way from Kulangsu to have my—"

"Come back tomorrow." He took the stool from me and started tying it, together with everything else, onto his back. "Weren't you listening?" He gestured with his mouth toward the street.

I was about to curse him when a half-unfurled roll of calligraphy paper hit my mother-in-law in the shoulder. As she bent over, coughing, the scribe ran toward us, waving his arms and shouting, "Aiya! Aiya!" Behind him, his unattended table toppled over and his brushes, ink sticks, and grinding stone scattered across the pavement. I rubbed my mother-in-law's back until she stopped coughing. Then I picked up the roll of calligraphy paper and ran, paper streaming out behind me like a kite tail, to help the scribe save his writing implements and his rickety table. By the time we finished, no one was left in the temple square except a monk who was tying things down. It looked as though I had no alternative but to abandon my plans and head back to Kulangsu.

The going was easy at first. The sidewalks had cleared out, and the bluejackets and policemen were too busy rushing down Zhong San Lu to even notice us. Then the military police appeared, and we ducked into an alley and wove our way through back streets and alleys to the bund. With so many Japanese Navy troops in the streets, I thought our own navy must have been attacking. But when we poked our heads out of the last alley, there were no Nationalist Chinese troops in sight. Collaborationist police had formed a cordon around the Crane River Hotel, and the bluejackets were interrogating its guests in the street. Wind whipped up from the water, and the people waiting in queues tried to steady themselves by bending their knees and holding on to each other. Even the policemen seemed glad to lock elbows. Everyone knew how powerful an October typhoon could be.

My mother-in-law and I braced ourselves against the side of a building, glad for the solid feel of granite against our shoulders. With the howling wind for cover, people spoke openly about the murder of a councilman, a member of the Special Amoy Municipal Government. Someone who claimed to know the facts spoke the dead man's name, and all around us people spat and swore, for the man he named was notorious for his ill-gotten wealth and his subservience to the Japanese.

We stayed in the alley long enough to hear that the suspected assassin and his accomplice—a young man posing as a pimp and a beautiful young woman—had most probably escaped sometime during the night. Then we pushed our way through the crowd, heading toward what would surely be an intense grilling by the guard at the ferry landing and a frightening ride back on a stormy sea.

The sea, in fact, was so rough that we were afraid we wouldn't be able to return until the typhoon abated. The Japanese guards didn't care, though. The man who operated the motor launch today was Chinese. It was a horrendous trip. My mother-in-law and I clung to each other, trying our best to hold on to the slippery ribs and bench of the boat as it pitched and rocked wildly, water streaming over the bow and gunnels. After we landed, leaning into the wind and sloshing through water that overflowed the storm sewers, I tried to apologize. "I'm so sorry, Mother-in-law," I shouted over the roar.

*   *   *

By the time my mother-in-law and I returned, Ah Kwai and Su-lee had already shuttered the windows and pushed the furniture against the inner walls. They'd rolled up the carpets and wall hangings and tucked away the vases and figurines and photographs, anything that could be damaged by the storm. Somehow, Su-lee heard us pounding on the gate and ran out in the rain to open it for us. Ah Kwai was waiting inside, her arms full of towels. She wrapped them around us and ushered us through the unrecognizable rooms amidst a torrent of scolding and a promise of soup before bed.

Now, halfway through the night, everyone but me seemed to be sleeping while I sat bolt-upright on my pushed-back bed, my hands clamped over my ears as I tried in vain to mute the angry scream of the wind. When in heaven's name would it stop its high-pitched whoo-whoo-ing? The whining and the banging of the shutters was like an army of angry ghosts. I squinted and scrunched my shoulders. I'd lived through scores of typhoons before, enjoyed them even—the wind's nerve-tingling energy, the huddling inside, the sense that it would all be over in a few hours and we could congratulate ourselves on having survived. Tonight was different. I had a bad feeling about this typhoon.

Finally, exhausted, I dropped my hands and fell back on the pillow. If my mother-in-law caught pneumonia because of today's outing, I'd have no one to blame but myself.

25

*A*s it turned out, it wasn't pneumonia that laid my mother-in-law low; it was bronchitis. She was already looking pale the day after our trip to Amoy. And before the branches and leaves scattered and broken by the typhoon had been cleared away, she was coughing and dragging herself around the house and garden. It went on for more than a month, her cough so deep and ugly I wanted to cry.

I took her to see Dr. Kao, and I bought the medicine he prescribed for her. But I didn't have the courage to write to Yu-ming. Finally when she was out of danger, I inserted a brief, sanitized summary of her illness into the middle of a cheerful letter. I described her bronchitis as a bad cough from which she'd fully recovered. I didn't mention that I'd taken her into enemy territory in an attempt to find a fortune-teller I liked. If he'd been at home, I would have confessed it to him. Face-to-face, I would have been able to make him understand or at least forgive me. But with so many miles and months between us, I was afraid. Besides, by the time I wrote, she was fine. Both of us could relax. Or so I thought.

And from all outward appearances, she did seem healthy—a little pale, her breathing somewhat shallow, but that was to be expected in the weeks following such a serious case of bronchitis. Then one morning as I was sitting at my vanity brushing my hair and thinking of one thing and another—Yu-ming's next letter, Ah Tou's new tooth, how long it had been since I'd tasted a mango—I heard a low, gravelly moan from my mother-in-law's end of the hallway. An early morning nightmare, I guessed. Except that it didn't stop. I put my hairbrush down and followed the sound to her room, and there I found her curled up on her side, her quilt up to her ears. I pulled it back, and a wave of trapped heat hit me in the face.

"What's this?" I demanded, directing my ire at God and fate and whatever ancestors might be responsible for the little red spots on her neck. It wasn't fair. I'd finally stopped worrying about her, and now ... Was I going to have to start all over again?

She fluttered her eyelids and tried to raise her head. "Could you close the curtains, dear? It's so bright in here."

The curtains were only half-open and the sky outside was overcast, but I didn't argue. I went to the bathroom across the hall, and when I came back with a bottle of aspirin, she was burrowed under the covers again, only her black eyebrows showing above the quilt. I raised her to a sitting position and wedged a pillow behind her back. Then I handed her the aspirin. She tried to swallow them, but they wouldn't go down. So I crushed them in a spoon, mixed in some water, and fed it to her a little at a time.

"I'm sorry," she said. "So much bother."

"No, Mother-in-law. How could you be a bother to me? I love you." Had I ever told her how much I loved her? And not just for Yuming's sake.

That morning I stayed with her without a break, feeding her crushed aspirin and wiping her face and arms and neck with a towel dipped in a basin of cool water. By lunchtime, her fever was still high, and I considered asking Dr. Kao to come. I hesitated, though. I didn't think he'd agree when she'd only been sick for a few hours.

On the other hand, bent over my mother-in-law's bed, a few hours was beginning to seem like a very long time. When Ah Kwai came in with some cool water, I handed her the wet towel and stretched my tired back. The uneven plaster on the wall and ceiling was covered with strange little shadows. A gecko skittered down the wall. He stopped, his sticky suction toes holding him upside down. If he was hungry, he'd just have to wait. I hadn't heard a mosquito in the room for hours. Earlier Su-lee had brought up some rice and pickles with my tea, but the smell of disease was so nauseating that I'd only eaten a few bites before telling her to take the rest away. Now my stomach was rumbling like thunder in a steep-walled valley.

Shameful neediness. You'd think that when someone you loved was sick, you wouldn't even think about food. You wouldn't care that your back was tired or that you'd been doing the same simple tasks over and over with no results. I was brooding on my hunger and musing on all the things I'd planned to do that day when I heard Mother call for Ah Kwai.

What was she thinking? Why would she call for her now? Didn't she understand how sick my mother-in-law was? I was the one who needed Ah Kwai's help. Mother could do without her for a few hours. I stifled an angry sigh and took the towel from Ah Kwai. "Go on down," I said. "Go." Glaring at her back, I splashed the towel into the porcelain basin and wrung it out. Was I the only one in this house who cared whether my mother-in-law lived or died?

Ah Kwai ran downstairs and then, from the sound of it, started back up. Suddenly I stopped my silent whining. The footsteps and grunts coming from the stairway belonged to two people, not one. It seemed that once again I'd underestimated my mother.

She was panting as she hobbled through the doorway and made her way to my mother-in-law's bed. "Ping," she said, taking my mother-in-law's hand, "how do you feel? I want you to tell me everything."

She could have just asked me. She didn't need to torment my poor, sick mother-in-law, who was struggling to blink her eyes open and squeeze out an answer.

"My head aches," she finally mumbled before sinking back onto her pillow.

Still Mother wasn't satisfied. She leaned in and touched my mother-in-law's shoulder. "Yes?" she prodded.

"Mother," I whispered. This was no time for a detailed investigation.

"What else?"

"I..." My mother-in-law opened her eyes. "I feel hot sometimes. Sometimes ... very cold. It hurts ... to ... turn my head." She lay there for a long time with her eyes closed. Then, her words barely audible, she added, "I want to throw up."

Ah Kwai ran for a bucket, arriving back just in time.

Stomach flu. That would explain the fever, the headache, the sensitivity to light. I wasn't sure how the rash fit in, but if it was stomach flu, that was something I understood, something all of us had at one time or another. You were sick for a day or two, and then you were fine. Tomorrow or the next day I'd be able to write to Yu-ming. It was only a touch of the flu, I'd say. Bad for a while, but it didn't last long.

For the rest of the afternoon, Mother stayed upstairs, counting her beads and giving advice while Ah Kwai and I tended to my mother-in-law. I didn't open the window and the curtains until late. By then, the air in the room was so stale and the air rushing in from the garden so fresh that we all stopped what we were doing and breathed it in. Ah Kwai arched her back and Mother folded her fan.

I rubbed my shoulder. "Do you mind?" I asked my mother-in-law.

She gave a slight shake of her head, and where the lilac-colored light fell on her chest, I noticed that her rash took on a purplish cast.

"Ma." It was the children, banging on the door and jiggling the knob. "We're hungry, Mama." Ah Chew's perennial cry.

"I'm sorry, ma'am," the amah said. "They ran away from me."

"Mama, Mama." Ah Tou's sweet baby voice pulled my heart away from my mother-in-law's sickroom. "Mama. I want my mama."

Mother shifted her weight and grunted.

"You look tired," I said. "Why don't you go downstairs and rest. Ah Kwai can fix dinner for you and the children."

"Yes," my mother-in-law croaked. "Feed the babies." It was the first sentence she'd uttered in hours. An encouraging sign.

Mother nodded and signaled for Ah Kwai to help her up.

Illness can be dramatic or dull, terrifying or—from the spectator's viewpoint—unremarkable. As far as I could see, nothing about my mother-in-law's condition was changing. So how could it hurt if I went down to dinner and left her in Su-lee's care?

Later, since she'd been sleeping most of the time and hadn't vomited in hours, I decided that Ah Kwai, Su-lee, and I could take turns watching her. Certainly that couldn't hurt.

During the night, her condition may have worsened. If so, I didn't recognize it. Her rash may have spread and coalesced into larger blotches, but it was nearly dark in her room. How could I see it?

Early the next morning, a delayed December dawn about to break through, I was wiping her brow when suddenly she opened her eyes and reached for me. "Why?" she wailed.

"What, Mother-in-law?"

"Why didn't you write a will?" Her voice sputtered and cracked. "Protect your wife and son."

The back of my neck turned to ice. Whom could she be blaming for leaving her and her son unprotected? Her husband was long dead.

I put my ear close to her lips, but this time I couldn't understand a word. She seemed to be speaking Mongolian. As I backed away, she made a clicking sound at the side of her mouth as though she were urging her pony to gallop. Frightened, I ran out of the room and down the stairs. "Ah Kwai, Su-lee. Go stay with her," I screamed as I threw open the front door. "I'm going for the doctor."

I should have gone sooner. The thought propelled me at a mad dash down the lane, our gate swinging wildly behind me. I skidded around corners, dodging children and women and old men. When I reached Dr. Kao's gate, I pounded and rang the bell. Finally his maid opened it a crack.

"It's too early," she hissed. "Come back later."

"No. I have to see Dr. Kao. It can't wait."

She shook her head and tried to close the gate, but I pushed on it with all my might and tumbled inside.

"Miss, miss." She jumped in front of me, blocking my way like a faithful guard dog. "You can't go in. He's sleeping."

Did she think that would stop me? I pushed her aside and strode toward the front door. "If you don't wake him, I will."

She caught up and tried again to stop me. Once I was inside the house, though, and within sight of the stairway, she could see how serious I was. "All right," she said. "Wait downstairs. I'll tell him you're here."

I heard his feet hit the floor, and within minutes Dr. Kao was ready to go.

All in all, I was only away from my mother-in-law for thirty minutes, forty at the most. No time at all. No one could have brought the doctor back faster than I did. And yet, during those few minutes I was away, something had changed. At first I took it as a sign of improvement. She was resting—no more delirium, no more babbling in Mongolian. Ah Kwai and Su-lee were standing back from the bed, which I assumed meant that they were making way for Dr. Kao. I expected that he would look at her and then prescribe a cure. After that, everything would begin to be all right.

I was certain it would. If my sixth sense—or even my eyes—told me otherwise, I refused to look. I ignored the fact that Dr. Kao didn't ask her how she felt, and when he shined his little light in her eyes and touched her pulse points, I failed to deduce the obvious. So when he turned to me and told me he was sorry, I didn't understand what he was sorry for. "She's gone," he said, making his opinion perfectly clear.

His opinion. That was all it was. She couldn't die just like that. So quickly. While I was out getting him. This doctor, who always cared for our family, who went to school with Yu-ming. Who should have known better. "Her pulse is weak," I told him, "hard to detect. Try again, doctor. You'll see."

He unbuttoned the top of her gown and motioned for Ah Kwai to open the curtains.

"No," I said. "It's too bright for her. She doesn't like ..." But Ah Kwai had transferred her loyalty to Dr. Kao, it seemed, because she opened the curtains wide so that there, in the thin light of early morning, even I could see I'd brought the doctor too late. My mother-in-law's skin was the same lilac color as the previous evening's sunset. The rash on her chest and neck and arms—now that I finally saw it in the light—stood out like a shower of blue cyanide crystals.

Dr. Kao shook his head. A virulent strain of meningococcal meningitis, he said. It wasn't unusual for it to develop so fast. "I'm sorry," he said once again. Then he advised us to disinfect the room and our skin and our clothes and to keep the children away from my mother-in-law's room. Finally he gave me special instructions on how I should wash her body to prepare it for burial.

*   *   *

Afterward, my only wish was to shake her back to life. I wanted to cling to her and scream and cry. To run and run until I couldn't run anymore and then to collapse in a puddle of tears. I couldn't, though. I had duties to perform. Her body had to be washed. She needed a casket and a burial site. And with the Japanese occupying the land beyond Amoy, she couldn't be laid to rest on the mainland beside her husband. She'd have to be in the little wartime graveyard here on Kulangsu, the field that used to be a children's park. And every moment, the duty I dreaded most of all was hanging over my head. I had to write to Yu-ming. This time I couldn't procrastinate.

In the evening, I sat down at my desk and searched for words. *I regret ... I'm sorry ... bad, no, terrible news ...Oh, my dearest, I don't* ...But how could I tell him that the mother he adored had died in my care? In the end, I simply wrote the truth of it and sent the letter quickly before I could change my mind.

After that, I still had the funeral to organize. It had to be digni-fied. Yu-ming would want all the rituals to be performed perfectly, in a manner befitting both his mother's rank and that of her father and husband. She was, after all, the daughter of a general and the widow of a champion of the old civil service examinations, one who had achieved the rank of mandarin first class and the position of ambas-sador. Someone had to be sure everything was done correctly. And, in Yu-ming's absence, it was all on my shoulders.

I pressed my sadness into a wafer-thin, diamond-hard package in the bowels of my belly, and I did it all—all the decision-making and organizing, all the greeting and speaking, thanking and witnessing. And then, five days later, when it was over—my mother-in-law laid to rest, the mourners gone home, I still had to hold myself together just a little longer so I could write another letter to Yu-ming.

It was late in the evening when I took out my ink stick and stone. I'd made a list of those who came to the house to pay their respects and those who attended the funeral, and I'd committed their words of praise and consolation to memory. Despite the passage of time and my mother-in-law's lowered estate since her husband's death, every-one we knew and many we'd nearly forgotten made an appearance. I ground a large quantity of ink, and then I dipped my brush in and wrote all their names and what they said. As with the first letter, I told Yu-ming only the details without comment. Both letters must have read like messages from a bureaucrat, the characters so mechanically written I could barely recognize my own handwriting. This letter was three pages long, the rows of characters tight against each other.

When I was finished, I chose a chop and took the lid off the porcelain red ink container. Usually I simply signed my name, but this letter required the formality of my personal chop. I pressed the carved face of the stone against the ink several times, tested it on a clean page, and then pressed it firmly onto the paper below my sig-nature and waited for the sticky red ink to dry. Finally I slid the letter into the envelope I'd prepared, and for a moment I felt a weight lift from my shoulders. Then, suddenly, my knees buckling beneath me, another more sinister weight, a huge tsunami of sorrow, crashed over me, and it was all I could do to walk to my bed and fall into it.

December 1941

26

Sometime before dawn the invasion began. It was December eighth on our side of the International Dateline. A year after my mother-in-law's death. By the time most people even had an inkling of what was happening, the Japanese had landed on Kulangsu and started moving from the bund into the business district. I must have heard something in my sleep because I got out of bed, tiptoed across the room, and opened the window. At first, the lane and nearby houses seemed exceptionally quiet, as though everyone were listening for something. Then the sounds of the invasion began to make their way around and over and through the buildings, trees, walls, and hills, misshapen sounds that when they reached our side of the island, were felt more than heard—the stutter of boat engines, the low-pitched shouts, the *rat-a-tat-tat* of running boots and shooting guns.

Who would rescue us? I wondered as I threw on my clothes. Maybe America would send marines or Britain, a battleship. Hurrying downstairs in my soft-soled Chinese shoes, my intuition told me that this time there would be no rescue.

Ah Chew was already in Mother's room, standing beside her bed, shivering. "You see," she couldn't resist saying the moment I opened her door, "even though he's white with cold, he doesn't dare climb up."

I didn't answer. A few days earlier I'd scolded him for running to her bed in the middle of the night, told him that a boy of three years was too old to sleep with his grandmother. I wasn't inclined to soften my view now. "No wonder," I said, lifting him up and squeezing his toes. "He doesn't have any shoes on."

Mother sighed. "Why don't you help me up?"

Her arms were as cold as Ah Chew's feet, but neither of us suggested closing the window. "The Japanese bombed a British gunboat early this morning," she said as I reached under the bed for her silk shoes. "It was anchored in the Huangpu River in Shanghai. Ah Kwai brought me the news a few minutes ago."

It could have been an isolated incident, I thought as I stretched the slipper over her broken instep. A bombed gunboat on the Huangpu River didn't necessarily mean the Japanese were making a concerted move on all the international settlements.

"Also, an American gunboat," she said as I helped her down from the bed. "The Americans didn't even put up a fight."

"In Shanghai, you mean?"

She nodded.

I couldn't believe it. When had the Japanese become so brazen and the Americans and British so helpless? I moved her screen over for her to dress behind, ignoring her little sniff of scorn as I opened it. If she wasn't concerned about protecting her modesty and Ah Chew's innocence, I was. He wasn't a baby anymore. Then, as though this were any other day, she began her habitual morning deep breathing exercise, raising her arms then forcefully lowering them with each exhalation.

"What's wrong, Mama?" Ah Chew asked as he curled and uncurled his cold little toes.

"Today, Ah Chew, you must be a big boy."

"Yes, Mama." He stopped wiggling his toes and bravely sat up in Mother's chair.

"Do everything I tell you. Everything your grandmother says, also," I added. "Remember, you are the son of a Chinese army officer." I turned back to steady Mother, who was wobbling on her small feet.

"Just hand me my tunic," she said. "I need to get dressed."

I was still buttoning her tunic when Su-lee burst in, a tea tray balanced on her hip. "The Japanese are marching into the foreign parts of Shanghai," she said breathlessly. "Ah Kwai told me to tell you."

For a split second I felt a rush of relief—relief, I suppose, that all those years of anxiety and dread were over. We wouldn't need to worry any more about losing our freedom and security. They would already be gone. Through the half-opened window, the view of our yard was a confusion of fog-obscured leaves and branches, walls and gates, all of them neatly squared-off by the window frames and mullions. Last year's pods still hung dark and twisted on the leafless tree outside the window. The branches cut the view into still smaller pieces—an irregular mesh inside the squared-off grid. A wisp of morning fog floated in the lane. Too high to hide our chipped brick and the brownish-green moss crawling up our posts, it hovered near the Lims' wall, smoothing out its imperfections. Occupation couldn't be too bad, could it? People in Amoy and all those other cities, Peking, Nanking, Wuhan, weren't they enduring it?

Su-lee's high-pitched voice cut into my blurry thoughts. The next-door maid, Jing-jing, heard about the troops entering Shanghai from the washerwoman on the other side. "Her master, or someone's master, heard it on the wireless." Like everyone else, Su-lee, who in all likelihood had never seen a wireless set, revered any information that came over one. She started to pour our tea then stopped. "Oh, ma'am! They can't bring tanks and lorries onto Kulangsu, can they?"

"No," Mother assured her. "Blessed be Buddha for our narrow lanes."

"Blessed be Buddha," Ah Chew repeated.

Su-lee picked up the teapot and poured a twisted rivulet of tea, golden as the braid of an Englishwoman. How I hoped Buddha had kept a few more blessings in reserve!

That first day we weren't required to open our gate to the invaders, but they were everywhere. Before our morning rice porridge was warmed, they had spread out across the entire island, proclaiming their newly acquired authority and the "New Order" for China. The first contingent of bluejackets that passed our house stopped every few hundred meters. One of them shouted through a megaphone in broken Chinese that warriors from the Land of the Rising Sun were liberating us from Anglo-American imperialism and that, for Kulangsu, today was the beginning of a new era of cooperation with our brother-nation, Japan. While he was haranguing us, other members of his team put up large-character posters. They plastered one on the wall across the street from us that declared, "Asia for the Asiatics." Another farther down boasted of Japan's great victory over the United States of America and all the Western imperialists.

By then, we already knew about the attack on the American fleet in a place they called Pearl Harbor. We heard the news over the Japanese-controlled radio station, and then we heard it confirmed from wireless reports that were passed over walls by maids and mistresses alike. Old Mr. Song, who usually spent his mornings in a teahouse exchanging gossip with his friends, leaned over the wall in his back garden like a servant boy and told us that the Americans who lived on the corner, Mr. and Mrs. Bradley, had been ordered not to leave their house. "The dwarf pirates pasted a sign on their gate," he said in a whisper that was louder than ordinary speech. "Then they left a guard with a rifle behind to stand watch. Next will be the barbed wire."

"Auntie," Yun-yun gasped. "How will they get food and fire-wood?"

She frowned. "Their maids of course."

"So?" Mr. Song jerked his head, frowning as though he thought women were incapable of carrying on a conversation without being prodded. "What have you heard?"

"They imposed a curfew. Did you know that?"

"Yes, yes, yes. What else?" He stuck his little finger in his ear and shook it.

I told him about the gunboats on the Huangpu and the Japanese takeover of the International Settlement and the French Concession in Shanghai.

"Yes, yes, yes, yes," he kept saying. "I knew it," he mumbled, kicking a basin filled with soaking clothes. "I knew it. We should have gone to Hong Kong or Manila."

Later that day we learned that Hong Kong and Singapore had also been bombed and that the Japanese had destroyed American ships in Manila Bay and American airplanes at an airfield north of Manila. The news just kept coming. The foreign section of Tientsin had been taken over, and the foreign concession at Chinwangtao.

By evening I couldn't think anymore. And I couldn't stop thinking. I went up to the roof and waited for darkness to deepen around me. A tomcat yeowled and yeowled, finally tapering off into silence. I stared at the receding black sky and the ever-increasing assortment of stars—miniscule dots of light in an immensity of darkness. I was afraid I'd never see Yu-ming again, never—not until one side or the other surrendered. And I couldn't imagine that our army would ever stop fighting for a free China or that Japan would ever voluntarily leave.

The word wobbled out to the stars and back again. *Never.* I shook my hands in front of my face. Weren't four-and-a-half years long enough? *Never.* A time span as incomprehensible as the constellations. And yet, wasn't I already losing Yu-ming? Hadn't I been losing him all year long? I slid down onto the cold tiles and leaned my back against a concrete pillar. After his mother's death, Yu-ming's letters had been ... well, cold. He never once accused me of anything. In fact, he insisted on thanking me for looking after his mother and providing her with a proper funeral. He would always be in my debt, he said, which made me feel more like a usurious banker than a wife. I didn't want gratitude, I wanted love. And gratitude for what? Letting her die? My thoughts stalled there and repeated themselves in an endless, wordless loop that was leading nowhere at all. A chill was seeping through my buttocks and up my spine, and still I sat there, doing nothing. *Nothing ... nowhere ... never.* Suddenly I slapped my hands on the tile and jumped up. Better to follow Scarlett O'Hara's example and put off thinking about it all until tomorrow.

*   *   *

After December eighth, everything was different. Our island wasn't ours anymore. Strangers patrolled our lanes. They set up barricades, plastered our walls with photographs of American warships burning and sinking while airplanes emblazoned with the rising sun tilted their wings and escaped untouched through the smoke. On corner after corner we saw the incontrovertible photographic evidence of their victories. And the victories kept on coming. On December ninth the Japanese struck Bangkok. On the tenth they conquered Guam, obliterated the American navy yard in Cavite, Philippines, and sank two British ships off the coast of Malaya. The following day their soldiers landed at Legaspi on the island of Luzon, and two days later they attacked the American navy base at Subic Bay.

Meanwhile, the Japanese assigned to Kulangsu devoted their efforts to ransacking pantries. They took bags of rice and flour—far more than they themselves could consume, presumably so they could sell the excess back to us at black market prices or send it on to Japan. When it was our turn, we stood watching helplessly as they confiscated our food and urinated on our carpet. Oh, for a heavy, sharp sword! I thought, my leg twitching to kick one of them between the legs and my tongue clamped down on oaths I longed to shout.

After they left, I went upstairs. Ah Mei was sitting on the floor, arranging beads and colored rocks from her box of treasures in a circle around her doll. Ah Chew had my old toy soldiers set up on his bed, one column marching down the middle while the opposing army waited in ambush on the pillows he'd placed on either side. "Wait until they're closer," he whispered to the men on horseback. "Get ready." As he moved the column into the trap, Ah Tou watched intently from the other side of the bed. "Attack!" Ah Chew shouted. "Kill! Kill!"

"Kill!" Ah Tou cried, clapping his hands.

Ah Chew couldn't move his cavalrymen fast enough and they tumbled off the pillows onto the enemy. Ah Tou grabbed some in each hand and bounced them forward, shouting his nineteen-month-old's version of "kill!"

I shook my head. How glorious those mock battles of my childhood games had seemed! The little foot soldiers, so brave, my mounted archers so skillful. And my generals. They were brilliant; their every move dictated by sound strategy, love of country, and loyalty to the true emperor. Now it was the Japanese pilots who felt the thrill of battle. It was they who, after dropping bombs on the American fleet, turned back and saw billowing smoke and flames, and shouted, not *kill*, but *banzai*.

Back in my bedroom, I pushed open the shutters, slamming them against the wall. They swung back, and I shoved them again and stomped out onto the balcony. Glorious? Not this war. It was petty and mean. It was loneliness and hunger and humiliation. I kicked the balusters and then hobbled back inside, slamming the doors behind me. Ah Chew was wasting his time playing chivalrous war games. Better to throw the toy soldiers out the window. When I returned to the nursery door, though, and saw him telling his baby brother how to set up the next battle, their faces fierce with childish concentration, I sighed and threw up my hands. Let them pretend. Let there at least be heroes and grand strategies played out on my child's bed.

Halfway down the stairs, I heard Mother and Ah Kwai discussing food. It made me want to scream. We were like nomads, our whole lives taken up with the search for food and the fear of starvation. As I hurried past Mother's door she was asking Ah Kwai about a crock she'd buried. "How much rice do you think it holds?"

"About ten *sheng*."

"And the canister under your bed?"

"Five *sheng*."

I shook my head. Here we were, the enemy's stench still fresh in our nostrils, and they were already deep into planning the practical details of our occupation. Well, good for them. As for me, I'd rather have a sword. I slashed the air over the kitchen table and kicked its leg. Ah Kwai had already mopped up the muddy Jap footprints and swept together the spilled grains of rice, undoubtedly saving every last one.

I grabbed my quilted jacket and went outside. Su-lee was in the courtyard squatting in front of a basin of dirty clothes, underpants and blouses breaking the water's surface between reflections of clouds, a bar of soap in her dry hands. "What will we do now, Young Mistress?" she asked. "Will we have to eat the carp?"

The carp? What was she thinking? It just showed how much we'd spoiled her that she would ask about them. No matter how much affection we had for the carp, especially the two big ones that were almost as old as she was, they were just fish. Had she forgotten how her parents had been forced to sell all their children during a famine? *Are you Chinese?* I wanted to shout. "No," I told her instead. "At least not yet."

Someday, though, we would have to eat them. Tears filled my eyes as I approached the pond. The fish were hidden under the lily pads and elephant ear. Little swords of sunlight flashed up from the water. I threw out a handful of food, and immediately the carps' gaping mouths broke the surface, bunching together like a bouquet of bubbles. Like so many things, these fish reminded me of my mother-in-law. Time after time, I'd stood beside her at this pond, each of us throwing out a handful of food. The last time was only days before she died. The sky was sunny, her bronchitis was gone, and I was filled with happiness. After weeks of worry and guilt, I felt as light as a soap bubble. Now, as the fish circled, waiting for more food, I wondered as I had so many times since she died whether my mother-in-law would have caught meningitis if she hadn't been weakened from the bronchitis.

"What will happen next?" I whispered, wishing she were there to answer. What would she say about General Tojo Hideki? Would he be more ruthless than his predecessor? I held a pinch of fish food over the pond. A mass of fish swished their tails and slid their scaled bodies over each other. I opened my fingers, and they went into a frenzy. "In the presence of a little dried meal," she would say if she were here, "they lose all dignity." As they continued to fight for food, I imagined what else she might say. "America and Britain are injured tigers now," she'd be sure to point out. "Only time will tell how hard they will fight and how much of their fighting will be to our benefit."

By now, the fish had finished their food and gone back to hiding under the lily pads. Only the orange one, grandmother to the rest, stayed on top. Now and then I caught sight of the familiar black spots on the long white back of her mate. Perhaps it was cool enough now to stop feeding them for the winter. I wondered what my mother-in-law would advise.

Pushing my shirtsleeve up to my shoulder, I reached into the water. I felt for the root of an elephant ear plant and carefully dislodged it. For some months, we'd been cooking and eating elephant ear tubers. Each time we pulled one up, another grew to take its place, sometimes two.

27

"*They've* arrested Old Kao."

Pei-lu was waiting in our sitting room. I stepped through the door and she jumped up. "Your old tutor's friend. The poet."

"I know who he is, but ...." It didn't make sense—although nothing should have surprised me by now. During two short weeks of occupation the Japanese and their lackeys had harangued and threatened us. They'd confiscated our food and shortwave radios. They'd shut down our newspaper and imposed a curfew. Now every time we passed a sentry, we had to bow and show our papers. Still, I couldn't imagine anyone wanting to arrest that gray-bearded old poet. "I don't understand," I said. "Who would want to arrest him?"

"The *Kempeitai.*"

"But why?"

Pei-lu let out an impatient puff of air. "He's an intellectual. These days, that's reason enough. The point is ..." She grabbed my hand. "Your old tutor is his friend. We should go to Teacher Wei's house and warn him."

I nodded.

"Bring a jacket. It's cold out."

I grabbed a faded blue jacket off the hook next to my red swing coat and put it on.

"Don't forget your papers."

I was already opening the small drawer in our medicine-and-herb chest where I kept my identity card. "Just a minute," I said. "I want to bring something for Teacher Wei and his mother." I ran to the pantry and put a few things in a basket.

"Let's hope we don't meet any Japanese along the way," Pei-lu said with a grim glance at the small bag of rice and jar of pickles in my basket.

I shrugged. We could only hope. These days, with the whole world at war and Kulangsu clamped in a Japanese vise, our ambitions had become laughable in their modesty. No more dreams of saving the nation. Today, if we were lucky, we'd be successful in warning Teacher Wei.

Outside the door, we stepped into a cloudy, gray-white world that didn't belong to us anymore. The lanes were unnaturally quiet. People walked on cats' paws, easing their doors open and closed. They spoke in hushed voices. Pei-lu and I tried to make small talk, but we kept stopping ourselves, weighing our words for the possibility that unfriendly ears might misinterpret them. Not that we ever talked about resistance or street theater anymore.

Nearing Teacher Wei's house, having abandoned any effort at conversation, we were listening to our own footsteps when a man's voice broke through the stillness. "This will be my chance to atone!" he said, his voice so emotional, so incautious that we stopped walking.

"It's Chang Ti," I whispered. "Maybe we should come back later."

Pei-lu shook her head. "We're already here."

"For my moderation," Chang Ti bellowed. "For my excessive lack of excess."

I knocked, softly then a little louder. It seemed that with Chang Ti it was always one storm or another. I was about to knock a third time when the door opened a crack.

"Ah? It's you," Teacher Wei's mother cried, throwing the door open, her face forming itself into a complex map of smile wrinkles. "Our favorite young miss. Madam," she said, nodding to Pei-lu. "Come in. Come in. Have you eaten? Jing-hai," she called, "your favorite girl student is here with her friend."

I set my basket on the table and stepped in front of it.

"What's this?" she demanded.

"Nothing, Auntie. Only a small bag of rice and some pickles."

"No, no. We can't accept it. Jing-hai," she called again to Teacher Wei, trying to raise her voice above the plaintive tones of Chang Ti's polemic.

"I'm put to shame by your valor," he was saying. "And now you want me to skitter away like a timorous little mouse." If he were a little more timorous, I thought, perhaps he would lower his voice.

"An Lee!" Teacher Wei exclaimed. "Miss Hung, welcome. Come in, come in."

"Look." His mother frowned, pointing a crooked finger at the basket I brought.

"An Lee, my dear, we can't accept food from you in these times of scarcity. You have your family to consider."

"It's nothing, teacher. A mere token."

"We'll talk about this later. Please come into the sitting room. I believe, An Lee, you're already acquainted with my guests." The two men were hazy figures in the glare of wintry sunlight and the cloud of cigarette smoke. Chang Ti spun around and offered us a perfunctory good morning. The man in the traditional blue gown turned and bowed. When he raised his head, I was surprised to see that it was Fan Ho-fu. He had grown a literati's goatee, but his eyes were unmistakable.

Teacher Wei introduced Pei-lu. And Fan Ho-fu, giving no hint that they were already acquainted, folded his hands and bowed again. "Perhaps," he said, "you ladies can help me convince my good friend here to come away with me."

Chang Ti frowned and crossed his arms. "Just leave me alone."

"But, Ti . . ."

"No. I won't turn tail. It's too late. A true patriot would have joined the resistance years ago."

I glanced out the window. Why didn't he keep his voice down?

Fan Ho-fu raised an eyebrow.

Only Teacher Wei, it seemed, had patience for this poet of the less-than-excessive excesses. "My young friend," he said gently. "What's right for one man may not suit another."

Chang Ti stamped his foot.

"Come," Teacher Wei said, "let's all sit down." He ushered Pei-lu and me to his armchairs while Fan Ho-fu brought more chairs in from the kitchen. Pei-lu and I looked at each other. This wasn't a good time to talk to Teacher Wei about Old Kao's arrest.

"I tell you, Ti," Fan Ho-fu said as he set one of the chairs down near his friend. "You're too sincere to be a secret agent. You have absolutely no ability to dissemble."

Chang Ti swung around. "Like you."

"Yes. Like me. Tell him, Miss Liu, how easy he is to read."

I sat back in my chair. If he was trying to get me off balance, he was going to be disappointed. "It's true," I said. "Chang Ti's talent lies more in the realm of sincerity and deep feelings than in that of cold-hearted deception."

Chang Ti lurched toward me, glaring. "Coldhearted? How could you call it that? Deception for the sake of China's survival is an act of love."

"I'm sure Miss Liu didn't mean to impugn anyone's character." Fan Ho-fu looked sideways at me as he picked up his pipe. "Or the warmth of his heart." He crossed his leg and lit two matches.

"And when the hell did you start smoking a pipe?" Chang Ti asked.

"Calm down." Teacher Wei took his young friend by the elbow and maneuvered him into a chair.

"You see." Fan Ho-fu held the matches to his pipe and sucked. "You don't even realize that the person wearing this gown would use a pipe." He winked at me. "A man in a cream-colored suit and hat, on the other hand, would prefer to use a cigarette holder. Especially if such a man were posing as one who dealt in, shall we say, harlots." He waved out the matches and dropped them in the bowl beside him.

As far as I was concerned, he didn't need to explain why he had been dressed like a pimp that night Pei-lu and I saw him and Cricket going into the Dancing Phoenix. It was clear that, in terms of both resistance and performance, the two of them had gone far beyond street theater. Especially so if, as I suspected, they were the ones responsible for the assassination of the collaborationist councilman at the Crane River Hotel on the afternoon of the typhoon.

Suddenly Fan Ho-fu jumped up. He settled his pipe on the pipe rest, swooped across the room, and snatched the tea tray away from old Mrs. Wei. "Auntie," he said, "this is too heavy for you."

My, I thought, how easily he changed both his clothes and his manners.

Chang Ti was another story. He could no more change his appearance than he could veer away from a train of thought. He was still glaring at his friend's back and clenching his fists. "You underestimate my talents," he said. "And my determination to give my life for China."

"Ti," Teacher Wei said. "No one questions your love for China."

"I only regret I wasn't there when they closed down our magazine."

Fan Ho-fu smirked. "It's a good thing you weren't. I doubt if you would have been able to keep a rein on your runaway emotions."

"You think so little of me." Chang Ti slapped his chest with the flat of his hand. "I'm not afraid to die."

"And what about torture?" Fan Ho-fu asked. "How much of that do you think you could withstand before you let slip the name of a friend or colleague?"

"Huh?" Chang Ti's face turned white. "I would never betray you."

"Not me, my friend. I'll be gone in a few hours. Never to be heard from again," he added with a touch of drama. "Now, enough of this talk. We're distressing the ladies with our raucous behavior."

"We're not so easily distressed," I said. "What's a little argument in the middle of all this desolation?" I spread my hands and shrugged, smiling with what I thought was a minimum of bitterness. "In fact, your debate is a welcome relief from the silence and dread outside."

"I'm glad you find us so entertaining," Chang Ti said.

"Sorry. I didn't mean …"

Pei-lu stood up. "We'd better go. We're interrupting your discussion."

Fan Ho-fu lowered his eyes. "On the contrary. We can only benefit from your gentle presence."

"No need to play the gentleman's part." I leaned forward, resting my hands on my knees. "You do have a safe means of escape, I hope."

He gave me a disgusted look.

Of course. I knew he'd have things all planned out. Still …

Pei-lu shifted her weight and looked at me. "May I make a few comments before we go?"

"Yes, of course." Teacher Wei and Fan Ho-fu nodded their assent while Chang Ti turned his back and looked out at the sea. It was so dull and flat today under the gray-white sky that until now I hadn't noticed the ship that floated on its surface. Only one ship today.

Pei-lu pushed her hair behind her ear. "It's universally accepted," she said, "that our country needs poets to inspire its soldiers and people. Within an occupied city, however, a poet's usefulness is severely limited."

Chang Ti never would have let her lecture him this way at one of our KCRL meetings. But here in Teacher Wei's house, where they were pretending not to know each other, he seemed to have no objection.

"If the poet isn't forced to write propaganda for the enemy," Pei-lu continued, "he might escape official notice by confining himself strictly to safe topics such as childhood reminiscences, cheap love stories of the mandarin duck and butterfly variety, or historical commentary. But with Mr. Chang's history, it is far more likely that he would be arrested." She took a step closer to Chang Ti. "I think, sir, you should take your friend's advice. It's clear that he and Teacher Wei love you."

Chang Ti's back shook with emotion, and when he turned around, tears were running freely down his cheeks.

Pei-lu backed away. "I'm sorry. It's getting late."

I wondered about all the details of their escape, how they would get past the sentries and checkpoints, where they would go now that nearly every place I could think of had fallen to the Japanese. They'd have to find their way into Free China.

"An Lee." Pei-lu waved a finger. "Shall we go?"

It didn't seem possible that one could simply decide to leave occupied territory and then do it. Even though Yu-ming was in Free China, it didn't seem real anymore. "Yes," I said, "we really should go."

Chang Ti stood at attention as we left the room, nodding and mumbling, good-bye, good-bye. Fan Ho-fu put his hands together and bowed. "It was a pleasure, ladies," he said without any winks or verbal flourishes.

On Teacher Wei's doorstep, finally I had a chance to warn him. "Be careful," I said. "We have news that Old Kao was arrested."

"Yes," he said. "I heard."

"So ..." I blinked back tears. "You promise, you'll be very, very careful?"

"Yes, An Lee. And you, too, both of you. Take care of yourselves and your families."

We assured him that we would.

As we walked away, our footsteps echoing behind us like distant kettledrums, I was aware of being back in the gray-white world of the occupation. "I think you convinced Chang Ti to leave," I whispered.

"He wanted to be convinced."

I smiled. Chang Ti with all his melodramatic ways could be so annoying, but I was going to miss him. "Well, it looks like this is definitely the end of the KCRL."

She shrugged. "It died a long time ago."

Maybe so, but until now, I could always imagine that someday we'd go back to it—after her husband's anger died down, or after Ah Tou and then Pei-lu's little girl were born. After her mother got well. After I recovered from my mother-in-law's death. Yet I must have known for a long time that the KCRL was dead. Now there was no denying it.

"Sorry," Pei-lu said as we zigzagged around a couple of boys. "I hope I didn't rush you back there. My alarm clock went off. She slowed for a second to open her jacket and show me the dark spots at the tips of her breasts. "I have to get back to my baby." Unlike most women in our circle, Pei-lu had chosen to nurse her own child. "I've got all this milk," she liked to tell anyone who thought she should have hired a wet nurse. "Why not use it?" It wasn't a popular thing to do, and yet, her example made me feel inadequate.

I hurried along beside her, thinking of my sweet Ah Tou and matching her step for step.

After we went our separate ways at a corner just past the public bathhouse, I slowed down and filled my lungs with great open-mouthed gulps of air. You'd think loss would make you lighter, but it was just the opposite.

1942

28

*C*hapter two of *Outlaws of the Marsh* had a single illustration: a full-page ink drawing. The boys, leaning in to get a better look, pressed their sweaty little bodies against me while across the room three slivers of sunlight slipped between the shutters adding three more beams of heat to the room's already unbearably hot temperature.

"Ball." Ah Tou fell on my lap so he could touch the picture of the ball. It was about to be kicked by "Kao the Ball," a scoundrel who would soon gain favor at court because of his soccer-playing prowess.

"The royal prince," Ah Chew said, pointing at the man in a Tang-style hat, his robe embroidered with an imperial dragon.

"Yes. Prince Tuan. Now you boys sit up. Mama has to blow her nose." I handed the book to Ah Chew and turned away to blow a large glob of yellow-green mucous into my handkerchief.

"The eunuchs." Ah Chew pointed to the other players in the royal soccer game. "One, two, three, four, five, six, seven eunuchs. You count them now." He poked his little brother.

Normally I would have swelled with pride at Ah Tou's lisping attempts to count. Today, though, I was too groggy and stuffed up to feel anything.

"Ball." Ah Tou kicked the air. "Kick, kick, kick, kick."

I folded my handkerchief and coughed into it. It was the heat and humidity that made me feel so miserable with this cold. I took the book back from Ah Chew. "The ball sailed past Prince Tuan and….'" I stopped and blinked my stinging eyes. I didn't want to read anything more about Kao the Ball—not about his stupidity or his undeserved advancement. Certainly not his nimble kick and twist. Not now at least, when I felt so heavy and slow.

Ah Chew tapped my arm. Ah Tou flopped onto my lap.

"No," I said, struggling to free myself from the tangle of their arms and legs and the weight of their moist bodies. I felt like I was drowning, my limbs tangled in seaweed, flabby, amorphous sea monsters weighing me down. "It's time for Ah Chew to write a letter to Papa."

"No!" He jumped up and glared at me. "I won't!" A Genghis Khan–like ferocity gleamed in his narrowed eyes.

"It's your duty as a son."

He lowered his eyebrows even further. Suddenly he turned, stomped to his little table, and sat down.

"You think life is nothing but stories?" I asked, pushing my advantage. "Do you think all you have to do is open your mouth like a helpless infant and suck up the tales I read to you?" I recognized the petulance in my voice, but still I kept on. "You're not a baby anymore." My temples were pounding. "Any son of Han Yu-ming, grandson of Han Gang, should be able to write a simple letter by the time he's four years old." Why did he always resist? He understood these stories, memorized whole sections of them. He never objected when I sat him down to practice reading. Why should he always get so belligerent when I tried to get him to write?

I pulled out Ah Mei's little chair and sat down across from him. "Okay," I said, writing *Dear Father* in large characters for him to copy. "Okay. What do you want to say?" I dabbed my nose while he stared, straight-backed and tight-lipped, at a spot two inches above the paper. "Ah Chew!" My anger was turning murky, a poor match for the compressed heat I sensed inside him. "Think of something."

"Ah Mei never has to write to Father."

"Ah Mei is sick." I opened my fan and cooled the air between us.

"Even when she doesn't have chickenpox, you don't make her."

"Just think of something or I will."

His chest heaved, and then suddenly it stopped. "Dear Father," he said finally, "we don't have any meat."

"You can't write that." I picked up my brush pen. "I'll have to choose the words then," I said.

"Mama. Wait. I want to tell Father . . ." He picked up his pen and gazed thoughtfully at the ceiling. "I want to say . . . I like my soccer ball."

As soon as Ah Chew finished his scrawling, off-kilter attempt to copy my sample letter, I took the book upstairs to read to Ah Mei.

"I have to scratch," she cried the moment she saw me. "Mama, Mama. It itches too much. I have to scratch."

"Don't scratch. You'll make ugly pockmarks if you do."

"Ugly, ugly." She picked up a hand mirror from the side table, looked at her reflection, and burst into tears.

"Give me that. Don't worry, sweetheart. You're still beautiful. It won't be long before all the spots are gone. Your skin will be as smooth as ... the petals of a mountain camellia."

The flicker of a smile. Then she moaned again, rolling and writhing from one end of the bed to the other as she clawed the air over her blisters.

"Don't scratch. I'll call Su-lee and you can have another cold starch bath."

Two days later, spots appeared on Ah Chew's chest and then on Ah Tou's.

It was June, six months into the occupation of Kulangsu and the hottest June anyone could remember. It wasn't just that we were already miserable under the enemy's evil hand, plagued with inflation and hoarding, unemployment, fear, and hunger. No, the air was fiery hot. We waited for evening, hoping the heat would disperse. But it seemed caught between the mountains—between Tiger Head Mountain and Dragon Head Mountain, between the Great Southern Warrior and the Po P'ing Range, trapped under some invisible heavenly roof, demon-sent and foul with the stink of rot and disease. Most nights the electricity was cut, the ceiling fans over our beds still and silent. Thankfully, the children were able to ignore the heat and their itching chickenpox long enough to fall asleep—even if they did wake up halfway through the night. But I wasn't a child anymore, and the heat often kept me awake.

On those long, sleepless nights, I would sit at my desk fanning myself and writing to Yu-ming. The rituals of writing comforted me—wetting my brush, flicking water onto the grinding stone, circling my ink stick round and round. From experience, even by the light of a candle, I could tell when the ink was thick and black enough. Then I'd dip my brush in, wipe it against the stone, and pause for a moment, my brush perpendicular to the table, before writing the same greeting I'd been writing for more than four years: *Dearest Yu-ming*. It was becoming harder and harder to think of anything to write after that. I'd already told him about Ah Mei's chickenpox, but I hadn't mentioned that Ah Chew and then Ah Tou also caught it. They didn't have cholera or scarlet fever or meningitis, but still, their chickenpox was just one more piece of dismal news. Being the bearer of bad news might make Yu-ming stop loving me. If he still did.

No, a thousand times no. I couldn't think that way. He still wrote, didn't he? He still asked how I was, how the children and Mother were—which, on the other hand, only brought to mind that other question he always used to ask? *How is Mother?* His first question, always the first. If only he'd been here and seen how impossibly fast her illness progressed. ... If we could have mourned together, his head on my lap, my tears falling on his neck, maybe then I could be sure he loved me.

I circled my ink stick over the stone until the ink was black as the darkest hell. And still my mind was a blank. Finally I put the brush pen down and blew out the candle. When he left, I was young, a tender flower. Now I was twenty-six years old, nearing thirty. For four years he hadn't seen me in the daylight. When he did, I wondered, what would he think? I started to climb into bed and changed my mind. Perhaps there would be a breath of air on the roof.

When we were courting, we sometimes held hands on the roof. I wondered if he remembered. The first time he took my hand, the moon was as thin as a lady's plucked eyebrow, almost the same as it was now, except tonight it was lower, a fishhook hanging over the sea. I walked to the edge of the roof and gazed at its silvery reflection. I thought about the dress I had made for Yu-ming's homecoming four years ago—the powder pink silk brocade with a design of white chrysanthemums. Someday, when the war was ended, I would wear it to a party.

The tiles under my bare feet were still warm, but the thought of silk against my skin made me feel cooler. Now that my cold was almost gone, it was hard to believe I could have let something as insignificant as a cold cause me to lose my temper with Ah Chew. I remembered the last thing Yu-ming told me before I walked him to the ferry four years ago. Take good care of our children and our mothers and the maids.

"I'm so sorry," I whispered. I stood there awhile, feeling the hollowness of sorrow and regret. Then I went inside. I still had the rest of them to care for. And I was determined to do my best.

And yet, despite my sincere desire, before twenty-four hours had passed, I'd gone back on my rooftop resolution.

It was my zeal for the children's welfare. That was how I'd like to explain it—that my mind was so caught up in worrying about their health that I couldn't pay attention to anything else. And it was true. I hated seeing them confined to bed, their sweet faces disfigured by spots and scabs. Ah Mei alternated between trying to get up and run around and hiding because of her "ugliness." Ah Chew was frantic to scratch, always jumping wild-eyed from his bed and dancing frenzied circles around the room. And poor Ah Tou, he just lay in his crib, weak from fever. I was worried for them all. Under our present conditions, even an ordinary childhood disease like chickenpox could be dangerous. Disease and death were everywhere. Only a week earlier Mrs. Ma's grandson died from scarlet fever. Worst of all, my friend Ling lost her beautiful little daughter during an outbreak of typhoid. I had good reason to worry. It was no excuse, though, for the things I said in the kitchen that day.

I was sitting at the kitchen table, fanning myself and drinking tea. Ah Kwai was scrubbing a large white radish, and Su-lee was at the other end of the room, cleaning hulls and pebbles out of the uncooked rice. "How can we expect the children to be healthy," I grumbled, "when they don't have enough nourishment? And where is Su-lee's goatherd? We haven't seen him in more than two weeks. Maybe he gets paid more elsewhere."

"Young Mistress!"

"He must be sick," Su-lee said. "Or…." She turned away and stared into the pot.

She might as well marry her goatherd, I thought. She hadn't been any safer here since the invasion than she would have been with him. I blew on my tea. Unfortunately, goat milk wasn't our only problem. The Japanese had taken most of our good rice and we'd eaten the rest of it. Now all we could buy was broken, moldering rice mixed with rubbish. "If only we had some meat for the children," I muttered. "That's what they really need to regain their strength. There must be some meat out there somewhere." I turned to Ah Kwai. "Are you sure you've tried everything?" Until then, I'd never questioned her about the shopping. Ah Kwai was brave and smart, and she was loyal to the marrow of her bones. But at that moment, my reason was overcome by passion. I glared at her and crossed my arms. "Surely," I huffed, "if you truly made an effort, you could find something."

She lowered her eyes. "Yes, Young Mistress."

The following morning, Ah Kwai was gone. She went to the market, Su-lee said. By noon, when she still wasn't back, I knew what had happened. She'd gone looking for meat. I should have known she would.

It was the hottest part of a blazing hot day when I set out to look for her. Her nephew, Yun-yun, insisted on coming along. At first, since most people were inside resting, we couldn't find anyone we could ask about her. Finally, an old woman fanning a baby in a doorway said she saw her but it had been early in the morning. At the bund, a man playing chess under a tree told us he saw her when he was setting up his board. She was hurrying along Lingtow Jetty. After he finished putting his pieces in place, he looked up again and saw her bow to the Japanese guard and board the ferry to Amoy.

Not long after the December eighth takeover of Kulangsu, the regular ferry to Amoy had been put back in service. Yun-yun and I bowed, showed our identification, and walked on board. I wasn't sure what to do once we got to Amoy. It was a large city, most of its inhabitants, strangers. To them, Ah Kwai would look the same as every other kitchen amah. Keeping our eyes open and looking for any small clue that might lead to her, we headed for the nearest market. As we peered into the alcoves and alleys, shadowy figures whispered of blackmarket rice for sale. No one seemed to have any meat, though, and with the passing hours, my fear and remorse grew. Ah Kwai had suckled me at her breast. If anything happened to her, it would be my fault. Again. I rushed from one place to the next, but it was like searching for a needle at the bottom of the sea. We stopped to catch our breath in front of the Hong Kong and Shanghai Bank, now referred to as an "enemy property," its tall, proud Sikh guards replaced by Japanese military police. She must have gone farther than Amoy City. But where?

"We have to start home," I told Yun-yun. "Otherwise we won't make it before curfew."

He sank to the ground, tears rolling like beans down his cheeks. Since the day he arrived at our gate, Yun-yun hadn't heard a word from his parents. Even if they were still alive, it was unlikely he would ever see them again. Without Ah Kwai, he would be alone in the world. "Come on," I said, pulling him up. "Maybe she's already home."

We hurried down Zhong Shan Lu to the ferry landing and crossed the harbor. As we started up Kulangsu's main street, merchants were already rolling their heavy metal shutters down. A group of men jostled past us, laughing and talking. One of them turned around to tell a joke and walked backward into some men, lost in their grief as they carried a coffin out of the coffin shop. It was the Widow Ng's five sons, and by the mournful slope of their shoulders, I guessed that the coffin was meant for their mother.

* * *

It must have been more than an hour later when I finally heard the gate. I ran down the stairs and into the kitchen.

Oh, happy sight: Ah Kwai with a smudge of dirt on her forehead and a withered celery stalk sticking out of her rattan bag. "Sorry, sorry, sorry." The words burst from her mouth like rice porridge from an overflowing pot. "I'm so late. Sorry, Young Mistress." She bowed her head with each "sorry," but her sweat-streaked face looked more proud than contrite. She dropped her bag by the sink and pulled out a stool. "Don't look." She wagged her finger at Yun-yun, lifted one foot, and pulled her loose pant leg above her knee. "I said don't look." She affected a frown for Yun-yun's sake. Then, laughing, she raised her pant leg up to her hip.

A large bundle was strapped around her thigh. Quickly she unwound a length of twine. Something wrapped in waxed paper remained stuck to her leg. She tore it off, and as she held it up for us to see, blood dripped from its corner.

"Meat," Yun-yun cried.

"Pork," Ah Kwai said. "I bought it in a village on the mainland. Just look at this." She took off the waxed paper and peeled back a bloody layer of cotton cloth. "I wrapped it in three layers of cotton and covered it in paper, and still the blood dripped down my legs. She laughed. "It looked like I was having my monthly flow." She held up her hand and looked at Yun-yun. "Not for your ears."

It was a large piece of pork back, and she had one of equal size tied to the other leg.

"Oh, Ah Kwai!" I said. "What if you'd been caught by the Japanese?" I should have said more—thanked her and told her never to risk her life that way again. But I was too tired and relieved to think straight. "Ah Chew is going to be so happy."

29

*E*very night for a week we had pork for dinner—pork dumplings, pork ball soup, spicy ground pork with tofu, stir-fried pork with pickled cabbage, pork with rice and pork with noodles. Who wouldn't be happy? Who wouldn't grow strong eating such food? And every afternoon, bathing the children, I watched the evidence of their illness fade away. The spots, which had grown into pimples and then blisters, soon became scabs. Then they dried up and vanished. One day I slid my hands over Ah Mei's wet back and found it absolutely clear. "Beautiful skin."

"Yes," she agreed, examining her arms, "I'm beautiful again."

Ah Chew dropped his towel and twirled so I could see his naked glory. And Ah Tou, leaning over to examine himself, put his finger in his belly button, smiled foolishly and announced that he, too, was beautiful.

"Tomorrow afternoon as soon as it's cool enough," I told them, "we'll go for a walk in the Bird Garden."

* * *

After six months of occupation, we'd learned how to get by as best we could. We still worried and cried and raged. But we also played with our children and met with our friends.

Our next game of mahjong was at the Hungs' house. For years, their house had been a meeting place for our leading citizens—Chinese and Europeans, merchants and government officials, all of them intent on speaking with the president of the Chamber of Commerce. After Hung Li-son's assassination, though, his widow's house became uncomfortably quiet. Walking in the door, each time I half-expected the house to look the way it did before. Then I'd remember that the lucky jade plant was missing all its branches on one side, and the black lacquer screen with its mother-of-pearl peacocks, coral plum blossoms, and jade willows was nowhere to be seen—probably sent back to Japan to grace the sitting room of some Japanese officer.

The reception room was dark now, almost austere. The drapes had been patched and one of the sofa cushions was missing, but the white doilies were still on the arms and backs of the chairs, each one carefully placed and sparkling clean.

Ling hadn't joined us since her daughter's death, but we were expecting her today.

"Don't worry," Chi-chi said when she saw me glance at the empty chair. "She promised she'd come." Reaching in her handbag, she pulled out a package of cigarettes, tapped up a couple of sticks, and offered them to Pei-lu and me. "You two. Come on. When are you going to start?"

"When I decide to," I said.

She laughed. "Sounds like you, An Lee." She shook the pack in front of Pei-lu, one more time. Then she took one herself and lit it.

"Oh well," she said, clicking her lighter shut. "Ling will smoke with me."

I scooped up a handful of peanuts and watched the smoke escape from her ruby red lips—the same red as her nails and the lacquer finish on her lighter.

"You painted your fingernails," Chi-chi said.

I ran my thumb along the chipped edges.

"You need more than one coat. It lasts better that way."

Pei-lu looked at her watch. Last time Ling promised to come, she had a crying spell and backed out.

I bit my fingernail and spit out the flecks of polish. I did hope she'd come, and at the same time, I was afraid to see her. I bit another nail. It was so quiet without the tiles clicking. If she didn't hurry, before long we'd be discussing the battles on Guadalcanal or the Japanese push to control the railway corridor from Shanghai to Thailand. We might as well, I thought in an irrational rush of pique. If we were going to be reminded of Ling and her dead little girl, why not discuss all the rest of it? The skyrocketing price of rice and the latest outbreaks of smallpox and cholera. I squeezed my hands together until my fingertips were bright red. Before long we'd be talking about all the men we knew who were dead or missing in action.

"Why don't you let me do your nails with my new polish," Chi-chi said quickly. "I can paint them before you go so you can let them dry on the way home." She leaned down and took a bottle out of her handbag. "Do you like it? It's called *ruby glow*."

"While we're waiting," Pei-lu said, "we could compose a group poem."

Chi-chi rolled her eyes.

"Or I could read one of Lin Yutang's essays."

"Go ahead," Chi-chi agreed. "Choose a humorous one, though. In Chinese."

The essay Pei-lu chose had a promising title: "Half-naked in a Room of my Own." Her voice rose and fell with the description of the great author's dusty, book-lined room. A Buddhist oil lantern hung over his couch. Bamboo swayed outside his window. Suddenly Pei-lu stopped reading.

Ling had entered the room on cat's paws, hesitating halfway. I almost didn't recognize her. Her hair hung limp and dull against her pale, thin face. She tottered forward, her ankles looking too fragile to hold her up. "Sounds like something by Lin Yutang," she said, holding the back of a chair to steady herself.

She sat down, and immediately we started stirring the tiles. For a while, each time I glanced at Ling, she would look up and attempt a smile. Eventually she stopped looking up. Concentrating on the game, I thought, until I noticed how flushed her cheeks had become.

"I have an extra fan," I said, taking a carved sandalwood fan out of my bag.

She accepted it and fanned herself a few times. Then she seemed to forget, and her cheeks grew even brighter. We'd only finished one game when she sat back in her chair and hid her face in her hands. "I can't do it," she sobbed. "I have to go."

"Come on, Ling," Chi-chi said. "Just one more game."

"I should go, too," I said.

Chi-chi opened her mouth to object, but Pei-lu cut her off. "That's fine. We can play again later. Chi-chi," she added quickly, "I wonder if, since An Lee has to go, you could paint my nails instead."

"Sure. In fact, while your nails are drying, we could try to do something about your hair. Or maybe your makeup."

"Just the fingernails," Pei-lu said.

Ling and I walked in silence for a while. It was a strange sensation. She'd always been so chatty. "I'm glad you came," I said finally. We turned onto a shaded street of three-story houses with tall trees overhanging the walls. The blossoms from a large frangipani lay scattered across the lane and in the gutter—a day's worth of fallen flowers, some already half-brown, others still fresh.

"I couldn't concentrate anymore," she said.

"You did fine." She'd lost every game, but then, Ling was never the best mahjong player. We walked over the frangipani flowers, our feet indiscriminately crushing wilted and fresh ones alike.

We walked another block before Ling spoke again. "That's not what I meant," she said, her voice starting to choke up. "I mean it takes so much concentration . . . not to cry." Just saying the word sent tears down her cheeks. "I'm so tired," she said.

I looked at the gates and windows and shops on either side. The door of the Ngs' noodle shop was locked. "They must have run out of flour again," I said.

"That's not it."

I handed her a clean handkerchief and she blew her nose.

"They're in mourning."

Poor Ling? She must have lost track of time. It had been months since their mother died.

"The second son," she mumbled dully. "Two days ago."

She must be wrong. The Ng brothers were the strongest men I knew. They'd always been there, in the same noodle shop, stretching and cutting those great long strips of heavy, wet dough. She had to be wrong. But there it was, a white mourning ribbon newly nailed to the doorpost.

We stopped by the tobacco and paper store so Ling could pick up some cigarettes.

Everyone smoked, it seemed—Chinese and Japanese, soldiers and coolies, sophisticated men and modern young ladies. A harmless pleasure in the present scheme of things. She bought a package of Lucky Strikes and we left.

"Wait," I said. "I'll be right back." I walked quickly back to the counter, impatient for the customer ahead of me to finish his transaction. "A package of Lucky Strikes and a box of matches," I said when it was my turn.

Outside, I noticed the smell of burning tobacco everywhere. Smoke curled up from pipes. It drifted out from windows and seeped through doors, its smell as familiar as the sea, as ordinary as urine and mold and decay—common beyond noting.

The lure of the cigarettes snuggled against my ribs had already spread into my chest and belly. *Don't even think,* they said. *Step into my satin boat, lie back, and let my silken threads pull you into the current. Relax and float with me.*

Ah Kwai had dinner ready. Afterward, I went in to wish my mother a good night. I still pretended I didn't know that she smoked, but the smell of cigarettes permeated her room. She was in her favorite chair, her head bent over a pair of goldfish she was embroidering on the yoke of a dress for Ah Mei. She asked about the mahjong party and my friends. Then, as I was leaving, she looked up from her needlework. "Ah Chew was unusually quiet today," she said. "Maybe he's getting sick. Would you check on him, dear?"

"Certainly, Mother." She needn't have asked. I always checked the children before I went to bed.

As I expected, Ah Chew was just fine. He was perspiring from the heat, but no more so than the others. I brushed the strings of damp hair off his face and waved my fan over him. Ah Chew was her favorite. She probably wouldn't have noticed if Ah Mei or Ah Tou had had a quiet day. I fanned them, too. Then I folded my fan and slid it into my purse beside the cigarettes.

In my room, I didn't bother to light a lamp. I went straight to my dressing table, sat down, and opened my purse. Tearing open the package, I dug my fingernails between cigarettes, pulled one out, and lit it. Even before it touched my lips, I felt better. Even before the singed, airy remnants of tobacco reached my lungs, I felt the pleasurable release of desire satisfied.

I lit a candle. Then, leaning on my dressing table, I blew a tiny cloud of smoke at my reflection. I inhaled and my cheeks hollowed. The cigarette tip turned a glowing red. I exhaled, this time more slowly, the smoke escaping through the small opening in my puckered lips. Too pale, I thought, so I balanced the cigarette on a saucer and reached for a tube of red lipstick. Stretching my lips tight, I traced their outline and filled in the rest. Then, I picked up the cigarette and let my lips relax into the full roundness of a carp's mouth, the plump softness of a ripe tomato. Each time I inhaled, my eyebrows lifted like flyaway wings and the fiery glow moved closer to my fingers.

Fire. It was my element. Combined with dragon, it was the most powerful birth sign, a combination that happened only once in sixty years. I puffed my fire stick red to remind myself that the year of my birth, nineteen sixteen, the year of the Fire Dragon, conferred enough strength to survive our current trials, even without Yu-ming here beside me. The fire was only centimeters from my fingers now.

I stubbed it out in the saucer and sat watching the smoke trail off. My eyes, looking back at me from the mirror, were blacker than twice-ground ink, grave beyond all accounting. I jumped up and lit the gas lamp. Then, blowing out the candle, I sat back down at my dressing table. What a meager collection of jars and bottles I had! Lipstick, perfume, face cream, rouge, nail polish—one of each, and most barely used. I skimmed their cool hard surfaces with my fingers, ending with the nail polish. I shook it and applied a coat. Then I blew on my nails and waved them in the air. So slow to dry. No wonder I seldom painted my fingernails. I liked the red color, though, and the shine.

When I was sure they were dry, I lit another cigarette and stepped out onto the balcony. Scattered squares of yellow light shone in our neighbors' windows. Someone appeared at one of them, paused, and went away. Before the occupation, on a clear hot night like this, people would have been out in the lanes enjoying themselves. Now, they stayed indoors. I finished my cigarette and waited in the shadows, listening for the sounds of Japanese boots on the paving stones. When the curfew patrol had come and gone, I went inside and got ready for bed.

Yun-yun had been the latest one to run afoul of a Japanese patrol. I don't know how he could have neglected to put down the bag of rice he was carrying and bow to them. If he was afraid of losing the rice, that was exactly what his negligence resulted in, that and a swollen cheek and eight hours in jail.

I climbed into bed and forced my eyes shut. My stomach growled and my leg twitched. My heart beat heavily against my eardrums. I tried to relax, but it was no use. I got up and went into the bathroom. Leaning against the wall, I tried not to think about the long list of deadly diseases the Widow Ng's second son could have caught or the ways he could have been killed. Instead, I examined my imperfectly painted nails. He was only one of some tens of thousands of residents of Kulangsu, neither a relative nor a close friend. I had no reason to dwell on his death.

I felt for the pack of Lucky Strikes I'd brought with me, tapped out a cigarette, and struck a match on the grout. I watched the flame for a while. Then, blowing it out, I sat down on the floor and cried. I cried for the noodle maker, and for my mother-in-law and Ling's little girl, sobbing out loud until I almost choked. It shouldn't be like this. I shouldn't be alone. I hugged my knees, blubbering as hot tears dropped on my feet and mucous streamed from my nose and slid down my legs. I was too young to be alone, untouched by my husband. Another wave of sobs shook me, and I struggled to breathe. Too young.

Curling up like a baby, I cried and cried—for myself and my loneliness, my ruined life, my virtual widowhood. Wrapped in a shroud of sorrow, I couldn't stop.

Finally, when my tears were exhausted, I wiped my eyes on my nightgown, lit another match, and looked around me—at the package of cigarettes, the water pitcher, the towel, the worn bristles of my toothbrush. How self-indulgent I was! How unrealistic! No one could say how long this war would last, but one thing was certain. In war, only the strong survive. I stood up and pushed the bathroom door open. All right, I told myself. No sense wishing for another life. It was my fate to live in a time of war, and I bloody well was going to be one of the survivors.

30

*T*he process of strengthening one's will is a cold, narrow thing. It cuts you off from dreams and intuition, maybe even from luck—in short, from everything I needed in those days before Ah Tou got sick. I didn't have any dreams to warn me, no sense of foreboding. It was as if I had no connection to my own son, my little Ah Tou, the one I loved most of all.

It began with a fever—not so high at first, no worse than Ah Chew's. Just another cold. When it went higher, I reminded myself that they'd all had fevers before and recovered. I brought him some aspirin and a glass of juice. I lifted him to a sitting position and held the glass to his lips. "Hurt," he said, clutching his throat and turning away.

"Try a little, sweetheart," I urged. "Just a sip or two." If Ah Chew or Ah Mei had resisted me that way, I probably would have scolded, but Ah Tou was more delicate. It wasn't his fault he felt pain more intensely. I fanned him for a while, and then I called down to Su-lee to help me move his crib into my bedroom so the others wouldn't catch what he had.

Two days later he started vomiting, which meant that he needed his fluids more than ever. Still he didn't want to drink. I may have pushed too hard, and maybe my face betrayed my exasperation, but I never shouted at him. His throat didn't look that bad—a little grayish, but not the least bit red. Of course, I had no idea what to look for, and without forcibly pulling out his tongue, I had no way of getting a good look at his throat.

That wasn't the point, though—not that he wouldn't open his mouth and say "ah," not that I didn't know gray was worse than red.

The point was, I should have known how sick he was. If I hadn't been trying so hard to be strong, every cell in my body would have screamed with knowledge.

It was Mother who finally sent Su-lee for the doctor. An hour or two later, I came to the same conclusion and went looking for Su-lee. "Didn't you know?" Ah Kwai gave me a puzzled look. "The Old Mistress sent her to fetch the doctor."

I ran back upstairs, suddenly afraid of leaving Ah Tou alone. I rubbed the back of his neck, and he closed his eyes and, despite his cough and his labored breathing, seemed to fall asleep. The hours dragged on.

Finally Dr. Kao came. He wiped Ah Tou's face with a crumpled handkerchief and leaned over his bed. It was the same posture he'd assumed a year and a half earlier in the room down the hall. His hands moved from Ah Tou's forehead to the pulse point at the side of his neck. "How's our young patient?"

Ah Tou's mouth opened in alarm. His eyes shone like an animal in a trap.

Dr. Kao clicked on a small light. "Say 'ah,'" he said as he depressed Ah Tou's tongue with a flat stick. He leaned close, almost touching Ah Tou's cheek with his nose. Then he clicked his light off and straightened up.

"He has diphtheria," he said. He opened his bag and took out a syringe. He laid the bedsheet aside and pulled down Ah Tou's pants. "Luckily, I still have some penicillin. I don't have the antitoxin, though." Ah Tou didn't notice the needle prick, but as soon as Dr. Kao pressed the plunger, his body jerked, and he struggled to get away, letting out a twisted, muffled scream that was all the more heart-wrenching for having to force its way between the swollen walls of his throat.

"Penicillin is in short supply," Dr. Kao said as he wiped the needle with alcohol. "We have the Overseas Chinese War Relief Committee in Manila to thank for this particular shipment." He wrapped the needle and put it away. "It's not enough, though. It never is." He turned to go. "I'll be back tomorrow afternoon."

"But, doctor. Is he going to be all right?"

"We'll see."

* * *

245

"He only said, 'We'll see,'" I complained to Mother that evening.

"He spoke in haste. Dr. Kao must be tired these days. By the look of him, he doesn't get enough to eat. The same as you." She squeezed some lime on a slice of papaya and held the plate up. The flesh under her arm jiggled.

"Tired or not, why would he make such a vague comment?"

She looked at me and then at the papaya. Her gaze was maddeningly serene. Her forehead didn't have a single wrinkle. "Perhaps modern doctors are taught not to make promises." She put the plate down and scooped out a spoonful of orange papaya flesh. "You shouldn't worry. Penicillin is a miracle drug. Besides, you said he was doing better. You said he drank some tea and ate some rice gruel."

"Only a few small bites."

"With heaven's blessing, it will be a few more tomorrow."

"But, Mother, he's still burning up. And what's this antitoxin Dr. Kao doesn't have?" Suddenly, outside, a low rumble reverberated in the night—the distinctive sound of a Japanese soldier clearing his throat. Two sets of boots clicked on the cobblestones as the curfew guards passed by.

"In the morning," Mother said, "I'll tell Su-lee and Yun-yun to carry his crib down to the sitting room. It's cooler downstairs."

"No. Let's do it now. I can sleep on the sofa."

During the night, when I wasn't pacing, I sat in the rocking chair and listened for his breath. By morning he was better. I fed him rice gruel while Mother stood at my elbow, praising and encouraging him, smoothing his hair. "Come on, dear," she urged. "Open for your ma."

I touched his lips with the spoon, and he started to open his mouth until he was distracted by Ah Mei padding down the stairs. "Mama, Mama." She was barefoot, her hair uncombed, Ah Chew close behind. "Ma. We couldn't find you. Where were you?"

"You're not supposed to be in here. Both of you, go back upstairs."

Ah Mei's eyes filled with tears.

"Go!"

She turned and fled, but Ah Chew stood firm. He glared at me, his eyebrows nearly covering his eyes. "I'm allowed. This is not your bedroom."

"It is now. Now you go upstairs and get dressed."

At midday it rained, a short but heavy downpour that briefly cooled the air and then turned to steam. I walked to the window, leaving Ah Tou for the moment with Su-lee. A puddle was all that remained, its shiny surface framed by a dull, scalloped dampness. In the center was a reflected miniature of our porch—its white pillars, its fuchsia bougainvillea, the arm of a rattan chair. All at once, the puddle flared with the white-hot light of the sun and the miniature was gone. Why had heaven chosen to torture us with this scorching hot weather, this year of all years, when we were already suffering from enemy occupation?

"Ma'am!" Su-lee had propped Ah Tou up on some pillows so she could give him sips from a glass of warm tea mixed with water. "Ma'am, look at this!" She held up a white handkerchief with a reddish glob in the center. "From his nose."

I ran over and took it from her. Quickly folding the bloody mucous inside, I wiped his nostril. "It's all right, baby. It's all right."

"Ma, what . . ."

"It's nothing, sweetheart." The fear in his eyes was terrifying—ancient and knowing. "Well, look at this," I said in a sunny voice. "What a good boy! You drank so much tea for Su-lee. Let's put it aside now and you can take your nap."

As soon as he'd closed his eyes, I grabbed Su-lee's hand and pulled her into the kitchen. "Where's Dr. Kao?" I whispered. "He should be here by now."

"I don't know, ma'am. Do you want me to get him?"

"Tell him Ah Tou is worse. He needs another injection."

Waiting, always waiting. The ceiling fan groaned in slow, unending circles, and all around me in the hills and valleys of the room, mosquitoes played their guerilla games, hiding and attacking, buzzing, buzzing. Mother and Ah Kwai came in and out—Ah Kwai on her silent servant's feet, Mother jostling my nerves with her prayer beads and her cane and the flat pounding of her legs on their tiny feet.

Somehow, Ah Tou managed an uneasy sleep until a new burst of rain woke him, gasping and coughing. I picked him up and took him to the window where he could look out. But the rain frightened him. It was loud and dazzling, ten thousand swords aimed at the earth. Turning away, I caught a glimpse of Ah Kwai running through the rain to open the gate for someone. It was the goatherd, without his goats. He hadn't been around for months. If Ah Tou hadn't been sick, I would have thought to be pleased for Su-lee; I would have told Ah Kwai to invite him in. As it was, he simply went away.

My ears roared with the sound of the rain—a single, sustained note, refusing to change and move on, and at the same time a million rushing notes measuring the moments, too fast, too fast. The rain rhythms must be disrupting my perception of time, I thought. Otherwise Ah Tou's heartbeat wouldn't seem so fast. It wouldn't seem that Su-lee had been gone so long.

The gate creaked and then clanged, cutting through the haze of sound. At last they were back. I hurried to the door and opened it. Su-lee climbed the stairs, dripping. "I'm sorry, Young Mistress," she said.

"Where is he?"

"I went to the clinic, the way you told me to, and …"

"Where is Dr. Kao?"

"He wasn't there, ma'am, so I went to the hospital."

"Why isn't he with you?"

"They wouldn't let me see him. They told me to wait."

I was ready to explode. What a stupid rice bucket! But with Ah Tou shaking in my arms, I had to hold my tongue.

"I asked them many times, Young Mistress. Finally they told me to go home. They said he couldn't see any more patients today."

What a fool I was! I shouldn't have sent Su-lee. "They won't dare keep me out."

Ah Kwai stepped in front of me. "No, Young Mistress. You stay with second young master. I'll get the doctor."

Hours later, when Ah Kwai returned, she couldn't look me in the face and her tongue was thick with apologies and excuses. "I tried everything, Young Mistress. I explained how sick he was."

I wanted to scream. "You should have said he was getting worse."

"I did. I thought the man behind the desk was listening. He was so polite at first. He asked me questions and wrote down the family name—slowly since he had two fingers missing on his right hand. When he finished, he told me to sit down. I refused, of course. I said it was too important. An emergency. He sighed unpleasantly. They had many emergencies every day, he said, especially today. I told him Dr. Kao was our family doctor, and we were expecting him at our house this afternoon. That's when the man started raising his voice.

"'Please,' he said. 'Wait over there.' Still, I didn't back down. I was careful not to shout, but I told him plainly that our little Ah Tou had diphtheria and it couldn't wait. He put his pencil down and glared at me. Then he started naming off all the diseases and injuries he could think of. The large purplish scar on his cheek became horrible as he spoke. 'Do you think the patients with smallpox can wait?' he asked through his teeth. 'And what about those with dysentery, typhoid, and malaria?' He didn't pause for an answer, just kept telling me about patients, as though it were my fault that an old woman and her grandson came in with burns over half their bodies or that a man had his gold coin stolen and his ear nearly cut from his head by one of the dwarf pirates. What could I do about any of that? And, ma'am, he even told me about a twelve-year-old girl who was violated and whose private parts needed to be repaired in an operation. He was too angry by then to remember he was a man speaking to a woman. That's when I decided to sit down for a while. Let him cool off."

I clenched my fists and turned away.

"No one told me he left," she said, her voice breaking.

"What?"

"Dr. Kao. He went out another door and no one told me. I could have followed him to his house. And now it's too late."

"He's at his house?" I ran to Ah Tou's bed.

"It's too late, Young Mistress. The curfew."

I wrapped a quilt around him.

"No, Young Mistress. Wait. We'll go in the morning."

Then I swung him up onto my back. I wrapped the carrying cloth under his bottom, crossed it over my chest and around my shoulders, and tied it securely in front.

"The guards are everywhere. They'll arrest you."

I pushed past Ah Kwai. She tried to grab my elbow, but I spun away from her. "An Lee," Mother cried, "it's pouring down rain."

I flung the door open and ran out. We were no more than twenty paces from our gate, the rain pelting us, cruel on Ah Tou's feverish body, when I heard them. *"Tomare!"* They came out of nowhere, barring my way with their rifles. I stopped, but still they shoved me backward, spitting Japanese words in my face.

"Let me go," I pleaded. "My baby is dying." The urge to run was nearly irresistible, but I knew that if I did, they'd shoot me right through Ah Tou's back. "My baby," I said again, backing away. *"Akachan."* Wasn't that the word in Japanese?

Moonlight outlined their forms—monsters in the black and white of night, their steel helmets slick with rain, their teeth and armbands eerily white. One of them jammed his rifle against my chest, pushing me to the ground. Suddenly his grimace turned to a leer. He took one hand off his rifle and reached for his pants. Before he could fall on me, I rolled to the side and jumped up, only to be stopped by the second MP. "Go home!" he shouted in Chinese. He pushed my shoulder with the butt of his rifle and then, twirling it around, slashed my thigh with his bayonet. Stumbling, I backed away from him.

"*Bakayaro!*" his partner swore. I looked up to see his rifle trained on me just as I felt Ah Kwai's hands grabbing me under the arms and pulling me and Ah Tou through the gate and up the walk.

"No! Let me go!" I cried as she pulled me into the house. Ah Kwai and Yun-yun held me as Mother and Su-lee untied Ah Tou. Su-lee took him, and Ah Kwai pushed me down on the sofa. As she ripped open my pant leg, blood pulsed from my thigh. With it went all my strength and any hope of getting penicillin for Ah Tou. "I'm his mother," I said, marshaling just enough energy to get to my feet. "Give him to me."

"Not yet," Mother said.

Everything started to turn black, and quickly, to keep from passing out, I dropped my head between my knees. I couldn't faint, not now.

"Sit down, An Lee," Mother commanded. "We have to stop the bleeding. Ah Kwai, quickly, go get a bottle of brandy and a needle and thread to sew up her leg. Su-lee, dry the baby off. Children, you stay back. It's only a cut."

"Ma!" Ah Mei shouted from the doorway. "Look at your leg."

I glanced down and, seeing the blood and exposed flesh, I felt a wave of nausea. I had to keep control of myself. I had to be strong so I could keep Ah Tou alive until morning.

The rain that night was intense. No wind to speak of, and yet afterward, I remembered feeling the presence of a great wet wind, powerful as a typhoon, deafening in its fury. It stays with me, in the hair roots of my memory, a wind exploding against the walls of our house, trying to get in. Mother insisted I was in shock—whatever that meant. Certainly, I was shaking for a while. But didn't the brandy take care of that? Ah Kwai maintained that I was outside my body. That's how she explained my not flinching when she sewed up my thigh.

She said if my spirit had been present, I wouldn't have been able to stand the pain when she stitched together the deeper layers of flesh. Later she apologized, explaining that if she'd sewed only the top layer, it wouldn't have held. I didn't contradict her. She wouldn't have wanted to know that I felt every stitch. Besides, how could I have explained it—the agony of the pain and, at the same time, my distance from it?

They even accused me of being crazy—temporarily insane. I heard Mother whisper it to the others, to Ah Kwai, Su-lee, and Yun-yun. "Don't let her out," she ordered in a hiss. "She doesn't know what she's doing." And they believed her. They wouldn't listen to anything I said. When I tried to take a step toward the door, they formed a blockade, their six hands reaching out to pluck Ah Tou from my arms. I begged them to let me past. I twisted and dodged and pushed against them. I shouted and scolded and demanded. Was that insanity? No, a thousand times no. I understood the risk. How could I forget it with the gash from the MP's bayonet still burning in my thigh? But risks have to be weighed against risks. And I knew what I saw. I knew what it meant.

He couldn't swallow. Maybe a drop or two dribbled down the constricted passage of his throat, but that was all. When they wouldn't let me out, I was forced to sit with him in my lap. Ah Kwai squeezed water, drop by drop, from a clean cloth. Most of it pooled in the bottom of his mouth and dripped from its corners. I would have sat dribbling water down his throat all night long if that could have saved him. Little by little, though, I could see that his throat was closing not only to water but also to air. I couldn't let that happen. I had to try to slip past the curfew guards with him. It wouldn't be easy, but it was a risk worth taking. I tried to convince Mother. Then I tried force and trickery against her loyal troops. To no avail.

Finally I turned my back on them and walked in circles, glaring at the walls of my cage, an impotent rage boiling inside my skull. Ah Tou wheezed in my arms; his chest heaved against mine. "Ma." He forced the syllable out, a heartbreaking cry that pierced my soul.

"Mama's here, my sweet." I sat down and cradled him. "Everything's going to be all right."

"Ma," he gasped, his eyes wide with questions. And over the roar of the nonexistent wind, the frightening rasp of his struggle for air ricocheted fear from wall to wall. The sound still echoes in my ears— menacing and sad and far away.

"It's all right, dumpling. Close your eyes and rest." I patted his bottom and rocked back and forth. "Mama's here." Trusting me—oh, horrid mother's lie—he closed his eyes while I, helpless as a turtle in a whirlpool, held him and rocked and patted. I dripped water into his mouth and it dribbled out the corners. I murmured words of love and comfort, and he twitched and heaved in my arms. His racing heart drummed inside him, reverberating on my belly.

"Lord of heaven!" I cried. "Please come down and save this innocent child." But heaven had turned its back on us. Oh! My baby! My baby! His little heart fluttered against my breast, faint and fainter still as I held him close, trying to warm his cooling body with my own. "Oh, my precious one. Don't leave me."

I touched his innocent face, my heart crying out to heaven. And his spirit slipped away. Light and silent as a dust mote on a moonbeam. My heart grew fingers to hold him; my spirit opened wide to swallow him. Don't go! it cried, even as he slipped away. Don't leave me alone. My baby. My sweet, sweet baby.

They say I didn't know he was dead, that my grief-numbed mind wouldn't allow me to understand it. This they deduced from my so-called unresponsiveness, or so they say. They told me he was dead, and I didn't respond. I stared into space, they say. Or they contradict themselves and say—all this behind my back—that I continued to talk to him and touch his face and hair long after he died. What really disturbs them—still, even now—is that I wouldn't give him up when they told me to.

They make me sound crazy. "Poor An Lee, rocking that dead child through the night. She simply refused to give him to me," they say, whichever one of them is telling the story. "I tried to take him from her, but she wouldn't let go." Every one of them tried, even Yunyun, even Mother. You'd think Mother would understand. When Father died, she didn't just walk away from his body, did she? The hair, the skin, the eyelashes. She must have wanted to hold on to the little she had left.

Because the moment you let them go, they're gone forever.

Over and over again I touched his little fingers and toes, the bottoms of his feet. I laid my cheek against his and whispered to his hovering spirit. Drinking dry the consolation of his body, I ran my fingers over his silent, still belly and through his hair. Oh, Ah Tou! My baby. Where are you?

Through the night, rocking, rocking, the heat draining slowly, imperceptibly from his body, I held on to him. And then, at one particular moment in time, I let him go.

31

"Teacher Wei is here to see you. I'll help you dress." Without so much as a sideways glance, Ah Kwai hustled past my bed, drew back the curtains, went straight to my bureau, and took a cotton slip and a pair of nylon panties out of my underwear drawer. "You can't go on letting your old teacher climb the stairs to your bedroom," she said with an authority that could only have come from Mother. "Teacher Wei is a distinguished elder. He shouldn't have to come up to you when you could easily go down to him."

I stared at the ceiling, fully aware of her disrespectful tone. A gecko, immune to the laws of gravity, skittered upside-down across the ceiling. My mind rolled back to the typhoon, checking. No, I couldn't recall any geckos flying through the air.

Ah Kwai draped a dress over her arm, a yellow-and-white floral print with apple-green piping. "Sit up, Young Mistress," she said, enforcing her request with a hand behind my back.

Why today? I wondered. As soon as the question formed itself, an answer appeared. Of course. The forty-nine days of deepest mourning were already over. Strange how my mind carried on without any instructions. It was like an automatic factory, churning out thoughts even while its manager slept.

Ah Kwai threw the quilt back. "This will be good for you," she said.

Uncovered, my nightgown bunched around my hips, the air grated cold on my smooth legs and my grief-thinned skin and skittery nerves. I imagined my head back on its pillow, my body curled into itself, my hands clutching the quilt, pulling it up to my ears. And yet, I remained where Ah Kwai put me. She slid my legs to the side, and I let her put her hands under my arms and stand me up. "I can dress myself," I said, even as I raised my arms and let her lift my nightgown over my head.

When I was dressed, my hair combed, leather shoes on my feet, she appraised me with a self-satisfied smile.

"I'm cold," I said. She opened a drawer and took out a sweater.

Today (was it morning or afternoon?) I'd be expected to talk. Although I hadn't counted them—it was the one task my mind wouldn't perform for me unbidden—I assumed the forty-nine days had been used up, and now I was expected to dress and talk. No more lying in bed while Teacher Wei recited poems to me. It might have been acceptable then, but from now on, it would be improper.

Seeing my teacher, by habit, I fell into the normal routine of greeting. I invited him to sit down and thanked him for coming.

"You look well," he said. "I'm glad."

I curled my lips into a smile. But if politeness required more, if by chance it was my turn to choose a topic of discussion, the ability eluded me. I could sit down, though. That was something I could do. I made my way to a chair beside his, my leather soles scuffing across the tile. "Please, teacher," I said again, "please sit down." I should pour him some tea. The thought floated through my head like a small white cloud. The table between us was bare, another fluff of mind-breath noted, not a book or a page of poetry on it. If he had nothing to read, then one of us would have to talk. I could ask about his mother, or about Chang Ti and Fan Ho-fu.

Teacher Wei cleared his throat. Suddenly I was afraid of what he might say. *Please, no,* I thought. *Don't ask me about Yu-ming. Please don't ask about my baby.* "Teacher," I said quickly, opening my eyes wide in an effort to contain the gathering tears. "Teacher, tell me, what have you heard about Fan Ho-fu?" I blotted the corners of my eyes and blinked. *Why did I ask about Fan Ho-fu?*

"I believe he's still alive. Only yesterday I spoke to a man who knew someone who saw him."

Yesterday. My mind jumped to another measurement of time. Three weeks. That was how long it had been since I'd heard from Yu-ming. I curled my fingers around the handle of the teapot. Then, forcing the muscles in my arm to contract, I lifted and tilted it until a stream of golden liquid spilled into Teacher Wei's cup.

He tapped the side of it in thanks, and then—just in time—put his hand under my wrist. The tea was already at the rim of his cup, domed and ready to spill over the side. He waited until the teapot was safely on the table, and then continued. "From what I understand, Fan Ho-fu has become a master actor. One day he is a peasant walking barefoot between fields of rice; the next, he is a beggar." He lifted his teacup with both hands and sipped carefully. "I heard a story about someone—this man thought it was Fan Ho-fu—who stole some Japanese uniforms, regulation tunics, and leather boots complete with sabers and pistols. He and his little band of partisans convinced a group of Chinese puppet soldiers to stack their rifles against the wall. Then he ordered them to follow him while his associates commandeered a lorry, loaded it with the enemy's weapons, and drove off."

Teacher Wei crossed his legs and smoothed his gown as though waiting for me to comment. When I didn't, he straightened his back and continued. "It was predictable that Fan Ho-fu would become a successful guerilla. His writing always seems to come from the hearts of a multitude of imagined characters rather than from his own." He stopped and adjusted the buttons on his gown.

I closed my eyes and sighed. I was so tired. It was so much effort to sit here in the parlor and try to talk. I just wanted Teacher Wei to leave so I could go back to bed.

"It's going to be all right." He leaned closer to pat my hand.

The warmth from his hands flowed like honey into my veins. "No one says his name," I suddenly found myself blubbering. "They go on with their daily affairs as though Ah Tou never existed. Even you, Teacher." I pulled my hand back and, feeling an unaccustomed surge of energy, jumped out of my chair. "You say it's going to be all right. But how can it be? I'm his mother. Don't you know what that means? Nothing can be all right ever again."

"An Lee."

"And where is Yu-ming, Teacher?" The words now wouldn't stop. "Tell me, where is my husband when I need him? If other men can sneak into occupied territory and dress as pimps and beggars and Japanese officers, he should be able to do the same thing. If he is so brilliant, why doesn't he devise a way to visit his wife and children?"

"I'm sure he would if he could."

"He never saw him, Teacher." I fell to my knees, sobbing, help-less to stop. Or not so helpless. Even then, I suppose, in the midst of my tears, I could have stopped. I could have taken a deep breath or walked in a circle or concentrated on a thumbnail or a spot of light. I could have splashed cold water on my eyes or forced my lips into a closemouthed smile. I wanted to cry, though, to sob until my appetite for grief was sated, my tears totally dried up. And yet, what I really wanted was not the comforts of grieving. It was Ah Tou.

"I'm sorry," I said finally, taking the handkerchief Teacher Wei offered and blowing my nose.

"It's all right. Why don't you sit back, and I'll read to you." He poured my tea and then reached into his gown and pulled out some neatly folded pages. He moved his chair so it was facing mine and sat down. My eyes fluttered and then held as I anchored myself, focusing on his hands, on his eight fingers splayed on the back side of the still-creased papers—four fingers on each side ending in four knuckles from which a fan of four thin bones ran down the back of a hand, meeting, almost meeting, at a wrist, which was another bulging bone under the horizontally wrinkled skin. The veins, blue under the thin skin, crossed over the fan of bones, tributaries meeting and combin-ing before heading up the arm, disappearing under the white cuff, the blue cotton sleeve. A voice, my teacher's, familiar in its tones and over-tones, in the formal rhythms borrowed from classical literature, the scoops and plunges—a bush tit's flight, ripples within waves, nearly predictable, hypnotic.

The tune washed over me, but the meaning rushed on by. Now and then it sprayed me with a stray word or phrase: *stairs, a tattered bandana, a room facing the lake.* My eyes fell slightly out of focus, so that Teacher Wei's long, tapered fingers began to look like Yu-ming's. I blinked and saw once again an old man's prune-wrinkled knuckles.

A red lacquered table. I looked down at my hands, at the short fin-gers resting on the yellow and white of my dress, the fabric draped like a banner between my knees, the banner's length proclaiming the extent of my unladylike posture.

Like a willow leaf. It must be his boat, drifting on the lake's sur-face like a willow leaf.

Alerted by a flash of tears, I pulled back from the scene. I blinked hard and pressed my knees together.

Teacher Wei glanced up and then back at his papers. I tried to listen by the sentence and the paragraph, but the words wouldn't hold together . . . *from his quiver of arrows* . . . *through the head of the third goose.* How could I make sense of it? What did this hunter of geese have to do with the woman in the room overlooking the lake? And what about Ah Tou, who was always in my mind but nowhere in Teacher Wei's story?

"Teacher," I said. "Could we stop here?"

"Of course, An Lee."

"I'm so sorry. You're so good to... Would you like some more tea?"

"Thank you. But maybe you'd prefer to rest now."

"Yes, maybe so."

*   *   *

In the weeks following Teacher Wei's visit, my friends stopped by. Chi-chi was the first. When she came, I was downstairs shuffling around the sitting room. She said some words of greeting and sympathy. Then we locked arms and walked out onto the lanai. When she tried to pass on some gossip, her quick movements and the brightness of her red-lipped, rouged face and her jade earrings confounded me. "You know, An Lee," she said as she prepared to leave, "you ought to get another permanent wave. It would give you a lift. Besides, the hairdressers need work. Think of it as a kindness to their malnourished children."

It would be easier, I thought, when Pei-lu came to call. She was more sensitive than Chi-chi. She'd know better than to talk about malnourished children. Sensitivity, though, turned out to be no easier to bear than its opposite. Pei-lu kept censoring herself. She'd open her mouth, only to close it again, leaving all the painful words she couldn't say hanging between us like a toxic fog.

I didn't think Ling would come. Why would two grieving mothers want to see our reflections in each other's faces? She did come, though. She said she was sorry; I thanked her for coming. She commented on the weather; I asked her to sit down. We listened to the rain and gazed at the shiny bits of falling water. At the door, she turned back and spoke my name. *It will get better.* Perhaps that was what she thought she should say. If it was, she couldn't follow through. I wouldn't have believed her anyway.

My poor little Ah Tou. I couldn't stop thinking about his suffering. Nor did I want to forget. I challenged myself to remember the ghastly images of him struggling to breathe. Forcing myself to gaze directly into the tiger's eyes, I dared my memories to be as ferocious as they really were. Even the worst, though, lacked substance. I told them to go ahead and pierce my heart, to dig their bloody nails into my belly, to scratch out my eyes. Where was my flesh-and-blood adversary?

When Yu-ming's letter finally came, it was the children who brought it to me. I heard a knock on my bedroom door and then Ah Mei's voice. "Mother," she said softly, "may we come in? I have a letter from Father."

How timid they'd become! Afraid to enter my room without permission. They opened the door, stepped inside, and stopped, heels together like schoolchildren preparing to recite. I glanced from Ah Mei's round, black eyes to Ah Chew's almond eyes and saw the same glint of sadness. Their hair was neatly combed—Ah Chew's slicked to one side, Ah Mei's parted on top, two short pigtails sticking up, the ends spraying out like water from a fountain. Ah Chew was dressed in clean blue shorts and a striped shirt, Ah Mei in her lavender dress. They could have been going to a party or for a walk in the park. Suddenly they looked so old, their legs so long. Had they grown when I wasn't watching? How old were they anyway? "Ah Mei, Ah Chew, how old are you?"

"Six-and-a-half, Mama."

"Five. I'm five years old."

"That's right, children, six-and-a-half and five. Good for you." I wasn't losing my mind. I didn't want them to think I was. Someday I'd be the same as I was before. I pulled back from the thought, frightened by all it entailed. Children demanded so much. Always, always they wanted their mama, to listen to them, read to them, settle their disputes. From morning to night they needed to be watched and scolded, fed and taught. So many things to teach them. Worst of all, they needed their mother to be a certain way, always the same—not crying or staring or shouting at them to go away and leave her alone. I wondered, would I ever be that way again?

"Well, let's see what you have," I said, neither smiling nor frowning. I held out my hand. "Let's see what your father has to say."

259

32

*T*he autumn equinox came and went, then Double Ten and after that, November and Dr. Sun Yat-sen's birthday. I was caught in the flow of it—bumped up against all the blooming, fading newness of life. Carried ever farther from my son. The sun rising and setting, the moon waxing and waning, while my Ah Tou stayed the same, buried forever beneath the sod.

The weather was cooler now, the sky often overcast. From my balcony the trees and rooftops in the distance melted together, fading finally into the white sky. A trail of smoke curled from the cigarette I kept hidden behind the balustrade. I couldn't see Ah Kwai, but I knew she was downstairs somewhere with the gold we dug up last night. Some children were making their way home from school, a parade of innocence ahead of my avaricious half-brother-in-law—if, indeed, anyone was innocent anymore. Occupation had poisoned us all— those who sold and those who bought on the black market, those who ate and those who starved. If we would live, we had no choice but to buy rice from men who consorted with the enemy. And Fen, the biggest operator of them all, was the one capable of procuring the best rice, such as it was. Even his rice these days was often so old that you could squeeze it to dust between your thumb and forefinger but at least it wasn't rotten.

I stared at the spot on the lane in front of the Bradleys' house until the children became moving blurs and my cigarette burned my fingers. I dropped it and stamped it out just in time to see Fen rounding the corner. His jerky gait was unmistakable. The bile rose in my throat just to look at him. Ah Kwai already had the gold. Let her take care of the transaction. I could watch from the balcony and save myself some unpleasantness.

"*Bakayaro!*" he shouted in Japanese, cursing the bearer who was several paces behind doubled over from the weight of his burden. "Keep up." He stopped in front of our gate. I jumped back into the shadows, my heart pounding like a rabbit in a bag. I really ought to show my face, I thought without moving. He *is* my half-brother-in-law. He rang the bell, and still I remained stuck. My stomach swirled with the impossibility of deciding. Su-lee was walking toward the gate now, drying her hands on her apron. She looked up and, seeing me, gestured with her chin. It was a small thing, but somehow it released me. I came inside and started down the stairs.

Prosperity had fattened Fen's belly, but it hadn't done anything for his scrawny neck. "Sister-in-law," he said when he saw me. "Have you eaten rice?" In Fen's mouth, our customary greeting became an indictment of our need and a cocky reminder of his power over us.

"Yes, thank you. And you?" I asked simply, no clever quip, no ironic double entendre to subtly put him in his place. "Have you eaten rice?"

"Yes, of course." He rubbed his belly and frowned in mock dismay. "Eating rice is an occupational hazard." He ran his fingers through his hair, smoothing it down on one side, leaving the top to stick up like a broken cock's comb.

"Sir," Ah Kwai said, "we have the agreed-upon amount."

"An amount that is considerably below my cost," he lied with a straight face. "Deals like this are going to ruin me."

Ah Kwai handed me the gold and stepped back. Behind her Su-lee and Yun-yun bowed their heads.

"How is my half brother?" Fen asked, picking a nonexistent piece of food from between his teeth. He knew how to stir up my anger, but today the fire I needed to deal with him lay suffocated under a load of ashes.

"My husband is fine." I looked at the bearers squatting beside the bags of rice. Their lumpy knees shone white through their sallow skin.

"I suppose Yu-ming is still dreaming of defeating the Japanese. He always was stubborn."

"The gold," I said, holding it out to him, the dead weight cold on my palm.

He sprang forward and plucked it from my hand. "Now, me," he said, smiling, "I'm a practical man. I don't make a habit of wasting my time on lost causes." He tucked the gold inside a pouch at his waist. Then he snapped his fingers, and the bearer jumped up. "Get going," he hissed. "You'll get paid after the next delivery."

I should have felt a sense of relief at Fen's departure. Instead I felt nothing. Coming or going, alone or in company, nothing could relieve the unrelenting heaviness. I watched Ah Kwai and Su-lee struggle to lift the bag of rice onto Yun-yun's back, Yun-yun sinking under its weight before jogging off to the kitchen. What was happening to me? I didn't recognize myself, didn't know how to get back to myself. What if I never found a way? Stumbling, I made my way into the house and through the kitchen. What if I was losing my mind?

I hurried through the darkened hallway, past the statue of Ma-tsu and up the stairs to my bedroom. If only Yu-ming would come back. That would change everything. I opened my bedroom door. *My* bedroom. Did the tongue of my mind know something my conscious mind refused to admit?

I yanked open my desk drawer and threw his letters on the bed. They were proof of his existence. *February 1942, June 1939, January 1940, September 1941, December 1938, October 1942.* There it was, his most recent letter. Proof. Not only was he still alive, but he wrote about coming back—or at least alluded to it. Didn't he? My eyes scanned the page, jumping up, down, up, down. I turned the page over. Didn't he promise somewhere that the war would be over soon? No, no, that wasn't it. He said he would be leaving Chungking soon and coming here. I had to slow down. The characters weren't making any sense. Always this numbering of his paragraphs, as though he were writing a report to his superiors. Where was the warmth in that?

I threw the letter down. A man who truly loves his wife doesn't number his paragraphs. A phrase caught my eye and I picked the letter up again. "I grieve that I couldn't perform the duties a son owes to his mother," he wrote. "I'll be forever grateful for all you did to see that she had a proper funeral." The words seemed to come from a Confucian manual on proper behavior.

Slowly I closed my fingers over the letter, crumpling its soft airmail paper in my palm. I didn't deserve his love. I climbed onto the bed, my knees crushing his letters. I was the one who let them die. I put a pillow over my head so I wouldn't have to think about it.

All through the muggy days of August, September, and October, sleep had been my salve. All I had to do was close my eyes, and I could escape into a shifting, featureless place where darkness ruled and time didn't matter. In November, though, my sleep began to turn against me. I never knew whether I would find blessed nothingness behind my closed eyelids or a frantic mélange of racing images. Some nights I couldn't sleep at all. I couldn't even stay in bed. I ran up and down the stairs, into the kitchen and out onto the lanai, all the while pressing my lips together to keep in the unholy sounds that strained to escape.

One early morning I dreamed of seeing Ah Tou on a narrow jungle trail. I was marching to Burma with our army, and he was sitting beside the trail with another woman. He didn't recognize me, and our commander was shouting for me to keep going. I was trying to shoot a poisonous snake over Ah Tou's head when Ah Chew came into my room. He coughed, and the dream began to slip away.

"Go away," I said.

"But, Mama . . ."

"I said, go away. What do you want from me?"

"Nothing, Mama."

It was a lie. They all wanted something from me. But I couldn't give it. Didn't they see that? I didn't belong in this world, in this century. If I'd been born in the Song Dynasty or the Ming or the Ching, people would have understood my grief. Back then, a grieving woman could jump into a well or slit her throat. I pulled the quilt over my head. My heart pounded in my ears. A belt of pain tightened around my chest. Maybe I was dying. Maybe that was the only way to be free of this unreachable desolation.

I rolled to one side of the bed and then the other. Like snakes, the bedcovers wrapped themselves around me—stinking, damp, reptilian arms that held on even as I fell to the floor.

"Mama."

"You again." I untangled my legs and stood up.

"I'm hungry, Mama."

I straightened my nightgown. Suddenly I was wide awake. "Well, so am I."

Ah Chew pattered across the room and stood directly in front of me. "Let's cook our own breakfast. Please. Can we?"

"Okay, okay. Just wait for me to dress." I found a housedress and some slippers. Toast with marmalade, maybe. For Ah Chew, rice porridge with some side dishes—spiced tofu, preserved cabbage, chopped peanuts.

"Hurry," I said, whisking past him.

"Can we cook noodles, Mama?"

"Why not? Noodles with tofu and dried mushrooms."

"Also dried shrimp. Okay, Mama?"

"Sure. A dozen recipes for noodles ran through my head: egg noodles, rice stick noodles, bean threads, noodles with pork, chicken, quail eggs, or shrimp, with celery, cabbage, carrots, bamboo shoots, snow peas, bean sprouts. I thought of the ground peanuts, sliced scallions, or fried, fragrant shallots I might sprinkle on top.

Ah Chew couldn't keep up. Before he reached the kitchen I'd already put the mushrooms and shrimp in separate bowls of water to soak. "Ah Chew and I are cooking today," I told Ah Kwai, who was taking a bag of bean sprouts out of her marketing bag. "We can use those." I dumped some on the counter. Then I picked up a bunch of scallions. Rice wine, sugar, soy sauce, sesame oil, a little cornstarch in water. My hands flew to keep up. I washed the scallions, cut off their white, dangly roots, and sliced the bulbs and the green tops. When I wanted to, I could be a whirlwind in the kitchen.

Ah Chew kicked off his slippers. Curling his toes around the drawer handles, he climbed onto the counter and sat cross-legged next to the bean sprouts. I noted how quickly he snipped off the brown tails and separated the sprouts into two piles. He couldn't keep up with me, though.

I untied the twine around the rice stick noodles and put them to soak in cold water. Yes. I really was a whirlwind in the kitchen. After I finished the noodles, I would make wintermelon soup for the midday meal. Then I would make spareribs with black beans, if Ah Kwai could get some, or steamed fish. I could even make a dessert…almond biscuits or toffee apples.

I slid the sliced scallions onto a plate with the back of my knife and took out the tofu. I cut it into perfect strips and then perfect little cubes. I squeezed and halved the mushrooms, drained the shrimp and the rice noodles. Ah Chew snipped off the last bean sprout tail. The oil was hot. We were ready to cook.

Fire flared under the wok and steam rose to the sky while one thing after another whirled around my wok, crackling and blushing to perfect doneness. I transferred the noodles to a large serving platter and dished some up for Ah Chew. Then I went to the pantry and got the can of Yunnan ham we'd been saving. Slicing it into paper-thin pieces, I marveled at the perfect, even sound of the cleaver on the chopping board. Then, with Ah Chew's almond eyes watching me, I pushed the ham aside and reached for the snow-white wedge of wintermelon. The golden seeds in its center were wet as dewdrops, sparkling as tears.

"Young Mistress," Ah Kwai said, reaching for my cleaver. "Why don't you sit down beside the young master and taste the noodles. I'll cut the wintermelon."

"No, no. Let me do it. I'm not hungry. Besides, I need you to go to the market. I need spareribs or fish. Try to get both. I need the spareribs right away. Otherwise I won't be able to make them tender in time for the midday meal."

"I may not be able to find either, Young Mistress."

"Yes, you will. I'm sure you will." Why was she opposing me? I stamped my foot. "I don't care what the price is. Ask Mother for more money."

Still she didn't move. She tightened her lips and frowned.

"What's wrong?" I raised the cleaver and brought it down hard, precisely in the center of the wintermelon wedge. "We can spend money once in a while. Haven't we scrimped enough?" I put the cleaver down. Ah Chew also was frowning. "Today," I said, smiling and waving my hands at my brilliant idea, "we're going to celebrate a new chef. Ah Chew is going to help me cook everything."

He put his chopsticks down and ran to my side.

"You'll help your mama with everything she needs?" Ah Kwai asked slowly. "You won't leave her alone?"

Ah Chew moved closer. "Yes," he said. "I promise."

Waiting for Ah Kwai, I had to improvise, inventing never-before-seen dishes with the ingredients I had at hand. Ah Chew stuck to my side. For the first time in his life I had to encourage him to eat. "You don't have to help with everything I do," I told him. "Go sit down and eat."

"I want to help, Mama. I want to learn."

"Who's going to eat my food then?"

After he gobbled down his noodles, I gave him some vegetables to wash. Then I let him watch. I didn't have time to train an assistant. I was flying. I moved so fast I couldn't feel the tile under my feet, couldn't feel the feet under my legs. Each dish I cooked added to the tangle of smells—fragrant, pungent, savory, sweet. Each platterful of food I placed on the table added to the confusion of colors and shapes. I sprinkled a pinch of salt on the sliced lotus root and mushrooms in the wok. A few quick stirs and it was done. "Where's another platter? I need it now." I picked up the wok handles and swung around. The odors and colors were a maze that wouldn't hold still.

I don't know what tripped me. How can I say when I couldn't feel my feet? Somehow I let go of one of the wok's handles and grabbed the table. It happened too fast. The mushrooms and lotus root slices spilled on my legs and the little kitchen table tipped over, dumping all the platters of food I'd just cooked onto the floor. Sauce and vegetables, shrimp and broken china lay around me like a nightmare landscape of vermilion and amber running into hills of chartreuse and brown and jagged white and blue mountains. On my hands and knees, I towered over it, a pathetic giant in a field of destruction. I leaned on the edge of the toppled table and hauled myself up.

"It's all right, Mama," Ah Chew chirped, plunging barefoot into the middle of it.

"No!" I shouted as he bent at the waist and started sweeping the scattered noodles into a pile with his fingers. "Get away. You'll get cut." I stumbled through the hot shambles of my banquet and lifted him up and out of the way.

It was a disaster scene, a stinky mass of garbage. I scooped it up with the dustpan and threw it in a pail. I was absurd. I slipped in the muck, staining my clothes and cutting my knees and hands on the broken china. I righted the table and leaned on it, exhausted. "What's the use?" I cried. The cleaver and the butcher knife were still on the floor. I knelt and picked up the knife. I tested its edge with my already bleeding thumb as I eyed the veins on my wrists. "It's too difficult," I said. I looked at Ah Chew. "Don't you understand? Mama wants to die."

"No, Mama." He walked toward me, holding me with his eyes. Then he stopped and held out his wrists. "Kill me instead, Mama."

Spring 1946

33

You wonder why I'm thinking about all these things now, with the Japanese War won and Yu-ming returned. Why dwell on it, you say, now that it's over? I can only laugh. Over? It's not over. Everything that happened still exists, doesn't it? Ah Tou is still dead; my mother-in-law is still buried in the little wartime graveyard that used to be a children's park; and I am still the same woman, wounded by eight years of war and occupation. When the Japanese War came to Amoy, I was only twenty-two. Now I'm thirty. Thirty years old. This has been my life. What else do I have to think about? I suppose you think I should just sit back in my sedan chair and enjoy the scenery—as though traveling through these mountains ought to be a pleasurable experience. Well, let me tell you, it isn't. I've been riding over these roads that are little more than trails all morning and half the afternoon. I've been jostled and jolted, nothing to look at except the rocks and trees and the sweaty, skinny back of the sedan chair carrier. Isn't it natural that all these thoughts about our "solitary island" period and the occupation should enter my mind?

You've assumed, rightly, that we're leaving Kulangsu. So, you'd like to say, it's a perfect time for me to fill my mind with sweet reminiscences of our house and Kulangsu's lanes and shops and beaches. You needn't worry. I remember every square meter of Kulangsu. Besides, we'll be back. We won't live in Foochew for long—a year, maybe two or three.

But if this is going to be such a long, uncomfortable journey, you persist, why not sing or recite poetry along the way? Why not think about the future or about the happy times before the war? You don't seem to understand that I could search up and down the thread of time and still not find a place where happiness isn't threatened by sorrow. It's all bound together. You can't simply cut out an offending segment of the thread and reattach the dangling ends. As for the poetry...who knows? Tomorrow I may decide to sing or recite poetry. Maybe. It's my choice, you see. And today I choose to let my thoughts come as they will.

Look, up ahead, the sedan chairs have stopped. The road is getting steeper. The bearers have put their chairs down and taken out the cubes of opium they keep wrapped in banana leaves. They squat and lick it, staring into space. Opium makes the rich lethargic, but on these mountain roads, men use it for stimulation. The new amah looks back at Ah Mei and Ah Chew in the second sedan chair. Together, my children weigh no more than ninety pounds, tiny for a seven- and a nine-year-old. But then, which child isn't small for his age these days? The amah—her name is Chu-chai—smiles at them. She's trying to get them to like her. She thinks she can get them to forget Su-lee.

My bearers have caught up to them now. All our sedan chairs are resting precariously on boulders at the side of the road. "We can get out for a minute," I say. "Come on, children. Quickly." I climb out of my sedan chair and hobble over to them. Ah Chew has already scrambled over the side, but Ah Mei waits for me to lift her out. We shake our legs and rub our behinds. Ah Chew kicks a rock down the mountainside and then starts gathering pebbles to throw at trees.

It's mid-afternoon, not the most likely time for bandits or Communists to attack. Besides, we're not an attractive target for them, not in relative terms at least. All we're carrying is food for the journey and a change of clothing, a toothbrush, and a comb for each of us. Everything else we need we'll get in Foochew. Mother, Ah Kwai, and Yun-yun will look after everything we left behind.

"Little Miss," the amah calls to Ah Mei. "Look. Over here." She's squatting at the side of the trail beside some wildflowers. She unwinds their tendrils and disentangles a vine from the bushes, looping it around her arm.

"Break it off," I warn. "Don't pull up the tuber. It's toxic."

"I know, ma'am. Gloriosa lilies are my favorite flowers."

"We can make a crown," Ah Mei suggests.

"Yes, one for you and one for your mama."

"No, thank you." It pleases me that Chu-chai likes this humble little plant. Gloriosa lilies are easy to overlook, and yet so lovely with their yellow-tinged red flowers.

I lean over and sift through the rocks at the side of the trail. Chu-chai is a cousin of Ling's cook. She's in her thirties—a little older than I wanted, but healthy and good-natured. Still, I miss Su-lee. I was tempted to keep her on, for my own sake. But even if her goatherd does turn to the Communists, as Mother predicts, at least with him, she'll have a chance to make her own life. I throw one of my stones, squarely hitting a tree. Ah Chew turns around and raises his eyebrows. "Now I'll hit the tree behind it," I say. "You see? That one." My rock finds its mark. I stand back, and Ah Chew hits his tree. "Okay," I say. "That's enough. Get back in your sedan chairs."

This north-south road has been traveled for over a thousand years. In places, the mountains have been cut into and even blasted to even it out. Still, this section must be as steep as it ever was. "No," I say, changing my mind. "Let's walk for a while. Chu-chai, I want you to hold Ah Mei's hand. Make sure she doesn't fall over the side." I grab Ah Chew's hand. "Watch your step," I say.

Obviously, it was a laudable thing Ah Chew did that day in the kitchen—offering, like a filial child in some ancient story, to die in my place. I wouldn't have killed him, of course—or even myself. I don't think I would have killed myself. I did want to die, though. Sometimes a feeling like that becomes so overwhelming, that it has to be experienced in the world outside of your head. Dramatized, if not actually enacted. The incident I'm referring to was almost four years ago now. Sadly, it wasn't the last such episode. Remember, what I'm talking about here are not actual attempts to kill myself. Otherwise, wouldn't I be dead now? No, as I said before, I just needed to give form to the way I was feeling. So empty … The emptiness just seemed to stretch on and on. I felt cold and dead, sadness like a rock inside me. Anyway, I didn't kill myself.

I don't expect the sadness will ever disappear. Today, though, I'm barely aware of it. Look. See this coral-tinged light and the fluttering leaf shadows on my arms. Listen to the sigh of the mountain. Even on a bed of sorrow, a person can lift her head to enjoy the bird trills and the fragrances of sun-warmed rocks and snowy jasmine blooming out of sight.

Ah Chew and I are sure-footed as we pick our way over the rocks and exposed roots, nimble as two mountain goats as we step across the furrow that was cut down the middle of the road by last year's monsoon rains. Actually, when you think about it, the suicides in history were rare. Those we celebrate in poetry and opera were notable precisely for being so unusual. Most of us Chinese desperately want to live. It's our duty. I still remember what Ah Kwai told me when she thought I might be involved with the resistance. The primary duty for every Chinese, she said, was to survive.

Every time I look at this road, it changes. The mustard-colored earth from this morning is gone. Now the blue-gray chips of granite under our feet are cobbled into a fine, reddish-brown dirt. Even the ditch is different. This one that runs along the uphill side has been scoured. The only silt I see is confined to the occasional low point. The slabs of granite separating the ditch from the road have long ago settled into their respective positions—tipping up or down, growing one variety of moss or another. The bearers' minds and bodies must be filled up with this road. After all the times they've traveled it, their calves must recognize the angle of every slope, their minds instinctively compute the distance between each and every curve.

My legs are beginning to hurt, but I don't want to stop. Not in the midst of this climb, so satisfying with its left, right, left, its steady upward movement. Not yet. What is it, the hill ahead I want to crest? The indeterminate something around the next corner.

"Mama." Ah Mei gives me a pained look.

I shake my head no before she can ask. When we reach the top of this switchback we can ride again. Or maybe the next hill. When we've walked enough.

It's almost like being on the sea when the bearers get a good rhythm going. That's what comes to my mind once I'm back riding in the sedan chair. I'm thinking of the first time we went to Foochew, when Ah Mei was only a baby and Ah Chew wasn't conceived yet. Like my father, I was born to be a sea traveler, and yet, that trip was the only long sea journey I've ever taken.

I stare at the bearer's dull black hair and hug my belly. I've changed my mind. I don't know why I thought a minute ago this felt like sailing. Even when they're in rhythm, it's uncomfortable. I should have told Yu-ming before he left for Foochew that I was pregnant. All this jerking isn't good for the baby. We could have gone by sea. This time of year it would have been all ripples and gentle waves rocking us, the sea giving way to our bulk—not like this unyielding earth. The earth seems to be fighting us, returning blow for blow, sending the bearer's steps up their legs and spines, into their shoulders, down their arms and into the sedan chair and us.

I would have told Yu-ming about the baby, but he left before I knew for sure.

We've turned off the main road and onto a trail. Banana leaves and fronds from fern trees brush against our arms and shoulders. At midday, from the reclining position of my sedan chair I had to close my lids against the sun's brightness. Now I watch the darkening overhead canopy and look for glimpses of a violet-tinged sky through the lacy green latticework. I remind the children to put their sweaters on, raising my voice over the chorus of cicadas. The only other sound is the *slap-slap* of the bearers' feet against the trail.

As the maze of shadows around us darkens, we head in the direction of a temple where we'll spend the night. Unfortunately, by the time we get there and get settled in, the light will be so dim I won't be able to read. I hear myself sigh—a mournful dove in a world of cicadas. All day, I realize, I've been looking forward to finishing the story I started last night.

Somewhere water, eager in its downhill plunge, clamors to be heard. Then the trail descends, and we see the stream—flashes of sunset silver in the dark, secret water. The bearers' footsteps slow as they cross a bridge made from a split-down-the-middle tree trunk. They carry us up the other side. We turn a corner. Then, suddenly on our right a sheer granite wall rises up, a large-character, red-painted poem chiseled into it. The characters, which end fifteen feet above the trail, read:

Mountain flowers gaze at high Heaven.
Cliff trees hold firm to deep earth.

The story I have tucked in my bag is by Fan Ho-fu. I wish I could finish it tonight—see where it's leading, how it ends. I'd like to understand his mind, I suppose, see what he means by writing this kind of story. It's so different from his others. They, too, were in the vernacular, and this isn't the first time he's made peasants the main characters. But in earlier ones they faced obstacles that were either of their own making or caused by the Japanese. In this story, it's our own government and its army that cause problems for his hero, an idealistic young man who seems to have ties to the Communist bandits in the hills. Of course, none of this means that Fan Ho-fu has become a Communist. For the sake of a story or poem, he has always had the ability to become anyone he wanted.

We pass through an open gate and onto the temple grounds. A scattering of lonely stars blink in the indigo sky. How pleasant it would be to sleep under the stars! If it weren't for the cold and the danger of tiger attacks, we wouldn't need to go into the temple.

The bearers lower our chairs beside a small pavilion housing a large bronze bell. While they rest and lick their cubes of opium, I take out our blankets and Chu-chai unwraps the rice and pickles we have left from lunch. The children, in a spurt of energy—the inevitable prelude to sleep—run in circles around the bell. Ah Chew taps its rim with his knuckles.

"Sh." I gesture toward the upturned sedan chairs resting against the side of the temple. "Some people might be sleeping inside. Come on. Your rice is ready."

We eat in silence, listening to the monotonous singsong of a priest chanting prayers for the dead. Then we clean up and start toward the temple. Its silhouette is small and ordinary-looking against a plum-colored smudge of light. The chanting stops, and a white-bearded figure in a maroon robe emerges, a topknot protruding from the hole in his hat. He bows and waits while I reach in my pocket for a donation. Then, tucking the coins in his sleeve, he bows again and glides away toward a low building.

At the temple stairs, a fruit bat sweeps past our heads. Ah Chew takes my hand, and we start up. The closer we get to the doorway, the stronger the smell becomes and the tighter Ah Chew grips my hand.

"It's all right," I whisper. "We'll get used to it." Like me, Ah Chew is sensitive to odors, and this concentrated blend of incense, mold, urine, and decaying flesh is truly overpowering, especially in contrast to the fresh mountain air we've been breathing all day. We step inside and pause. Several people raise their heads. The rest stay as they were—unmoving forms laid out on the temple floor. The dead are easy to distinguish from those who are merely sleeping. They're laid in neat rows, their bodies straight and equal distance apart. No knee is bent, no arm up-flung. No body huddles close to lend warmth to another. I search among the living for a space that will be large enough for the four of us, but the temple floor is small, and we arrived late.

"There, ma'am," Chu-chai says, pointing at a spot that doesn't directly touch a corpse. We spread our blankets out on the stone floor and lie down, the children on either side of me, Chu-chai next to Ah Mei. I lie flat on my back, a small pillow roll tucked in the curve of my neck. The children, resting their heads on my arms, hug me from either side. Overhead, the beams shudder. Someone coughs; another snores. The air throbs with the sound of breathing and not breathing.

Ah Mei pastes herself to my side and clamps her arm tight around my waist. I free my other arm and caress her softly, massaging and sliding my fingers lightly over her skin until she relaxes.

I can feel Ah Chew's little body shivering against my other side. He's trying to be brave, trying to be the man his father tells him he is. It's a dangerous world, Yu-ming tells him. Boys need to become men as quickly as possible. Returning from the Japanese War, Yu-ming immediately began calling Ah Mei and Ah Chew by the formal names we chose for them. He had no use for baby names. Before long he was teaching Ah Chew fighting techniques and how to shoot a gun. He was an apt pupil, but Yu-ming didn't notice how hard it was for a small child to behave like a man. Now, for example, Ah Chew would like to cry, but he can't. The only one he dares cry around is his grandmother.

"Come here," I say, putting my arm around him again and holding him close.

"Mama," he whispers, still shaking.

"It's all right."

"But...." His eyes are wide open.

"But what?"

"It's...." His whole body shivers.

"What? Tell me, what is it?"

"It's...a white gentleman."

A ghost. This isn't the first time he's seen one. Unfortunately, he's like me in this respect, too—able to see and understand things others can't. "What did your grandmother tell you?" I say, reminding him.

"She said..."

"You remember, don't you?"

"Yes, Mother. She said I shouldn't be afraid of ghosts, that if I didn't harm them in life, they wouldn't harm me in death."

"Yes. That's right." It was several months ago when she instructed him about ghosts. She must have sent him out to buy cigarettes, and he must have stayed away too long. He had a habit of stopping to talk with the shopkeepers and children along the way. Being late, he must have decided to take a shortcut through the cemetery. I heard him tell Mother that he saw a foreign woman wearing a long white dress float over the gravestones.

"All you have to do is remind this ghost that you never harmed him and that you wish him well," I say, using the same words Mother used.

"Yes, Mother."

"Sh. Quiet," someone hisses.

I put my lips close to Ah Chew's ear. "The white gentleman can hear you whisper."

"I know."

These children of war, they know so much. Even the few whose parents tried to shelter them inside their houses have seen too much. Well, let them see it, I say. Let them understand the cruelty of war. I close my eyes and listen—not to the snoring, but to the sounds beyond the temple walls, the hoot of an owl, the creaking and sighing of bamboo. And I think about some of the things my children have seen, especially Ah Chew. He's a boy, and he's brave, but he has always been sensitive.

I remember the day he came home with traces of tears still on his cheeks. It was during the time we called "the dark world." Our ration of rice had been cut again, and inflation was running wild. The price of smuggled rice was 600 or 700 times what it had been and heading higher. He found me in the kitchen cleaning rice with Su-lee. "Mama," he said, studying my eyes as though to see if I was strong enough to hear his news. "Another one of the noodle makers died. I saw his brothers carrying the coffin."

He didn't talk about the Ng brothers after that. To a boy wandering the streets, they'd been an everyday example of manly strength. The Widow Ng's five strapping sons—that was the way we always referred to them. When we were a few months deeper into "the dark world," I saw another coffin in front of their shop. It was only a matter of time before the Widow Ng's fourth son died. And by then, the only son who was still alive had just enough energy to drag his brother's body out onto the doorstep.

34

You learn to let sleep happen, to simply close your eyes on the enemy—yes, even that enemy who is patrolling your streets, drunk perhaps or climbing over someone's wall, intent on ravishing the women inside. No matter. You have to sleep. You have to learn how to slip away to a place where loneliness and fear recede a little, just enough for you to fall asleep. Or rather, you wait for that place to find you.

The candles are beginning to flicker out. An ancient cold infused into the slabs of granite beneath me seeps through my blanket. As you wait for sleep—something else I know—you must not exclude anything, not even, tonight, the corpses that share the floor with me, their confused, angry spirits newly released and lingering nearby. They thought they should have been safe after the Japanese left. I understand their complaint. I leave it at that. I don't want to argue, even though anyone with eyes to see knew that the end of one war only meant the intensification of the other. And we all knew that in the long run this war was the one that mattered. We have no name for it. We don't even call it a war. But our soldiers have not laid down their guns, and those officers who, like Yu-ming, have taken other jobs still have their military uniforms hanging in their closets. They still follow orders.

Ah Mei turns over. Her knee pokes my side. "Ba-ba-ba-ba-ba-ba," she says, a sleep-babble that sounds like "daddy, daddy, daddy."

Two more days, I think, and my heart skips a beat. Only two more days and we'll be together again. So many, many times I've thought of it, gathering in with the arms of my longing everything it contains, pressing it pure and exquisite, expecting absolute pure joy from our togetherness. I know. That's foolish. Dangerous. Yu-ming is only a man, after all. He's not a mold that fits around all my corners. He isn't a river that will forever flow into the basin of my emptiness. I know.

When he came back after the Japanese War ended, that was my trouble. Too many years of longing had burned away reasonableness. This time, though, when we're together again in Foochew, I'll remember that we are two separate people with our own moods and views. I sit up on my elbows. Ha! I can't help laughing at myself. All these days, it hasn't occurred to me that the house and furniture he's been choosing for us in Foochew won't be the way I imagine them. It's true. I've constructed a complete—a completely unrealistic—picture of the place that's waiting for me. In my mind, I see it as an updated, roomier version of the flat we had there the year Ah Chew was conceived—sunflower yellow curtains, a view of the park from our kitchen table, an airy sitting room with an overhead fan, a green sofa and wicker side chairs, straw-colored needlework on the cushions.

I laugh again. Someone near one of the pillars raises his head. I was the one who decorated that flat. We went out together to find it. This time Yu-ming will choose something sober and inconspicuous, a house that suits his new position as an executive at a shipping company and at the same time doesn't engender jealousy in a time when everyone is maneuvering for advantage in an unsettled world.

Well, this is not the way to fall asleep. I put my fingers under Ah Chew's head and gently move him away from me and onto his little pillow. Then I slip into my Chinese shoes and tiptoe away. Yu-ming is right to choose a modest house on a back lane. I saw for myself what happened in Kulangsu after the Japanese withdrew. All those years of suffering had left us with stomachs full of every kind of poison…fear and regret, unfulfilled ambition. Worst of all, revenge. Those who tried prematurely to establish themselves in the new order often became a target instead. Fen was one of the clever ones. He was well aware of how much he was resented for his dealings with the enemy and his exorbitant prices, and he wasted no time escaping to Hong Kong.

The candles have burned themselves out, but there's enough light coming in through the open windows for me to pick my way over the sleeping and dead bodies. I pass through the doorway and down the stairs. The air in the courtyard is still, and yet the sound of movement is everywhere—a great, constant whispering of leaves or water; it could be either. I stop and listen. The sound seems to be coming from the treetops and from the mountainsides. I imagine heaven is breathing life onto the earth—war or no war.

I feel a flutter in my womb, a foot perhaps. The baby's first kick. Smiling, I touch the spot in greeting. *Your father is going to be pleased when I tell him about you,* I whisper. *And for you it will be easier. Your father will be at home. Watching you grow, he will know what he can expect of you, and that will be enough.*

Crossing the courtyard, I realize how simple my hopes are for him. Fat, pinchable cheeks, chubby arms and legs, a happy life. I'm confident that as a child born in the Year of the Dog, he'll be loyal and reliable. I haven't felt the need of a fortune-teller, and if I haven't dreamed of white tigers or an immortal reborn as a monk, I shrug it off. I've lost my taste for producing a hero.

The smell of death is behind me now. In the distance, a wolf howls. Insects and frogs sing under the whispering trees. I think again that we should have insisted on going by ship to Foochew. On the other hand, Yu-ming had just been appointed to his new job. He wouldn't have wanted to take advantage of his position. Besides, he was in such a rush. They already had his airplane ticket, and if he'd missed the flight and had to go by ship, he would have risked the possible embarrassment of getting seasick. I shake my head. They should have hired me instead. Imagine, a shipping executive who gets seasick. Still, I think, changing my mind again, if I'd told him I was pregnant, he would have found a berth for us on one of their ships.

The building on my left must contain the dining hall and kitchen. I walk around it, past the back door where three large earthen pots filled to the brim with water sit, their surfaces quivering ever so slightly with my footfalls as the roundness of the moon reflects in one pot after the other. Padding across the courtyard's packed earth, I'm drawn toward the fresh scent from beyond the outer wall. I open a gate onto a path that's suffused with moonlight. The invitation to follow it is irresistible. I won't go too far. If the path veers into shadow, I'll turn back.

Even though I've learned how to sleep, on some nights I don't feel like sleeping. Yu-ming says I've changed, that my moods tend more to the extremes than they used to. I argue with him, insisting that I'm exactly the same as I ever was. I'm afraid he'll think there's something wrong with me. I remember the way they looked at me the night Ah Tou died, what they said afterward.

So far the path is easy to see. It's all smooth rocks and packed dirt, wide enough for two people to walk side by side. I try to ignore the shadowy areas under the bushes and trees, try not to imagine a bandit or a wolf hiding there. I'm fine until the path runs snug up against the mountainside. Three meters above the ground, the jagged rim of a ledge shines with a brightness that belies the deep darkness behind, an unknowable space that could easily hide a pair of crouching tigers. My heart pounds in my ears. I strain to hear something, even though I don't imagine tigers would announce themselves by growling or shuffling their feet. Unlike the white tigers I dreamed of when I was pregnant with Ah Chew, a hungry tiger ready to pounce wouldn't let me see the flash of his yellow eyes. I consider turning back. Instead, I hurry under the ledge, accepting the possibility of a tiger attack along with all the other dangers I constantly live with. Before long I'm out of the shadows walking in the open again. I round a corner, and there, atop a small knoll, is the silhouette of a graceful pavilion. The prize at the end of the trail.

I climb the pavilion's stone steps, pass through its empty center and walk out onto the fenced terrace...my moon-viewing platform.

During the day this small balcony would be a perfect place from which to enjoy a panorama of mountains, hills, and valleys, maybe even the sea in the distance. Now, looking down, everything is gray and black. A low, orange moon is queen of the sky. Tonight she's perfectly round. A fleeting thought tells me I don't belong here, that moon-viewing terraces are meant for lovers to gaze at the night sky until the moon's light lures them into each other's arms. Surely, though, just as many solitary travelers have come here, and surely it has occurred to them that their lovers, though far away, might be watching the very same moon.

I rest my hands on the stone railing and study the moon's face. I'm looking, not for the three-legged toad or the legendary hare who sits under a cassia tree pounding and mixing the secret ingredients of immortality, but for Yueh Lao. I stare and stare, and finally I see him. He's perfectly clear, bending toward the earth, one arm extended, the other raised to throw his invisible red thread. Tonight and every night the thread thrown by the moon-bound God of Marriage will tie together a man and woman who are destined to marry. I fill my lungs with the pure, cool night air and think about destiny—one husband for one wife. No concubines, no divorce. This night, on my moon-viewing terrace, Yu-ming waiting in Foochew, our child growing inside me, I believe in our destiny, Yu-ming's and mine. And I believe in him. I watch thin, feathery clouds form over the moon and just as quickly disperse, and I remember what I always knew—that no man was more loyal to his father's memory or to his mother than Yu-ming, no man more respectful of his teachers. I remember how faithful he has always been to his many friends, and I know without a doubt that he will always be faithful to me.

By the time I get back to the temple, the moon is white and thin. A concentrated stew of smells greets me on the steps—night-blooming flowers, mold and sweat, decomposing flesh, and open chamber pots. Inside, I shiver as I look around for my spot between the children. The decades of damp that have settled into the walls and ceiling radiate over the floor like a cloud. Walking into it, I feel a cold, angry energy. *None of this is my fault,* I tell the newly released spirits. I have my own dead. I don't tell them that, though. Knowing how many people have suffered more than I, I don't want to invite comparisons.

Picking my way around the bodies, finally I see my children. I tiptoe past another pair of children sleeping peacefully inches away from a corpse that smells like he's been here all week. On the other side of Chu-chai, a man is laid out flat, his feet uncovered, his toes splayed like the bones of a lady's fan. I step over him and he snorts. "Sorry," I whisper. "Excuse me."

Ah Mei and Ah Chew have swallowed my space. My blanket and pillow are crushed between them. I kneel beside Ah Chew and pull him, blanket and all, away from Ah Mei.

Suddenly he's on his feet, poised in a martial arts posture, knees bent, one leg half-raised, his hands rigid. "Mother," he says, frowning deeply and holding his stance. "Don't touch me when I'm sleeping. You might get killed." The exact words his father uses.

"Sh. Lie down," I whisper. "Go back to sleep."

This is the state of alert Yu-ming brought home from the Japanese War, a lesson he ostensibly taught his son, a child who has been alert to danger since the day he was born. I stretch out next to him and reach for Ah Mei. Her sweet moan rises and is lost in a roomful of snores and wheezing. Outside, the cicadas hum a Buddhist prayer. *For my son,* I tell them, *for my little Ah Tou.* A wolf howls in the distance.

And soon I'm drifting, pulled by invisible threads toward an inconspicuous house where a shipping executive with army uniforms in his closet waits for the day when he will welcome his wife and children home from the war.

End.

CPSIA information can be obtained at www.ICGtesting.com
Printed in the USA
BVOW02s2251210115

384272BV00002B/322/P